EX LIBRIS

VINTAGE CLASSICS

HERE BE DRAGONS

Stella Gibbons was born in London in 1902. She went to the North London Collegiate School and studied journalism at University College, London. She then spent ten years working for various newspapers, including the *Evening Standard*. Stella Gibbons is the author of twenty-five novels, three volumes of short stories and four volumes of poetry. Her first publication was a book of poems, *The Mountain Beast* (1930), and her first novel *Cold Comfort Farm* (1932) won the Femina Vie Heureuse Prize in 1933. Amongst her works are *Christmas at Cold Comfort Farm* (1940), *Westwood* (1946), *Conference at Cold Comfort Farm* (1959) and *Starlight* (1967). She was elected a Fellow of the Royal Society of Literature in 1950. In 1933 she married the actor and singer Allan Webb. They had one daughter. Stella Gibbons died in 1989.

STELLA GIBBONS

Here Be Dragons

VINTAGE BOOKS
London

Published by Vintage 2011

2 4 6 8 10 9 7 5 3 1

First published in Great Britain by Hodder & Stoughton Ltd in 1956

Vintage
Random House, 20 Vauxhall Bridge Road,
London SW1V 2SA

www.vintage-classics.info

Addresses for companies within The Random House Group
Limited can be found at: www.randomhouse.co.uk/offices.htm

The Random House Group Limited Reg. No. 954009

A CIP catalogue record for this book
is available from the British Library

ISBN 9780099529361

The Random House Group Limited supports the Forest
Stewardship Council® (FSC®), the leading international forest
certification organisation. All our titles that are printed on
Greenpeace approved FSC® certified paper carry the FSC® logo.
Our paper procurement policy can be found at:
www.randomhouse.co.uk/environment

Printed and bound by CPI Group (UK) Ltd, Croydon, CR0 4YY

FSC
Mixed Sources
Product group from well-managed
forests and other controlled sources

Cert no. SGS-COC-2953
www.fsc.org
© 1996 Forest Stewardship Council

To

ROBERT and SELENA

CONTENTS

CHAPTER ONE

SANCTUARY IN HAMPSTEAD

"IT's so exactly *like* poor Martin to go and lose his faith *now*, when everybody else is finding theirs," said Lady Fairfax.

This sounded witty. But even her niece Nell Sely, who was sitting upright and quiet on a dressing stool, and who added to the handicap of being not quite twenty that of having arrived in London for the first time from the depths of Dorset only yesterday, felt that it was not true. Martin Sely, her father and Lady Fairfax's brother, was not a man who did a thing when everybody else was doing the opposite, and Nell thought the remark was the kind that Aunt Peggy made when she was appearing on Television.

"Don't you agree, poppet?" Lady Fairfax turned suddenly from the mirror with her six-million-viewers smile, and Nell smiled back. "There's Magda with my milk," her aunt went on, "open the door for her, will you." She bent forward and began to paint her eyelids.

When Nell came back with the milk, and had put it down in a place from which her aunt with a faintly irritable smile removed it to one of greater safety, Lady Fairfax went on: "But do tell me—how do you like the house? Of course it's hideous" (*but you and your mother won't mind that*, she was thinking as she spoke, *because you have the typical English bad taste which is no taste at all*)—"those red-brick Edwardian-Gothic houses *are* coming into fashion again . . . if you care about fashion. I don't suppose you or your mother do, do you? I know Martin doesn't. Well, parsons never do, of course. (Oh dear, I keep forgetting he isn't one any more.) Of course strictly speaking the only thing to do with that type of house is to *keep* it Period. Chintz covers and water colours in gilt frames and so forth. I think it was a mistake to paint the inside all those raspberry pinks and pale blues but the Palmer-Groves *would* do it. (It was a pity they split up. They were dears.) And they were such good tenants that I let them. But the road is charming, isn't it? overlooking the Heath at the end. It will remind you of Dorset." She glanced at the clock. "It really is too bad of that little wretch Gardis; she's supposed to be back sharp at six and it's nearly half past. And don't you adore Hampstead already?"

She leant forward to draw a line along an eyebrow and went on without waiting for the answer which, in any case, Nell would not have been able to give:

"How's your mother taking it all? I'll let you in on the ground-floor about something, Nell; I'm just a little bit afraid of your mother. Old Hampstead family and all the rest of it. Your father and I, you see, don't come of an old family from *anywhere*, and I came up the hard way." The mirror glass, bamboo furniture, indoor plants, and exotic printed stuffs which decorated her bedroom did not give much notion of how hard the way had been, unless it was implied by contrast. "But I admire your mother. She's so clever. (My God, how I envy *brains*.) Did she mind coming back to Hampstead, do you think?"

"I don't think so. She didn't say anything about minding."

"I thought she might have minded meeting people she'd known as a girl . . . now she's had a parson-husband thrown out of the Church . . . but I suppose there aren't many old friends left now. It must be . . . what is your mother? Fifty-three? It's getting on for thirty years. Those old aunts of her's who had the house in Frognal, what was its name—Vernon Lodge—they died, didn't they?"

"Oh yes. When I was very small. Long before the war, I think."

"And the house was sold and pulled down . . . I remember. (Hold this for me, poppet, I must have it near my face.) There are some Willett-built houses on the site now, I saw them the other day. (I'm interested in properties in Hampstead; I'm going to buy all I can. They're a wonderful investment. Always good to let or sell.)"

If Nell's mother, Anna of the *brains*, had been in the room, she would have been as little capable as her daughter of tracing to its source the impulse which caused Nell to say in a moment:

"My mother sent you her love, Aunt Peggy, and asked me to say how kind it is of you to let us stay there."

"Oh well, poppet. It was empty; you might just as well have it. You couldn't stay on in Dorset, could you; with furious Bishops and so forth." She smiled at Nell, glanced again at the clock, then said to herself, "I shan't get those letters done before I go, now. (Undo that varnish for me, will you; yes, that's right, the blacky-red one. I must do my nails.) Of course, that house is what I still think of as *home*. I love *this* house, it's so pretty, and Twenty-five Arkwood Road is so awkward to run (I did warn your mother in my letter), as well as being over fifty years old, but Charles and I went into that top flat the day after we were married—in July 1934, that was, and we had exactly one day's honeymoon because we were appearing n a—thank you, dear, I shall have to give you a job as dresser, I think—(yes, and I've something *really* important to tell you before you go—) in a team radio show that was doing quite well, and we daren't miss turning up for it because it might be our big chance. Charles and I were always having big chances in those days."

She held out her hand and inspected the finished nails. "Poor Charles."

Nell's silence was due to a number of feelings. One was embarrassment, for poor Charles was not dead but divorced; another was sympathy, for her aunt's grief at the situation must be continually renewed by the (now rather infrequent) sound of his voice on the wireless and the sight of his face in the kind of newspaper that Nell herself had encountered yesterday, when unwrapping the fish for lunch. "That's your uncle, Charles Gaunt," her mother had said with a note of amusement in her voice, pointing with a long, work-roughened finger at the lofty brow, firm chin, and reader-regarding eyes. Nell herself was amused now, being unable to vizualize his face except under a veil of fish scales.

"And we kept the flat on all through the war, of course, only we were away so much. I was entertaining the troops and Charles was in the Navy and John was evacuated . . ." She turned herself round, facing Nell. "How long is it since you saw John?" she asked.

"Oh, a very long time. It must be quite ten years. Not since that afternoon you brought him over to tea when we were at Hinchcombe Parva."

"I remember. He *would* nag at you to tell him what you liked doing best in the world, and you got all haughty. And your mother tore a strip off him for gloating over a squashed frog in the road. I was down there opening a fête at Bath." She turned again, smiling, to the mirror. "He looks just the same, except that he's three feet taller. *Beautiful* little boy."

Nell, who could remember nothing about the occasion except that it had occurred, looked polite.

"But he's a bit of a worry to me, I must confess." Lady Fairfax did not sigh but her voice did. "Nothing serious, you know. He'll settle down. His father and I have great hopes of what National Service may do for him. He's due to go into one of them next September. But meanwhile he does nothing but wander round London with *the* most tatty crowd of little pseudo-bohemian boys and girls. Won't try to get a temporary job, won't say whether he *wants* to go into one of the services, won't even write."

"Does he—can he write?" Nell's voice was a little awed.

"My dear, he's *brilliant*." Lady Fairfax turned round, lipstick poised at mouth. "Quite remarkable. It's not just my maternal prejudice. I showed some of his stuff to Phillip Lousada (I suppose even Dorset has heard of *him*?) and he was really impressed; I got the impression, do you know, that he was actually a little envious! I had to steal the stuff out of John's precious portfolio to get hold of it at all, because he never lets anyone get even a *smell* of his writing, and when I told him about Lousada being impressed the little beast was furious with me and said he should hope so. Then he went off into the night. That was a week ago and I haven't seen him since."

"Does he live here or with—his father?" asked Nell, feeling her way amidst the shoals.

"He hasn't lived anywhere for the last year, since he left Grantfield. (No, I'd better be frank. It usually saves trouble in the end. They sacked him. General irresponsibility, idleness, bad influence, and what-have-you. I wish now we'd sent him to a progressive school. They were made for his kind. But they *are* so dotty and messy.) No, he doesn't live anywhere permanently, and that's one of the things that worries me. He's rooming with a friend just now, I think. I believe he looks on Twenty-five Arkwood Road as home, if he looks on anywhere. Oh, and by the way, I want you and your mother to be very kind and keep an eye on old Miss Lister for me. Daisy Lister. She's away in hospital at the moment, recovering from an operation, but she lives in that cottage whose back-door opens into your garden, down at the end. She's a protégée of mine."

"The little one that looks like a gardener's cottage, with the door behind the bushes?"

"Yes. It really was a gardener's cottage years ago. She won't be any trouble. She's near-gentry and madly independent, except for being a complete slave to an enormous cat. I've kept an eye on her for years. She's lived in that part for years, too—it must be *seventy* years, because she was actually born in the big old house that was pulled down to build the whole of Arkwood Road, so she really *does* come of an old Hampstead family. She was quite alone, all her people having died or married and gone away, and when the estate was sold and the house came down, she bought Number Twenty-five, which was then, of course, a new house, and moved into the ground-floor flat. She was letting the three other floors when Charles and I moved in, (damn, now the milk's got cold. That *always* happens, every night, and where that little b—— Gardis is—really she's *impossible*. Useful father or not, I'm packing her back to the States as soon as I get a solid excuse.) Where was I? Yes. Well, when the war came everybody cleared out of Number Twenty-five, leaving Miss Lister holding the fort alone. She got grubbier and grubbier and more and more stubborn. Just would not *budge*—bombs or Government or *anything*; she saw it all through—blitz, buzz-bombs, rockets and what-have-you. She was delighted to see us back after the war, and let us rent the top flat for next to nothing. (Charles and me, that is; John was boarding at Grantfield—and we were so busy fighting our way back into the B.B.C. that we couldn't have him back for the holidays; he used to spend them with those people he was evacuated to at Marlow—terribly dull types but of course he loved falling in and out of the river all day.) So, much later on, when I'd begun to do really well on T.V., I suggested to Miss L. that she should sell the house (which I'd always adored, as I told you) and move into what had been the gardener's cottage of the old house, which she'd allowed to get derelict. Number Twenty-five was looking pretty awful by then, too. But I managed to get our war-damage claim settled rather well, and I fiddled a lick of paint for the cottage as well, and then Charles and John and I moved into the top flat again. Only we were only there for about six months. By that time Charles and I were breaking up. Come in!"

Her famous voice sounded irritable and sharp. She did not look round as she spoke, but went on putting the finishing touches to her face. Nell, however, turned towards the door.

It opened slowly, and slowly a girl wearing a longish coat of some shaggy fur came into the room, pushing a black knitted cap back from her white bulging forehead as she came. She looked at Nell immediately and smiled, with her full lips, painted the pale red of pomegranate fruit. The smile pushed her white cheeks up into cushions, and gave her the look of a bad little girl, a child conspirator, with eyes long and black and liquid as a Japanese doll's.

"Now, Gardis, this is really too bad, you know . . . (oh . . . my niece, Nell Sely. Gardis Randolph, *alleged* to be my social secretary). You're nearly an hour late. I shan't get my letters done this evening. I pay you a damned good salary even by American standards and if you call this giving value for money I don't."

"You're right, Lady Fairfax. It's simply terrible of me and I deserve bawling out. I could blame the British rush hour but I won't. I'll just take off my coat and get started right away," she answered, in a low voice whose r's announced that she was American.

A smaller room opened off Lady Fairfax's, and into this she went, peeling off her coat and throwing it, with her cap, onto a chair as she passed Nell. Down fell a magnificent mane of hair, in a black cloud which reached to the middle of her back.

"And put on a decent dress, please," Lady Fairfax called. "Those trousers look simply terrible and when did you last have that sweater cleaned?"

Nell heard a quiet laugh which she thought did not sound particularly amused. After a pause came the sound of typing.

Lady Fairfax was now ready and inspecting herself for flaws, holding the mirror to the back of her head and turning herself this way and that while making unhurried, considered twitches at her short dress, which was of silk velvet of so dark a red that it looked almost black. She did not touch the curls which were arranged like a spaniel-dog's ears on either side of her lively and determined face, because they were in perfect order; their premature grey rinsed with blue allowed the columnists to point out three or four times a month that Peggy Fairfax had blue hair and golden eyes. She was inspecting herself, but thinking about Anna Sely and Nell.

She had never got on really well with either of them; and perhaps the conviction that, after poor Martin had made such a hash of things, they would shrink even more into the narrow circle of their family life and not expect to be taken up, or about, by herself, had influenced her when she had offered Twenty-five Arkwood Road, rent free for as long as they pleased, as a sanctuary for the afflicted family.

Poor, poor old Martin; the loved elder brother; the swimmer, the Rugby-player, the all-round athlete; poor sick Martin, whom she had last seen at Lyme Regis where he was recovering, on money supplied by herself, from pneumonia. He had looked ill, and he had looked old. If Peggy knew anything of psychiatry—and somehow, like most of us nowadays, she seemed to know something—Martin the muscular Christian, Martin the once-born and the healthy-minded, was going from now on to be an invalid. He would steadily build a wall of ill-health, apparently frail but actually impenetrable, between himself and life, and behind this wall—(she soon began to say to her friends, because really if one did not laugh about it one would cry) he could cower cosily with his imaginary sin.

She carefully smoothed one cheek with the side of her finger. Already she was feeling relief from the worry about Martin and, to some extent, his tiresome womenfolk. They were safely established in Number Twenty-five, where she could keep an eye on them; they had crept up to London and away from Dorset and the Bishop's displeasure (that was how Lady Fairfax thought of it), and were settled near at hand in Hampstead, and now the viewers, the million-eyed Argus who did so love it when you showed any signs of jumpiness or strain, or slipped up, would look in vain for signs of imminent collapse in *her*. Good. She put down the mirror quickly and turned to Nell.

"That's everything, I think, apart from *the* news . . . oh. No, there is one more thing. The top flat—that door at the top of the stairs, the one that's locked. . . . "

"The one with . . . 'Charles and Peggy Gaunt' on it?"

"That's it . . . well, Charles is mad keen to have it back. Apparently it isn't enough for him to have a cottage in Wiltshire that has appeared in *Vogue* and *Country Life*, with Margie—that's his new wife—running round it waiting on him hand and foot; he wants a *pied à terre* in town as well. Well, he isn't going to have my flat. It's *mine*, and I'm going to keep it. I don't want to bother your mother just yet by letting it, because naturally she's been through a pretty bad year and she'll want some peace and quiet, but I might want to let it later on, and anyway why *should* he have it? *It's my house.* Just because we shared the flat once . . . well, anyway, I'm telling you this because I want you to have the gen if Charles comes snooping round trying to get in. If once he *did* get in, it might be difficult to get him out again without a court case, and I don't want that; it isn't good publicity for me. So if he *does* turn up demanding to go up to the flat and telling some yarn or other any time during the next few days, 'phone me *at once*, and I'll come and cope. I've got one key, but the worrying thing is that he's quite capable of sneaking up the stairs and taking a wax impression of the lock—or John is. That quite clear?"

Nell nodded, trying—rather unsuccessfully—to take all this in.

Lady Fairfax got up from her dressing table and walked over to the bed and picked up a velvet coat. Then she looked at her niece.

"Nell, do you know what your parents' income is?"

The Selys had been always bitterly poor, but they had never fallen into the habit of talking about it. Since Martin's illness, Anna had taken Nell a little into her confidence about their affairs, because she had been really worried, but Nell could not discuss the subject without embarrassment.

"Mother has . . . a little under a hundred-and-twenty a year of her own, I think, Aunt Peggy. She didn't tell me what Daddy's last living . . . brought in . . . I don't think it was much . . . "

"That we may *safely* assume," Lady Fairfax said. "It never has been. Then wasn't there some legacy, left to your father a little while ago? I saw it in *The Telegraph.*"

"Mr. Owen's legacy, yes. He was at Oxford with Daddy and they were friends. It was three hundred pounds. But that was quite a long time ago, Aunt Peggy; it's nearly two years now."

"Do you know if your mother has received any dividends lately?"

"I don't think so." Nell's voice was low and her tone reluctant. The typewriter in the next room was silent. Was Gardis Randolph listening? She felt unhappy and ashamed and a little angry with her aunt as well—which was ungrateful, of course.

"I see." Lady Fairfax was opening a drawer in a cabinet. "Now here's ten pounds and I want you to give it to your

mother with my love. (*Don't* give it to your father; I know
what he is about money; he isn't mean but it never occurs to
him that people *have* to eat four times a day.) Tell her she's
not to worry about paying it back. And now for *the* piece of
news, the reason I rang up and asked you to come here this
evening. You *have* kept up your typing and shorthand, haven't
you?"

"Yes. Yes, I have, Aunt Peggy," Nell answered, *not* wondering what was coming next. She had guessed, and she had turned
a deep pink, which Lady Fairfax, one of whose tasks it was on
Television to explain the Youth of England to their elders and
to themselves, no doubt put down to embarrassed gratitude.

"Good speeds at both? What are they, should you say?"

"Oh . . . a hundred at shorthand, and fifty at typing,"
Nell said casually. She could almost feel a pair of Japanese-doll
eyes boring through the wall at her, and see their ironical
glitter. A hundred? said the glitter. And fifty? Fine.

"That's quite good. Nothing extra-special but it will get by.
I'm relieved to hear you've kept it up; I always knew that
course at Claregates would come in useful one day."

Nell said nothing. Her ten years at that boarding-school of
some reputation and considerable bracingness in tradition had
been made possible only because of Aunt Peggy, who not only
possessed some pull with the most important of the Governors
there, but had contributed, even in her most hard-up days, a
quarterly cheque. As for the shorthand-typing course, taken
during their final year by those fallen spirits who had not
proved 'bright' enough to win places at the Universities or
even get into the Upper Sixth, Nell remembered both its
wearisomeness and the ease with which she had mastered it.
But she had not kept it up. And now . . .

"Now you can use it," Lady Fairfax announced. "I've got
you a job."

"Thanks *awfully*, Aunt Peggy," Nell said, with the right
emphasis, but cheeks growing pale.

"Yes. It's five pounds a week, not much, of course, by pres-
ent-day standards, but it's a small firm, just starting, and you'll
be starting too. They'll pay you more later, I expect. It's
largely run by a friend of mine, Gerald Hughes, and he gave
me to understand that he's rather 'making' the job for you
just to please me, so you'll do your best and not let me down,
won't you, poppet? The firm's called Akkro Products, Limited,

and you'll be in the Accounts Department. They're in Lecouver Street, off Tottenham Court Road. An exciting part of London, country mouse." She smiled.

The typewriter had started again. "What do they make?" asked Nell . . . and indeed she would be interested to hear.

"Oh . . . well, I'm bothered if I know exactly. Plastics of some sort, I believe . . . But he's an up-and-coming lad, our Gerald, and it's a lively little firm. Very nice cloakrooms. I had tea with him there once (not in the cloakroom!). I know it's rather springing things on you but—"

A clock struck seven. "Gardis! Go and see if the car's there!" called Lady Fairfax, and Gardis came out wearing a black frock at the sight of which her employer exclaimed in disgust: "That dress! It might have been under your bed all night!" Nell heard the unamused laugh again as Gardis ran down the stairs.

Lady Fairfax went on: "She likes going about in those terrible sweaters and trousers, but she knows I disapprove, so she keeps a black frock stuffed in her desk and pops it on whenever I complain . . . what do you think of her?" An eye cool and sharp as a seagull's was turned upon Nell; Peggy Fairfax the T.V. personality was collecting data about Young America from Young England.

"She's awfully pretty," Nell answered cautiously, but even as she used the word she felt that it was not the right one.

"Oh . . . pretty." Lady Fairfax shrugged. "I think she's like a baby golliwog-witch. Her people were very kind to me when I was over in the States at Christmas, and as there'd been some fuss (over a rather terrible young man, I gather) and she was crazy to study art over here, I asked her to come for six months as my secretary. (Only the social side, of course. No one girl could cope with my fan-mail.) But she's quite hopeless. No idea of time and can't even spell. She was at Bennington over there, I believe, but she's completely uneducated."

"Aunt Peggy, when do I start with—Akkro Products? And what time? I'm awfully sorry to bother you but—"

"It's quite all right, darling, and you aren't bothering a bit. I know how you feel. You've been chucked into something without warning and you're scared stiff. But everything's taped . . . Gardis will give you all the gen when I've gone. Now don't let's talk any more because I've got to relax. I'm going to this film première, *Girl In The House*, and the Royals will be there . . ."

Nell was still sitting on the dressing stool. Lady Fairfax sat on the bed and stared at the dark green wall with hands placed palm upwards in her lap, and the softly-lit luxurious bedroom became very quiet. The mirror-glass ceiling reflected the violet carpet in a thousand dim and glittering cubes. Nell remembered that less than two days ago at this time she had been walking along the road to Morley Magna under a grey evening sky between budding trees, looking down at the lonely valley through the clear lonely air, but found no difficulty in realizing that she was where she was. She had found Morley Magna dull and half-dead. Aunt Peggy, using an expression Nell had come across only in the stories of L. T. Meade which her mother had owned in childhood, had called her a country mouse, but she was more than prepared to become a town one if given the chance, and she was not 'scared stiff' about the job that had been thrust upon her; she was annoyed. Grateful, of course, but very annoyed.

"Where *can* Gardis have got to?" Lady Fairfax was murmuring. "It really is extraordinary. Let her out of your sight for one minute . . . "

"Car's here, Lady Fairfax," and up the stairs bounded Gardis, all secretarial efficiency and smiles.

"Thank you." She got up from the bed. "Were you getting it off the assembly line?"

"I just went down to the corner block to see if it was coming," and Gardis returned to her typing.

"Well. Now, Nell poppet, good-bye and good luck. You start next Monday morning. Ring me up soon and let me know how you're getting on. And ring me up *at once*, night *or* day, if Charles comes snooping round after the flat. Oh," she paused at the door, having bestowed on Nell as she passed her a delicious-smelling kiss, gracefully unhurried and presented with her two hands cupping Nell's surprised face, "if you hear anything of John you might ring me up, too. Just remind him that I *am* his mother."

Nell had never heard of exit-lines, but it occurred to her again as Aunt Peggy went out of the door that this was the way she spoke and behaved while appearing before her public. Then she forgot it. *Monday morning. Next Monday!* And this was Friday evening. She got up off the stool and advanced upon the half-open door whence came the sound of the typewriter, determined to begin asking Gardis for the . . . what was it her aunt had said? . . . j—something . . . at once; presumably Gardis would give her all the details about Akkro Products. But before she got to the door Gardis appeared, wriggling herself, snapping her fingers, and rolling her eyes as she sang to a peculiar rocking rhythm—

> "Unfair to Gardis, unfair to G.
> Fairfax's Flour go off to de première
> And never say good-bye to me . . . "

She stopped, and they looked at one another. Nell opened her mouth to speak.

"Is that yours?" Gardis enquired, pointing to something lying on the bed.

"Yes. Why?" Nell's tone was neither defiant nor flustered; ten years at Claregates, whatever they had not done, had made her quite capable of dealing with malice or bullying, and here she recognized the unmistakable aura of both.

"Oh . . . nothing. Thought it was a dead cat. Don't mind me, I'm just a crazy girl." Her manner changed and became pleasant and business-like. "Now I expect you want to know all about your job, don't you. I've got it all here. Come on in."

Nell followed her into the little room, which was prettily furnished in pink and black as a miniature office, even down to Gardis's portable typewriter which was enamelled Shocking Pink.

"Fairfax's Flour has the office right next to her bedroom so's she can lie out and just rela-a-x while she dictates," confided Gardis, searching about in a singularly untidy desk, "park your fanny; shan't be more than a coupla hours."

Her voice was low-pitched and chuckling, and Nell had the impression that she emphasized these qualities; she also felt that, although what Gardis said was amusing, if confusing to someone fresh from Dorset, it was not good-naturedly so, and neither was it *real*: it was as if she were making fun of Americans who talked like that on the pictures. She was muttering as she searched, and Nell caught a word which she had heard the carter on Deywood Farm use when the horses were obstinate about being put into the traces. She knew that it was a bad word but not what it meant.

"Why do you call my aunt 'Fairfax's Flour'?" sh
thinking it better to say something.

"Because she's married to Sir Barclay Fairfax who made
money out of flour." Gardis's voice was now clear and u
affected as Nell's own, "Didn't you know it?"

"I knew she had married someone very rich. I didn't know
that he made his money out of flour. I've seen Fairfax's Flour
advertised in the country."

"I guess I've lost it," Gardis said, looking up from the desk
where she was sitting, and whose contents were now scattered
over the floor, and under her eyelashes at Nell. Nell said
nothing, and she went on with the search, "And I had it
typed so *nicely*."

At last she got up. "No use, I'm afraid. It's gone. Would
you like to see one of my pictures?"

"Let me look." Nell went over to the desk. "What does it
look like?"

"It was all carefully typed . . . " Suddenly she slipped a hand
into her skirt pocket. She pulled out a crumpled sheet and held
it up with her eyes glittering maliciously, "Why, there it is!
All the time."

She gave it to Nell, who took it quickly and after scanning it
and seeing with relief that all the details—address, telephone
number, hours, salary, name of firm and that of her aunt's
friend, Hughes, seemed to be there, put it away in her dis-
gracefully shabby bag.

"I guess you'd better come and be secretary to Fairfax's
Flour instead of me," said Gardis, who had sat down again.
"Fairfax himself is up north now, but he has a roving eye, as
you say over here, and if I were his type I wouldn't be safe.
But I shouldn't think you're anybody's type. And—honestly,
I'm telling you for your own good—ankle socks in Town!
I've seen some sights but that beats all. Now come and look
at my picture."

While she was speaking she had been carefully taking out
from a portfolio-case a small canvas stretched on wood.

"Oh, I nearly forgot. Fairfax's Flour said be sure to tell you
not to be late on Monday morning, because if there's anything that does make Mr. Hughes hopping mad, it is lateness.
And she said to tell you he could be a devil to work for.
So I'm telling you. There," holding up the picture. "Like
it?"

ibit with Nell but hypocrisy was not. She
think it's too weird for words."

Gardis's tone was dashed rather than
eyed her picture lovingly. "The man who
: art-school I'm attending says I'm de-
e rapidly and making a real advance.
..⌐ I said that about your coat and your

..⌐gain Nell shook her head. Her wardrobe was in fact a sort
of Record of the Rocks, whose strata recorded the stages of
her father's life-work. She had had to rely for clothes, apart
from her school uniform, largely upon whatever the eldest girl
at the Big House in the village where his living was had
finished with; thus, Rosemary Bratton at Hinchcombe Parva
had supplied the pink taffeta trimmed with rouleaux which
was Nell's best dress; Diana Frazer-Finch the grey flannel
suit she was wearing on this March evening; and Elizabeth
Prideaux, with whom she had been at Claregates and to whom
she still wrote and who occasionally replied from her finishing-
school at Châteaux d'Oex, had given her *a fur jacket*. It was
only bunny, but it was so soft and warm that she never put it
on without seeming to feel, coming out from it, a breath of
Elizabeth herself; her pouter-pigeon figure (known to the
Claregates Sixth as Prideaux's Pride), her passion for scent
and young men, and her frank, free tongue. This was the
jacket now lying on Lady Fairfax's bed which Gardis had
affected to mistake for a dead cat.

"Then I suppose it's just æsthetic ignorance; you don't
know much about art. Fairfax's Flour told me you've always
lived in the country, isn't that so?" Gardis had put the picture
away and was now quickly taking off her dress. The undergarments revealed were so scanty and torn as to justify to Nell
her own slight alarm at the beginning of the performance
(they seemed black only in the sense that they matched their
wearer's hair, but the dustiness and stains of the trousers and
sweater she now resumed by no means reassured Nell as to
the essential purity of the rest).

"Yes," she answered and added rather rashly, "and this is
the first time I've been to London."

"Is that so? You must get dear little John to show you the
sights. He *specializes* in London. He's writing a novel five times
as long as *Gone With the Wind* about it."

"I don't suppose he'll want to show me the sights. Do you know him, then?"

"Oh, he's around from time to time. Fairfax's Flour is crazy about him and I hate his guts and he hates mine. So now I'm going off to a party and I only hope he won't be there." Gardis was standing by the door, wearing the shaggy fur coat over her trousers but no hat, with her hair screwed up into a knob so tight and so high that it strained the skin of her forehead backwards. She looked at Nell for a moment.

"You'll get home all right, won't you?"

"I should think so. Why?"

"Because I'm in a hurry. Fairfax's Flour did tell me to put you into a radiocab, with the fare back, and the fog's coming up quite thick, but . . . "

"Of course I shall be all right."

"Be seeing you, then. Don't let me down with Akkro Products, will you, poppet. Good night." She ran down the stairs. In a moment Nell heard the front door shut with a reverberation hinting that she enjoyed a loud noise.

Nell stood in the smart, softly lit room, looking without seeing them at the gay bottles and jars on her aunt's dressing table. They glittered, like the ceiling and the pots containing exotic indoor plants, and Nell, who was suffering the onset of a feeling familiar to her at Claregates, waited crossly for the glitter to swim into that of tears. It did not come. She swallowed a lump, was relieved to find the feeling receding.

The luxurious quiet house smelt faintly of roasting chicken as she ran down the stairs and let herself out. Who on earth could be going to eat it?

CHAPTER TWO

BOY IN THE FOG

THE fog, which she had supposed to be a spiteful invention on the part of Gardis, turned out to be a fact. It had come up within half an hour like an invasion of ghosts. The road was unnaturally silent and distant footsteps were muffled; thick yellow haze veiled the street lamps, which in this backwater of St. John's Wood were the old-fashioned kind that do not

burn chemicals, and the end of the tree-shaded little road
was invisible. She could just detect the sound of the distant
traffic.

Nell naturally did not share the native Londoner's resentment of a thick fog in March, four months out of season, and
found it pleasantly exciting. Having an excellent sense of
direction she turned to the left without hesitating, and walked
quickly on under the big wet bushes and leafless lime-trees
hung with silent glittering drops, and was so busy resenting
Aunt Peggy's interference while telling herself she ought to
be grateful, that she did not begin to hear, until she had come
almost to the end of the row of smart brick houses with
their blue shutters, the leisured, curiously individual, tread of
feet keeping pace, on the hidden other side of the road, with
her own. They sounded full of meaning, somehow, in the
quiet.

She glanced across into the yellow dimness. Could she see
someone there? a tall black someone? She thought that she
could just make out a white face. And then, as she looked, it
was no longer there. Had the footsteps stopped? It didn't
matter now if they hadn't; she had reached the main road, and
cars were crawling cautiously along, hooting and sending
their glaring headlights into the writhing yellow mist, within
a few feet of her. No-one would knock her on the head now,
though a car might knock her down. Her mother had remarked
before she left, with a surprise not untouched by distaste, that
people seemed to get knocked on the head all the time in
Hampstead nowadays; there were three cases this evening in
The Hampstead and Highgate Express, which Anna's family had
always taken, and which she had ordered to be delivered at
the new house, with a reckless disregard of its costing threepence a week, soon after their arrival there.

Nell forgot the footsteps as she walked on, for if her imagination had not been slightly stirred out of its constitutional
sobriety by the move to London and glimpses of London's size
and strangeness, she would not have thought them meaningful
or even noticed them; yet her inward ear had heard faithfully.
Full of meaning they were, and meaning for herself.

Parsons' children are seldom fervently religious, and Nell
was no exception, but she had almost unwittingly absorbed one
Christian tenet. Years of wearing shabby cast-offs, eating plain
food in humourless company, and general going-without, had

schooled her in taking no thought for the morrow. She went
on up the broad sloping pavements of Fitzjohn's Avenue,
bordered with magnificent Edwardian mansions of red brick
in decline which had once given it the name "Park Lane of
North London"—with her brief depression put behind her,
and thinking only of the prospects ahead, while following her
mother's instructions to just keep straight on, both going to
St. John's Wood and returning. The cars glared and hooted
and crawled in the choking mist; homeward-bound workers
passed her with handkerchiefs held over their mouths, and
soon Hampstead's big trees began to loom and drip over-
head.

But she was finding it difficult to keep her thoughts on one
subject. First she would think about Miss Lister, and recapitu-
late the story's details to tell to her mother, who preferred to
be primed about people's backgrounds; then she would run
over the warning about Charles Gaunt's designs upon the top
flat, and then, always with the same small shock, remember
that she had a job. She started on Monday. She would have
to spend most of the week-end doing shorthand. Her typing
was not so neglected, because she was accustomed to banging
out the Vicar's Letter and list of psalms and hymns for the
Parish Magazine on her father's thirty-year-old Remington,
but her shorthand was really weak. Oh damn Aunt Peggy,
thought Nell, as she went past the long narrow passage with
the nostalgic name of Shepherd's Walk, which leads through
to Rosslyn Hill, I wanted to find a job for myself.

The fog was thicker here than ever, and the road much
quieter, for the homeward-bound procession of cars was dying
down and they crawled past at less frequent intervals. She was
walking quickly past a row of small houses with silent tree-filled
gardens, when she heard the footsteps again. They were
unmistakable. But this time they were on this side of the road
and they were immediately behind her.

Nell *was* a little frightened. But she was far more cross. She
whirled round and stared into the yellow haze which shut her
in like a writhing impalpable wall on all sides. Yes, there was
the tall dark shape and the white face. It was standing still,
looking at her. She could just make it out by the hazy orange
light of a lamp some distance away.

"What do you want?" she called, rather threateningly, in
her thin pure tones with the note that seems to shut ladies off

from the warm and vulgar world. She actually took a few steps towards the motionless shape.

"Don't be so *absurd*," a beautiful deep young voice said petulantly out of the fog, "don't you recognize me? I'm your cousin, John Gaunt," and the figure began to move leisurely forward.

"Oh," said Nell, relieved but still cross, "hullo. How could I possibly recognize you? I've only seen you once about ten years ago."

"I recognized you. By your walk." He was holding out his hand, and, having pulled off her worn glove, she put hers into it and received a firm shake. "How you do tear along; I've been behind you all the way up Fitzjohn's Avenue and I could hardly keep up with you. I saw you come out of my mamma's house, and you were darting along in just the same way that you did that afternoon."

"Then why on earth didn't you speak to me, instead of . . . "

She head a low amused sound. "I didn't want to frighten you."

"But surely it was much more frightening to prowl along like that . . . "

"*Need* we go on about it? It is so boring. Let's walk on, shall we?" and he gently touched her arm and began to move forward.

Nell went too, and for some moments they did not say anything. She was still annoyed, and now she was shy as well. This was the first time that she had ever walked beside a young man, unless that occasion were counted when Nicholas, Elizabeth Prideaux's brother, had taken her to the marquee for lemonade one Open Day at Claregates, and although she was not looking at him now, she had taken such unconscious pleasure in the sight of John's white skin, fair hair cut in a manner quite unfamiliar to her, and sleepy-looking eyes whose colour she could not distinguish, by this light, that the image was still floating before her mind's eye . . .

'Young man', indeed! He was quite two years younger than herself. He was a little boy. And although his mother said that he was brilliant, she had also hinted that he was giving his parents trouble, while his behaviour this evening had been of the kind always dismissed by Nell's own mother as *tiresome*.

Having replenished her self-respect, which had shown

surprising and unexpected signs of being depleted, she turned to him intending to say something amiably patronizing, and experienced precisely the same shock of helpless delight as before.

"How are you liking Hampstead?" he was asking in a social voice, "My friend Benedict Rouse says that *Camp But Enchanting* ought to be embroidered on its municipal banner. You must meet him soon. You'd like him. He'd like your bones, too. They're awfully small, aren't they, Nell, like some delicate bleached baby rabbit . . . and *don't*, whatever you do, let anyone persuade you to do anything to your hair. It's the kind that *ought* to hang in a straight little curtain like that and it's absolutely my favourite kind. I say, are you all right? You look quite green."

"I'm all right, thanks. Perhaps it's the lamps," said Nell, who had in fact suddenly become very hungry, "what a weird light, isn't it."

"That's exactly the right word." He glanced at her approvingly. "How Edgar Allan Poe would have liked them, wouldn't he? (I adore that kind of anachronism. I find them all day long.) Didn't you think dear little Gardis is like someone out of a poem by Poe? Ligeia, or the girl in the *ghoul-haunted woodland of Weir*? She's already in some of Benedict's poems."

"Are they engaged?" said Nell.

Afterwards, she realized that she had known before she asked it that it was a silly question, but the truth was that almost every remark, assumption, phrase and circumstance outside her family circle which she had encountered during the last two days was strange to her, and the only way in which she could meet each occasion was by making some pleasant, ordinary comment. She could not continually betray ignorance; she could not continually demand to be enlightened. If much of what her aunt, Gardis, and now John, said, was unintelligible to her, she could at least congratulate herself on having concealed bewilderment beneath a brisk, sensible manner. This time, however, the method brought shattering results.

"Don't be so bloody suburban," he said coldly. "They're lovers."

There was a pause. They had reached Hampstead Tube Station. People were wandering or scurrying in and out of it, or hanging about waiting for their dears. The lamps and shop windows of the steep narrow High Street glowed through the

thinning fog and the cafés were full. Nell saw to her slight
dismay that the station clock said ten minutes past eight;
she had been told not to be later home than a quarter past
seven. Putting the recent shock out of her mind, she turned
to John.

"I say, I must get back. They'll be wondering where I am."
But she was remembering as she spoke, *it's absolutely my favourite
kind.*

They were standing near the newspaper man on the corner.
Looking up at her cousin she realized both how tall he was,
and that a look of uneasiness, almost of distress, had come on to
his face.

"Oh, don't go yet. Can't you telephone them and say you're
with me? We'll go and drink coffee at an Espresso."

"I don't know the number. You see . . . "

"Oh really, Nell. It's under Palmer-Grove. Here, I'll look
it up for you."

She followed him into the station. As he strode ahead of her
she studied his clothes, odd indeed to eyes accustomed to the
soft rough tweeds of the true country, rather than the duffel-
coats and jeans of the Home Counties. He had trousers of
dark green corduroy, and a thick blue polo sweater showed
above the collar of a very dirty trench-coat. Under his arm he
carried a worn and bulging portfolio of good leather. His head
was bare. That *was* an odd haircut. Nell did not know that
much of her wish to go on looking at him came from the
beautiful shape of his head which the odd cut so well displayed.

"Here," he said, indicating a number with a finger, long as
his mother's, but dirty, "and do hurry up. I want to show
you an Espresso bar."

While she made the call and re-assured the not-very-active
fears of Anna, who seemed only anxious to get back to the
Mémoires d'Outre-Tombe, Nell was feeling, rather than thinking,
how singularly at home she was with John.

They had been together now for perhaps twenty minutes.
They had exchanged none of the customary exploratory
remarks. His manner was neither friendly nor attentive, and
his conversation was largely incomprehensible and could be
brutally shocking. (She was still tingling from the revelation
about Gardis . . . if it meant what Nell supposed it did mean
. . . or was it only the London way of saying that they were in
love . . . ? But she thought not.) She was pleased that they

were going to be together for a little longer. How hungry she
felt. The slice of home-made cake and cup of weak tea swallowed
four hours ago might never have been, yet her appetite, fed
from babyhood on starch, which is cheap, rather than proteins
which are dear, was generally content to skip supper altogether.
Could this unusual appetite be due to the Hampstead air?

When they had taken the last two seats in a long, bright, hot
room crammed with youngish people wearing bright untidy
clothes and all staring into each other's faces while they talked
at an immense pace without stopping, he said:

"I'm terribly sorry but can you pay for yourself? I've only
got a shilling and this marvellously good coffee costs ninepence
a cup."

"Oh—yes, of course—only I'm afraid I've only got a shilling,
too."

"That means we can't have any cakes. Cakes are sevenpence
each. Oh well . . . "

"Couldn't we . . . " Nell's lack of experience in issuing in-
vitations to young men caused her, in spite of feeling so
surprisingly at ease with him, to pause and swallow, " . . . have
our coffee here and . . . go home and have something to eat
there? There is . . . some cake, I think."

"We might. I'll see . . . oh, there's someone over there I
know. I can probably borrow from him."

While he was bending persuasively over the beard, red face,
and rough coat which was all that Nell could see of the someone, she looked curiously round at the young, bold, alive, and
sometimes—she saw with sheer disbelief; it *must* be this peculiar
light—dirty faces of the Espresso drinkers, set off by brilliant
checked shirts, white jackets fastened by wooden links, black
'jumpers' (as Nell called them) and, in the case of the women,
exaggeratedly severe or flowing manner of arranging the hair.
Coiffures and beards played a large part in the exhibiting of
their personalities, and did not always look quite clean. Were
these, Nell wondered, *artists*? and felt slightly awed.

"That's all right." John sat down again opposite her.
"Chris lent me half-a-crown. His woman is in work this week.
You must meet her; she's very beautiful and she washes-up
for a living."

"Does she?" Nell's bewilderment with the world now being
revealed to her expressed itself in a tone slightly tart and
cautious.

"Yes, she does. Don't sound so suburban. Now . . . isn't that a wonderful taste?"

She was not extending her caution to the sipping of the blackish-gold liquid in a transparent cup, which she indeed found wonderful. She nodded in enthusiastic silence, and an addict was born. John authoritatively selected two oozing cakes from a trolley wheeled up by a waitress, and for some moments, spinning them out, they ate in silence. This was the second time that he had called her *suburban*. What exactly did he mean?

"How is it that you only have a shilling?" he asked, when the last blob of synthetic cream had gone.

"Well . . . " beginning to colour, "we're . . . rather hard up just now and my mother thought I wouldn't need more than that to get down to Aunt Peggy's—your mother's, that is—but anyway I walked."

"You need not mind talking about money to me, you know. If you're going about with me and going to meet all my friends, you must stop having false and silly ideas about that. *We* usually haven't any money at all, and when we do have it's very little. Most of the time we're starving. You'll be amazed at how little food and sleep one can do with."

"Shall I?" said Nell. She could think of nothing but the fact that they were to go about together. But then she remembered his age. And his manner could be offensive. "I'm starting a job on Monday," she added in a busy tone, "so I don't suppose I shall have much free time"—but he did not seem to have heard, for he went on—

"You really must get out of that habit of answering in *questions*. 'Does she?' 'Shall I?' It sounds so bloody irritating and rude."

"You're *very* rude," she retorted, "and it sounds simply frightful to keep on . . . using that word." Her voice tailed off. He was leaning forward with both hands in the air.

"Your béret looks horrible on the back of your head like that." He twitched it over to one side and set it at a terrific slant. "*That's* how you want to wear it. Like Ewa Bartok?"

"Who?" But Nell left the béret untouched.

"Ewa Bartok the film star. If you can't afford proper clothes; long full skirts and low heels and metal jewellery, you should copy Ewa Bartok. She knows how to make horrible little suits like the one you're wearing and old raincoats look marvellously romantic." He stopped. Then he went on in what Nell was already thinking of as his social voice, "By the way, how is Aunt Anna?"

"Oh . . . very well, I think," she answered, rather thrown out by this abrupt change of subject.

"I was thinking . . . I'd like to see her again, and Uncle Martin too. I'm still hungry, aren't you? I think I will come back with you after all. What sort of cake is it?"

"Oh . . . home-made." Pale crumbling slabs, sparsely set with sultanas as pale, floated in her mind's eye. She did not want to risk his comments on them, but she did want him to come home. He was looking at her consideringly with now widely-opened, light grey eyes. And, perhaps because his expression was candid and gentle, she remembered something.

"Well, do come, then," she said, "I know" (this was an exaggeration) "they would both like to see you. Oh, by the way, I've got a message for you; from your mother. She said if I saw anything of you would I ask you to ring her up, and she said . . . "

Her voice tailed off again. He was looking exceedingly angry and she had said the very wrong thing.

"*Bloody* parents," he said violently. "I *did* ring her up ten days ago. Why can't they leave one *alone*? I don't want to *hear* what she said. She said she was my *mother*, I suppose. Well she is, but I didn't ask her to be nor my father *either*. And as for *you*, Nello, you had better make up your mind here and now and once and for all whose *side* you are on."

"I'm not on anyone's side," she said, after a pause. But of course she was, after only half-an-hour.

"How cowardly you are." However, he did not sound cross with her; his tone had suddenly become absent. "Let's go, shall we? There's such a beastly strong light in here."

When they were walking up the dim, steep, leafy back streets into which he immediately led her, complaining that the glare in the High Street was even worse, he began upon his mother's impertinence in finding her a job.

"It was sheer interference, why couldn't she leave you to find one for yourself? You *would* have. (You've got lots of character; I can see that. It makes me feel safe with you. Only you must never use it on *me*.) Why must she *butt in*? You'll hate Akkro Products. I've met Gerry Hughes at one of her parties and he looks quite damned with trying to get on. You won't

get a thing out of being with him, you know. *Must* you turn
up there on Monday?"

At some point in his tirade he had taken her arm, and now
she was matching her swift pace to his leisurely one as they
dawdled up and down the dim little alleys of lanky white
cottages and past silent gardens whose spring flowers glimmered
through the thinning fog.

"I shall get five pounds a week," Nell said.

"Well? Is that so necessary?"

They had paused in a hilly road whose end simply went off
into the darkness. "It's patchy, isn't it," he murmured, meaning the fog, and indeed here it had almost gone, "look, that's
the Heath. You can see the lights in the Vale of Health pond."

She looked at the strip of bright, wild, emerald grass edging
the dark, then beyond it, off and away, into airy blackness.
The wind blew in her face a smell of coldness and earliest
leaves. Low down, lights of crystal and gold were reflected in
still water; farthest away of all, some glittered so high that they
might have been up in a cloud.

"Yes, I've got to earn some money for the parents," she said.

"Oh . . . parents." But the outburst which she had impatiently expected did not follow, and they strolled on, Nell remembering how she had looked at her mother that evening and it
had been as if she had seen her for the first time.

Anna had been standing in the cold, crowded hall under the
unshaded bulb of the light, wearing the shabby woollen clothes
which had been her only style of dress ever since Nell could
remember, and her hands had looked red and her hair grey,
and the lines in her vigorous, weather-roughened face harsh and
deep. Nell had just come down from speaking to her father
where he lay in bed with his detective story under the light of
another unshaded bulb (all their lampshades at Morley Magna
vicarage had crackled into pieces when they were taken down
for the move) and he had looked unkempt and listless and old.
The two of them had looked old. And it had occurred to Nell,
while she was putting on her béret at the despised angle in the
icy bedroom where she had been warned not to light the electric fire, that if she did not set to work to feed and clothe the
elder Selys properly, they would quietly expire. She had told
herself not to be silly: that her mother was unusually strong,
and her father recovering, in body at least, from the illness
which had nearly taken him, but the feeling had remained,

and she intended to act upon it as soon as possible. She had
felt a warmer element entering into her rather reserved
relations with her parents as a result, but her aunt's high-
handed action had damped it all down, and now she could
feel nothing but impatience and an anticipatory boredom
about her shorthand.

"Here we are ... " she said, as they turned into Arkwood
Road.

"I know that. I was born here, you know." He was looking
up at the comfortable ugly red-brick fronts trimmed with
white stone.

"Where are you living now?" she asked, and as she was
making conversation from slight embarrassment at the
possibility of being seen by her mother arm-in-arm with a
practically new cousin, rather than seeking information, she
became justifiably annoyed when he replied repressively that
she would not know where the room he shared with Benedict
was, even if he told her. It was an unmistakable snub, and
at the same time he withdrew his arm.

They had stopped in front of Number Twenty-five. As she
made to open the gate, he stepped back.

"I don't think I'll come in after all, do you know. Do you
mind very much—I do so *hate* seeming rude."

"Of course I don't," Nell declared with briskness, "I've got
shorthand to do, and we haven't even started to get straight
yet." She bit soberly on her disappointment. She added,
"Good night. Thank you for the coffee, it was awfully good,"
and was turning away when he said slowly:

"I don't know ... perhaps I will come in after all. May I?"
and began to follow her up the front steps.

Nell shrugged, and put her key into the front door. Then
she stopped. She turned and looked down at him. "John, how
did you know that your mother had found me the job? I
didn't say so, and she said you haven't seen her for a week."

He looked up at her as he stood with one foot advanced
upon the step. "Didn't you say so? I think you did, you know,"
but Nell shook her head.

"Oh well, I heard it somehow. Perhaps she told me before I
walked out. Does it matter? It *is* so boring. Are you going to
keep me standing here for the rest of the evening?"

She turned away and put the key in. He was lying; she had
not said so. But this caused no equivalent decline in certain

feelings she already had for him. She opened the front door.
Behind her, she heard him coming leisurely up the steps.

Anna Sely had gone back to her book. She was sitting at the
kitchen table, leaning forward with hands pushed into her
curly grey hair, walking about in the mind of François de
Chateaubriand.

The kitchen was painted chalk-white and raspberry-pink,
and if she had been imaginative she would have felt an
atmosphere of Continental pleasures lingering there; created
by foreign travel posters pinned on the walls and by the ghosts
of olives and gnocchi, Brie and salami, which had been eaten
there by the Palmer-Groves, those admirers of the Continent
and its ways. There might also have silently echoed the discussions about art, and, towards the end, the deathly bitter
arguments about who was to have the children . . .

Anna felt nothing of this. She was roaming the red-draped,
spice-scented chambers of a long-dead Frenchman's imagination, and even so she was hearing the mellifluous French and
following the thought expressed, rather than receiving a series
of pictures, but beneath her customary slightly drugged
pleasure in the act of reading (for Anna read as chain-smokers
smoke) something unusual was going on.

For many years, now, she had observed only those facts
connected with herself which were practical and could be
dealt with by an action; such as her need for a clean overall,
or for her shoes to be mended, while thoughts and feelings
passed within herself unobserved. When occasionally they
threatened to be painful (and for months now the word
unhappy had been rising nearer and nearer to the surface of her
consciousness) she turned them off instantly; without hesitation; as if they had been some mechanical device. Only the
restlessness which drove her without pause from one clumsily-
performed domestic task to the next might have hinted, to
that observer interested in psychology whom nowadays she
never encountered, that she was not at peace. Few of us are,
but Anna seemed so unaware of her own lack—and yet to
need peace so much.

Her quick, well-bred voice, summarizing the contents of a
paragraph full of complex facts in the newspaper while her
long fingers, stained with garden and kitchen work, moved
undeftly among the tea-cups, sounded full of strain. She

sewed with big clumsy stitches while crouching forward in her chair—or blundered about the series of cavernous cold rectories, ceaselessly at work, keeping them reasonably warm and clean. She gardened, growing splendid flowers and vegetables which she regarded with a critical satisfaction; she even carpentered, and mended fuses; and once, during the three months that someone had lent the Selys an old car, drove it and repaired it and changed its tyres. In church, and of course she went to church automatically and often, her thoughts were busy with details of house-running. She was never still or quiet except when she was asleep.

This had been her state of body and mind for a very long time: almost since, inexplicably giving up those prospects of an academic career of solid cleverness which had caused her professors at the London School of Economics to approve and be proud of her, she had suddenly married Martin Sely, five years her senior, and newly ordained, and just established in his first living.

This evening, while she sat reading in the kitchen, she had been remembering. That was a most unusual thing for Anna to do; and she was also uneasy, which was even more unusual. Memories were flocking into the grey head sunk between the roughened hands; drifting, lightly touching her spirit, troubling her faintly. She had actually got so far as giving herself a reason for her odd mood; it was coming back to Hampstead that was responsible; that first sight of the Heath yesterday, looking just as green and brown and blue under the cold spring rain as it used to look thirty years ago, had—upset her. She had felt herself as two people, while the car was going up the familiar High Street: the cheerful, handsome, clever girl living in The General's House with her parents, and the shabbily-dressed, ageing wife of a silly old parson who had lost his faith and been turned out of the Church, on her way to live in a house lent by his sister out of charity.

It was most confusing and Anna did not like it at all.

It had made her feel so peculiar that it had prevented her from starting work on the house. Their furniture, deprived of the familiar background which had somehow lessened its shabbiness, was scattered up and down the pale blue staircase and on the navy-blue or black floors, with old chairs, whose forlorn state had been taken for granted for years, looking fit only for the rubbish-heap as they stood against the raspberry walls.

"I'd no idea we owned such a collection of junk," Anna had remarked to Nell while the removal men were carrying the things in, but she had not added *I wonder what the neighbours must think*, because such an idea would never have entered her head. Miss Meredith, of The General's House, had had no neighbours in the usual sense, surrounded as she had been by old friends of her parents, and their children with whom she had grown up, living in Hampstead's old white mansions shaded by Hampstead's beautiful old trees; and in the country the Selys had for years been separated by poverty, the fact of their being a parson's family, and something in Anna's own temperament, from making casual acquaintanceships. Even her dutifully performed parish work had brought her neither liking nor friends.

At this moment the wife of the no-longer Reverend Martin Sely felt a strong disinclination to begin arranging those thread-bare carpets and slowly-disembowelling chairs and curtains faded to mere drabness. She had been out that morning to the public library, which she had found astonishingly good, and come back with an armful of books for herself and her poor old Martin, and now she wanted only to read. Outside, coming into the quiet of the house, she could hear a bell ringing sadly through the fog for some late Lenten service (Compline, perhaps; she had heard that during the soon-to-be-relinquished guidance of Dr. Wand many London churches had tended to grow Higher). And the sound added a vague feeling of guilt to her thoughts. There was another sound which had been coming to her for nearly two hours now; ever since she had impatiently pushed aside the remains of their scanty tea and settled herself, with a sense of relief, to read; a sound deep, persistent and soft which might almost have been her own thronging memories made audible; muffled; diffused; throbbing very faintly over the quiet gardens where white and yellow spring flowers glimmered through the drifting mists; coming up through the fog lying on the marsh to Hampstead, outspread upon its hills. *Of course*, thought Anna, not lifting her head to listen nor taking her eyes from the page, *it's the traffic down in London. I'd forgotten. I used to hear it when I was a child.*

Upstairs the front door closed. In a moment she heard footsteps coming down the kitchen stairs; then Nell's voice— "Mother? Are you there? Here's John—John Gaunt, you know. John, here's my mother," and they came into the kitchen; a plain young person and a beautiful one, both noses pink with cold and fog.

"Hullo, John. It must be quite ten years since we met. How are you?" Anna got up, pushing Chateaubriand aside, "How is your mother?"

"I really don't know, Aunt Anna, I haven't seen her for nearly ten *days*. All right, I imagine; she usually is. Margie, that's my new mamma, says she looks like an advertisement for Cornflakes (Margie has to make these bitchy remarks; she's naturally rather a nice little thing but my papa encourages her to be spiteful because he feels it's more interesting)."

"I see." Anna had a habit of saying this when her thoughts had gone to practical details while anyone was talking, and she had not heard what was said; in this case, it was just as well. "Nell, are your feet wet?"

She also had the habit of fussing mildly over Nell, who had been a small and unusually white baby whose difficult rearing had added considerably to the toil of Anna's days and nights. She was by no means 'wrapped up' in her daughter, but she still saw to it that Nell herself was 'well wrapped-up'.

Nell shook her head.

"You look cold. I'm sorry there's no fire . . . do sit down, John . . . we can't go upstairs, there's nowhere to go . . . what *have* you done to your béret, Nell? It's falling off you."

"I made her wear it like that, Aunt Anna. It looks more elegant," said John. Nell snatched off the offender and cast it on the dresser.

"Nonsense," Anna said. She looked at him as he lounged on the chair into which he had sunk. "Don't loll like that, my dear boy, you'll get curvature."

"I'm sorry, Aunt Anna," sitting meekly upright.

There was silence for a moment. Anna was trying to think of something to say. She was not at a loss generally but his appearance was really so peculiar that it seemed to increase the bewilderment of her feelings. She found herself wishing suddenly that she were knitting in the drawing-room at Morley Magna. What had he done to his hair?

John said suddenly. "It's simply freezing in here. Shall I make some tea?"

"Tea? But we had tea hours ago." Anna did not catch Nell's irritated glance. "There's a piece of cake in the tin if you're hungry."

"I am rather. I've had nothing all day. I would really *rather* have tea. Where do you keep the tin? I'll make it."

Anna had not prepared an impromptu meal for anyone since the days when she had visited the studios of her college friends with the Poetry Book Shop rhyme-sheets on their whitewashed walls. She laughed now, but said, "Very well, if you really want some and don't think it'll keep you awake. Why haven't you had anything to eat all day? Is your mother away?"

"I'm not living at home now (are these the cups? . . . and the sugar's in here, isn't it . . . I know my way about because I used to come here when old Miss Lister . . .)"

"What did you say?" Anna's tone was impatient. "Don't mutter, please. Where are you living, if not at home?"

Nell heard him, while she superintended the kettle, giving a cautious and vague account of his lodgings (somewhere east of Camden Town, wherever that was) followed, under questioning, by a list of the things he was *not* doing. She could see that her mother thought it odd, but she was convinced that Anna did not know how very odd it in fact was. Nell, who had been followed in the fog, felt that she herself did at least *suspect* the advanced state which the oddness had reached.

"Then if you only work occasionally (no, I won't have any, .thank you, it keeps me awake) and aren't taking classes anywhere or training for anything, what on earth are you doing with yourself?" Anna demanded at last, sitting upright with elbows on the table and looking at him rather severely. She detested idling, especially idling and planlessness in the young; although some of her friends in youth at L.S.E. had been idle and indecisive, their brilliance had excused them. Was John brilliant? She would have been prepared to swear that he was not. He seemed half-asleep.

"Oh . . . I wander about London, looking at things . . . I work quite hard sometimes too. I've just finished a job slicing bacon at Selfridges for three pounds a week . . . that was hard enough work and hours to satisfy even an *adult*. And I'm writing a novel, you know."

"I didn't know. It sounds very grand," Anna said dryly. She began to gather together the tea-things. "Nell, you're drinking that tea much too strong. It will give you indigestion. Put some more milk into it."

"Doesn't it? That's exactly the right word." He beamed

with satisfaction and glanced affectionately towards his portfolio, lying on the dresser.

"What's it called? What is it about? Will it be a best-seller?"
Anna, slapping the cups into the sink, darted a 'comical' glance
at Nell.

"It hasn't a title yet. It's about London. Yes, one day it
will be a best-seller, only not quite in the sense that you mean,
Aunt Anna. Would you call Dante's *Inferno* a best-seller?"

"Dear me! You are aiming high, aren't you. I should call
that a classic and a work of genius."

"Precisely," said he politely, and got up from his chair.
"I must go, I'm afraid. I've got to meet someone who's going
to give me a job . . . Thank you so much for the tea, Aunt
Anna, I hope you'll let me come again, often." He picked up
his portfolio, and Nell saw him glance quickly, almost stealthily, round the kitchen. "I wish the bloody Palmer-Groves—"
and then, as Anna stared at him coldly—

"I beg your pardon . . . the *idiotic* Palmer-Groves hadn't
painted it this sickly colour."

"I think it's rather jolly," said Anna, excusing his slip with
the thought *showing off*, "even your Uncle Martin thinks so."

"It was nicer before. How is Uncle Martin? Can I look in on
him before I go?"

"Oh, getting better. But he still isn't himself. No, better not,
I think. He may be asleep. I'll tell him you asked after him.
(Nell, see John out, will you?) Good-bye, John. Come and see
us again soon. Perhaps you'll condescend to read us some of
your masterpiece."

They left her laughing to herself over the cups in the sink.
When they were in the dim, cluttered hall he said very quietly
to Nell: "I'll go at once, because you're wanting to tell her
about your job . . . (if you're *really* bent on turning up there;
I think you're being bloody silly) . . . But you don't mind if I
just fly up and look at our flat, do you? I won't be two seconds."

Before she could speak, he was gone. She had no idea that
he could move so fast. He darted up the faintly-lit stairs without making a sound in his rubber-soled sandals on the un-
carpeted boards, and she stood there staring after him, feeling
vaguely uneasy. She did not know why. Somewhere, at the
back of her mind, there was a sensation of warning.

He could not have been as long as ten seconds, if he was longer
than the promised two. When he reappeared he was smiling.

"It looks just the same. The bloody P.G.s haven't sloshed their paint all over *our* front-door. I've had a lovely time. I'll take you out to meet some of my friends soon but *first*, I suppose, I must earn some money." He paused.

Nell's cold hand was hanging at her side. Now she felt it gently lifted, John's head came down to meet it, and it was softly kissed. She said not a word. Surprise drove out all other feelings.

"Don't *do* anything to yourself, will you? I like you as you are, except for your clothes, which are *horrible*. But I'll tell you what to wear later. I'll ring you up soon. Good-bye, Nello darling."

The front door opened and closed. She heard his footsteps, those unmistakable footsteps, going slowly, now—down into the street, and saw through the glass panels in the door his tall, dark shape receding. The footsteps died away.

Nell went up to her room to put away her own outdoor clothes. She was still so surprised that it was an effort to remember what she had to do next, and she was conscious of nothing; not the chill of the neat shabby room, not the muffled roar of distant traffic going past in the High Street, not the glare of the unshaded light; she could feel nothing but this surprise, and the pressure of his lips on the back of her hand.

"Nell? Don't tell me that *you* are going to start mooning about, now. Do you want any supper? Surely not, after all that tea." Her mother, who had come upstairs to find out if Martin Sely wanted a hot drink before going to sleep, looked in at the door.

"No; I had a cake with John. Mother, what do you think? Aunt Peggy has found me a job."

"Oh?" Anna did not sound pleased. She came into the room and sat down on the bed. "What sort of a job?"

"I don't know. With a—some people called Akkro Products, Limited. The manager is a friend of hers. I start on Monday."

"On *Monday*! But I shall want you to help me here. I can't get this place straight by myself—though it is so much smaller than Morley. I call it rather high-handed of your Aunt Peggy."

"Her secretary gave me this." Nell handed her Gardis's crumpled paper, and Anna studied it with an expression which, in one who did not come of an old Hampstead family, would have been accompanied by a sniff.

"Tottenham Court Road. H'm. When I was a girl that wasn't

too bad; there were big furniture shops, and interesting people living in Fitzroy Street; but from what I saw from the taxi on Wednesday it seems to have gone right down. I think I must ring Peggy up." But Nell interrupted her purposeful rising from the bed with—

"Mother, it is five pounds a week and we . . . do need it."

"That's Daddy's business and mine, dear. I don't think he would want you to take this job. You know he has never liked the idea of your working at all. In some ways, bless him, he's very old-fashioned, and just now you know he mustn't be upset or worried."

"But you wouldn't mind my doing it, would you?"

Anna stood at the door looking at the daughter for whom she had felt a slight, impatient contempt since Nell failed to distinguish herself academically at Claregates. A scholarship to one of the Universities, even to London, would have been so useful, and Anna, a constitutional storer-away of facts, failed to understand that other people might not find their acquisition so easy. What difficulty was there in memorizing figures or working out a theorem or writing a paper? Nell, poor child, was rather a disappointment.

However, this evening she only looked rather forlorn, standing there in her old grey costume and her grey socks. She certainly was smaller and thinner than most girls of her age; she had not inherited the rosy colouring and curly hair of both her parents, and she was no beauty, although Anna had always admired the clear pale complexion that set off the light blue of her eyes; the blue of the ribbon called in Anna's girlhood *bébé*. (Anna's own complexion had been admired, before the garden and the chickens and the weather took their toll of it.) Perhaps it was the straight hair that made Nell look forlorn.

"No, I shouldn't mind," she said, more gently than usual. "And we *do* need the money. (I can say these things to you, now that you're nearly grown-up.) I've been really worried about money. Five pounds a week won't go far in Hampstead; I'm appalled by the prices here; but it would be very useful—in fact, Nell, I think we shall have to let you do it. But I'm not sure about your qualifications. I expect you've forgotten most of your shorthand, haven't you? (Don't look so dismal, child.) I suppose that's what they'll want you to do?"

"I'm not looking dismal, Mother." Nell's tone stopped just short of irritability. "I was thinking that I haven't any

clothes. And I'm sure these socks are wrong. I've been looking
at people this evening, and no-one wears them except foreign-
looking girls."

"Well, we certainly can't afford to buy you any new clothes.
And what's the matter with the socks? They'll wear for ever.
I haven't decided to let you do the job at all, yet, I must
consult Daddy, of course, but if you do—surely no-one wears
elaborate clothes in an office?"

"No . . . " Nell's tone expressed doubt; she was prepared
to bet on no-one's wearing hand-knitted grey socks either. The
youthful secretaries and receptionists pictured in *Vogue*,
smuggled into Claregates by Elizabeth Prideaux, were not
elaborately dressed, yet Nell possessed not a single garment
remotely in the same style.

"I wish you would consult Daddy tonight, Mother. I want
to telephone Akkro Products early tomorrow morning and
tell them I'll be there at nine on Monday."

"You're going too fast, Nell. I can't disturb him tonight;
he's just settling down. Besides—"

"Oh—!"

The exclamation was not despairing or passionate. It was
merely impatient, and before Anna could protest, Nell had
darted out of the room and across the landing. Anna heard her
tap on her father's door; it opened, and she went in and shut
it behind her.

"Really!" said Anna, aloud. She was considerably taken
aback. She stood there, looking round the bedroom whose
tidiness was in such contrast to the rest of the house, feeling
annoyed and very surprised, but not so angry as she felt that
she should be. She had always known that Nell possessed a
quick temper and a strong will, and she had always insisted on
Nell's controlling the one while she herself mastered the other.
Any rudeness, any defiance or disobedience, had been curbed,
during Nell's childhood, by her brusque heavy hand, and
Claregates (Anna had always presumed) had finished the
training that home-life had begun. One of the results of this
method was that Anna had also begun to despise Nell, aged
nearly twenty, for not asserting herself. She did not know this,
but it was so, and now there mingled with her annoyance a
reluctant—satisfaction.

She had a dim sensation as if one of the responsibilities, those
many responsibilities of her married life which had begun by

fascinating her by their novelty, and the ease with which she had accepted and dealt with them, and ended by overwhelming her selfhood, had begun to remove itself. A burden had lifted; only slightly, but it had. Yet the novelty of Nell's defying her for the first time in nearly twenty years added another note of strangeness to her disturbed, idle, upset mood. Had she not felt herself surrounded by the familiar roads and trees and houses of Hampstead, spread all around her outside in the foggy night, she would have been—unhappy?

She suddenly shrugged, switched off Nell's light, and went downstairs.

"Daddy? I'm sorry to disturb you but it's important. Aunt Peggy has got me a job, doing typing and shorthand with a firm in Tottenham Court Road. It's five pounds a week and I start on Monday. You don't mind, do you?"

The shabby room was illuminated only by a dim bedside lamp. The carpet had not yet been laid and was rolled up near the window, and pictures were stacked against the walls, while the rest of the furniture stood about unarranged. In the midst of it, Martin Sely's red face under his grey, almost white, hair looked out from an untidy bed covered with shabby bedclothes. A book lay face downwards on the counterpane.

Nell stood looking at him, standing slightly beyond the ring of light.

"I see. And now will you repeat that all over again, please? *Slowly.*"

While she was doing so, with a touch of red in her cheeks, he lay with his head turned sideways and his eyelids lowered, apparently listening. But he was not really listening; he had heard the first time; he was experiencing that shame which, now his constant companion, sometimes seemed to him like an actual malevolent spirit; one of those about whom he used to read in the Bible, without a second thought as to its nature and powers.

"Nevermore!" When he and Peggy were young, they used to laugh at that stagey old poem of Poe's, but now the reiteration, because he knew what it meant, seemed to him not funny but terrible. The sober joy of duty done, the cheerful acceptance of God's good, if mysterious, world . . . Nevermore. Easy sleep—Nevermore. Calm waking—Nevermore. The comfortable words and the good cheer and the peace that passeth understanding—Nevermore, Nevermore. And he was ashamed, too, of having spoken like that to his Nell, who would never set the Thames on fire but who was a good child. (The innocent small joys of family life—Nevermore.) And now, thanks to him, she had to go out as a typist.

He slowly lifted his eyelids and looked at her. The thought of having to make a decision confronted him awfully. He could feel his will becoming lax, and melting as he lay. He controlled an impulse to let his lips part in a silly, trembling smile.

"Yes . . . well . . . I suppose it's very kind of your aunt . . . but I've never wanted you to take a 'job', you know. There's always been plenty to do at home, hasn't there . . . but of course . . . this house is so much smaller than the—the vicarage at Morley, isn't it . . . what does Mother say about it . . . you've told her, of course . . . does she think it would be a good idea?"

His deep voice had once given fitting expression to an unusually robust constitution, but now it was so quiet that it seemed to rumble in his chest, suggesting the image of a sea exhausted on the morrow of some titanic storm, while the notes of emphasis, interrogation, approval or warning were almost lacking. It seemed to be an effort to him to speak at all.

"Yes, I know, Daddy." Nell made no attempt to deal separately with his comments, "but you see it's the money. It is five pounds . . . and I have told Mother, and she says it would be useful." She was feeling slightly impatient. First Mother, and now Daddy. Caution and secrecy and fuss. They had hardly any money; very well; why not admit it? and be thankful that she had the chance of earning some.

"It isn't only a question of £. s. d., Nell; these things have to be considered from other angles, you know—from every angle, in fact. What kind of people will you meet in this work? Will they be . . . "

The word *Christians* died upon his tongue. What was he?

He knew that he was only prolonging the discussion because he did not want to give way; to appear weak; to let his daughter see how much he wanted that five pounds a week. To be sure of two hundred and sixty a year! (less tax, of course, less tax. Say two hundred a year). What a relief to know that there was something coming regularly into the house besides Anna's fluctuating hundred and twenty! He would have to swallow his pride and let the child do it, and later on, when he was better, he would get a job himself—address envelopes, become a crossing-sweeper (poor Martin's idea of Honest

Work, like his ideas about everything else, was out-of-date).

"Ordinary people, I suppose," Nell said a little loudly and for the second time. She wished that he would give her a kiss and say that the money would be very useful and wish her luck. She was not looking forward to Monday. *An office* had always sounded, to her, the dullest place on earth.

"Well, dear, you will have to be careful, you know. There are some strange kinds of people in London nowadays . . . does your aunt know this man, the manager, really well? . . . I wish she had consulted us first . . . "

"She's so busy, Daddy." A composite picture of Gardis; her aunt's painted fingernails, the pink typewriter and the mirror-glass ceiling appeared in Nell's fancy, displacing for a moment the face which had lingered there since the shutting of the front door. "She really hardly has time for anything . . . ordinary."

"No . . . I suppose not." (Two husbands. And he had gathered from his sister that she still kept in touch with the first one. Peggy. Lady Fairfax the Television Star. Queer girl, queer people.) "It was kind of her . . . I hope you thanked her." The colourless mumbling voice sounded tired and his fingers moved towards his book . . . "Yes, well, I suppose you may do it . . . try it for a week, anyway, and we'll see how you get on." He did not look at her as he spoke, but took up his detective story.

Nell made herself say, "Thank you, Daddy." Then she kissed him and darted out of the room. She liked darting: it had been an effort to her to loiter along in step with John that evening. John! As she skimmed downstairs she glanced at the white telephone in the hall, which was to her now the most interesting object in the house.

"He says I may, Mother," she announced to Anna, standing surrounded by crates and straw and boxes with a book held up very close to her face under the shadeless glare of the drawing-room light. "I say, hadn't we better get this a bit straight? Supposing someone came?"

"No-one will." Anna came reluctantly out of Chateaubriand, "but I suppose we may as well. Aren't you tired, dear? It's been such a long day."

Nell, glancing at her in surprise, said truthfully that she was not, and for an hour they worked on the room, Nell taking the chance, while she darted round, of telling her mother about old Miss Lister, and Charles Gaunt's possible designs on the top-floor flat.

About eleven o'clock they decided that the room now looked
what they called presentable, although Anna shook her head
over their mild late-Edwardian possessions displayed against
peacock-green walls. Then she went up to bed. But long after
twelve, Nell was sitting in her room, copying *n* hooks and *shun*
hooks and revising dots and vowels and abbreviations, with
an expression on her face as cross as it was dogged.

CHAPTER THREE

THEY WERE BOTH BREATHING FLAME

ABOUT a quarter to nine the next morning, having bolted
her breakfast and made her bed and taken up her father his
tray, she was banging away on the ancient Remington while
her mother took a prolonged preliminary survey of the garden,
when the front-door bell rang.

Nell said *damn*, shook back her hair, and flew out into the
hall. The pale face floated more clearly before her mind's eye.
Supposing—? But no; he would have attracted her attention
in some way through the open window. Front-door approaches
were not his line at all.

"Oh—good-morning," said the handsome, grey-faced,
elegantly-dressed man who stood on the doorstep, "I expect
you're Nell, aren't you? We've never met but I recognized you
from . . . Peggy's description . . . I'm terribly sorry to disturb
you at this ungodly hour but the fact is we're going to be fellow-
tenants. I've got the flat at the very top of the house," and as
he said it he began, so unobtrusively that only someone on the
alert would have noticed, to incline himself over the threshhold.

So here he was. Aunt Peggy had been alarmingly right. This
was the face last seen by Nell under a coating of fish-scales, and
what on earth was she going to do about it?

"Oh . . . how stupid of me. My name is Gaunt, Charles
Gaunt," he added. This time as he said it he looked round—
for now, Nell could not imagine how, he was standing in the
hall—for somewhere to put his dark hat and dark walking-
stick and pale gloves, but there was nowhere, unless he cared
to hang the one and rest the other upon the enormous reproduc-

tion of Rosa Bonheur's *The Horse Fair* leaning against the terra-cotta wall.

"Rather chi-chi taste the Palmer-Groves had, don't you agree?" he said pleasantly and glanced past Nell into the drawing-room. It seemed to her apprehensive eye that he was already in it. Where, if this went on, would he end up? In the top flat, of course. She did not look at the telephone but all her thoughts were upon it. How—*how* to warn Aunt Peggy?

Mr. Gaunt was now looking up the stairs.

"Do come in, won't you," said Nell, leading the way into the drawing-room. He followed, but rather slowly, while she wondered what to do. "Er—I expect you would like to see my mother." (Mother. That was the idea. Get Mother; shut them in the drawing-room; creep to the telephone . . .)

"Oh, please don't bother. I expect she's very busy . . . I really only came to 'take possession'."

He laughed. That is, his mouth opened and his teeth showed. His yellow eyes looked dull and miserable and cross. "I know my way about the house, you know; I used to live here." The Gaunts, father and son, seemed determined to assert their claims over Arkwood Road, thought Nell. The situation was difficult, but she was not an ex-parson's daughter for nothing. She dealt with him as she would have done with some tiresome morning caller at the vicarage.

"Oh, but I know she would like to see you," she said firmly, and was flying out of the room when a slow step sounded outside and Anna's face looked round the door, all enquiry at seeing so much masculine elegance decorating the drawing-room at this hour in the morning.

"Oh, here is my mother," trying not to sound thankful, "Mother, you know—Mr. Gaunt—don't you?"

"Of course. How nice to see you again," Anna said, regarding him with that amused interest with which the well-bred but unfashionable contemplate those connected however remotely with the arts; Nell wondered if it might also be caused by a memory of fish-scales, "and how nice of you to call. I was just inspecting the garden. We only moved in two days ago and I have scarcely looked at it yet."

"My dear Anna, it isn't nice of me at all and this is a terrible hour to invade a fellow-creature's house but the fact is I've come to 'take possession' of the top flat. I—"

"*Oh*," said Anna. It was a sound charged with meaning

as she said it; with lips made round and such a distinct note of doubt that he stopped, in full spate, and looked at her cautiously.

"Why '*oh*'?" he said, but evidently decided against letting her explain. "I'm in rather a desperate state for a *pied à terre* in London, you see; our house near Wilverton (do you know Wiltshire at all? It's a delicious county and we have delightful neighbours, Edward Early, the actor, has a place near us, and we see quite a bit of 'Pogo' Fairlie, he has that absurd house all over griffins, I expect you saw the photographs recently in *Vogue*) our place is uninhabitable at the moment owing to burst pipes and a leaking roof and what-have-you (it's very old; seventeenth century) and I've been coming up every other day and sharing with a fellow-hack in Russell Square while poor Margie camps out in the village . . . but now. that you're in possession here Peggy has very generously decided to let us, Margie and myself, that is, have the flat upstairs. It is furnished. All our stuff, Peggy's and mine, that is, is still there. (She thought she might let it, you see, at one time.) So all I have to do is to take possession."

He stopped, smiling with all his teeth and holding out to her his hand, in the palm of which reposed a Yale key.

"Why are we standing up?" enquired Anna, "do sit down, won't you?" and she sat down herself upon a large bale of faded chintz. "Nell, get Mr. Gaunt a chair."

"Oh, call me Charles, for God's sake," he said, declining with an impatient movement the offer of a cane affair whose seat needed mending. (Nell had given up the idea of telephoning. Unless she shut the door he would hear every word, and even if she did, she could not be certain of privacy.)

"Peggy hasn't said anything to me about all this, Charles," Anna began, looking up at him, "in fact, we haven't seen her since we moved in—"

"She probably forgot. She lives in such a perpetual crescendo since she rocketed to fame on T.V. that she can no longer vizualize the ordinary pattern of existence as lived by normal people. Have you really been here two whole days? I judged from the picturesque confusion that it was last night . . . you *poor* housewives . . . you know, of course, that I'm your ardent champion on the air?"

"We used to hear you quite a lot. We haven't heard you lately." Anna's tone was perfectly placid, but he looked at her suspiciously. (Blast all women who could not be summed up at sight.)

"I haven't *been* on the air lately, dear lady; that explains it." He paused, while his grey face twitched. "But I won't bore you with a recap. of all the hoo-ha there was some months ago . . . and I really must get upstairs and open the place up . . . but what it boils down to is that I'm being given a second chance . . . oh, they're not going to let me broadcast to all *you* unlucky people. They're quite adamant about *that*. I'm to be allowed to creep back into the fold via a little programme to the Continent called *What's Wrong Over Here*. It's to deal with things which might be 'ordered better in England' . . . proving there's nothing wrong at all, really . . . damn foreigners . . . what do they know about it anyway, and so on. I'm to be groomed into a kind of poor man's Gilbert Harding, or so I gather."

He frowned ferociously and protruded his jaw, while Anna and Nell gaped in fascination. Both shared a passion, seldom discussed and of course never indulged, for the theatre. Any acting, however crude or poor, captured their attention as instantly as if they had been small children.

He relaxed, and gave them his savage mechanical smile.

"Do you usually make tea about this hour in the morning? I know most women like it . . . don't let me stop you, if you do . . . I'm going upstairs now . . . I've taken up enough of your time as it is."

"Tea?" Anna was following him to the door while Nell, keeping herself in the background, wished that he would hurry up so that she could get to the telephone. "We only finished breakfast an hour ago."

"My god, whatever ghastly hour do you have it?" pausing halfway up the stairs. "I'm not usually up before eleven."

"At a quarter to eight," Anna said, "and I rather dislike tea at any time. What I really like is good tap water. But that's not easy to find nowadays."

"You *dislike tea*? My dear lady, you are unique. You should be signed up at once for *What's My Line*." He was looking down at them, and as he mentioned the panel game they both saw a look of extraordinary venom cross his face.

"If you run into my husband—" Anna sent her voice soaring quietly but easily up the well of the stairs as he disappeared, "just explain who you are, will you? He may think you're a burglar."

"So he is," Nell said in a stage whisper, "or as good as. Mother, is it safe to telephone Aunt Peggy?"

"Of course, if you feel you must. But really—! I wash my hands of it all; I'm going down to wash dishes instead. It's between you and your aunt; I know nothing about it. I only hope they won't *come to blows*."

In the quiet hall, while shafts of dusty sunlight shone on the bare boards, and vague noises of slamming doors, bumping, and windows opening came from the top of the house, Nell listened at the telephone.

"Lady Fairfax's home," said Gardis's pleasant official tones; this was her version of giving the number and exchange, "Who? Oh. (And how are we this morning?) No, you can't. 'Cause she's just gone out. Yes. In her car driven by that dirty Jamaican bastard she's given a job to. (I can tell you I nearly took the next 'plane home when I saw *him*. I was born well South of the Mason-Dixon, you know.) Where? 'Fraid I don't know. *Nor* when she'll be back. You're welcome. See you some time maybe. 'Bye."

But even as Nell, wondering what to do next, put back the receiver, she saw a shadow come up to the glass panels and heard the bell ring. She opened it to Lady Fairfax.

"Poppet"—She was given two scented and painted cheeks, one after another, to kiss, which she carefully did. "*Is he here? He is? I knew it. My poor people, I thought; only arrived two days ago and *Charles* moves in on them. *John* rang me up late last night, and that was quite enough to warn me that something was in the wind. He never rings unless he can't resist gloating over me. He doesn't say anything, of course, but I know from his voice that he'd got his own way about something. And he's simply dying to get back into the flat. (He has a real fixation on the place.) But I don't see why he *or* his father *should* have it. They haven't treated me so well—where's your mother? No, don't disturb her. This is all very tiresome for her anyway."

She stopped, and threw back her head. And there, before Nell's eyes, her face became silently brilliant, as if a light had been set going within her that caused her personality to glow. The transformation seemed to extend even to her hair, and the poise of her short powerful neck. She smiled, and Nell saw her as she appeared nightly to her many million viewers. She put her hand in its violet glove on the banister rail.

"I can tackle friend Charles by myself," she said, and went quickly up the stairs.

Nell returned to her typewriter. It was as well that she should be heard industriously banging away, and if, in the pauses of tackling friend Charles, Aunt Peggy caught the sound, her approving ears could catch no echo of the 'gloating' voice, talking to his mother over the telephone, that was echoing on in Nell's mental ear. She knew now that she had been a fool to let him come into the house. He might even—she stopped typing, and slowly coloured—he might even have taken the key from some hiding-place upstairs which he knew of. He had not been gone long enough to open the flat, much less to look at it, but he had been gone quite long enough to find a key. After all, Aunt Peggy had said that he was 'quite capable' of doing something sneaky. Nell's typing increased in speed and vigour while the long clear line of her lips almost disappeared into her flushed face. She had been made a fool of, and the fact that she could still feel the pressure of his mouth on one busily-banging hand did not make her mood any sweeter.

Peggy Fairfax, being the mischievous grown-up child whom her viewers loved, almost tiptoe'd through the open door of their former sitting-room and said, "Hullo, Charles," to her ex-husband's back.

She kept her voice quiet but she was incapable of murmuring; her softest sentences came out in a kind of crystal miniature of the normal pitch; and it was these tiny 'asides', uttered while she and he had been appearing on a radio programme some eight years ago, the married pair in a team that discussed current problems, which had brought her the beginnings of fame. Audiences had begun to listen delightedly for 'Mrs. Gaunt's asides'. Now that she was one of the six top-flight Television stars in the country she still indulged her viewers—judiciously, of course, and after detailed discussion with her agent and advisers—with these naughty-girl, impudent undertone comments. As she spoke to Charles Gaunt her voice held precisely the note most likely to anger him. She knew that she was being unwise but she could not control herself. Really, he and John were behaving like a pair of *skunks*. After all, they were two to one.

"Oh . . . hullo." He did not turn round at once from the bookshelf he was studying, but she saw him suppress a great start. His nerves were still bad, poor Charles; yet she was

pleased about it, as well. What of her own nerves? Didn't she
have to live the disciplined life of a ballerina, a boxer, a nun?
She was simply not in a *position* to *have* nerves, and this proved
how far she had come from the days of *Ask Me Another*.
She wasn't complaining; she was only telling herself that she
too lived under a strain: that he was not the only one.

He had turned round now and was looking at her. She
opened her mouth to begin, not quite knowing what she was
about to say, but eager to stop him from beginning, when she
saw the room.

He was seeing it too; she could tell that he was, and that was
why he was keeping quiet; seeing the shabby cream paint and
the ordinary yellow walls and the few good pieces they had
chosen together and paid for by halves; seeing, over it all, the
familiar ten-o'clock light associated for both of them with breakfast in dressing-gowns, the papers, and arguments over John.

She actually moved a step forward to break the moment of
quietness and its spell; not because she 'could not bear it'
its reminder of 'the old days' but simply because she really
must get things settled at once; in an hour she was leaving for
Manchester, to open, that afternoon, a new T.V. department
at a branch of a big multiple stores.

"Charles, you are a swine," she said irritably, "how did you
get in? I could have sworn you hadn't a key."

"I hadn't. But I've got one now. You didn't acknowledge
my letters so I got to work myself. I warned you I should."

"I didn't read your letters. I told Gardis to burn them or
put them down the lavatory or something."

"You can thank her for my having it." He took the key out
of his pocket and held it up to her on its ring and chain. "*She*
types your letters; she saw the amiable John when she went
out last night to see if your car had come (he was hanging
about your place, apparently), and told him to tag on to Little
Cousin Nell—which he did; got into the house by using his
famous charm and took the spare key."

"From the nail by the meter."

"Exactly."

"I'd forgotten we always kept it there," she said slowly.
"That's surprising, you know. I'm always supposed to have
such a head for detail."

"Two years is a long time, at the pace you and I live now,
Peggy."

"Oh don't be so sickening!" she burst out. " 'You and I, Peggy'! You make me tired. I think it was a filthy trick, simply filthy. I'm not so surprised at John, because I know he'd do anything to get back here, but I'll sack Gardis tonight."

"In spite of her useful new step-papa? Sponsor for one of the best-known brands of toilet-paper in the States?"

"Oh, I'll find some excuse. She knows I'm not satisfied with her. (Who would be?) And you'd better let me have that key back, Charles."

"Don't be a fool, Peg. Give in gracefully. You used to be generous on a shoestring; you can afford to be now. What are you making? Two thousand a year? And all Fairfax's money behind you if your Public suddenly cools off? (They do, you know. I've had some.) Let us have the flat. Don't be a bitch-in-the-manger."

"You once told me I made my career on a shoestring too. Don't try soft-soaping me. That I will not stand."

"All right, I won't then. Use your brains. You don't want a court case, do you? I know I haven't the shadow of any legal right to the place; so what? You'd win your case but how about the publicity? Your dear Public likes to picture you as a mischievous little girl. They'll like picturing an old meanie who does her unsuccessful husband out of a three-pound-ten-a-week top flat, because she's jealous of his new wife, even better, won't they? And what about the life John's been leading for the last eighteen months? They'll enjoy hearing about that, too."

"Leave John out of it. I'll deal with John."

"You've dealt so successfully with him up till now, haven't you? He needs a damn good hiding and two years under an old-type sergeant major. That might make something of him. If he goes on as he is now—"

"Perhaps it will—the Army, I mean, or the Air Force . . . but don't let's start on John, Charles. You know how we always end up . . . Are you going to give me back the key?"

"Oh, shut up for God's sake . . . like something out of *Rigoletto* . . . of course I'm not. (You've got to hand it to John. He's bright enough. If he could pull himself together . . .) You can always have the door padlocked, of course. But I'll take good care the whole of Fleet Street and Broadcasting House knows about it if you do."

"Poor Charles," she said, where she stood by the window looking out over the quiet leafy road and distant Heath, "you're so envious, aren't you." Her tone was pensive rather than mocking.

"Not envious. A bit sore, perhaps. Another kind of woman might have taken her husband up with her."

"I did try, at first."

"You 'tried'! Yes, you did, didn't you . . . forcing me down people's throats until they almost screamed at the sound of my name . . . you were so tactful, you were so apologetic when I didn't do as well as you'd hoped . . . and all the time you were on the up-and-up yourself, standing on me and kicking me aside when you'd got where you wanted . . ."

She was watching him. Now she interrupted in a gentle tone, as if his violence had caused her own to disappear.

"But none of that's true, Charles. It's just that you haven't got star-quality."

"And neither have you, by God," he said very loudly, out of a red face, "and you wouldn't be where you are now if we didn't live in an age when T.V. blows up a personality like a cheap balloon. . . . The whole thing's utterly artificial. I made more *real* reputation with *The Aftermath* than all you and your friends on T.V. put together."

"Oh, now let's talk about *The Aftermath* . . . that masterpiece that nobody under fifty's ever read or heard of . . . you talk about *my* reputation being artificial—your's is just *dead*."

There was a pause. The room looked calm and pretty and did not lack signs that people of culture had lived there. The words hung in the air, and rang on, and on, in the mind's ear. Their silent sound shocked the two a little. Charles said in a moment, sitting down on the divan with a sigh:

"Peg, it costs me twenty pounds a week to keep Hayter's going; just to keep it going, with food for myself and Margie and the dogs, and a bit of entertaining (yes, I know that goes on the Expenses Account but you know how things mount up as well), and I'm being perfectly frank with you; I must have a *pied à terre* in London if I'm to get back on the air. It's a new programme—they're going to try me out on it, and if I'm any good I'm going on a publicity tour through the Benelux countries next month, building up goodwill. You know how little work I've done lately. I don't mind telling you it's been a hellish time for both of us. Margie's been a brick. In some ways she's not the right wife for anyone who means to get to the top but she does her best to keep up, poor kid, and I'm grateful. But it's been difficult, damned difficult, for both of us, and now I've got the chance to get back on the air and drop this blasted hack-work for the Sunday rags, I've *got* to have somewhere in London. And I *can't* afford six guineas a week for a furnished place, yet I've *got* to have somewhere presentable. (You know how it is.) Now will you be a sport? I can't put it in any other way. Let me have the flat? It's lying idle, you *can't* need to let it, it's doing nothing, you might just as well. Will you? I think you owe me something."

"I suppose John will come here and live with you," she said.

"Oh, John . . . " He gestured impatiently. "I don't know, I suppose so. He seemed very keen to get back here when I mentioned that we might. But you can never tell with John."

Lady Fairfax did not seem to hear what he was saying. She was holding her wrist to her ear and distractedly shaking it.

"My watch has stopped! Blast the thing. Charles, what's the time? Is yours right? I limited myself to half an hour for this business . . . "

"It's a quarter to ten," he said.

"Oh . . . I must go at once . . . " She was halfway to the door. "I've got someone coming at ten past . . . " Her voice sounded absent and in some way her personality and her attention seemed no longer to be in the room. "Very well, you can have it. It's against every single wish and principle that I've got and I think you and John have behaved like a couple of swine about the whole affair but I'm sick to death of arguing and I simply haven't the *time* to do anything else about it . . . don't you find that, Charles?"

She turned for a moment, as she stood at the door, "Don't you find there's never a minute for *anything*? I loved it at first, it gave me such a feeling of being really alive, but sometimes now it does get me down a bit . . . it's frightening."

He shook his head. "Males are better fitted for the rough and tumble. I find it exhilarating."

"I'll let you have something in writing," she called as she hurried down the stairs.

He leant back, and lit a cigarette. He was experiencing strong feelings of satisfaction and triumph. His knowledge of Peggy's nature and habits had served him well; how much in character that last, generous, flung-back cry had been!

First put to her a strong case, then tire her out with her own anger and resentment, then appeal to her common-sense. He had done it so often in the past, and had so often in the past been rewarded by an unexpected gesture—like the one she had just made, which gave him more even than he had demanded. Ah, he was a psychologist. Why was he wasting his gifts? He thought of *The Aftermath* and all at once the cigarette tasted bitter.

"Oh—dears—do forgive me for bawling for you like that," Peggy, poised at the front door, was saying rapidly to Anna and Nell, "but I'm in the most desperate hurry. (Can't even stop to see my Marty. Kiss him for me.) I'm letting Charles and Margie have the flat. (Yes, I know . . . after all I said . . . but I *am*. Haven't time now to tell you why.) You must tell him I said he's to pay you a pound a week. (Yes, you *are* to, Anna. It's ridiculous. He can afford it. Let that little Margie cut down on her costume jewellery—I ran into them at the Wine Amateurs Society's dinner—and she was in dark green and looked exactly—but *exactly*—like a Christmas tree. About sixty-five strings of Dior crystals—you know.) So you tell him I said so . . . about the pound, I mean. Nell, poppet, you absolutely cannot work for Gerald Hughes in ankle socks."

"No, Aunt Peggy." Nell glanced triumphantly at her mother.

"She has stockings, of course. But we keep them for the really cold weather."

"What do you call this?" Lady Fairfax shuddered in the carpetless hall. "What sort of stockings?" she added suspiciously, and, on hearing they also were hand-knitted, shook her head.

"Won't do, darlings. The mind boggles. Look," opening her bag, "here's a pound. (Oh, don't be so *proud*, Nell. Look on it as a sub. on your first week's salary if you must.) Now you fly out to a nice little shop in the High Street called Gaze's, and buy yourself some *thirty denier nylons*. Got that? Thirty denier. Now there's nothing else, is there?"

Two pale violet gloves were pressed for a moment against the brow under the dark violet cap while Lady Fairfax shut her eyes.

"No, that's all, I think. Nell, telephone Gardis and get her to arrange for you all to come to lunch one day next week—oh, damn; *you* won't be able to, of course—well, for drinks one evening about six, then. That really is all, I think. 'Bye, darlings."

She ran down the steps and did not pause to wave. They heard her say, "Home, quickly, please Robert," and saw her fair smiling face turned once more towards them as the car glided away.

"A black chauffeur," Anna said, as they shut the door. "Aren't there any white ones wanting jobs? And why must she say ''bye' like that? It sounds idiotic."

"He's a Jamaican. She gave him the job to set an example because his family was starving. She told me about it last night. Mother, can you get the nylons for me? I don't want to go out."

She was hoping that John would telephone.

"I don't want to either, Nell. I really must start on the garden."

Nell was quiet for a moment. Then she said:

"But there's nothing for lunch, is there?"

"There's that piece of cheese. I could make a Welsh rarebit for Daddy and you and I could have milk and bread and jam."

"I'd better go," said Nell, and went upstairs for béret and coat. Supposing he did telephone. Let him find her gone out.

As she sped down the steps in search of sausages and apples, banishing angry thoughts of him by turning over in her head plans for nourishing and cherishing the parents, a vague disturbance at the upper windows caught her attention. She glanced up, and was in time to see the face of Charles-for-gods-sake, as she now thought of him, looking noble and remote above a fluttering duster. He gave her a cross smile and wave of the lowly object and disappeared. Nell remembered the fish scales: *Is this the face that launched a thousand chips?* she thought, and went on down the road laughing.

After all, he was coming to live there now; in the same house. There would be plenty of opportunities to show the silly little boy what she thought of his behaviour. She would be firm but dignified.

CHAPTER FOUR

THE OLIVE-COLOURED CANAL

THE premises occupied by Akkro Products, Limited, was a tall, thin, ancient house of brown brick, one of a row over-looking, from a side street, the tidy ruins of something called Whitefields Tabernacle, and a little green public garden. The hour was precisely nine o'clock; Nell had just heard it strike from somewhere; a vaguely religious sound tolling quietly through the roar of the traffic of Monday morning. The house did not look as she had expected a place devoted to commerce to look, and she was still slightly shaken from having tem-porarily parted with her stomach in the new fast lift at Hamp-stead, and from having counted eight black men (? Jamaicans) on her way from Goodge Street station. But the address cor-responded with that on Gardis's paper. She crossed the road and went in.

"It's Mr. Riddle," said a girl of about her own age seated at a desk behind a wooden barrier marked *Enquiries*, having heard her name and business. "Upstairs." She turned back to her papers.

"I'm to ask for Mr. Riddle, do you mean?"

"Mr. Riddle. That's right."

"Where do I find him?"

"Mr. Riddle." The girl showed signs of impatience. "Up the stairs."

Nell was feeling impatient herself. She ran up a flight of dusty stone steps, glancing at closed doors as she went. She met no-one. There was a distant sound of typewriters and a sharpish smell like celluloid or Aunt Peggy's nail varnish. The windows were unexpectedly clean, revealing the clear blue spring sky. Then she saw a door marked with the pregnant name. She opened it rather quickly and went in.

"Here, here, we're very full of energy this morning, aren't we?" cried a fat man perched on the edge of a desk. "When she's been here six months she won't run up the stairs like that, what's the betting, George?"

A pair of watery eyes looked across at Nell. Their owner was sitting at the desk. The room was small and rather dark and stiflingly, startlingly hot. A small gas fire, looking as if at any moment it might burst into flames, so red and quivering was it, hissed madly in the black fireplace. There was a strong and triumphant smell of cigarette smoke: very, very old: old: this morning's—for both gentlemen were smoking, although the seated one was doing so with less abandon than the perched one—and even future, for it was possible to deduce that the room would never, as far as human thought could reach, smell of anything else.

"Good morning, Miss Sely," said the elderly one, conveying reproof. "You are a few minutes late but we'll excuse that as it's the first morning. I am Mr. Riddle and you will be working for me. This is Mr. Belwood, our Chief Accountant." (Mr. Belwood made a mock-obsequious inclination of his head and brandished his cigarette.) "The Ladies Cloakroom is on the next landing. Now if you will kindly hang your coat and hat behind the door, we will get to work. That is your desk, in the corner near the window. I suppose, like all young people, you like fresh air."

"Yes," said Nell, and Mr. Riddle gave a faint start. He stared at her, and she saw that the word had been a mistake. I ought to have just smiled, she thought, but honestly, *what* a fug. Had her tone conveyed possible future rebellion even as his own had conveyed disapproval? It soon became clear that it had.

"Oh, so you're a 'fresh air fiend' are you?" said Mr. Riddle; not threateningly, not sarcastically, but in the voice of somebody taking up one more burden in a harassed existence; "well, I can't say that I am. Give me a cosy atmosphere any time. Belwood, I've got some work to do."

"Lord yes, and I must be blowing." Mr. Belwood heaved himself off the desk, smiling at Nell. "Lovely person your aunt, Lady Fairfax, isn't she? My wife raves about her."

"She is very kind," said Nell. She was removing the cover of a typewriter whose newness, gleaming black enamel, and white and scarlet keys did something to restore a confidence in the solvency of Akkro Products (and the regular payment of five pounds a week) which their premises, and the seediness of Mr. Riddle, and the blowsiness of Mr. Belwood, had somewhat shaken.

"Br-r-r! Touch of frost in the air this morning, isn't there, George?" said Mr. Belwood, adding as he went out, "Cheer up, Miss Sely, the first ten years are the worst."

Nell stretched out her legs, in their nylons, under her desk. It was a cautious movement; so might a prisoner in the stocks have tested his powers of extension. She caught sight of her feet; her best black shoes were all wrong, of course, but the nylons undoubtedly made a great difference. She felt more cheerful. Resting her hands on the keys, she looked across expectantly at Mr. Riddle.

But in spite of Mr. Belwood's heartening badinage, and the nylons, and various signs of the firm's prosperity, and even certain hints of a modified approval of her own efforts which presented themselves during what seemed the longest morning of her life, she flew out of Mr. Riddle's room at one o'clock with a relief which should have warned her of the future. A wailing cry pursued her—"Miss Sely, aren't you going to try the firm's lunch? We provide an excellent lunch at the Rosita Café, next door but one, for two shillings—Miss *Sely*—" But she ignored it, and ran upstairs to the Ladies Cloakroom.

There she found three thin, pale girls, with hair dressed like South Sea Islanders (Old Style), banging powder puffs against their faces in front of a large, bright mirror. Over the two pink washing basins, the chromium taps which gushed splendidly hot water, the machine providing a fresh paper towel for each arrival, and the device for doling out liquid soap, there hovered a dry, sour, rotting eighteenth-century smell which had lived for two hundred years in the walls and under the floor.

The three girls looked at her with sly suspicion and alarm, and, after some exploratory preliminaries, warned her not to try the office lunch. It was sawful. They only had it themselves, it appeared, because a collective authority named Mum insisted. Then one of them said in a half-undertone to the others that she supposed *she* would have *her* lunch with her auntie at a posh place in Oxford Street, and they all looked at Nell and giggled. Having applied Claregates's grave politeness to the situation, and seen them reduced to resentful silence, Nell went out to sit in the small green public garden.

For her lunch, she bought a cheese roll which she ate in the open air. Her offer of four pounds ten shillings a week to her mother had been accepted by Anna without protest, and Nell knew better than to mention the subject to her father. But now that Mr. Riddle had spent ten minutes in explaining to her about deductions for Income Tax and Insurance and so on, she knew that not even by lunching daily for fourpence, a thing which she must get used to, could she give her mother what she had promised. She would give every penny that she could. Later on, when the weather was warmer, she would walk to work and save the fare.

She sat under the budding trees, watching old men feeding the sparrows with crumbs, and plotting to get back before Mr. Riddle and to open the windows, for it appeared that, although he recommended the canteen lunch to the junior staff, he himself patronized a restaurant at some distance away, from which he sometimes returned a few minutes late. He had told her this while winding himself up in a singularly dismal muffler of darkest grey, very thick, wool, which matched his knitted gloves; not excusing his lateness; merely imparting an impressive fact.

She had time for a run past the jewellery shops of Tottenham Court Road before she turned her steps again office-wards. Lumps of cheese-roll sitting on her chest did something to lessen her pleasure in the ear-rings made like tiny bowls of fish, or baskets of fruit, or golden bells, and she was shaken by irrepressible hiccoughs while admiring the pink, white and yellow undergarments in the shop windows, but she liked Tottenham Court Road. It was a bright spot in the day's undeniable drabness, and, if she were questioned that evening about its respectability, she would not mention the black men.

"Miss Sely this room is quite *cold*." Mr. Riddle entered at four minutes past two, to find Nell, looking frail, typing diligently in a breeze that rustled the papers on her desk. "We must have the window closed at once. I cannot stand a draught; a draught is the one thing that gives me a cold, and I've had five since the autumn and I don't want any more."

He shut the window with an authoritative slam, relit the stove which Nell had dared to extinguish, and sat down at his desk, and fixed her with a fretful eye.

Boss's Pal's Relation, that was the category Miss Sely was filed under, and, instead of being, like most of them, hopeless, she showed signs of being efficient. She would probably hold down the job, annoying little chit that she was, with nose still pink from the wind that had rushed in through the open window. Mr. Riddle felt in his bones that he had not heard the last of her liking for fresh air, and, with the thought, he was certain that he felt a tickling in his own nose. He brought out his handkerchief and managed to head off a prophetic sneeze.

"Have they moved in upstairs?" Nell asked her mother casually that evening at supper, her experiences at Akkro Products (Anna referred to them as "your work") having been briefly related by herself, and the revised arrangements about her contribution to the housekeeping having been heard with some dismay.

"Margie, as he calls her, arrived about tea-time. He came down to let her in. It's a good thing they have their own bell; I certainly shouldn't want to be always answering it for them. As it was—"

"Oh, John hasn't come, then?" Nell was bolting bread and margarine with limpid eyes fixed on her mother's face.

"I don't think so, no. I haven't seen him. As it was, Charles got hold of Daddy this afternoon when Daddy had come down to see the garden, and told him that although there was *absolutely no question* of their *expecting* us to take telephone messages for them, they would be 'most tremendously obliged' if we would just answer 'the thing' whenever it 'kept on and on and on', because it might mean a job for him. (Oh, yes, I remember now; John *hasn't* come; because Charles said that he would be seeing him later this afternoon and would give him a cheque for me, and John would bring it in later. A month's rent in advance, he said.) And John was to give me a spare key for the flat, too, in case 'the thing' *did* 'go on and on and on'. Charles was just 'dashing', he said."

"They seem to dash a lot," said Nell, who rather envied them.

It had been enjoyable to come back to Hampstead; up from the grime and crowds and petrol vapour into the narrow old streets with lively people walking homewards in blue spring twilight under the big, brown, bare old trees, but now the evening stretched before her. He had not telephoned during the last three days. Why should he come tonight? Everybody said that he was so keen on Arkwood Road and the flat: why, then, hadn't he been near it since Friday? As for keys, the less said about him and keys the better. And Akkro Products was as dull as she had expected.

He neither came that evening nor telephoned.

Nell was rather concerned about her own foolishness, for she could not stop going over and over in her mind, at every hour of the day, every word that he had said to her. It was not much consolation that she could no longer remember his face.

But on Thursday evening, by which time it seemed to her that she had been working for Akkro Products ever since she had been born, and she was beginning to recognize various Hampstead beards and pony tails seen in the cafés on her way home each night, she had stopped to look at Frances Harling's shop in the High Street, where the jewels in ancient brooches and necklaces gleam with a myriad watery fires. A low voice behind her said, "Hullo. I've been waiting for you," and she turned round and there he was.

Different clothes, this time; a long pale jacket reaching far below his hips, and darker trousers. He looked very stiff and white about the neck.

"Were you? Where? I didn't see you."

"Can you come to a party? Benedict's giving one, and I want you to meet some of my friends."

"Well—I must let my mother know. And what about supper? And I haven't . . . this won't do for a party, will it?" glancing down at her skirt.

"You're always thinking about food, Nello. I've seen Aunt Anna and explained. She's pleased for you to be going to Odessa Place, I think." He smiled. "As for clothes, you do dress bloody badly of course but then most girls do. You ought to dress like dear little Gardis."

"In that awful old jersey and slacks?"

"I meant when she's dressed for a party," coldly. "There'll be food there, if you're so ravenous, but don't expect sandwiches and that sort of bull. Now we'll walk to Canal Terrace."

"Isn't it at your mother's house?"

"Of course not. But I let Aunt Anna think it was, because, if I hadn't, she might not have let you come."

They walked down, through the clear dusk, into London again; through long quiet roads, where the thrush sang among the chimneypots, that gradually became long grey streets where children played on the pavements under the yellow or mauve light of tall cruel lamps. Down here spring was already losing its early freshness, and the air was beginning to fall back into the familiar London weariness. Nell had been glad to leave it, an hour before, but now she walked beside him, checking her pace to his, content to listen to his praise of Gilbert and Sullivan's operas, and his humming of this or that air when she confessed ignorance of them all.

So he led her imperceptibly away from the main streets and lights and trolley-buses into the back ways; the short, silent, dimly-lit alleys of little pale houses where plaster was peeling from the walls and lights glimmered faintly behind dull blue or green curtains, and the wireless distantly yet raucously played or sang the same tune from one house to the next. As Nell walked past the ground-floor windows, under old lamps whose faint glow scarcely pierced the still night's heavy dark, she saw, without seeing, as each mean shallow bay approached, a vase of withered daffodils or a plaster statuette set upon a small round table. But the streets grew dimmer, and soon there were no more lights in the front windows. These people lived in their warm kitchens overlooking the trampled gardens.

They came at last to a mouldering terrace of white cottages; very old, standing above the broken iron stumps where there had once been railings; dark windows whose lamp-reflecting glitter defied the eye to see within; chimneys twisted as if in some disaster; shut doors that had a sealed look. These faced a piece of waste land, rutted, and scattered with newspaper and rubbish, and the coiled-serpentine shapes of old tyres. Beyond this, black buildings towered softly against the orange sky, and hidden traffic faintly roared.

"Here we are," said John, and stopped in front of a door that stood open. He looked at her, and she looked back at him. She could just make out by the dim light that he was smiling. It was at this moment that Nell began to know there was not going to be much ordinary happiness between herself and her cousin John. She did not yet know that she would have to become used to, and to put up with, the fact.

"Afraid?" he asked.

"Of course not. Why should I be?"

"I thought you mightn't have seen a place like this before. It's not on the pictures, you know. It's real."

Nell looked past him down the passage. It was black and it smelt. "I suppose if you've been living here it can't be too bad," and she stepped over the threshhold.

Somewhere at the end of the passage a door opened. A shaft of light shone out and she caught a glimpse of a small, dim, cluttered room full of people, all staring towards the door. There were two or three of them; sitting quite still; not talking.

"All right," said John, and a woman's voice called back, "Oh, it's you. He's been expectin' you this hour. She's up there too. I don't know what's—" the words were lost as someone shut the door.

"I'll lead the way, shall I," and he went ahead of her up the stairs. Nell followed, picking her way over holes in the oilcloth and broken boards, and thinking now that her clothes might be unsuitable for the party merely because they were clean. Who was 'she'? Not, she hoped, Gardis. She was trying to forget the faces of the people in that room.

They came to a landing where she could just make out several closed doors by the faint glow filtering through a skylight; she thought that it must be reflected from the street. John went across and knocked on one.

They waited. She wrinkled her nose against the composite smell of stale cabbage, onions, dirty carpet and, from a half-open door on her left, something worse. "You know," he turned to her, half-whispering, "I should have told you about Benedict. In my opinion and that of a lot of my friends, Dylan Thomas and Day Lewis are going to be very minor figures compared with Benedict Rouse. (Betjeman may be able to keep his end up: I don't know: but he does express the spirit of the age, in some ways, while those other poets don't.) And Benedict has such wonderful technical ability. His ear is exquisite—in the precise sense, I mean."

He stopped, and listened. There was a movement from within; what kind of movement Nell would have had difficulty in saying. It included something that might have been laughter; and it was also a kind of stirring, as if something were waking up. When in response to a call she followed John in, she saw a low, grey, bare room almost filled by a great bed. The blackened brass of its frame winked in the light of two candles guttering in the air from the open window, and on it was lying a young man, who turned a long, smiling face towards them. Nell had to summon all her small store of recently-gained London sophistication, when she saw, streaming over his naked chest from the head of someone humped recumbent under the coverlet beside him, a mass of black hair. To Nell it looked dismayingly familiar.

"Hullo," he said. He pushed the hair aside onto its owner, who did not move, and sat up. "I thought you weren't coming. How do you do?" to Nell.

"How do you do?" she said.

She wondered if the walls of this room often heard the phrase,

which was associated by herself with rare visiting clergy, rarer
tennis parties, and meeting friends' parents on Claregates
Open Day. It seemed unlikely. But Benedict had a how-do-
you-do voice.

"Do sit down," he said; he had got off the bed and was now
rapidly pulling on a shirt, "John, shift those magazines off
the chair, can't you."

"You mustn't let Nell make you conventional." John slid
a mass of *Picture Posts* onto the floor and inclined the broken
chair towards Nell. "Is there anything to eat? She is ravenous—
as usual."

"I was just going to cut some bread and butter. Will you
make the coffee?"

"Can't Gardis do that? I'm tired." He sat down limply on
the forlorn rusty web, once a carpet, which covered the floor
and leaned his head against the wall.

"I'll do it. I'm not tired," said Nell, and was disconcerted
to see a black eye like a snake's open amidst the mass of hair
on the bed. Gardis was not asleep, and she was finding something amusing.

"The things are in the cupboard, if you're going to be so
kind," said Benedict.

"Coffee stinks," observed a voice from under the coverlet,
"how about some gin?"

"I've no money for gin," said Benedict, who was moving
about, and getting bread out of a cupboard.

Nell did not know that one of the distinguishing marks of
the poet's face is its lining and marking, even in youth, by
the tides of passionate feeling. These may be the mild, moon-
swayed neaps that blanched the face of Coleridge, or the
scorching, sterile ebbs that pinched up the face of Swinburne,
but always they leave their mark beside the mouth and on
brow and cheek; and here, in the face of the smallish, slender
young man; on his high forehead where the brown locks
strayed, round his suffering eyes, was the authentic wrack.

"You have got money too, I heard it go jingle-jangle,"
Gardis was saying.

"I want that for food, thank you."

"Bourgeois . . . " she said drowsily. John, finding the floor
uncomfortable, had taken Nell's chair while she was at the
cupboard, and as she went to and fro between room and
landing, filling a kettle at a tap which sent, taking its own time,

a scanty stream into a leaden sink on the floor, she heard him lecturing Gardis on her Hollywood notions about artists.

" . . . I admit that you have to *go* to the limits in order to create anything permanent, but you need not *stay* there. Look at Flaubert. *He* said that the proper *milieu* for an artist was the middle-class one. I don't say that I agree with him (and in any case French middle-class life is so different from its English equivalent) but he lived that life himself and he was a wonderful artist."

"All this class-stuff . . . And what a collar! You look like something out of *The Seven Little Foys*."

Gardis was now sitting up on the bed, screwing her hair into its knot. She had contrived to put on her clothes, Nell *hoped*, while lying under the bedclothes; she *feared* that she had dressed herself in front of the young men during the prolonged filling of the kettle. Perhaps she was afraid that Nell would give a report to Lady Fairfax. But I can't imagine her being afraid of anything, thought Nell, kneeling on the floor by a rusty gas ring whose feeble flame seemed to work under the same principles as those which animated the tap.

Benedict was glancing at her now and then with approval. He liked her childish appearance and practical manner, while her thinness and her straight brown hair, the colour of a dead leaf, refreshed in him that spirit (like that of most poets, his nature contained some dozen or so spirits) which perpetually craved coolness and freshness. Even his passion for Gardis could not always reconcile him to the sight and touch of her small feverish hands—which seemed never to be quite clean . . .

" . . . good heavens, no-one's going to mind you being a 'Commie', as you call it, over here," John was saying contemptuously now to Gardis. "We still possess some remnants of freedom in *this* country. I'm always telling you to *be* a Commie, if it makes you feel any better."

"Maybe I will, then . . . I often feel like one. Only if they *did* find out back home . . . you people haven't any notion how far back they trace you—ten years, fifteen years, maybe. Then if you've written a preface to a Commie's book, or been seen around with Commies, or helped one in any way—wham. They've got you . . . 'Tisn't quite as bad as it was a year or two back, but . . .

"What are your politics?" she demanded, turning suddenly upon Nell.

"Conservative," Nell answered, without looking up from her midwifery to the kettle.

"Wha-a-a-t? You admit it? You admit right out you're a Fascist reactionary?"

"Of course she's a Tory. So would you be, if you'd always lived in the country and been a parson's daughter (Church and State, you know). Leave her alone." John's tone was authoritative.

"But I never heard anyone admit *right out* that they were a Fascist. It's *thrilling*." Gardis was sitting on the bed hugging her knees, and Nell did not know if the black eyes fixed on her were mocking or not. "Coming to the powder-room?" Gardis asked suddenly. "It's across the landing," and Nell, although she did not know exactly what a powder-room was, thought that she would.

She followed her out of the room, and John shut the door firmly behind them.

Gardis pranced ahead into the place smelling of something worse. They had to strike matches; Nell grazed herself against a terrible rusty bath filled with yellow newspapers, and saw in the flickering light the blue damp oozing in patches out of the walls. Mould, and damp dust, and decay and worse . . . Gardis, who had not troubled to shut the door during her own tenancy, leaned against the lintel and seemed inclined for a chat. Nell shut it with decision. Afterwards, while they were tidying themselves, Gardis murmured slyly: "Do you like those boys in there?"

She was holding a match high above her head so that Nell could see. There was a mirror on the wall, so old that its last traces of beauty had been broken down into the strange repulsiveness attaching to domestic objects of great age; all that was left of the bows and roses that had once decorated the frame were some wires and fragments of plaster, whose gilt had turned almost black. God alone knew where it had come from; it might even have reflected a white wig towering above a face covered thickly with red and white paints, but now it only cried out to be taken down, down from the oozing wall, and destroyed. Yet its degradation was not quite complete: the few patches of silver left on the blotched surface returned the fragmented images of the two girls with touching purity and faithfulness.

"Do you?" Gardis repeated.

"I like Benedict." Nell turned away from the glass. "Shall I hold one for you now?"

"(If you will.) Oh, Ben. He's . . . no use. Are you a virgin?" She was using her lipstick, but her eyes slid round to laugh at Nell, who found herself capable of giving a nod. Then she swallowed, and said: "Are you?"

"Haven't been since I was fifteen,"—there was a glint of surprise in the eyes—"If I told you how many men I've had you'd die. And do you like dear little John? He's a stuck-up snooty specimen of a typical Britisher, isn't he?"

"He *is* my cousin," Nell said repressively. The question did not embarrass her, for she had never thought about her true feelings for John. He was silly, and he was untrustworthy, and he had behaved badly. This was his official rating. It was family feeling (she told herself) that made her give a note of protest to her reply now.

"I don't see how that makes him any better . . . let's get out of here. I'm afraid we'll both catch something . . . You'd better gargle when you get home. I shall." It annoyed Nell that every now and then Gardis prevented herself from seeming completely detestable by saying something almost kind. It made relations with her less straightforward.

A far-off, solemn, major note was rolling faintly through the open window as they came back into the room.

"Ten," said Nell, surprised.

"That's Big Ben," said John, now lying on the bed, "the wind must be this way; we don't often hear him 'live'.."

"Can I help?" Nell had gone over to the table where Benedict was laboriously adding to a pile of bread and butter. "What a lot you've done. How many more people are coming?" She began to spread butter on the waiting slices.

"Chris, I think. He said he might. He's absolutely desolate without Nerina, of course," said John. "No-one else. Don't look blank, Nell. It doesn't become you. What's the matter?"

"You said—'a party' . . . "

"Aren't you having a swell time?" Gardis's voice sounded mocking, as she bustled about with her official secretarial manner collecting cups.

"Yes . . . I only thought . . . "

"This is a party," John said coldly. "Anywhere where a few people meet to talk and see one another is a party. I warned you there wouldn't be a lot of suburban bull."

Nell felt herself snubbed. But really—! as her mother would say. So this was all there was to be, except for Chris, who was 'desolate'. And was she enjoying it? She could not truthfully say.

She liked Benedict, but the partly incomprehensible talk and peculiar manners of the other two disconcerted her, while John seemed to have one manner for use in public and another manner for use when he and she were alone together. Realizing suddenly that she had been looking at him ever since she came back into the room, she looked quickly out of the window and said, "Oh!"

"What? Oh, the canal," Benedict put down his knife and came to stand beside her, "isn't it lovely? It's black now, by daylight it's usually olive-green. When you see it from the other side, as you're going past on the bus, with these little white houses standing above it, it's even better."

"It must look like Venice," she said.

He smiled. "The houses in Venice aren't often white, they're usually russet-colour or pale grey."

"Have you been there often?"

"I was living there last summer. I had a job as a waiter in a hotel."

"Oh. It must . . . have been very interesting."

"She means *how shocking*." It was a biting voice from the bed.

"I don't." Nell turned to him and spoke sharply. "I would a jolly sight rather do that, anyway, than work in an office."

"Not want the job that kind Auntie got for us?" said Gardis. "Naughty, naughty."

"Well—" John sat up, prepared for argument. "*I* think it's bloody *trahison des clercs*. I'm always telling him so."

"It's better than working all day at something literary . . . If I did that I shouldn't want to write poetry in my spare time. I should want to get drunk," Benedict said.

"You'd want that anyway," from Gardis. "Jesus! Who let the kettle go off the boil? And where's the Nescafé?"

"I'm awfully sorry, it took such ages," Nell said guiltily, "while we were tidying I put it in the grate."

"Well, you can go right in and boil it up again."

"The gas went out, it wasn't anybody's fault," said Benedict fretfully. "John, have you got a shilling? Gardis, then? Oh *hell*."

"I've got one." Nell produced a neat purse.

"Oh . . . thank you." He snatched it and put it into a black metal case that was fixed on the floor and turned a little wheel. The ring began to hiss feebly.

"A match. A *match*. Haven't *any* of you got a match? I hate the smell and it'll be all over the room."

Again Nell supplied what was wanted, from a box hurled in a corner which she had noticed, and when the ring was lit, the kettle replaced, Benedict said to her:

"I'm sorry. I've been working all day and haven't eaten. I don't usually forget but I got so . . . John, you don't want those damned candles now, do you. I know you hate light as a bat does but I can't see to cut the bread."

"Do you want to? I know Chris's appetite, but there's enough here even for him. Oh, here he is. Come in," John called.

Nell looked up from the kettle, and saw a huge boy in rough clothes edging himself into the room. 'Boy' was the word for him, for although his thick bright beard glinted in the candle-light, the cheeks above it shone like apples. He muttered something in a hoarse shy voice and sat down in a corner.

"How's Nerina? When's she coming home?" John began charmingly at once, and Nell saw Chris's face light up.

"She's all right," he mumbled. "Not for another three days, though. They've asked her to stay on."

"Oh, well, that's good in one way, isn't it?" He turned to Nell. "I've told you how lovely Chris's woman is, haven't I? She's doing a week's washing-up and waitressing at a café in Southend, living in."

"I'd a' been down there too," Chris turned to Nell as if to excuse himself, giving her a little bob of his head as if to introduce himself at the same time, "on'y I've got this here picture to paint for this old lady. I did start out one night walking, had to turn back halfway there. Shouldn't have been back in time next day, see. And it's ten pounds clear." He stopped. It was plain that he meant to keep quiet now.

"It's a portrait of her little dog," John said.

"Nell, come and help," said Gardis. She looked suddenly very cross, and as Nell handed round bread and butter and coffee, she wondered if Gardis were comparing the party with others she had been to in America or at Odessa Place, for certainly, now that Benedict had insisted on having the gas lit, the room had lost all its shadowy charm and looked, to Nell at least, merely squalid.

But no-one else seemed to mind. The names of painters and writers and musicians and poets went to and fro, and there were scraps of argument about politics, and many references from John and Gardis to 'my stuff'. Nell gathered that this was their painting and writing. She sat in complete silence, occasionally mixing fresh Nescafé for a cup thrust out impatiently by someone who neither looked at her nor stopped talking. In half-an-hour only one remark was addressed to her. Chris, who had been as quiet as herself, leant across and said hoarsely:

"Couldn't get a lift on a lorry, you see. The police might get on to us. John told you, I reckon." After a moment's reflection, Nell understood that he was still thinking over his unsuccessful attempt to walk to Southend.

No, of course John had not told her. She looked at him (she had not done so for three minutes or more) in some indignation. The police, now. What kind of company was this?

John, however, seemed to have ears for more than one conversation at once, and also to know (disturbing thought) when one was looking at him. Without turning, he stretched out his hand to her, interrupting for a second his impassioned discussion with Benedict:—

" . . . no bearing on it really because like dear little Gardis here Toulouse-Lautrec was only slumming . . . it's all right, Nell; no-one's going to prison; Chris doesn't want the police to recognize him because he and Nerina ran away together, and they're both under age . . . that's all, it's bloody parents again . . . and could get out of it whenever he . . . "

The argument continued. Nell heard the major notes roll out once more across the dark roof, and through the heavy night stained by the fires from chemical-burning lamps: eleven. She struggled with a yawn. It was probable, almost certain, that none of these people had to be up at half-past seven to-morrow morning. She wondered if it were 'done' to go home when one had had enough? They would probably be surprised that anyone *could* have enough. John would be offended, anyway.

Suddenly there fell one of those silences which occur in the liveliest conversation. She was opening her mouth to make some kind of a preliminary murmur about departure when he turned to her.

"How are you getting on with your distressing job? I'm sure it's as bad as I said it would be."

"It's very dull," answered Nell decidedly. They were all looking at her now.

"Why don't you walk out?" Gardis said. She was sitting upright on the bed, and had let down her hair again at a whisper from Benedict, lying full length beside her.

"I can't." Since frankness seemed in fashion Nell would be frank; she preferred it, anyway. "We've hardly any money. I've got to earn some."

"Your mother should work. Mine does. She runs a line of beauty-products called *Venus Inc.* (Should suit my mother. She's on her fourth husband.)"

"I don't think my mother could get a paid job. She does work very hard at home, of course. I don't know quite . . . what's going to happen, actually. Perhaps my father might be able to do something when he's well again . . . teaching, my mother thought . . . but . . . I've got to stick it for the time being, anyway."

"What do they pay you?" asked Benedict, and when she told him (having overcome some embarrassment) shook his head.

"That's very poor pay, especially as the work's so dull. You could earn more than that as a waitress. Are your legs and feet strong?"

"They'd never let me be a *waitress!*"

Nell's exclamation was lost in the laughter. John's went on longer than the rest and sounded malicious. She looked at him enquiringly. He only continued to laugh silently, and suddenly she remembered that both Benedict and Chris's 'woman' (she had a confused image of someone aged forty-odd with untidy black hair) earned their livings in this way. She coloured, but no-one else was looking conscious.

"Are they strong?" repeated Benedict.

"I don't know. Yes, they are, I think."

"He thinks you'd make a successful tart," said Gardis.

"His views on that subject have been coloured by someone else's proficiency, no doubt," murmured John—but it was only a murmur, and only Nell heard.

"It *is* possible to earn sixteen pounds a week at waiting. But of course to earn that you would have to work six days a week, Sundays as well. It can be brutally hard work, too. The scale of pay laid down by the Catering Trades Association isn't high either. But it's the tips that bring it up so. In some places the tipping is so good that people pay the proprietor to be taken on the staff," said Benedict.

"The parents would never let me," Nell said flatly, after her imagination had looked at sixteen pounds a week. That was all it saw. Sixteen one-pound notes, very clean and green and fresh.

"Of course they wouldn't. It's honest work (if you care about honesty). It's amusing. You'd meet crowds of people. You'd get exercise, instead of getting cramp all day in an office. To say nothing of earning more than three times what you do now. But all that doesn't count. And why? Because being a waitress isn't a conventional thing for an educated girl to be," said John.

"I said that she *could* earn sixteen pounds a week. I've known one or two people who did. But don't imagine that everyone does. I don't, for example. My—er—my heart isn't in my work, so to speak."

Benedict did not go on to say what Nerina earned, but a hoarse mumble came from the corner:

"Nothing like that. Crumbs! I should say not."

"I'm sure it would be more interesting than being in an office, anyway," Nell said, rather primly and politely. The idea was as amusing as it was fantastic, but the sixteen one-pound notes still danced before her fancy, sometimes in a cloud, sometimes in a neat row.

For the last four days she had paid her fares and bought her bar of chocolate out of a ten-shilling note rather reluctantly parted with by her mother. Some dividends, Nell gathered, were expected next month; until then the Selys must live on the remains of Aunt Peggy's ten pounds, and meanwhile were on short commons indeed. Mother really is extraordinary since we came to Hampstead, Nell thought; we never did get much to eat, but now if I didn't insist on having a meal at night we'd get *nothing*. And she's hardly begun on straightening the house. I wonder if she's Breaking Up? This mysterious calamity, which had in their turn overtaken all Anna's old aunts and various ancient creatures in the different parishes where Martin had ministered, had haunted Nell's childhood; she had lived in fear at one time, of seeing it appear in her mother and father.

She decided that she really must go home and said so aloud,

although a stomach pleasantly and unfamiliarly distended with coffee and bread and butter made her disinclined to move.

" . . . and so I would never be a waiter again. I think the being at people's beck and call is degrading," John was saying. "I'm not saying that it degrades *some* people. But *I* feel degraded. I would sooner slice bacon or—"

"You may be perfectly splendid at slicing bacon: as a waiter you were plain godawful," said Benedict. He turned to Gardis. "He used to *argue* with the people at his table about the topics of the day. It did me no good with the Italian people I recommended him to, I can assure you."

"John. I really must go home," Nell said urgently.

"Go *home*?" turning with an outraged stare. "But it's *early*. Let's go down to the Eldorado. I've got to see a man there who's going to give me a job. Have you any money?"

"Two shillings." She looked him in the eye.

"Oh. I thought we might have a taxi. I've been walking all day and I'm tired . . . Benedict, have you any money?"

"Not for taxis."

"And I must go home too. Fairfax's Flour is getting all worked up into a dough about my late hours," said Gardis.

It was decided after some discussion that they should, at least, all go out somewhere, except Chris, who decided to go home and slouched away. Nell was preparing another speech, as they walked towards the traffic lights in the main road, about *having* to go home herself, when John exclaimed:

"Here's a bus." Before she could protest, almost before she knew what was happening, she felt her waist gripped and he swung her up onto its platform; it had swooped to a standstill just where they stood. The conductor snarled, the bus glided forward at a terrifyingly increasing pace, and she looked back at the receding figures of Gardis and Benedict, to see them laughing and waving as they got into a taxi.

"Oh . . . " she said, disappointed in Benedict's firmness of character.

"*Up*stairs," said John, going ahead of her.

The bus rocked and swayed, careering along at a smooth and dreamlike speed. He made his way down the centre to the front seats, and she followed. They were the only passengers. He looked back to laugh at her, calling, "Who was it called the hansom cab 'the gondola of London'? The trolleybus is the poor man's stratocruiser," and as he slid into the front seat and she came up with him, put out his arm and pulled her close. "There." He clumsily kissed the side of her face. "Now we'll have a lovely time."

The pale and dark houses soared and fell, soared and fell as they glided by, and the green lamps sprayed out their poisonous soft light into the night—or the lilac ones cast their corpse-colour on the faces of the dark anonymous shapes waiting patiently below. The small round ruby and amber lights winked on, paused, winked off. The yellow globes banded with black winked, winked, winked; maddeningly, to eyes that had been looking at London for any longer than twenty-five years. But of course Nell was not maddened, nor even aware of their winking, for she sat within his arm; she felt its young thin hardness pressed against her shoulders; and smelled, coming from the cheek close against her own, a faint warm scent at once childish and unmistakably masculine. She was both happy and unhappy; because she had an orderly and sensible nature, she did not like the duality of her feelings.

"It *is* Dickens's London still, of course," he was murmuring, "but it's Dickens writing science-fiction. It's more sinister than anything he even imagined because it's more impersonal . . . no-one cares. No-one ever did, much, but now they're more afraid, too . . . this chap I'm meeting tonight is starting a paper dealing with *aquariums*, and he wants someone to take photographs for it and go round getting advertisements for it. He does most of it himself but he thinks he may be able to use another man . . . I must borrow a camera from someone . . . Toby has one, if I can find him. He doesn't often go into Eldorado's but he does go to The Coffee Dish and we'll go there tomorrow . . . oh blast. You're *working*. Do you terribly mind paying your own fare? I've only got one and six. I simply detest asking you."

"Then don't," said Nell, in trepidation, but forced by her own character to make some sort of a stand.

"But I must, Nello dear. If I don't we can't have any coffee. And at Eldorado's they're fussy if you just sit there without ordering anything . . . the fare's only fourpence. You said you had two shillings. Can't you manage on one and eightpence until you're paid tomorrow?"

Nell found that she would have to, for she seemed to be in the humiliating position of not being able to tell her Cousin John *no*. But she decided that next time (if there were a next

time, for he was neither predictable nor dependable) she
would really be firm.

When the fares were paid he set himself to entertain her,
making her laugh (Nell had scarcely laughed at all during the
past week) with stories about the co-educational school he had
attended just after the war, where, he said, the girls were all
terrible little tarts ("I dislike those free, frank, blithesome girls,
I like secretive well-behaved little ones like you, Nello"), and
went on, seeing the expression on her face, to explain the rami-
fications of a word which she had heard Elizabeth Prideaux
use, but about which she had never had the courage to enquire.
While she listened and laughed, however, there kept recurring
a sensation as if there were something pleasant at the back of
her mind; something desirable to be done, or secured for herself; and soon she remembered the sixteen clean pound notes.

"I suppose . . . " she said, in a pause in his reminiscences,
"your mother would be awfully fed up if I ever thought of
giving up my job?"

Best to put it vaguely. She did not trust him, why should she?
She suddenly remembered the flat, and the key, and the
whole mysterious, rather tiresome, business which, in the
novel experiences of the past few days, she had almost forgotten.
He might easily tell her aunt that she meant to leave Akkro
Products next week.

"If you mean, 'would she be shocked if you tried for a
waitress's job', no, I don't believe that she would. She's always
telling her horrible little Teenagers Panel to have initiative
and leap into life's battle, and that sort of bull, although I do
admit that she puts it rather well. She never sounds Victorian or
pi. She *is* Victorian *and* pi, of course, because she's so hard-
working and moral, but you would never suspect it . . . no, I
don't think she would make a fuss. But you don't want to be a
waitress, Nello. You would hate it."

Nell, as she followed him quickly down the stairs when the
bus stopped, was not so sure about that.

"My mamma should have got you a more interesting job,"
John said, as he armed her across a narrow, thronged street
bathed in a dark warm glare of light, and starry with the
winking and glittering of advertising slogans, "but of course
she isn't quite in a position to foist her relations on famous
people *yet*. (In a few years she will be—if she stays the course;
and I think she will.) It's the famous people who usually have

the interesting jobs to offer. Now don't talk any more, Nello, because here's the Eldorado and I've got to find this chap."

Nell suppressed a denial of having talked, and followed him as he pushed open a door set in a double-fronted shop curtained with dirty net.

She suppressed a shiver and a yawn. Two chromium sticks on the face of a wooden clock pointed at five to twelve, and the place was dim and quiet and very hot. She thought that it looked dull; there was no movement or laughter among the people sitting at the long tables covered in with glass, and the two waitresses in soiled white coats leaning against the sandwich bar at the far end of the room looked drowsy and dejected. But in a moment she began to notice things that she actively did not like: the ragged clothes, faded almost to purple, of a man at a nearby table whose sleeping head rested on his arms, and who had some disfigurement of his skin that made her turn away her eyes; and the expressions on the faces bending across the tables engaged in low-toned expostulation or argument. She did not like the cigarette butts trodden into the floor nor the trays choked with more butts and little heaps of bitter grey ash: the whole place was drifting and dry with smoke that got into her eyes and her throat.

"Can't you see him?" she asked presently, when John had obtained for them two cups of weakish brown fluid, and done a certain amount of peering at distant tables and even questioning of various men, all older than himself, who seemed to resent their interminable arguments and discussions being interrupted.

"Of course I can't see him. What an absurd thing to say and bloody irritating too. This is serious. I must have some money or I may have to borrow from my mamma . . . Tom. I think that was his name. Or Toby. And he always wears a green pullover."

"Perhaps he's late . . . " she said, struggling with another yawn. Her eyes were stinging painfully with the smoke.

"He might be . . . We ought to have come earlier. He only said he *might* be here. I'll just go and ask Reg, over in that corner . . . he may have . . ."

Nell watched him as he made his way between the tables, the tall graceful boy with a child's short delicate nose and a child's mouth. She wished that they were both walking home up Hampstead High Street. Hampstead people looked odd, perhaps, compared with people in Dorset, but they did not look, or sound, like the people in the Eldorado. Now and then as she sat there she caught a sentence from a nearby table that was spoken in English but for all its comprehensibility might have been spoken in Arabic, and somehow this was vaguely alarming.

"Any luck?" she asked, when he returned from an earnest five minutes with Reg, who had ginger sideburns and a suspiciously virtuous expression which seemed to be perpetually exclaiming, "Wot, *me*, guv'nor?"

"No. And if anyone would have seen him Reg would. He sells nylons in Berwick Market. You must meet him some time. Not now."

He looked whiter than usual, and sulky and exhausted.

"Oh. Don't you think we'd better go home, then?"

"Of *course* not, Nello. He's probably upstairs. (This place is a club, you know, and owns the entire house.) I'll just go and see. I hate to leave you but you'll be all right. Sit still; pretend to be asleep." He made his way across the room to the stairs, and again she watched him go.

He went up them and disappeared. In a few moments she began to dislike being alone. She felt conspicuous. She sat there, wondering if she would be molested. But no-one did molest her. No-one looked at her for longer than it took to sweep over her a bleared, over-bright or sunken eye in search of something more positive, and the next ten minutes taught her something that she was never to forget; she was not the molest-able type . . . any more, she supposed, than the pale girl sitting at the other side of the room under one of the dim lights, wearing a tweed coat, with straight brown hair falling from under a béret, and irregular features which a kindly observer might have called delicate. She was just wondering if the girl felt as out of things as she looked, when she saw that the far wall was a mirror. She was still looking amused when John came back.

"He's probably gone to Jumbo's. That stays open all night, too. We'll try there. I'll just leave a word with Stanley in case he does come in . . . "

He went across to the coffee bar and spoke for a moment with the yellow-faced and oily-haired barman, the indefinite-ness of whose age was increased by an attire which had pretensions to Bohemian carelessness. When he came back, Nell said:

"John, *I must go home.* It must be two o'clock."

"Don't be so *bloody* silly. It's only half-past one and I *must* find this man. I can work for him and collect copy at the same time. You absolutely can't go home yet, Nello. I want you to be with me. Are you cold? Here——" they were outside now and standing in the dark, silent little street, and he was unwinding the long muffler from about his neck, "——have this. It's beautifully warm," he began to wind it round her.

"I'm not cold, thanks. You have it. You haven't got a coat——"

The words were lost in kisses. He pressed her desperately against him, kissing her on the mouth and cheeks with despair, like a miserable child, and muttering, "Oh please, Nello, don't leave me. You've got to stay with me. You're such a comfort to me. You *must* come too."

So they went to Jumbo's, which was in a street off Golden Square and even smokier, dimmer and quieter than Eldorado's, and John enquired of Jumbo's handlebar moustache, which was behind the bar, whether that fellow in the green pullover had been in this evening.

It appeared that Davina might have seen him. She sometimes did. Davina, interviewed in a corner where she was sitting with a friend, told them she hadn't seen Tom for days. He might have gone to the country. He sometimes did. Nell meanwhile studied Davina's long and voluminous black skirt, dusty black sweater with a high neck, and the various huge pieces of metal hanging from her wrists, ears and throat, and remembered seeing Gardis similarly festooned. Evidently this was Fashion.

She glanced round the room, trying to overcome her sleepiness. The people here were of another type; younger, more peculiarly dressed, with faces more intelligent than those of the Eldorado customers.

"Tom Ennis," John was repeating, when they were outside once more. Nell, who was learning rapidly, did not exclaim, *Didn't you even know his other name?*, and, as they began to walk slowly down the dark, grimy and indescribably melancholy street, he put his arm round her and said:

"Didn't you think Davina wonderfully attractive? She's the best-dressed girl in The Coffee Dish. (That wasn't The Coffee Dish, of course. We'll go there sometime.) That's where she usually goes; it was just luck finding her in Jumbo's."

Nell, who retained a general impression of condescension and grubbiness, wondered if it really had been.

"What does she do?" she asked diplomatically. "Has she a job?" Perhaps Davina earned sixteen pounds a week as a waitress, and chose to squander it on yards of black stuff and lumps of lead.

"*Job?* Good *heavens*, no. Davina is pure Soho. She couldn't *stand* a job now, even if she wanted to." His tone indicated approval. "And didn't you think Jumbo an interesting type? Ex-Battle of Britain pilot. Of course, if the Battle of Britain had been nowadays I rather doubt if people would have fought. Certainly *I* shouldn't. (Not from any theory of pacifism. I loathe bloody theorizing.) But out of pure logic. Jumbo isn't intelligent, and not very what *you* would call honest either. When you can get him to talk about the Battle of Britain— which we don't often, because it's boring—he seems to take it all for granted. He's unimaginative. I suppose they had to be, or they would have gone mad. But I never intend to destroy *my* fellow-creatures. I'm much too soft-hearted. I wish you would buy yourself a skirt like Davina's."

Nell had come to the end of her patience. She stood still in the middle of the frightening little street and announced:

"John, I'm going home. I have to be at work at nine tomorrow and it must be three o'clock and we shall have to walk because I've no money and neither have you."

"But you *can't* go home yet, Nello. He may be at a room in Earls Court where a friend of Benedict's lives. And I've simply *got* to get this job. It's the most wonderful chance."

Nell turned and began to walk away.

"Nello—don't be cross."

"I'm not in the least cross," turning round, "I'm—I'm not at all cross. But I've got to get home."

"*Wait*, then—" He darted back into Jumbo's, and in a moment reappeared.

"Here—" triumphantly holding out a pound note— "Davina lent it me. Now you needn't walk, my sweet."

"How did Davina get it, if she hasn't a job?" Nell asked grimly when they were speeding in a taxi towards Hampstead, "is she a tart?"

"Nell!" He sat upright and withdrew his arm, "Davina is a girl with the very *highest* ideals. She's perhaps the purest and loftiest in her way of living of *all* my friends. Jumbo lent it to her."

Nell made up her mind to visit Jumbo at some time in the

future when she might be earning more money, and repay the
debt in person (for certainly John never would); then she
relaxed once more against his thin, muscular young breast
and almost went to sleep. He indicated, as they crept up the
steps of the house, the ghostly orange moon lying tilted on her
side between the branches of the trees, stopping for a moment
to sweep an arm round the arc of the sky as if showing Nell the
stillness, and the thin, dark air silent and asleep. She obediently
looked; and did not say how sad she thought the sight; then
they tiptoed on towards their beds and sleep. The taxi had cost
eleven shillings and that was how the night ended.

CHAPTER FIVE

NEVERMORE

DURING the greater part of the bright spring mornings, Martin
Sely lay in the bedroom he shared with Anna, reading, and
trying not to think.

The days had once been neatly divided by his duties to the
Church; now they were divided only by meals, and the hours
seemed shapeless, and long indeed. He tried not to anticipate
the sound of the bells that rang for Early Service, for Evensong,
and on Sunday for Matins, from the church at the end of the
road, and when Anna had decidedly announced her intention
of not going to church any more, he had remained silent. He
knew that Nell continued to go; lying awake in the grey April
dawns, he had more than once heard her making her way
quietly down the stairs before seven o'clock. He had envied
her, and his envy had made him ashamed, but he could chide
himself no more. The springs in him of all feeling, except a
sulky resentment at what had happened to him, seemed to
have dried up.

But he was still compelled, as if by some force within himself,
to recall over and over again the early weeks of his misfortune;
that first morning in Morley Magna, for example, in the garden
where Anna had done such wonders with Michaelmas daisies,
and he had admired them when he had stepped out for a turn
round the paths while Nell was getting breakfast after Early
Service. Oh . . . and if a thought can be a groan, his thought

was a groan now . . . he was seeing again, in the merciless eye of the mind, that spider's web, glittering with dew like a chandelier with its diamonds, and the strands so fine they were almost invisible. There might be something here for a sermon . . . subjects for sermons were not easy to find when one had been preaching about a hundred a year for thirty years . . . that spider's web, the last thing of earth that he had looked upon with the eyes of faith.

Conscious of a hunger which, though not acute, he knew would not be completely satisfied by the breakfast he would in a moment sit down to because cornflakes with milk, and bread and jam, were all that the Vicarage could run to, and he was a big man, he had looked closer at the web, stooping above the mossy path in his shabby clerical dress. The web hung motionless, sparkling in the early morning sunlight, between the stalks of the flowers. Then, as his eye moved across it with a reverent appreciation of the beauty and order of God's handiwork, he had seen beneath a narrow pendent leaf the spider squatting; had even thought that he caught there, in the tiny cavern of black shade, the microscopic glint of an eye. (At this point in the miserable recapitulation, like a tune ground out over and over again on a cracked record, there always came the mocking line: *I, said the fly, with my little eye, I saw him die.*) He had smiled then as the nursery rhyme came into his head—and it was then and there, at that precise instant, with the indulgent smile touching his lips and his stomach subduedly signalling its need of food—that something had been withdrawn from him.

It had begun to go—and he had felt it begin, exactly as light or warmth might withdraw from the air, but this air was within himself—before he saw, behind the spider, the trussed bundles that were the flies. He was looking into the spider's larder, which also was the handiwork of God, and, had it been left to him, even that sight would not have shaken his acceptance of God's world. But it had not been left to him, and slowly, so slowly, something was withdrawn from the deepest depths of his nature, and he was left exposed to the cold and the dark.

It was not . . . how often he had tried! during the next few months, to explain: to Anna, to himself, to the Bishop . . . it was not that the hideous sight of the bound and helpless insects following upon the beautiful sight of the glittering web had set up some undergraduate'ish questioning within himself of God's

Plan and Nature. No, it wasn't anything like that at all; he had never, even in the early days of his training, been troubled by such problems. Anna had sometimes teased him for being what she called a Muscular Christian; and he had taken the joke good-naturedly because he knew that he was not a clever man and because, after all, there were worse things to be than a games-loving parson, who had entered the Church because his father and grandfather had entered it before him. And he loved his Anna and he knew, without ever thinking about that either, that she loved him. That was why his wretchedness increased when he found himself unable to explain to her, or to anyone else, what had happened to him. There had been a withdrawal; and now there was a lack; and the nearest thing to it was the sun going in, leaving everything in coldness and shadow, but the coldness and shadow were inside himself, and he could no longer serve God at the altar or go on being a parson while he felt as he did. (In those days, he had still hoped that he would get better.)

That was all. And the weeks went on, and he did not get better, but rather got worse, because a dull despair crept up and lay within him, filling the places once occupied by the honest sense of duty done and God served.

He kept on: he preached and ministered; baptizing and marrying and burying in the small and rather surly village of Morley Magna, and as the load of his hypocrisy grew, his health, that hitherto perfect health, began to suffer; while Anna occasionally wondered to herself amidst her chicken-rearing and gardening and cooking whether her old Marty was still being tiresome about his vocation (at his time of life!), and Nell, amidst the busy boredom of her days, wondered if the parents would ever follow Aunt Peggy's suggestion and let her find a job in the nearest town. At last, following on a chill caught bicycling in cold rain to a parishoner whom his now over-scrupulous conscience drove him out unnecessarily to visit, Martin developed pneumonia; nearly died; talked of his misery to the man who had come to take over his work; and everything came out.

How kind they were to him at Gore House where his own Bishop sent him; where each of the fourteen bedrooms was so brimming with spiritual joy that, visitors assured one another, one did not notice the bareness and the cold. In this rest home and clinic for the spiritually perplexed, run by a young, clever

enterprising parson with the help of a wife cut from the same
piece of cloth as himself, Martin had been miserably aware of
the sweetness and joy all about him and of the desire to help.
But there was so much zeal and sparkling spiritual talk, such
beauty of bare blue walls and shining floors and cold pure-
sounding music and half-trees set with all their load of leaves
and blossom in great tubs coopered by the spiritually regener-
ated, that he was confused and unhappy, feeling himself more
than ever to be a dingy clot of dust, a negative unwilling thing,
amidst the joy and the brightness.

The founder of Gore House had devoted to him an entire
week-end, giving of his best as he always did, and trying
patiently to bring his keen joyous mind into the dimness of this
bewildered and (he soon began to perceive) obstinate one. The
man was certainly *exceedingly* obstinate. Was he also (the younger
man was asking himself after some seven hours of it) rather
stupid? At any rate, it was plain that this kind came not out
by prayer or fasting, nor by applied psychology and a touch
of spiritual healing either. All that Sely would say, at infrequent
intervals, was that he "did not feel it was right" to administer
the Sacraments while he felt as he did. It was like a stone wall
. . . and really the man was awfully like a donkey looking
dolefully over it!

As usual, time was limited by the demands made upon it, by
other cases, some of which were showing signs of being cured
of whatever was troubling them, and Martin's host felt that it
would not be fair to give any more time when two and a half
days had already been given with apparently no result. He
would see to it that the poor soul was most heartily and
efficiently prayed for. He blessed him, and sent him back to his
own Bishop with the regretful report that Gore House must
record another of its rare failures.

Martin's own Bishop thought it only his duty to let his deep
disappointment and displeasure be made plain. Then he sent
him away; out of the Church; into a poverty greater than even
the Selys had so far known.

At first this had worried Martin almost as much as his
spiritual unhappiness. It had seemed the last straw that not
only should the meaning of life have been taken away, but
that he had also been forced to give up his livelihood. Anna and
Nell were now exposed to the possibility of actual want. But,
since the morning that Peg had telegraphed the money, three

minutes (as she told him) after reading his letter, he had not really worried any more, for Peg would stand by them. She always had been a brick, and he felt, and knew, that she would go on being one, and later on, if he ever got back some of his former energy and strength, he could earn (his first rather dramatic notions about addressing envelopes had taken on a more sober colour by now) something by coaching boys for exams. This could be added to Anna's income and the money earned by Nell as a typist.

A typist. Peggy had said that Nell was secretary to a Mr. Riddle, but Martin preferred to face the fact that she was a typist: excellent girls, typists, no doubt, in their way, but as a class despised even as 'skivvies' had been in his youth, and he did not want to think about Nell's being one. He never asked her about her work, although he did once enquire of Anna if she were 'getting along in that place', and heard with some indignation that they were 'very pleased with her'. So he should hope; his quick, light-footed girl, who had skilfully helped nurse him while he was ill. They were lucky to have her.

"We really are straight at last," Anna told him one afternoon at tea, when they had been in the house about three weeks, "I hung up the infant Saint John, dear little thing, in Nell's bedroom just after lunch and that's the last thing to be done. More, dear?"

He passed his cup, while the faint look of distress, brought to his face by this mention of a name from the former life, slowly faded. Anna, who was sorry for her dear old boy but did not believe in humouring him to excess, went on:

"Of course her room hardly needs pictures, with that extraordinary desert painted on the wall by the fireplace, but I saw no reason why Saint John shouldn't go up there. Nell always has had him."

"A desert picture?" he said slowly, looking across at her while he sipped his tea.

"Peggy says that man who was here before us painted it. It's a *trompe l'oeil* . . . I knew what it was; didn't remember the name until Peggy told me how it came to be there." She did not add that she had refrained from explaining to Peggy what it was. It had been a sacrifice, for Peggy's particular brand of knowledge set her teeth on edge. To herself, she called it 'B.B.C.'.

"What are you smiling at, Anna? You look . . . "

"Nothing really amusing. Do you like this cake? It's a new recipe."

" . . . better, somehow, since we've . . . been here. You look . . . younger . . . "

"Oh, my goodness." She clumsily swept some crumbs off the mahogany cakestand, which needed polishing. "What on earth do you mean?"

The tone held no question but she, who used never to think about her feelings or motives, was interested, as well as embarrassed. Wrong, so wrong, to talk or think about oneself; *make the best of yourself and forget yourself; why on earth should anyone be interested in you?* The voices of past nannies and governesses sounded faintly within her mind. Yet nowadays it was a constant temptation with her to do both. What had changed her? The cold high air of Hampstead, in which she moved about as two people, a girl and a dowdy ageing woman?

"Well, I mean what I say, dear. You do look younger and better. You . . . I think . . . do you like it here, Anna?"

"I like Hampstead, of course," she answered decidedly. "I always have. The air suits me, better than in Dorset. And I enjoy wandering about the streets, and seeing what's new since my day and what's been changed or pulled down. I wish you would come too, one day, Martin. Now that the weather's more settled it would do you good."

"No, no, I don't want to, I can't do that," he said nervously, fidgeting in his chair. "Later on, perhaps."

She was silent for a moment, then began to collect the tea things and pack them on the tray. She was thinking that it was no use expecting him to go outside the house when he would not even venture so far as Nell's room on the top-storey-but-one to view the *trompe l'oeil*; but she herself had really enjoyed those excursions up and down the small hills of Frognal, remembered from her childhood as a place of gardens with a country spaciousness overhung by old trees, silent, yet gently astir with life. Here the white mansions had stood, diversified by many a bay window, and many a gilded clock and tower above their stable doors, and at that time still haunted by memories of the 'arbitrary and vexatious' Irish Lady, Miss Sullivan of The Mansion, who had offended her neighbours for many years by exercising her right to forbid carts and carriages to drive through the toll gates without her permission. Anna had heard stories about her from the aunts who had lived at Vernon Lodge.

These aunts, Nancy and Eleanor, had played an important part in Anna's childhood; their 'ways', the shady comfortable rooms of their house where the loudest sounds had been the click of the parrot's beak as he extended his grey claw for sugar, the quick authoritative rise and fall of their voices, or the sweet straightforward airs they briskly played upon their Bechstein; these sights and sounds had seemed to her then as unchangeable and eternal as the twin towers of the Crystal Palace rising twelve miles away from the blue mist of summer lying in the valley, or as the hills on which Hampstead stood. Now there was not a trace left of Vernon Lodge. Two Willett-built houses stood upon the site, and these were almost twenty years old. When Anna, a few days since, had lingered by their trim gardens, she had fancied she could distinguish between them a slight hollow where the roots of the mighty oak tree which she had so often climbed in childhood had been wrenched from the ground, but she could not be sure. Only the sweetness of the air was unchanged.

A door slammed downstairs (they were having tea in their bedroom) and Anna said, "Bother."

"It's Miss Lister, the old woman who lives in that cottage at the end of the garden," in answer to an enquiring look. "She came home from hospital this morning and I promised Peggy I would look her up. The door reminded me. I'll just wash up these few things and go . . . but it's a bore."

"Who was it that went out?"

"Just this minute? Margie, I think. She has been flying about all the week, doing something for Charles."

"What a lot of people come to the house, Anna . . . don't you think that a lot of people do? While you're out I'm always opening the door to strange-looking young people—"

"Friends of John's: yes."

" . . . and Margie, as you call her, is always forgetting her key. She seems . . . "

He did not finish the sentence, a habit that was growing on him with the habit of pottering about until past midday in dressing gown and slippers. He thought that the young woman who had, presumably, taken Peggy's place in Charles Gaunt's affections seemed rather a nice little thing, but naturally he

disapproved of divorce and more naturally he did not wish to
admire his sister's supplanter. And of course it was all rather
squalid.

"I wish she wouldn't wear those absurd pointed glasses.
They make her look like—Mephistopheles—" said Anna, with
an uncharacteristic flight of fancy— "and they are such bad
style; bright green, and all over imitation jewels. I believe her
sight's as good as mine. In fact she practically admitted to me
that it is. Dear, don't go down to the door if the stairs tire you.
Let them knock. They can go away and come back later;
they're mostly young, it won't kill them."

"I don't mind," he said vaguely, taking up his book again,
"I didn't mean that. Look in on me when you have seen the
old lady, won't you."

"I will."

Anna went firmly and heavily down the stairs with her tray.
She slapped through the washing up, and then went down the
garden to call on Miss Lister.

The path sloped between clumps of iris and wallflowers and
tulips, under the shadows cast by two noble sycamore-trees,
and the view went across a street of small grey roofs, rising out
of bright green foliage, to an abrupt fall; a drop of hundreds
of feet; to a landscape painted in purples, pewters and white:
London, spread out below upon its conquered marsh. Anna, as
she went, looked at the greening plants which interested her
more than a prospect she had known since childhood; then
turned her attention to Miss Lister's home. It must be years,
she thought, since the place was properly done up, but it's a
nice little cottage. Absently, without thinking the thoughts of a
good housewife, she stared at the grey rags of net at the windows while awaiting an answer to her knock.

Almost at once it came, in the form of a shout from within;
not loud, but having a note as of one encouraging resistance to
a siege by Redskins. In a moment the door opened, and revealed as much of Miss Lister as could be seen beneath a colos-
sal marmalade cat. She looked at Anna over the top of his
frantically heaving back.

"Good afternoon. Your knock upset my boy, I'm afraid.
He's terribly nervous."

"Miss Lister? How do you do. I'm Mrs. Sely from the house
at the top of the garden. I heard from Lady Fairfax that you
were coming home today and I wondered if there was anything

I could do for you." Thirty years of being a parson's wife had
not taught Anna to soften her blunt manner.

"It's very kind of you but I'm going out myself presently.
Just to get a few things before those devils close," and she
crushed her boy tighter against the small bosom of an unfresh
blue woollen dress and looked at Anna with some defiance.

"Do you feel quite up to it? I understood that you are only
just out of hospital."

"Oh, I suppose you heard that from Lady Fairfax, too."
Miss Lister's face, which had surprised Anna by its remnants
of a marked, if ordinary, prettiness, took on an expression of
pondering reserve. "Yes, the ambulance brought me home this
morning and I've had a lovely rest after lunch and very glad
I was to be back again in my own beddy-byes (be quiet,
Dandy). So I shall be quite up to a run up to the shops this
evening. I want some Tide and a pair of shoelaces—" extending
a foot in a worn size-two shoe—"and some Quaker Oats—
though those devils at Burnshotts' hadn't any yesterday when
Mrs. Carter—a very nice woman, not one of us of course but
very nice—tried to get me some. She got in everything for me.
(There's one woman in Burnshotts' who's a beast. I hope
she'll have left while I've been away.) And a small white loaf.
(How people can eat brown I don't know. It would choke me.)
Oh, very well, then, *go* if you want to." Here she launched the
cat into space and it flew up the stairs like a rocket. "Another
neighbour has been looking after him for me. It's very kind of
her but it's made him worse than ever. He *hates* strangers.
Can't bear them. Takes after me."

A smile flashed out, and for an instant Anna had a confused
impression of seeing a little girl of ten with grey hair and
wearing false teeth and glasses. "I'm an unsociable beast.
Always have been. My Daddy used to say, '*Daisy only wants her
own*'."

"Oh . . . well, if you're sure I can't do anything . . . "

"I'm as fit as a fiddle now, thank you, and I'm going to be
as cosy as a bug in a rug—*if* only the nice weather will keep on."

"Yes, it's so nice to see the garden coming on, isn't it. Er . . .
yes . . . well, if ever you want anything. Miss Lister, we are only
at the top of the path."

"I'm perfectly all right, thank you. Good-bye."

Miss Lister shut the door upon Anna with some crispness.
Then she hurried up the steeply-pitched stairs into a tiny

bedroom which might have belonged to a midget with no silly prejudices about dust, and peered over the ragged curtain at her caller's retreating form.

"Dreadful old shoes and her hair's almost as grey as mine. Doesn't pick her feet up. Slouches. Hope I shan't ever have to drag up the High Street with *her*," muttered Miss Lister. "And what the dickens has it got to do with *Lady Fairfax* when I come out of hospital? Comes of taking benefits from people. Wish Henry and Margaret had never gone. Not going to like this one. Wish my *other* boy would come and see me. Must take my darling nurses some chocs. Dandy, Dandy, Dandy. Milkums!"

CHAPTER SIX

BOSS'S FRIEND'S RELATION

"Your Aunt Peggy's ideas of near-gentry aren't mine," said Anna, relating her side of this incident to Nell that evening while they were seated alone at supper. "Miss Lister is nowhere near it; she's Trade; prosperous Trade I should think, but she has it all over her . . . there *isn't* any more, Nell. You've eaten it all. Your appetite has trebled since we came here. Have some bread."

"It blows me out." But she cut herself a thick slice. "Mother," she went on, cautiously, with only one of the many plans in her head revealing itself by the determined look in her clear eyes, "has Margie told you about the party?"

"What party?"

"This party tomorrow night. They're having some people in for drinks," said Nell carefully, "because Charles is going on this goodwill trip to the Benelux countries and they want us to go."

"I shan't. It's too short notice," Anna said decidedly. "Why couldn't she let me know sooner?"

"It *is* only upstairs, Mother."

"Chattering and cocktails . . . you've never been to anything like that, have you? I used to go to them, when I was about your age. (Not at home, of course. Your grandmother detested casual entertaining.) But my friends at L.S.E. used to give that sort of party."

She looked at Nell. She did not often do so, although her eyes rested upon her frequently, and she now thought that in spite of the trebled appetite she had not put on any weight, and that she was unbecomingly pale. "Are you still having nothing but chocolate for your lunch?" she demanded.

"I shall go," Nell announced, flicking the question aside with a tiny frown. "That's what I want to talk to you about, Mother. I've worked it all out. And I need some separates."

"Some *what*?"

"Separates. A top and a skirt. There's a shop in Oxford Street where I can get a top for less than a pound and a skirt for less than thirty shillings—I've seen them for days now and if you could let me have three pounds I could get them in the lunch hour tomorrow and wear them tomorrow night—*my pink's too tight and too short*," she ended, quickly and loudly, as Anna opened her lips to speak.

Anna said, "Oh. Is it?" and then for some minutes said nothing. Nell began collecting cutlery and plates, with some colour in her face.

Anna was annoyed. The pink had ample darts and a hem. Perhaps it was rather childish in style for someone aged nearly twenty, but nothing looked in worse style than youth over-dressed. No 'top' or skirt costing so ridiculously little as the sums Nell had mentioned could be anything but bad style (and here Anna, with the unselfconscious pride of the chaste woman who disregards her own beautiful body, straightened her shoulders. Of course a good tailor-made did set one off, but she had never been able to afford good clothes for Nell, whose slightness would not have been set off by tailored lines anyway).

"You couldn't have asked at a worse time," she said. "I don't get my dividends until the first, and you know how we're placed, and Hampstead prices are . . . "

"I'll pay you back . . . later on, Mother."

"How, I should like to know? You give me almost everything you earn now. And I don't like these chocolate lunches—"

"Perhaps I'll get a better-paid job later on." As Nell stacked plates on the lift, which she now sent trundling and rumbling down to the kitchen, she kept her back turned.

"Oh, later on. Well, I'll have to see . . . can't you manage with the 'top', as you call it, alone? You have your grey skirt, and if you buy a pretty jumper . . . "

Nell shook her head as she turned round. Her lips were set in a long, pale pink, determined line.

"Really, Nell. You're being quite childish. But I suppose you *are* nearly twenty . . . if you're really sure you can't manage with the top alone I suppose you must have three pounds. (It is very cheap, I must say. But I suppose . . . never mind). Here, you had better take the money now."

That evening Anna was troubled by an uneasy sensation at the back of her mind. Had she been both stingy and unjust?

Nell, going quickly homewards the next evening with a large parcel from C. & A. Modes under one arm, was thinking that she had had very nearly enough of it.

By *it* she meant Akkro Products, Ltd.: the unceasing struggle with Mr. Riddle about ventilation: a struggle which, he had hinted to her, would have been no more than material for brief and awful laughter between himself and Mr. Belwood, a kind of fee-fo-fi-fummish jesting before rebellion was quelled for ever—had she not been the niece of Lady Fairfax, who was a friend of Mr. Hughes, who was Mr. Riddle's boss.

When the first small spurt of interest in herself had died down, Akkro Products ceased to notice Nell more than it did anyone else employed there.

She told herself that she did not care, that she wanted none of Aunt Peggy's glamour reflected on herself, and if the job had interested her this would have been true.

But it was so dull! No-one, she thought, could possibly imagine how dull, except someone who had, for five mornings a week during the last three weeks, watched Mr. Riddle cocoon himself into his muffler at three minutes to one every day, and heard the tone in which he replied to her expressed hope that he would have something nice for lunch: *I expect it will be sausages as usual.*

The one bright spot amidst the gloom was The Islanders. Nell liked them; she also found them amusing.

She and they had been exchanging remarks on the shocking mortality among nylons, and disrespectful comments on this here old dripper, as Maureen called the neat device for dispensing soap, for nearly a fortnight. She had detected differences in the collective controlling entity called Mum, Sylvia's and Maureen's being ever so nice while Pat's was ever so nasty, horrible, really; she knew that all Maureen cared for in the world was Dickie Valentine singing 'The Engagement Waltz', and that she hurried home from work every night to change into her best clothes and lie on her bed, smoking and thinking about him in the dark. She knew that Sylvia and her boy were practically engaged.

She had once let the Islanders treat her to lunch at the Rosita Café (hunger, and a real desire not to be what Pat called a toffee-nose, having persuaded her); and here, while the Islanders, having poked disinterestedly at their plates covered in pieces of dry pastry and wet potato, soon pushed them aside in favour of cigarettes, and she had polished off her own plateful down to the last crumb, she heard them discussing another collective entity: ''e'; boys; an ever-changing population in the case of Pat, whose pale, degenerate Cockney prettiness and deep red hair were inherited from a Mum born before the days of free orange-juice.

The boy in Nell's own life came and went, too: sometimes she met him coming down the stairs as she entered the house at the end of the day, and he stopped to say something puzzling or irritating ("I see you've got your béret at the Cresta-run angle, Nello. That's right. Soon you'll be able to go without a hat at all"); or, above the lime-trees in the front garden she saw him cross the window as she went out in the morning, look-ing pale and busy; then he never noticed her. Sometimes on Saturday mornings she saw him, elegant and detached, in the High Street, shopping with Margie. Margie and Charles would 'dash off' into the country until Tuesday night, and John would fill the top flat with his friends. But he did not invite her, and she did not know whether the man who was running the paper about aquariums had given him a job or not. She certainly was not going to flatter him by asking.

She turned out of the High Street, and began to skim down Arkwood Road.

Something must be done about being at Akkro Products, and done soon. Only that evening, as she hurried thankfully with The Islanders over the threshold of the place—"She makes a pound a *day* in tips. Straight she does. And she gets three, so that's nine pound a week. *And* her lunches. *And* she works near home so there's no fares," Pat had said.

"My cousin was a waitress last summer. She had a nervous breakdown afterwards. All the running about. It was sawful, she said."

"It's smashing work if you get in a nice caff, though."

"I wouldn't like to do it, though. Would you like to, Nell?"

"Leave her alone. She's Dreaming of Thee."

"Your auntie wouldn't let you, would she, Nell?"

"Don't see it's any of her blasted business," said Pat, a remark with which Nell, although she said nothing, heartily agreed.

Sixteen pounds a week . . . A pound a day in tips—and more at holiday times. (Nell had casually drawn what facts she could from Pat while they were walking to the 'bus-stop.)

But why consider the idea? The parents would never let her. Go into another office, with a better salary?

I'm absolutely fed up with offices and I'm not going into another, if I can help it, ever again, thought Nell.

She looked up as she came level with the gate of Number Twenty-five, and there were Gardis and Benedict Rouse, sitting on the cracked black-and-white marble lozenges of the steps. Their clothes were elegant, but somehow their personalities had the effect of making the sober Edwardian façade suggest a Home of Rest for Romanies.

Gardis's immense skirt of white felt, patterned with scarlet strawberries the size of tennis balls, was spread about her in a cartwheel, and a stole of white felt similarly adorned was round her shoulders. Her sandals, mere twists of scarlet joined to a papery sole, had four-inch heels. The face above Benedict's dinner-jacket suggested that the afternoon, which, he told Nell, they had spent walking on the Heath, had not been a particularly happy one.

"Hullo. Still in your good British tweeds, I see, and it's nearly warm today." Gardis greeted Nell with this and a gesture towards her with one foot, "did you ever do any more about being a waitress? *All right*," as Nell made a frantic gesture towards the upper window where her mother could be seen gazing out at the apocryphal scrawls made by a passing jet, "she can't hear. I suppose you didn't, or kind Auntie would have heard about it."

"Are you going to the party?" Nell asked, coming up the steps and moving the parcel under her arm into what she hoped was concealment.

"We are. Dear little John invited Ben, and Ben brought me along. 'Pears there's going to be some B.B.C. folks there who might be useful to him. Are you invited too? What's in that parcel? New frock? Surprise!" and Nell had to make her way into the house past Gardis's attempts to open the parcel, while refusing her offers, which seemed half-genuine, of helping her to make up her face.

She was glad to escape. But she had taken the decision to get hold of Benedict at the party and find out from him just how she should set about getting a job as a waitress *if* at some time in the future, she should want . . . At least then she would *know*.

She stepped into the quiet hall full of evening light and shut the door behind her. There, standing at the top of the stairs, looking down at her, was John.

"Hullo, Nello darling, I've been waiting for you," he almost whispered as he came running down. "I hope you're coming to my papa's party?"

"Yes. Is Aunt Peggy coming?" She stood stupidly within the circle of his arm while he pushed puppyish kisses into her neck. From the top of the house there floated down authoritative cries and sounds of obedient feet hurrying: last-minute preparations for the entertainment.

"Of course not. She hates Margie's guts and Margie hates hers. (Do have some delicacy, Nello.) I say, I'm not going back to Benedict's room any more. He's chucked me out because I will talk while he's working. So I shall be here all the time now."

"Do you mind?" She ventured to rub her cheek against his, and learned that the thrice-weekly shave of which she had once heard him boast was overdue.

"Of *course* not, Nello. If there *were* any slight inconvenience—but there isn't—I should be proud to put up with it in the service of Benedict's exquisite technique. And you know I *like* being here, almost best of all my . . . did you like those poems of his that I pushed under your bedroom door, by the way?"

"Oh, was that you? It wasn't my door; it was Daddy's. (*He* didn't like them.) Yes, I did, rather. I thought they were awfully original, anyway."

"That's quite discerning of you, Nello," with an approving glance. "They're *extraordinarily* original. That expression of burning passion in delicate metres and light, precise words has never been carried so far in English before. Reading them is like having an icicle of blood go through you, isn't it?"

"Don't be so *horrible*," and she disengaged herself, from caution rather than from any wish to leave the circle of his arm. One of the parents might appear.

"Hadn't you better go and get out of that terrible coat?" beginning to follow her up the stairs. "Can I come and talk to you while you change?"

"No you can not," colouring, as she paused outside the door of her room. "I'm going to have a bath and all sorts of things . . . oh all right, then. Just while I brush my hair."

"I shall like that very much. (I adore watching people brushing their hair.) I won't stay long but may I just lie on the bed? I've been hunting all day for a man who's promised me a job and I'm exhausted . . . I can always bury my face in the pillow—if you insist . . . There are going to be a lot of B.B.C. creatures there tonight. (That's why Benedict's coming. He heard me say they were expected and he *asked* to come. I didn't like to refuse, but they'll do him no good; he ought to write like mad for three years and then die.) I hope my papa won't make another gaffe with them and get himself thrown out on his little ear *again*."

"What was it he actually did? I've never really heard." Nell turned her head to look at him through a raying fountain of silky hair.

"Haven't you?" He propped himself on one elbow, beginning to laugh. "Oh, it was wonderful. You know he built up his radio reputation on being The Housewife's Champion; buttering them up and verbally kissing their horrible little red hands and all that sort of bull; well, one day he got fearfully worked up about the price of mince or something and he said—he said—" rolling over and choking into the pillow—"*the housewife, staggering under her heavy burden, darting this way and that like some maddened animal*"—and of course billions of letters poured in from all over the country from horrible little housewives complaining that he'd called them animals. It completely finished him. It was like the fall of Lucifer. We all laughed like drains. Of course," he added, "it wasn't scripted or the B.B.C. would never have passed it. He lost his head and said it in an interview."

"You must go now," she said, when they had stopped laughing. "I want my bath. And I've got to see if my mother wants any help with supper."

"Oh, must I? What are you going to wear? Not some horrible pink thing? I loathe pink." He continued to lie where he was, with arms behind his head and dusty shoes on the coverlet, looking at her.

"No. *Will* you go away?"

"I suppose so. But how suburban you are. Don't expect much in the way of guests. There will be these B.B.C. types and some of Margie's advertising set . . . the women will all be very painted. (How vulgar paint is.) All right, I'm going. Thank you for letting me see you brush your hair," and he slid off the bed and wandered from the room.

As Nell went upstairs half an hour later towards the distant roar of voices, the dark yellow skirt rustled about her ankles as satisfactorily as if it had been real silk, and she only knew that the sleeveless jersey, of paler yellow, showed arms that were smooth and pale; their touching, childish fragility escaped her—on the whole—un-anxious eye. She wore her usual pink lipstick. (*How vulgar paint is.* But why should she always do what *he* approved?)

"Now you've overdone it, of course," he muttered, emerging unhurriedly from the mass of people packed tightly together in the small hot room, shouting their heads off in the radiance of the April afterglow, and approaching her where she stood by the door, "those things are more suitable for going to the ballet . . . but it was weirdly clever of you to choose yellow. It's most original. I expect you've never been to this terrible kind of party before, have you? You must come and say how-do-you-do to Margie first," and he began to steer her deftly through the crowd, "she's so busy working off all the spiteful things she's thought out for the past few days that I don't suppose she'll even remember who you are . . . she's in a permanent state of nervous tension, poor little beast . . . but she shouldn't have married my papa if she wanted to be nice and quiet . . . Margie, you know my cousin, Nell Sely, don't you?"

"Oh, John!" Margie, who was very small and very dark and very pretty, made a sparkling face behind the devilish sparkle of her glasses, whisking round from the people she was shouting at, "isn't he absurd?" to Nell, "of course we know each other. We meet on the stairs, don't we? Is he looking after you? Have you had something to drink? Sherry? Gin? Vermouth? . . . "

"Nell drinks tomato-juice," John said austerely, even as Nell accepted an enormous glass from a man who was struggling by ("If you drink that, Nello, you will be drunk. I am not trying to stop you. I am only telling you").

"Oh, let her have it." Margie turned back to her gabbling guests. "God knows she'll need something to make her enjoy *this* party (at her age I suppose one still *does* enjoy parties) and I'm sure you put on that pretty jersey expecting to meet a *lot* of glamorous people, didn't you?" to Nell, with a screwing-up of the eyes and a special smile. "Susan! Angel! When did you get back!" and she launched herself at a large woman in a cock's-feather cap.

As her cheek pressed the hot painted one of the angel, she was feeling remorseful at having said that to the poor kid; why shouldn't she put on something pretty and want to meet glamorous people (God help her); she was young and it was only natural; she couldn't have much fun living with that pathetic old father and her bossy snob of a mother . . . For an instant, as Margie plunged into an exchange of ecstatic interruptions with Susan, she clearly heard, and impatiently dismissed, her own mother's voice saying, *"Marjorie dear, that wasn't kind."*

"She is a bitch, of course," John was saying judicially to Nell a little later, as they stood in a corner near the improvised bar, so wedged about with people that they could hardly lift their glasses, "but not a *natural* one. People say that some years ago she used to be rather boringly sweet. But what I think happened was this: when she met my papa *first*, he was terribly down on witty career-girls because he'd had such a dose of my mamma. But after he married his sweet little Margie, he not only found her a bit *dull*, after my mamma, but *also* found that her nice, natural manner *bored other people*, and wasn't helping him with his *career*. So he told her she had got to turn herself into a witty bitch, and she has. That's all. (*Don't* say 'is it?')"

"I see," said Nell, who had drunk half the gin (with some effort) and who was liking its effect. But she had prudently put the glass down on a side table and was now watching, with some surprise, a large man stealthily pick it up, smell it, and shoot it down his throat.

"She was so much in love with him, you see. She made herself a doormat for him. (I don't know that she's so much in love now. How could she be, after two years of him?) But people absolutely *go* to their parties hoping Margie will say something outrageously catty, and of course she always does. But she never says those things to famous or clever or *useful* people; she just goes for stupid people and people who are beginning to slip up and young people, like you. She does it rather well, I think. But it's a frightful strain, keeping up a reputation as an amusing cat when you feel guilty all the time."

"Does she feel guilty?"

"Of course."

"How do you know? She . . . just looks as if she were . . . having a nice time and looking after her guests, to me."

"That, Nello darling, is because you're still rather green. But you soon won't be: I think you have a gift for seeing things and people as they are; rather soberly. I like that. Only you mustn't start trying it on me. I'm the exception, remember. *You must always see me as I want you to see me.*"

He smiled, and through the delightful haze of gin Nell smiled back. *Beautiful little boy* . . .

"Besides, it's my business to know about people . . . I'm a writer, a novelist . . . now I suppose you had better meet some of these terrible types. It will be good for you. I'll just . . . "

"Oh, there's Benedict. Could I speak to him, do you think?"

"I imagine so, if we can get him away from dear little Gardis for five minutes . . . yes, I know he isn't actually talking to her now, but do look at him; *chained* to where she is, like *Andromeda*, or perhaps *Prometheus* would be a better comparison . . . an absorbing but horrifying sight. What an affliction to be so undetached. Yes, you go over and talk to him."

CHAPTER SEVEN

"AND ALL MY DAYS ARE TRANCES"

BENEDICT, with no guard upon the expression of a face which, in any case, seldom concealed its owner's feelings, was standing silently on the edge of the circle which had gathered about Gardis.

She was entertaining it less by what she said, than by that effect of wise-cracking which a display of American teeth, and the sound of an American accent, creates rather easily today in England. The group looked gayer than it was. He, who felt even less gay than he looked, was recalling throughout all his senses, with a numbing pain, every detail and incident of the

afternoon they had passed together on the Heath—together!
yet for all she had comprehended of his feelings, he might have
been accompanied by a little animal, running beside him in its
black silken fell across the fresh grass of spring.

At their first meeting, two months ago, he had been instantly
enslaved by her air of being a bad, lost, impudent little girl
who had run away from home to busy herself with her own
affairs, and who cared nothing for the grown-ups she had left
behind; and as he had come, by the painful way of passion
exchanged without kindness, to know her better, he had learned
that this deliberately-straying child was her true self and that
her paintings were her beloved toys and her only pleasure and
treasure.

She was hopelessly—yes, she had told him, the analyst had
informed her parents that nothing could be done—immature,
unintegrated, inharmonious, schizo—helplessly, in short, *split*.
She had grinned, and said that she did not care if she were;
you got more fun that way. In the early days of their affair,
he had not cared either; telling himself that surely psycho-
analysis was the greatest kill-joy of the delicious pangs of love
since the Church had ceased to thunder, and congratulating
the creators of such characters as Dolly Varden and the whole
tribe of imperious, childish, irresistible charmers that their
books were written, and they themselves safely dead, before the
new 'dismal science' had spoiled the fun.

Then he had learned accidentally, that his particular
child was not nineteen, as he had supposed, but almost
twenty-four—no age if a girl were maturing nicely, but dis-
turbingly old if she were not maturing at all; and he had seen
her when she was in one of her helpless hysterical fits of crying
at the prospect of growing older; seen her hurrying frantically
away to have almost-invisible wrinkles massaged, and firm
young neck muscles rubbed with astringent creams; seen the
change in her expression when conversation turned upon age.
He had been made to swear that he would tell *everybody* that
she was nineteen; just nineteen; and he had kept his
promise.

Her terror and her weakness had increased his pity for her,
and his love. Yet there was in his passion at the same time a
strong resentment. This was linked in some way with 'his'
poetry, his own power to write it. His passion never prevented
him, of course, from doing so; pain, sleeplessness, jealousy,

longing, despair, never dried up the true springs of creation yet; but often he felt that something ugly was going on; some negative force was at work between Gardis and himself, which added anger to his pain.

It was indeed a negative force; it was the absence of joy. But he did not yet suspect it.

Someone was addressing him for the third time, he realized, when he came slowly out of the trance of suffering, memory and longing in which he was dreaming while he watched Gardis's face.

"I'm sorry? I beg your pardon," he said, when he had looked for a moment unseeingly into the eyes looking up into his own, "oh—hullo." He saw with relief that it was John's cousin Nell, and she was neither grinning at him nor shouting.

"I hope you don't mind, but I want to ask you something. It's about," and here, with a glance round, she lowered her voice so that the quick light tones reached him clearly under the uproar, "about what you said the other night about being a waitress. I'm fed up with my job and *I'm* going to try to be one. How do I start?"

"Well . . . " He hesitated, reluctantly rousing himself, "it's quite simple, you just—I say, can't we get out of this noise? Let's go and sit on the stairs."

So they went; with much difficulty, across the crowded room and out on to the draughty and more-or-less silent landing, and when they were seated on the pale-blue, chipped paint of the top-stair, with two glasses which he had snatched up in passing, he drank off half his, and, sighing, said without animation:

"Well, what do you want to know? I didn't say it was easy work, you know, and you don't always earn sixteen pounds a week."

"Yes, but that's all right. I know it won't be easy and it will be enough if I can earn about eight. But how do I start?"

"Just walk into any café or restaurant that doesn't look too low (you'd better begin at a respectable place—you don't want to get put off the whole thing right away) and ask if they need a waitress."

"Will it matter never having done it before?"

"Shouldn't think so. It doesn't for men, and you've got to start sometime."

"Where shall I try?"

"Well, not in Camden Town, or Aldgate or anywhere like that."

"I hardly know London at all, except round Tottenham Court Road, and of course Hampstead."

"Tottenham Court Road is definitely out. Hampstead's all right. Why not try one of those places in the High Street? Not a coffee-bar; one of those teashops that's always full of elderly ladies. That would do to start on. You don't want anywhere tough; you aren't a tough type and your parents might object," and he looked at her with slightly more interest, and smiled.

"They'll object anyway," said Nell, swallowing. "I was looking at those places on the way home this evening, as a matter of fact. What about The Primula? Do you think that would do?"

"Very well, I should think. Gardis and I had tea there this afternoon."

Every detail of its furnishings, and the very light that filled its low, wide, white room came before Benedict as he spoke, steeped in an irresistible soft enchantment and interest. "Yes, try there." His eyes had strayed to the open doorway, and were searching among the crowd.

"Thank you very much."

"Oh, that's all right. Good luck." He got up, and so did Nell. "And don't worry too much about what your parents say. Parents never understand, but some of them do try to. I realize now how good my father was about my not wanting to take over his practice (he's a doctor in Cornwall) and chucking medicine half-way through my training. It must have been terribly hard on him. But he was so decent about it, and we're still on good terms." He smiled.

"Wasn't it difficult, making up your mind?" They had paused at the door, before re-entering the packed, shrieking, grimacing crowd, as if willing to postpone the effort for a moment. His gleam of better temper had vanished and he looked crosser than ever.

"What the hell else could I do? I say, there's someone I must . . . I've got to talk to these B.B.C. people, that's really what I came for . . . I'll see you some time, I expect; good luck."

He began to shoulder his way towards two elegant personages dressed in palest grey and wearing horn-rims, and Nell remained in the doorway.

What he had said about parents, of course, was rot. It was
true that they never understood, but she was very sure that
hers would not even try to. They would only be horrified and
shocked. She suddenly felt inexperienced and lonely, and
wished that Elizabeth were there to help and amuse her, but
Châteaux d'Oex was six hundred miles away, and perhaps
if ever Elizabeth heard that that 'worthy type, name of Sely',
as she had called Nell, had become a waitress she might drop
her. The prospect added to the immediate lack of cheerfulness.

"Is there anything to *eat*?" demanded an old, musical voice
at her elbow, "you are taller than I am, perhaps you can see
. . . I've had four drinks, there's plenty to drink, but what I
like at this kind of party, where you have to talk a great deal,
is something to eat as well, because after a time it takes it out
of you so, talking . . . now could you get me a sandwich?
although I haven't seen any; there seem to be only those pieces
of pastry with things balancing on them . . . I'm sure you won't
mind . . . "

The earrings worn by the wonderfully elegant tiny creature
who murmured all this barely reached to Nell's shoulder, and
Nell had almost to peer under a mass of curling grey feathers
and blue hair to distinguish a *mignonne* monkey face, whose
ageless prettiness was uncertainly covered with orange, red
and black paint. Out of this contemporary mask smiled, also
uncertainly, two splendid faded eyes.

"Of course I don't. But I haven't seen any sandwiches . . .
will you wait here?" The eyes continued to smile vaguely, and
Nell rushed away, returning in ten minutes with an exiguous
square of pastry covered in greenish cheese to find the lady
gone.

It was true; there seemed to be almost nothing to eat, and
she entertained herself by collecting what food there was and
handing it to anyone who looked in want of it or who could
spare a second from their loud, quick, grinning conversation
to bolt it . . . it was amusing, moving from group to group and
noticing who needed what, and trying to supply it. She would
have welcomed some notice from the bright, elderly, successful
faces surrounding her on all sides, but the only one who said
anything to her but "nks', in return for a biscuit or a glass
(for she had now added that of wine-waiter to her rôle) was a
lady who looked at her and murmured rather wistfully

" . . . heavenly to see straight hair," which was not a very interesting *mot* to repeat to the parents after the ball.

Someone had opened a window; cool air was eddying the smoke about, and between the parted curtains there showed the lamps in the street and the night sky. Margie, standing still for an instant and rubbing one minute foot, slipped from its shoe, against her glass nylon, was glancing quickly about the room. She looked dog-tired. Her dark-blue dress sprinkled with silver droplets seemed to have drawn down all the colour from her face into its sombreness. The party was almost over.

"Do have a sausage roll . . . " Nell said, to an enormous bald man surrounded by smaller people who were gaping up at him admiringly as he roared and waved his arms about; it was a silly thing to do, for it stopped him in full flight. He paused, blinked at her, shook his head, glanced at his wrist, screamed, and at once swam majestically off towards Margie, pulling all the smaller people with him, and beginning to apologize for having to leave while he was still within six feet of her. Nell stood in some dismay, watching.

"Good God, why do you have to do this? Haven't you had a drink yourself? Where's John? John, why aren't you looking after Nell? She's having to be a waitress . . . can't *you* make yourself useful? Oh, must you? Well . . . yes, tomorrow . . . no, about a month. Yes, it is . . . I hope so . . . lovely to have seen *you* . . . "

It was Charles Gaunt, putting a distracted hand on her shoulder as he accompanied some friends to the door, jerking his head towards Margie to bring her into the group as he did so, and pushing Nell with him. John, leisurely approaching across the now almost empty room with a glass in one hand and an immensely long cigarette holder in the other, observed to Nell:

"I suppose you were getting your hand in."

"Do shut up," in a low tone.

"Why? There isn't anyone here who matters now that dear little Gardis has gone . . . do you like my jacket?" turning his shoulders about to display a white coat, "my papa's valedictory present. I am sure you don't. You are going to tell me that it looks weird."

"I do rather like it, as a matter of fact."

"It's too early in the year for it, of course, but I couldn't resist wearing it. I saw you talking to old Celia Costello. Isn't she wonderful? Do you know she's nearly eighty?"

"I thought she was rather horrid."

"Of course she is but she's wonderful as well. Why do you always want everything and everybody to be nice? I say, I must go. I don't want my papa . . . I'll see you some time soon, I expect."

It was difficult to realize that two hours ago this elegant creature had been kissing her neck in a lonely, in-need-of-comfort kind of way. Nell watched him skilfully and charmingly extricate himself from the remnants of the party, with an air of being about to come back to it at any minute. But she thought that he might not come back until long after midnight, if then; often she was aroused in the small hours by the stealthy closing of the front gate or that unmistakable step approaching the house in the quiet of dawn. She never spoke to anyone of these excursions and happenings. To learn his ways, to keep his secrets, gave her the feeling, which was becoming necessary to her, of sharing something with him. Certainly she could not be sure of any other kind of bond.

CHAPTER EIGHT

"AND ALL MY NIGHTLY DREAMS..."

THE last guest but one had gone. The room looked as repulsive as most rooms on such an occasion. Nell, realizing with embarrassment that *she* was the last guest, was opening her mouth to apologize and say "thank you for having me," when Margie cut in, in a flat voice:

"Will you be an absolute angel and help me cope with the washing-up? That wretched man's never turned up, blast his eyes . . . not that it would have been his job to wash up anyway, I suppose . . . but not even to let me know . . . if you're really going to be a saint, let's get it over, shall we?"

Someone had already been stacking some of the glasses on the draining-board in the kitchen, and Nell went to and fro, collecting the remainder, while Margie began the rinsing.

"Have an apron," she said, indicating two voluminous garments of blue linen embroidered with red. "This is mine and this is Charles's. He loathes washing up, of course, who doesn't, but he loves to cook and he's got quite a reputation. His *Oeufs à la Neige* and *Coq au Pâté* are quite famous; Phil Harben will have to look out."

Her voice rattled on, sounding slightly hoarse from never having stopped talking once during the last four hours, but the conscious sparkle in her face had been replaced by a shut-in exhausted look.

Nell listened without interrupting until Margie herself broke off her stream of chatter, gave a start and muttered, "Oh God, what's the matter now?" Charles Gaunt could be heard exclaiming and rustling papers in the next room. Margie fixed her eyes apprehensively on the door—while continuing to rinse the glasses. Suddenly, frowning and gnawing his upper lip amidst convulsive twitches, he appeared.

"Do you know anything about this?" holding out a letter with an accusing glare.

"That? Oh, heavens. I meant to tell you . . . "

"But it hadn't even been *opened*. It was lying under a mass of stuff. It's dated April the fourth and it's been here *ten days*."

"Oh Charles, I truly am sorry . . . I'm simply desolated . . . I remember now . . . it was that time we were up when you had to cover that show for *Home Choice* . . . there were some letters in the hall and I was in such a rush . . . I just brought them up and dumped them on the desk . . . I was tearing off to see Kitty about those old theatrical prints . . . and I simply never thought a thing about them from that day to this. It was *appalling* of me. Has anything absolutely frightful happened as a result?"

She stood there, her hands with their long red nails dangling at her sides, staring at him with a crushed yet also a 'this-is-the-last-straw-at-the-end-of-such-an-evening' expression.

"Only that I shall have to sit down at once and write fifteen hundred words for *Gracious Living* on 'Wines to Amuse Your Friends'. *The dateline is tomorrow*."

"Charles! How frightful." She fumbled in her apron pocket for the devilish spectacles and set them distractedly on her nose: perhaps to give herself confidence. The whole gesture suggested one of his nervous twitches, much enlarged.

"I'm glad you realize it. Leave all that now, will you, and get out your machine. I'm all in, and so are you, I expect . . . "

"Who says I'm all in?" tilting the spectacles with a tiny wink at Nell.

"—but I'm not in a position, nowadays, to turn down thirty guineas . . . we shall be on this until three this morning, I should think . . . there's a mass of stuff to be looked up—and the dates on the vintages had better be correct this time . . . "

"You know how sorry I was about that—"

" . . . oh, God, and now I can't tie it up with the advertising . . ."

"Won't they do that?"

"You know nothing keeps the wine people sweet like the personal touch . . . really, Margie, it's too bad, you know. Are you slipping up, do you think?"

She flung down the tea towel and went to get out her typewriter.

He lingered. He explained to Nell—speaking in a voice jarred with exasperation, whose every word could be heard in the next room—that he looked back on the days when he had had time for his own work as if they were a lost paradise. Of course, she wouldn't have read *The Aftermath*, his first novel. It had been written before she was born; it was about the men who had come home after the 1914 war and had had to adjust themselves to what in those days was called Civvy Street, and it had sold eighty thousand copies and made him a nice little bit of money. But he had had to keep it up, of course; not miss his market; follow up success—all the rest of the line—and damn and blast all the people who wouldn't or couldn't realize that a writer *had* to have time to digest his material— and of course, thanks to them, his second book hadn't done nearly so well as the first—*Hercules Bound*, it had been called, about industrial troubles and the General Strike of 1926— although Arnold Bennett—she wouldn't have heard of him either—had praised it in '*The Evening Standard*', and he'd had to take to journalism to keep the never-never man from the door, and then he'd let himself be persuaded by Peggy into doing a bit of broadcasting as well—and then there'd been *Ask Me Another*, and from the day he walked into that blasted studio until this he'd never had a minute; not even a spare half-hour a day to write the thriller he'd had in his head for the last three years—and it was damn good too. He knew it was. Almost certain to make a film—and then you were made. But what chance had *he* got of writing a line? with broadcasts, and articles for the Sunday rags, and the women's rags, and

goodwill tours here and there and all over the place? Not a
hope; not a hope in hell.

He was only telling Nell all this so that she might be warned
never to take on too much; burn up her health and her nerves
doing work she hated. She'd better look at *him*. He was enough
to warn anybody. Of course, if you could once get on T.V.,
especially on to a panel game, your troubles were over. You
could lie back and relax—and God knew that you didn't
have to be *good* to get on to a panel game . . . yes, your troubles
would be over.

He stopped. The hard light in the kitchen showed up the
weariness of his grey face and the dullness of his eyes. He had
not once looked at Nell as if he saw her, throughout all his
tirade, and now he stood looking down at the floor in silence.
She felt rather sorry for him: John's father.

"Charles? I thought you wanted to get started." Margie's
voice came snappishly from the next room.

"Yes, we must get down to it."

He smiled charmingly at Nell and escorted her to the door,
she receiving on the way there an absent wave of the spectacles
from her hostess. As she ran down the stairs she heard the
typewriter begin.

For some reason, she found it pleasant to see the parents
seated one on either side of the fireplace in the drawing-room.
Her father looked feeble and old, her mother only glanced up
long enough from *The Hampstead and Highgate Express* to ask
if she had had a good time? and returned immediately to its
columns; nevertheless, Nell thought that they compared well
with wonderful old Celia Costello, Gardis and poor Charles-
for-god's-sake, and the rest, and the conclusion influenced her
in deciding to stay another two weeks with Akkro Products.
Poor old things: they were only just getting used to the idea
of her having a job at all.

She announced that she was going down to the kitchen to
hunt herself up some supper.

"That reminds me," Martin looked up slowly from his book,
"this afternoon, while everybody was out and I was alone
in the house, someone rang up to say that they couldn't come
to the—er—party. It was someone named Patrick, I gathered,
who had promised to help *wait*. He had a cold; they all had
colds, he said, so none of them could come, and would I tell
Mrs. Gaunt. But the line was bad and I couldn't hear clearly,

and I'm afraid I forgot. Was it all right, do you know?" He looked anxiously at Nell.

"That was a firm that hires out waiters for parties—'Patrick', it's called, Margie said. No, it didn't matter—there was hardly any food to hand round anyway, and what there was *I* handed round."

As she ran down to the kitchen she almost expected to hear cries of "Waiting? What a peculiar way of earning a living. Nell, don't *you* ever do anything of that sort" but naturally the drawing-room remained sunk in the usual dull, but somehow comforting, hush which had pertained to all the Vicarage drawing-rooms in which the Selys had ever sat, and she was able to bolt a fried egg and think over her future plans without interruption.

The noise of the typewriter had stopped by three o'clock, so unless poor Margie (Nell now thought of her as poor) were engaged in re-writing the article by hand, the task must have been accomplished. Soon after, Nell heard the sound of the front gate opening, but lay still, refusing to creep to the window and peer out, while the soft night air, scented with hidden leaves, blew faintly into the room. By straining her ears she fancied that she could hear him making his way, with infinite cautiousness, upstairs, and presently, satisfied that he had come in, fell asleep again.

But in the garden at the back of the house, where brilliant starlight made every object mysteriously visible, he was sitting at the foot of the steps leading up to the iron balcony outside the drawing-room, trying to see exactly what he had done to his shin. Attempting to find a way in at the back of the house because he had mislaid his key, he had tripped, and sprawled almost the length of the flight. He was furious with everything, and when a quiet, grating voice behind him said sympathetically, "Poor old chap, did you tumble-down-dee?" he merely growled without looking up.

When he did look up, he saw what might have been a goblin, so small and bundled up was it. A scarf covered the head, and between its folds large bright eyes gleamed behind glasses; it had grey hair, and feet in a doll's bedroom slippers, and two tiny knotted claws of hands. He looked at it without surprise.

"Yes I jolly well did tumble-down-dee. I hope I didn't *disturb* you? I've been chucking pebbles at your window for the last twenty minutes."

"Have you? I didn't hear you."

"So I gathered."

"I was looking for my naughty boy. He *will* go out at night. I'm sure that vet. didn't do him properly. They ought not to *want* to go out at night when they've been done. Have some cocoa? I'm going to have a little cupsy."

"Oh . . . thank you. It's awfully kind of you."

This conversation had been conducted in a succession of piercing whispers. John now slowly gathered himself up, and, assuming the grave gentle expression which always accompanied his mood of feeling like a chivalrous young knight, followed Miss Lister noiselessly down the path towards the light shining dimly in her cottage.

It came from one candle, burning stilly in an old blue holder and sending her humped shadow towering and sliding across the faded walls as she closed the back door, and moved about between cupboard and gas stove. He sat in a broken Windsor chair with arms resting on the table and chin sunk in his hands, staring between eyelids heavy with sleep at the rusty row of saucepans, which looked as if none of them had been used for years, and the chipped cups, whose gilt gleamed faintly through dust, ranged along the dresser. The lovely place, the best place to be in of them all; no need to talk, to pretend, to try; no need to do anything but look, and dream, and almost to catch as it spun murmuring softly, hypnotically by, the moment itself . . .

"Where have you been, you naughty one?" she asked, coming to the table with the steaming saucepan, but her tone was merely playful; it held no curiosity at all.

"Oh—out and about. Heavenly cocoa. You are kind, Auntie Daisy."

"After the gir-hirls, eh?" She filled his cup.

"Not this evening." He sat very still, in furious impatience, smelling the mild yet rich steam while she filled her own: a young knight, a young officer of the 1914 war, did not gulp his cocoa before an old woman, or his men, had been served.

"I've got some biscuits somewhere. Damn," producing a limp object from a tin, "they've gone pammagy. *That*'s only fit to chuck on the fire," and she removed a rusty lid and threw the biscuit into the boiler. "There." She sat down at the table and drew her cup towards her and lifted it tremblingly to her pretty, withered lips. "This is cosy, isn't it? Just you and me."

"I'm perfectly happy." He drew the back of his square, powerful hand across his mouth and sighed unrestrainedly. "I don't know what I should do, without you, Auntie Daisy, and *here*."

"Have some more. Do. There's plenty."

"Oh . . . but what about you?" His eyes dwelt on the half-full saucepan like a greedy child's.

"Now you know I never drink more than one cup, dear. You have it." She refilled his cup. It was a ritual; the cocoa, the candlelight, and the things they said; and the tiny variations which occurred every time they performed it only added to the delicious sensation of permanence, and timelessness, which it gave him. He tasted the drink voluptuously, with some sense that had nothing to do with his five bodily ones, staring at the stilly flame of the candle.

"No, can't manage more than one cup now. Not what I was, you know."

"Nonsense, Auntie Daisy."

"Nearly seventy-three, dear. Can't believe it, sometimes."

"Neither can I. You look so wonderfully young."

"Oh, come off it . . . I wish Dandy would come in. Hate him being out at night all among the robber-pussies."

She got up and trotted to the door. While she stood there, peering out into the dim night where huge slow wafts of air wandered, calling softly for her cat, John stirred the sugar at the bottom of his cup and spooned it into his mouth.

His eighteen-year-old body could successfully keep at bay hunger and weariness and lack of sleep, but nothing could control the images of himself—vast, towering, perpetually changing their rôle but always appearing in sympathetic and romantic shape—which fled continuously across the mirror of his imagination; that mirror which he knew must be cleared of them before it could reflect, as he truly longed that it should reflect, the real things that he saw. To watch this great image pass and re-pass, commanding the love and veneration of all who saw it, was the secret food of his spirit, yet its presence also filled him with guilt and shame. Often he longed to be rid of it, and hidden from it in the place that was even quieter and more safe than this one; the place which he saw, and felt, within his most secret self at times when he was drifting away into the sleep of utter exhaustion.

It was a place where, as here, a dim light burned. And

someone was moving about there; almost silently, yet not creepingly or fumblingly, engaged upon tasks which he, in his part as passive watcher, felt to be both important and eternal. There never was, and never could be, a time when the figure and what it was deftly and silently doing had not been there; and the mild light had always burned, and the small sounds which comforted him had always broken the breathing stillness. And that was where, with what he thought of as *my deepest desire*, he longed to be, yet something stronger was perpetually driving him out from that place, into the real world, to watch and listen and remember. It was as if he were a mirror, which could feel, and which longed to be empty and quiet, but never could. Yet in the watching and listening and remembering there was also deep and delicate delight . . .

He awoke with a start. The old woman was standing by the table, looking down at him.

"Had a nice little nap?" she repeated.

"Yes. Sorry." He did not raise his head from his arms, and the languid eyelids, thick and white with youth, hardly lifted from eyes red with lack of sleep as he smiled at her.

"I suppose you've lost your key again. You ought to hang it on a long string. That's what I do. In my bag. Never lost it yet."

"I will. It's a good idea." A great yawn set him shuddering.

"I suppose you want the couch, as usual."

"Yes, please, Auntie Daisy."

"Come along, then. Dandy isn't using his rug tonight . . . they wouldn't thank you for knocking them up at the house when your father's got to make an early start tomorrow, you know."

"How do you know he's making an early start?" he asked, sliding his eyes round towards her without turning his head; he had got up from the table and was leaning forward, resting his hands on it, swaying, drunk with sleep—

"The milky-maans told me. We're great pals." Miss Lister's shadow, now made more grotesque by the addition of a rug which she had pulled out from under the dresser, was disappearing along a passage accompanied by the candle, and he slowly followed. It was irritating, the way she always knew everything, but so long as she did not talk to people about him —and he knew that she did not—what did it matter? Sometimes it was useful to know somebody who knew everything . . .

"There."

She put down the candle on a table with a glass top, where a thick film of dust almost concealed the trinkets of blackened silver arranged within, switched on the light, and began to arrange some old cushions on a couch covered with faded chintz. The drawing-room was even smaller than the kitchen, and, because of activities on the part of Dandy and his friends which should have been confined to the garden, it was strongly scented, and the hush of the dead hour before dawn, and neglect, and the past, lay over the walls gleaming softly in an embossed paper of cream and silver. Curtains and chair covers were of a cream-coloured chintz patterned with green leaves, moss-rosebuds and blue bows, and the stained and faded carpet was moss-green. He lay down, in obedience to her gesture, and settled his head luxuriously into the soft dirty cushion, and now he could see once more, as he had seen them very often by different lights and at so many different times, from where he lay, the dusty frills of the china shepherdess pirouetting on the mantelpiece, and the long fall of the withered yellow lace curtain, behind the green velvet one bloomy and furred with dust.

"My dear drawing-room. All from the old home. Awfully decent of your mother. Only I never get time to see to it. It's filthy. Often think I ought to have sold everything. But probably I wouldn't have got much. People are such devils nowadays. There. Take off your shoes. That comfy?" He nodded.

The air of the room was very cold.

"Like a bottle?"

"Oh please. Do you mind putting out the light?"

"With pleasure. It all saves money. Never use it in the kitchen anyway. But I can't see in here, I fall over things. There." Suddenly the glare vanished. "Shan't be a jiffy."

Her shadow dwindled away with the candle-flame.

The beautiful darkness, just softened by the candle's faint glow shining back from the kitchen. He stretched himself on the sofa, too short by half a foot for his length, and sighed.

When she came back he was asleep. She pulled Dandy's indescribable rug higher about his shoulders and put the bottle at his feet. Then, without another glance at him, she trotted silently away.

CHAPTER NINE

TWENTY-TWO AND FOURPENCE

"Miss Sely, you are doing quite well," Mr. Riddle actually had observed to Nell one afternoon. "You know where you are heading for, don't you, in about six years? Mr. Hughes's personal secretary. So keep it up. I am sure that your aunt will be delighted."

Dream on, old man. Nell is heading for The Primula café and sixteen pounds a week. She is not looking forward to giving notice, but she succeeds fairly well in keeping that particular fence at the back of her mind.

On the evening of the very Friday afternoon when Mr. Riddle had poured upon her the unction of his praise, looking competent about nothing and cool in her baggy grey suit, she might have been seen sailing into The Primula teashop.

Her nightly observations on the way home had shown her a slender form with neatly shingled grey hair moving authoritatively amidst the tables and receiving cash at the desk by the door. If this were the proprietress, she looked approachable, and might be prepared to give a chance to a beginner. Nell would have preferred a livelier place where they slapped the dishes about, but the respectability of The Primula might pacify the parents and her aunt.

The place was empty but for two lovers, gazing, in one corner, and the slender one, busy in another. Nell, thinking she had better not sit down, waited, and in a moment the lady looked up and saw her. She came across with a bright enquiring expression.

Nell swallowed. It was the biggest swallow of her lifetime and it was the last. She said coolly: "Good evening. I hope I'm not interrupting at a busy time . . . but do you want a waitress?"

She saw the bright expression change. It did not become contemptuous or wary. It became joyful and relieved.

"Great God Almighty, do we want a waitress?" said the slender one in an impeccable Cheltenham voice lowered to the pitch of Nell's own. "More than anything else in this blasted world at the moment. How soon can you start? My usual girl has walked out on me without a moment's notice—this

morning—in fact she's gone off with a G.I. (and I hope the
Iron Curtain gets her) after working like an angel for six
months. I'm single-handed except for the cook who's got
something unmentionable wrong with her innards and is
likely to fold up any minute, my washer-up, and the evening
girl. I suppose you're a student. Have you done this kind of
thing before?"

"No. I'm a typist. But I wanted a change. Office work is so
dull. I haven't any previous experience."

Nell did not add *I'm afraid*, or *but I can learn*. She neither
liked nor disliked the look of the slender one, but she thought
that it was easier to deal with a lady. So much, thought Nell,
could be taken for granted. (Wherein, as Kipling would have
said, she erred.)

"That doesn't matter. There's nothing to learn. You only
have to be quick as lightning and as tough as hell. I can't let
you smoke, I'm afraid, while you're working."

"I hardly do smoke, anyway."

"Good-o," said the slender one, pulling a ring up and down
a finger stained saffron with nicotine, "well, now, can you be
here at ten tomorrow? We open at half past for morning
coffees—(Hogwash! How they can, licks me). Where do you
live?"

"Not far—" Nell was beginning cautiously when the slender
one interrupted impatiently, "All right, all right, I don't
want to know, it's only whether you can make it on time in the
mornings."

"I live in Hampstead."

"Oh, jolly *good*. Well, then—"

"But I'm in a job now, you see." In spite of herself Nell's
tone was touched with agitation. "I have to be at work on
Monday morning as usual. But I'd love to come. Couldn't you
possibly hold it open for me until Monday week?"

The slender one gave a loud, despairing laugh.

"I could, I suppose. The weather's been so foul that we aren't
very busy. But it would mean doing most of the waiting myself
and getting my washer-upper to stay longer. (That's what I
was planning to do when you blew in, in fact, just until I got
someone else.) But I'd *like* to have you. (What's your name?
Nice name; I had a collie bitch once named Nell.) And
perhaps we could . . . I can only pay you two pounds fifteen
a week, you know. Catering Trades Association won't let me

pay anyone of your age—what are you? Twenty?—any more. But then there are the tips—"

Nell said that she knew all about the regulation wage and the tips. She could not help adding again that she would *like* to come.

"Yes, I can see that. Well . . . look here, are you working tomorrow at your office? Good-o—" as Nell shook her head, "then how about coming in for the Saturday and the Sunday? I'll pay you a pound a day and you'll get your tips and you can see how you like it. All right?"

"All right," Nell said. She had no time to think.

"Splendid. You be here at ten sharp tomorrow morning. Now all you want is a pretty little apron and some flatties— (and do put your hair behind your ears, child, or the customers may complain), and your tips ought to work out at a pound a day if the weather's fine. Don't for God's sake let me down, will you? Oh, and my name's Muriel Berringer. Miss."

"I'll be there, Miss Berringer. Thank you. Good night."

She was out in the street again, with an agitated stomach and two jobs. She marched down the High Street wondering what on earth she was going to say to the parents to explain being absent from home the whole of Saturday and Sunday? *Two* excursions into the country with two unexpectedly-arrived school friends? Or how about telling the truth and getting it over?

She compromised by leaving the house at half-past nine on the following morning, murmuring something to Anna about *shopping* and *not being home to lunch*. The deception was made easier because Anna had two days ago bestowed on her thirty shillings, telling her that she must buy herself some shoes; her only walking pair would not stand mending again. Presumably her mother thought that she was going off to town to buy them. As she fled down Arkwood Road, intent upon getting to the first draper's shop in the High Street and spending some of Anna's gift on 'a pretty apron', a derisive wolf-whistle brought her eyes up to the windows of the Gaunts' flat. There he was, hanging out.

"How you do 'hare' along," he called. "Where are you going? What's the matter?" in a surprised tone as Nell made warning faces. "Oh . . . I understand. Well, I don't approve, but good luck all the same."

How could he have 'understood' merely by seeing her make

warning faces? Perhaps because his own life was so shady, and peculiar, that it gave him a special instinct for guessing at the shady peculiarities in other people's, and what a very good thing it would be for young John, thought Nell, if *he* were at this moment setting out for college or an office or some sensible, regular, useful job.

Then she seemed to hear a low mocking voice saying, *How smug you are, Nello*, and as she turned into the door of Weeks's, her face was pink.

"Good child. Now go into the kitchen at the back and Mary will show you the trays and everything. I'm tied up here for the moment."

Miss Berringer returned to the telephone, and Nell, with the apron in a parcel under her arm, went through a curtained door and down a short dark passage into a low-ceilinged kitchen smelling strongly of coffee, with a view onto an un-beautiful yard. A large, sad-looking woman was sitting at a crowded table with her feet stretched straight out before her, surrounded, it seemed to Nell, by basins of water filled with peeled potatoes, colanders of lettuce, and plates piled with hard-boiled eggs. Another woman was standing by the sink, rinsing cups. As Nell came in they both stopped talking and looked at her.

"She'll be the new one," observed the woman at the table, sighing heartily, "Miss B. said she would be coming. Now Tansy, it's you that will have to show her everything, for how I will get the strength to get through the day unless I rest myself I do not know. Good-morning, dear," to Nell.

"Good morning. Er—are you Mary?"

"Mary it is, and this is Tansy."

Tansy, whose bleached hair and waspish face Nell did not like, came forward wiping red hands upon a damp apron and saying in broadest cockney:

"I'd better show you where everythink is, not but what you can't see most of it, stuck under the tables and all over the place, not that it's my business but you're likely to fall over it, being new. Well 'ere's the trays, and there's what goes on them. Mind and give them a nice wipe over every time they comes down, or you'll 'ave Lady Bottlewasher creating; very posh we are round 'ere, except where Staff is congcerned and they don't matter."

"Ah now, Tansy, you'll be frightening her," Mary sighed. "Do be excusing me from moving my feet, dear," as Nell, following Tansy on the conducted tour and trying to take in what was being said as well as what she was being shown, stepped carefully over those extended members, "but it's agony it is to disturb my stomach with the least movement."

"And these 'ere's the biscuits," went on Tansy, jerking her head in the general direction of a dresser laden with cups, plates and tins, "tuppence each for Bourbongs, wot I buy every blessed day of my life for my Julian in Marks's at one and two the 'arf. Well, I said to myself . . . someone don't arf know 'ow to stick it on. Mary'll be wanting to get on with 'er lunches so that's about all."

She came to a dead stop, went back to the sink, and resumed her work.

Nell, who had gathered from her commentary only the vaguest idea of where things were kept, had had to use her eyes, and now began swiftly arranging the trays for morning-coffee drinking, deciding that she could ask Miss Berringer later about prices.

Tansy finished the last cup, slapped the cloth on the draining-board, and crying, "I'm off. See you two-thirty," pulled on her coat and vanished through the back door. Mary told Nell that she had gone to do her shopping and get her Julian's dinner. She continued to offer mild advice and information upon the extravagance and untrustworthiness of Tansy's character, and the sunlight slowly travelled across the yard until it shone upon the colanders of green lettuce in the kitchen. It was a quarter past ten.

At this hour, Nell had been accustomed to begin looking at her watch and thinking drearily that it wanted two hours and three quarters to lunch-time. There was an agreeably relaxed feeling in the kitchen.

Now came a breezy, bustling sensation in the corridor, and Miss Berringer appeared.

"Biffing along all right? Good-o. Yes, that apron looks very nice; don't those little organdi things look better than that ghastly plastic, Mary? Now Mary dear, come up and get down to it. You've given your stomach or what-have-you a nice long pamper. People will be foaming in here for their lunches before we can turn round. *You* come with me," to Nell.

They went into the restaurant, which had been planned as a

parlour for a moderately prosperous family in the reign of
Queen Anne, and Miss Berringer showed Nell how to 'lay
up', or arrange the tables for lunch, leaving three out of the
eight small ones bare for the morning coffee-drinkers.

"There's only comfortable room for eight," she confided,
"we *could* take ten, but people would sooner not be cramped,
and if they aren't cramped they'll come back again. I like to
cater for the sort of people who don't want to be cramped. I
could make more money by shoving in those two extra tables,
but I won't. And I don't like the toiling masses in here,
either, so remember to discourage them."

The half-hour sounded from the parish church across
Hampstead's steep and crowded roofs. The Primula was on
the right side of the High Street for sunlight, and the flowers
on the mantelpiece were fresh.

"My sister keeps me in flowers," confided Miss Berringer,
"she has three acres of violets and anemones in Cornwall. Put
your tips into the begging-bowl here. (I was born in India. My
father was Army.) Now here comes your first customer. I'm
going to pip off and leave you to it."

In a moment, Nell knew why. The old gentleman in shabby
overcoat and check muffler had no sooner taken what was
obviously his usual seat in the sunniest corner, and fixed her
with his eye, than he exclaimed in loud dismay:

"Where's Betty?"

It was the perfect occasion for the Victorian catch-phrase
'Gone for a soldier', which the youthful Anna had learned
from her aunts' maids and passed on to the infant Nell, but of
course it would not do. "She has left, I'm afraid, and gone
abroad," she replied soothingly.

"Gone *abroad*? What d'she want t'do that for, eh? Gone
abroad? On holiday, d'y'mean? Of course she's coming back?"

"We aren't quite sure," Nell carefully avoided giving an
impression that she was waiting for his order or becoming
impatient, but stood in a relaxed attitude (although relaxing
was never easy for Nell) and smiled down into his disappointed
old face.

"You the new girl, eh?" and on hearing that she was, he
shook his head. "She was a very nice girl, Betty, an unusually
nice girl, you might almost say a *fine character*. Gone abroad.
Well . . . changes everywhere. Hampstead has changed almost
out of recognition. If I hadn't lived here all my life, first in

East Heath Road where I was born, and then during most of my married life in Redington Road, and now at The Pryors, with my brother's family since my dear wife—where has she gone, abroad?"

Instinct warning Nell that mention of Germany, West or East, might bring on an explosion, she boldly said that she did not know and was rewarded with a discontented order for 'my usual' which sent her hurrying to the kitchen.

"Is it Betty's boy-friend already?" said Mary, stooping with groans to take a batch of scones from the oven. "Him and his 'usual' . . . now what would it be? Scones or Bourbons? I think it was Bourbons it is, and two of them, but I'm not quite sure. Take him the Bourbons, dear, and try."

But there was that in Mary's grey eye which made Nell decide to take the scones, and she was rewarded with a mumble of 'nice and hot' as they disappeared into her first customer's mouth.

He lingered on until nearly eleven, while she successfully served five other coffee drinkers and, concealing excitement, gathered up one and sixpence in coppers. Her first tips. The money was cool and heavy in her hand; grimy, worn, common pennies and halfpennies that nevertheless seemed to her more real and satisfying than the neat packet of notes she had received at Akkro Products every Friday afternoon. She put them into the little bowl on the shelf at the back of the room, and took the last load of used cups back to the kitchen, where on Mary's advice she stacked them for Tansy to deal with on her return. She contemplated, wrestled with and decided against the notion of asking Mary why she had given her wrong information about the old gentleman's 'usual'. It might make trouble, and trouble on her first day there was something that Nell did not want; however, a note of warning went down against large, poetic-looking, fascinating Mary with the wet grey eye.

No sooner were coffees dealt with than it became time to stand by for lunches. Miss Berringer, descending from upstairs where, she told Nell, she had a duck of a flat and had been having a breather and a gasper, took over the finer details of cooking while Nell made herself useful by polishing glasses, writing menus, greasing basins for two large puddings, making custard under instruction ("I'd like to give them the real stuff instead of this packet muck but I can't afford the eggs, of course, and ten to one they wouldn't like it if I did"), and arranging various jugs, pots and dishes filled with prepared food to keep warm around the outer precincts of the electric stove.

Miss Berringer threw out information as she worked.

"We do two hot dishes every midday; can't manage more and it wouldn't pay if we did; now put some water in that jam; not too much but a little works wonders; fill up those dishes with it, not more than a dessertspoonful in each, and arrange them over there; Mary, if you nearly fall into that bowl of lettuce once more I shall have kittens; shove it farther under the table, will you; Nell, have you got a black dress? You ought really to have one; I don't mind particularly what you wear, but I know from experience that people are more likely to tip the waitress well if she *looks* like a waitress; otherwise you might be my niece, and they don't know whether to or not. Great God in Heaven, there's someone crashing round in the restaurant already and its barely half-past; go and stifle them, will you, Nell, and say lunch is coming up."

The morning flew by; the kitchen grew hotter and the pile of washing-up mounted, while Mary toiled groaning between table and stove and Miss Berringer apparently grew cooler, darting about with not a grey hair out of place; sometimes coming to the curtain which shut off kitchen from dining-room and advising Nell with a murmured word as the latter moved quickly between the tables with laden trays, but spending most of her time in the kitchen, assembling the orders which Nell brought back from the sunlit room now full of quietly-talking, placidly-eating customers.

Nell had no time to think whether she liked what she was doing. She had the sensation now and again of racing against the job, keeping pace with the demands that were made upon her speed and her memory, but not once did she have to say to an amiably expectant face, "I'm sorry—what did you say you would have?", nor did she receive a single scowl for keeping anyone waiting, and when at last, at a quarter to two, she sat down to a plate of indifferentish stew with hardish potatoes and cabbage à l'Anglaise on the corner of the crowded kitchen table, she was enjoying for the first time in her life the sensation of having worked hard and—yes, she had— enjoyed it.

Miss Berringer told her not to hurry over the weakish coffee,

that morning's brew re-heated. Hiccoughs were the reward of
waitresses who bolted their lunch, and hiccoughs either
amused or revolted the customers; Betty had been the only
waitress Miss Berringer had ever known who could bolt her
lunch and not get hiccoughs. Mary showed a tendency to
wonder, with a gleam in her eye, what Betty was doing now;
Miss Berringer shook her head lightly yet quellingly; and Nell
rested her feet and thought about the bowl on the shelf, which
was now full of coppers and even contained an exciting gleam
or two of silver. She had given up counting, for there simply
had not been time, and had dropped her loot into its place
as she passed on her way to and from the kitchen. She seemed
to have been at The Primula ever since she could remember,
and Akkro Products was a thousand miles away.

Soon, very soon, the teas were upon them. The kitchen cooled
down; Tansy returned and washed up, while relating a long
story about 'my Julian' which Nell only heard in snatches
because she was moving between restaurant and back premises
laying up; and just before half-past three she found time to
comb her hair and refresh her flushed face.

Mary turned out a batch of small cakes adorned with cherries,
and Miss Berringer produced from some cranny two iced sandwiches. An elderly man brought in a trayful of pink, green and
apricot-jammy 'fancies', and slammed them down on the floor
because there was no room anywhere else, while exchanging
badinage with Mary. Miss Berringer described the new
arrivals as pastry-muck which the customers insisted upon
having. There was a type of customer which she called Tea-
and-Pastries, and, she added darkly, a tea-and-pastries mind
to go with it. When she had gone upstairs, Tansy said that to
her mind the pastries was very nice; what was wrong with the
pastries? Her Julian was very fond of pastries. Lady Bottlewasher had some funny ideas. Nell's feet punishing her? Try
Tiz. You could get it at Boots. If Nell thought this was a rush,
let her wait till Easter, then she'd see something. Queues half-
way down the street and for the toilet too. If she was still here
at Easter, said Mary mournfully. The place wasn't so bad, it
might be worse, said Tansy, assuming what Nell was to come
to know as her shut-in face, and then sounds from the restaurant
indicated that the first of the teas were arriving.

The teas were quieter than the lunches. Presumably, as they
were mostly female and elderly, or young and in romantic

couples, they had not spent the morning in office or shop and were less in need of restoratives; be that as it may, the morning's sensation of keeping pace with demands was not repeated, and Nell had opportunity to enjoy the sunlight while leaning against a table in the only unoccupied corner, near the begging-bowl, which was to her the most interesting object in the place. She had no idea how much it contained, having lost control of the sum she was trying to carry in her head somewhere around half-past one, but she knew that whatever it was would be all hers, because Miss Berringer had told her that tips were only shared amongst the staff at Easter and the Bank Holidays.

She thought that on her way home she might buy something nice for the parents' supper—then decided that such a display of affluence might be imprudent. Yet sooner or later they would have to be told, for she liked working here; she liked it very much; and she intended, with every ounce of determination she possessed, to go on working here—if Miss Berringer would have her. As she civilly advanced to welcome a weak and cautious countenance which she rightly diagnosed as a Tea-and-Pastries, she wondered whether Miss Berringer was satisfied with her new waitress. That cheerful face with the delicate well-bred nose gave nothing away.

"Er—do you like China tea, Hilary? Good, so do I. China tea, please, and scones" (pronounced to rhyme with *bronze*) "no; no cakes, thank you." (Sixpence.)

"Tea and pastries, please, miss." (Twopence.)

"A pot of tea for two, please, miss, and scones," (pronounced to rhyme with *bones*. Twopence).

"Just bread and butter for one, please, dear, and a pot of tea." (Threepence.)

And on one awful occasion:

"Miss. This cup's got lipstick on it." (Twopence. Coals of fire.)

"Dirty cat," observed Tansy, impartially referring to herself, on Nell's giving her, with outward calm but some inward trepidation, the offensive cup. She proceeded to scour it, while Mary, sitting at the table bathing in tea, indignantly suggested that the complaining customer had left the lipstick there herself.

"It was a him," said Nell, sipping her own tea and eating one of Mary's characterless cakes. Mary said the more shame to him, the dirty beast, and before Nell had time to explain, the bell, which had an unearthly silvery note, summoned her again into what was now the tea-room.

It was getting on for five o'clock, but people were still coming in, attracted to the Heath by the first brilliant weather after the cruel winter, and Nell began to realize that she would not be away by six, having been warned that there would be clearing-up to be done after the teas were over. She would probably not be home until seven. She could only hope that her mother might have been out on one of those long rambles over the Heath and up and down the back lanes of Hampstead village which she lately seemed to enjoy, and not return until after Nell herself had arrived.

But at ten past six—"Put up the 'closed' notice and shut the blighters out," commanded Miss Berringer, running downstairs and putting a perky blue feather cap and expertly-rouged cheeks round the kitchen door, "I'm off. You be off too, Tansy; your Julian will be clamouring for his telly. (I still think you're making a mistake about that, but never mind.) Snacks all ready; that's right, Mary. And here's Mrs. Cooper. Nell, I'm glad to see you've survived your first day in the mad-house. See you tomorrow. Nighty-night, all." She was gone.

There was a silence. Then Mary said.

"You're not the only one that's making a mistake, Tansy dear. Where are we meeting the fancy-boy tonight?"

"Car was parked outside The Everyman, as per usual."

Tansy was twisting a scarf neatly round her head into a turban. Nell, who had been carrying out Miss Berringer's order concerning the *Closed* notice, caught only the end of this exchange as she returned to the kitchen, but she did see Tansy's lightning grimace of warning and she saw also a grin lurking on the face of Mrs. Cooper, the evening girl, a slim young matron in slacks, a dyed lovelock, and an immovable cigarette, who was leisurely combing her hair.

"There. She'll be tired, no doubt, after her first day," Mary said, surveying Nell with affected benevolence. She heaved herself to her feet. "Well, I'll be tootling. I hope I'll be seeing you tomorrow, but it depends on my stomach and that's the truth. Good night to you all, girls."

When she had made a leisurely exit, to which they paid formal tribute by watching in silence, Mrs. Cooper uttered a tinkling laugh.

"Poor Mary and her stomach."

"Yours is a young one; let's 'ope it keeps its 'ealth," Tansy said sharply. "Not but what Mary don't give one the creeps with 'ers. Well, I'm next. My Julian'll be thinking I've fallen down a hole. So long, all."

Nell began to think that she might be going, too. She said something pleasant to Mrs. Cooper, who was trying to change into a black dress without removing the cigarette from between her lips and who uttered in reply a peculiar noise whose intonation was, however, undoubtedly amiable in intent, and marched into the tea-room to collect the begging-bowl.

Standing alone in the wide, white, sunny room, with the homeward traffic rushing past up the High Street, she poured her hoard on to one of the tables and, sitting down, began in some excitement to count it.

Twenty, twenty-one, twenty-two. And four pennies.

One pound two shillings and fourpence. Hers: earned by this undignified pleasant work which she found hard on the feet but amusing, absorbing, and, in some way, satisfying.

She jingled the pennies in her hand; standing now in the white apron which already bore a stain of tea in one corner, and looking thoughtfully out of the window at the late sunlight shining between one of the High Street's sycamore-trees. I like being a waitress, she thought. Perhaps most people wouldn't, I don't know; all I know is that I like it, and I'm going to keep on being one, until I've saved enough out of my tips to start a tea-shop of my own.

The idea burst upon her without warning. At one moment she was a girl with no aim in life; counting pennies at the end of a day's work which she must keep concealed from her parents because it was 'not the kind of thing' educated girls did; living rent-free in her aunt's house, wearing shabby clothes, perpetually hungry because she had to lunch every day off a bar of chocolate or a fourpenny roll; worried about her parents' future; not knowing what she wanted from life; and given to bad attacks of loneliness about which she alone knew. The next moment she was a girl with a definite and sensible ambition in life, one which she could work for; ladies *do* run tea-rooms; parents and aunts could even approve. She saw the sign floating in the air, as she stared out of the window at the bowl of magenta and yellow primulas painted on a wooden board. The flowers had changed to roses; plain, large, pink roses. The sign said simply: NELL. HOME-MADE CAKES.

Sweeping the takings lavishly into her apron, she flew off.

"Well, did you get your shoes?" Anna asked, when they were sitting at supper in the shabby dining-room, with the very last rays of sunlight sparkling through the plane-trees outside the window and sliding over the ceiling. "Where did you get to? I didn't go out until half-past four this afternoon and you weren't back then. Daddy would like some more bread, dear," and, as Nell leapt to the sideboard to fulfil this opportune wish, "do you know, I saw a girl so exactly like you this afternoon in one of the tea-shops in the High Street. I was so late in going out that I wondered if I should have some tea, and I stopped to look there. (Terrible prices; I didn't have any, of course.) This girl was the waitress. She was *exactly* like you. It was quite uncanny."

"Was it?" Nell squeaked, beginning to hack at a second enormous slice of bread.

"She even had your white blouse and grey skirt. (But she was wearing an apron, of course.) I only saw her for a moment. She vanished at the back somewhere. But I have never seen such a likeness; it wasn't just that she reminded me of you; she might have *been* you."

Nell laid down her knife amidst the wreckage of the loaf, and turned round. As well now as later on.

"It was me," she said calmly, and, at the sight of their two slightly puzzled faces; safe, and embedded in the solidity of middle age, and not knowing oh! one *quarter* of what was going on all around them, she gave an irrepressible giggle.

"How could it have been you, dear?" Anna said at last, "you were in London buying your shoes. And this girl was the waitress."

"No . . . " Nell came back to the table, handed her father his piece of bread, and sat down, "I didn't go into London. I've been at The Primula all day, *being* the waitress. You see . . . " her eyelids just flickered towards her father, who had laid down his knife and fork, and she rushed on, "A friend of John's told me what a lot of money you can earn being a waitress. Sixteen pounds a week—"

"Sixteen pounds a *week*!" Martin's tone held a kind of sick outrage; he might have been speaking for all the underpaid schoolmasters and half-starved parsons and struggling scholars in the world, "*waitressing?*"

"Yes . . . " she turned to him quickly, "but not always, of

course. Usually it's about eight or nine—with tips, if you're in a busy place. So . . . you see, I've made twenty-two shillings today apart from the pound they paid me, just in tips."

She was darting glances from one face to the other; guessing, weighing, trying to tip the balance over into approval.

"That's where the cake came from," Anna said slowly. She had rested her elbows on the table and put her chin into her hands and was studying Nell. Her expression was thoughtful; no more. "I wondered. I thought you must have economized on your shoes, and I was going to blow you up about it. Though it's a very nice cake," and she smiled rather uncertainly; half at the 'walnut gâteau' which Nell had been unable to resist buying in a shop that was just closing, and half at the daughter whom, she had just decided, was a stranger.

Her feelings were extraordinarily confused. She was cross with Nell, and she approved of her independence and courage, and she was strongly aware of how upset Martin was, and over and above all other feelings she was shocked.

All the names from her past rose before her: Aunt Nancy and Aunt Eleanor, her father and mother, the neighbours in the large white houses under the great elms, the Lyddingtons, the Trevelyans, the Peytons. Most of them had died years ago, and their houses had been pulled down or converted into flats, yet her first thought was: *what will they say?* Anna Meredith's daughter has become a waitress. How extraordinary; how unthinkable; how shocking; Anna must have gone mad to let her.

Then, becoming amidst her whirling thoughts aware that Nell was looking at her with a mixture of anxiety and defiance, while Martin was still sitting with sunken head staring at his plate, she pulled herself together. She had been trained to think: she must see the situation, not as it theoretically was, but as it was in fact; and, in fact, it could not possibly have happened in the Hampstead of 1920.

It would have been unthinkable, as the marriage of a black man with an heiress of the Smiths or the Vanderbilts in the New York of 1895 would have been unthinkable; something which no-one ever even visualized because it lay beyond the bounds of imagination. Yet now, this evening, her daughter's being a waitress was a fact.

And was it such a shocking fact? Let me look at it *sensibly*, thought Anna; after all, I do come of a family that talked and thought about everything under the sun. Nothing was banned.

Suddenly she laughed. What a fuss! It wasn't insanity or theft. She put her hand quickly over Nell's.

"It's all right, dear. I'm awfully surprised. But I'm not cross. (No, I'm not cross. I ought to be, I suppose. But if I tell the truth, I'm not.)" She hesitated, now feeling very conscious of the sunken red face and bitterly drooping mouth opposite. Poor old Marty, always much more conventional than herself . . . "but I think you owe us an apology, you know," she ended—'gravely', so that he should feel she was ranged at his side, the loyal wife and prudent mother.

"Oh, I know . . . " Nell, who was also very conscious of the face, rushed into an account of how it had all happened: the unendurable dullness of Akkro Products, the tempting vision of sixteen pounds a week, the stuffy room, Mr. Riddle, Miss Berringer, the fun of seeing new people all day, and so forth.

Anna listened, thawing: the face neither moved nor made any comment. But at the end of the speech for the defence, which perhaps gained something in the ears of the jury because it was given in Nell's usual quick sensible style without any *flights*, by a piece of great good luck she, Nell, was able to produce what the aunts at Vernon Lodge would have called the *comble*; a kind of cap or summit which triumphantly topped off everything that she had, though not openly, been pleading for and trying to prove. She produced an evening paper (left, in fact, by a customer, on the popular table-in-the-window at The Primula).

"Look," she said, pushing a picture under the face's dejected nose, "she's an earl's cousin."

There she was; the Honourable Prudence Field-Marshall-Pepys, looking amused in a frilly apron while dancing rather languid attendance on the customers in a Knightsbridge Espresso bar.

"You see," said Nell, nodding, and was taking the paper away when her father slowly put out his hand for it.

"Yes . . . " he said, studying the picture through the spectacles which always needed a polish, "so she is. I hadn't . . . realized . . . but that doesn't mean that I approve . . . you see, Anna, it was so good of Peggy to get Nell this . . . job . . . that was partly what I was thinking of when I . . . you haven't *left* your job with these other people, have you?"

"Oh, goodness no. If I decide at the end of tomorrow that I

don't like it after all, I needn't do anything more about it,"
very cheerfully. She was glad that he could not see her cast-
iron determination to beard Mr. Riddle on Monday.

This, of course, led to a cry of 'Working on *Sunday*?' which,
however, developed no further because poor Martin did not
care to pursue the thoughts which any mention of *Sunday*
called up, and he heard in silence her soothing answer that she
would go to the seven o'clock, in the church at the end of the
road. Nodding, he pulled the paper towards him again and
began, after saying something about 'meeting rough people'
which she again soothed with a murmur, to read it.

Anna cleared the table round him. (She had fallen into the
habit lately of doing this. She found it tiresome, but he did so
hate being moved about.)

"You go off and amuse youself," she said, in reply to Nell's
offer of help. "I'll do this. You've been busy with tables and
things all day."

Nell skipped upstairs to her room.

Could this be all, then? No more going to be said? No
thunderings and wonderings, no anticipations of disaster, no
reproaches? (As for rough people, had the parents any idea
just how rough Gardis was?)

She felt relieved, but also rather sobered, for the parents'
unexpectedly quiet acceptance of her action had shown her
unmistakably that they were no longer the two figures of unshakable authority and importance which had dominated her
life for nearly twenty years. Ever since the arrival in London,
she had felt that she must take care of them, rather than that
they were taking care of her, and now she knew that she was
free to manage her own affairs. The idea, which was almost a
feeling, was decidedly pleasant.

As she sat down to begin a long letter to Miss Elizabeth
Prideaux, Les Rosiers, Châteaux d'Oex, France, she had a
mental picture of Anna and Martin feebly creeping and dozing
about downstairs which would have rather surprised them:
Anna was just thinking, as she washed up, that if Martin
really minded Nell doing this crazy thing she must be stopped:
she would have a proper talk with her tomorrow evening, after
the novelty had had a chance to wear off a little, and point out
all the disadvantages.

Among the *advantages* was the possibility of sixteen pounds a
week. Anna had to keep telling herself that the sum was

utterly fantastic, and that they would not want as much as that even if the child could ever earn it.

"Give notice? Is that what you said, Miss Sely?"

"Yes, Mr. Riddle." Nell's voice had begun as a squeak but she impatiently pulled it down again; she was only giving notice, wasn't she? Thousands of people must give notice in London every day.

"But why? What for? Your work is quite satisfactory."

"Thank you, Mr. Riddle."

"Then why do you want to leave us? What reason could there possibly be?" Then, before she could bring out the tactful arguments which she had assembled—

"This is a very nice firm to work for, you know. There are Prospects, if you work hard (Miss Driver will be getting married one day, of course), and you know all about our Pensions Fund and the Canteen. Next year we hope to have a Firm's Dance. It isn't what I care about myself, Mrs. Riddle not being fond of dancing and in any case my dancing days being over, but young people like dancing. *You* like dancing, Miss Sely, don't you?"

Nell moved her gaze from his face, which was beginning to unnerve her, to the floor. Was she expected to toil year in and year out with Akkro Products for the reward of one evening's hopping about during the twelvemonth?

"Don't you, Miss Sely?"

"It isn't anything to do with the firm, Mr. Riddle."

She tried to add something about having been very happy there, but rebelled. Why should she lie to Mr. Riddle? She had disliked every moment of it.

"Then what . . . I suppose you want more—er—money?"

"I do want more money but it isn't only that. Mr. Riddle, if you could tell me whom I give in my notice to, I could do it this morning. Before lunch."

The unmistakable note of yearning brought sharpness to Mr. Riddle's next words.

"I see; you're anxious to be quit of us." He paused; a disturbing thought had occurred. "Er—it isn't anything to do with our little argument about the window?"

"Oh no, Mr. Riddle."

"That's all right, then. Er—would you like me to speak to Mr. Hughes about a small rise? It would be only a small one, of course. I don't suppose the firm could manage more than two and sixpence a week. But even that mounts up in a year, you know: it would pay for one lunch at the canteen—"

"It's kind of you but I would rather leave, truly, Mr. Riddle. My mind is made up."

"Is it, indeed?" Some of the almost holy indignation which Mr. Riddle felt at hearing this, from a chit of a girl who had been pushed into a sound job to please a friend of the boss's, escaped him in the form of a sarcastic intonation. "Well, if your *mind is made up*, I suppose it's no use arguing. You had better ask Miss Driver if Mr. Hughes can see you just before one o'clock."

This was duly arranged; and the interview turned out to be a very different affair.

"Sick of it, are you?" said Mr. Hughes cheerfully, lifting a steely blue eye from some papers and fixing her, "well, you can go, my child. You haven't done too badly here and if you'd wanted to stay on we shouldn't have said 'no', but you realize, of course, that we only took you on in the first place to oblige Lady Fairfax. The job was more or less made for you. So you run along and find something more exciting. What's it to be? Modelling?"

"I'm going to be a waitress," said Nell.

She wanted to take the careless expression, which yet, she felt sure, concealed some natural annoyance, from his face.

She succeeded. The look was replaced by surprise, and admiration, in that order.

"Are you, by gum? Well, I take off my hat to you. You aren't afraid of work. But what's your family think about it? And what on earth do you want to do it *for*? Dirty, tough, monotonous job."

"Sixteen pounds a week, if I'm lucky," said Nell.

"Sixteen pounds a week, eh? Executive level. Well, you run along with my blessing, and when you've got your job and broken the news to your aunt, I'll come along and you can give me a cup of tea and God help you if there's lipstick on the cup."

"That would be the kitchen staff's responsibility, I should think," Nell said thoughtfully. She fixed him with a determined eye. "May I leave next Friday, please, Mr. Hughes? I really am anxious to get started." She had no intention of telling him that she had started.

"You're supposed to give us a month's notice, you know."

"Couldn't you possibly make an exception?"

"All right. I think you're a completely crazy child but I like your—er—pluck. And I suppose you want it kept dark for a bit, eh?"

"Yes, please."

"Right you are, then: no telling Aunt Peggy until you're earning sixteen pounds a week. She won't be any too pleased, I'm prepared to bet. Waitressing . . . " He shook his head. "I've got one like you of my own, just turned eleven, but she's booked for Sherborne and, we hope, for a university. She's rather bright. I hope *she* won't want to be a waitress."

Nell left the Presence feeling not completely comfortable. His tone had been pleasant, but it had not succeeded in hiding his disapproval, perhaps he had not meant it to; and she knew that this was based entirely on snobbery.

The week passed quickly, in spite of the shadow of Riddlesian disapproval, and at five o'clock on Friday she stepped across the dingy threshold of Thirty-eight Lecouver Street for the last time. She was free. She looked around at the bright, busy, exciting evening and the homeward-bound crowds. A decision to go off without saying anything to the South Sea Islanders had been, rather to her own surprise, reversed by herself at the last moment and she had just escaped after fifteen minutes of amazed questioning, head-shaking, and stories about cousins who had worked for three years without a Sunday off and developed varicose veins, mingled with warm good wishes and promises to drop in for a coffee, threats of demanding tea and pastries free of charge, and wonderings about whether she would have to wear a cap as well as an apron. But loudest and most frequent were the speculations about What Will Your Auntie Say?

This evening, Nell did not much care. Last Sunday at The Primula had been very exhausting, very stimulating and very amusing, and she had earned, besides her pound in wages, twenty-eight shillings in tips, and nothing now was going to prevent her from working at The Primula. She was to start tomorrow morning, Saturday, at ten o'clock, and when she was fully employed there her free day would be Monday.

When she opened her last salary packet, under the indulgent eye of the young lady in Weeks's who was serving her with five more organdi aprons, she found that she had cause for even greater cheerfulness. There, tucked in amongst the green notes, was a great, crisp, black-and-white Gothic beauty; a fiver: "With good wishes and good luck from Gerald Hughes and Akkro Products Limited."

Nell was too astounded by this piece of generosity to be touched by it; and in fact Mr. Hughes himself regarded it as an investment rather than a good-luck penny. How blood did tell; here was all the Peggy Fairfax drive coming out in the niece. If he knew anything about people, the Sely child would be running a chain of restaurants in ten years' time, and that might come in damned useful to the firm—plastic beakers, plates and spoons.

He also knew enough about people to know that she would remember his tip.

CHAPTER TEN

THE STREETS OF SUMMER

WHEN in later years Nell remembered this summer of her youth, she always saw in memory the hilly winding streets of Hampstead, and sunlight falling through green leaves, and, amidst them, John's face.

They would sometimes set out together in the morning, she to begin her day's toil with the coffees, and he presumably to indulge in those wanderings through London which, he frequently said, were necessary for his work.

"Nello? Must you 'hare' off like that? I'm just coming."

He would swoop down from the top flat, wearing some extraordinary collection of clothes—an immaculate striped blazer, blue denim trousers, a gaudy American shirt—give her a quick hug where she waited on the landing, and pull her down the stairs after him, telling her about some party to be held that evening in an attic or cellar which she must attend (she usually waited for him to telephone further details and heard no more about it), or some new friend who was going to revive the art of writing musical comedy in England. Sometimes he would lecture her about being a waitress, saying that she never had a moment to spare for him; that she was *necessary* to him, like the sights and sounds and smells of London; and

that her 'so-called work' took up too much of her time; that
she was hardly ever there when he wanted her.

This was sweet to hear, but like most of John's statements
it bore only a tenuous relationship to the facts, which were
that she often saved him an evening or a Monday afternoon
and never heard a word from him throughout the whole of it.

"Of course. I didn't want you *then*," was his usual petulant
comment when asked casually (Nell's own temperament, as
well as a kind of deer-stalking instinct, prevented her from
asking in any other tone) what had kept him or prevented
his telephoning? And he would add, "You see, you must be
there when I *want* you, Nello."

She was frequently very annoyed with him; impertinent,
casual, rather shifty boy. It made no difference to how she
felt, nor to their friendship . . . if it was a friendship.

She supposed that it was a friendship. They did not speak
of their feelings for one another, and she never looked into her
heart to see what was there; she only felt a constant longing
to be of use to him and to watch him as he moved and laughed
and spoke. It was the truest kind of love, the kind which longs
to give and to serve; and perhaps the delicate scents of May,
wandering that year on the wind down the streets of summer,
gave to him as much as she did. She was never to know.

She did know that sometimes he seemed to need her very
badly; she would return home after an exhausting, if satisfying
day's work and, going up to her room, find him sitting sullenly
outside her door on the stairs leading up to their flat. Why was
she so late? He had been here for hours. He was wretched;
she must stay with him.

Then she would be wrapped in his desperate clasp, his head
pushed uncomfortably into her shoulder, and thus they would
sit in silence for half an hour, only springing apart as Anna
came up the stairs, to see what on earth Nell was up to, and,
as the weeks went on, get a foretaste of the day's gossip from
The Primula which Nell would relate, to the reluctant amusement of Martin, over the supper table.

She did not know what was the cause of the fits of fierce grief
which overwhelmed John, although she sensibly explained
them to herself as being due to the way he lived; and not having
any settled career to take up when he left the Army, and the
influence of his peculiar friends, and irregular meals and lack
of sleep, and so forth. She thought his way of life shocking; it

was everything she herself disliked most—disorderly, planless
and uncomfortable, but some instinct prevented her from trying
to change him.

She seemed to know that any attempt to do so would drive
him away from her, and so, although she *did* want to see him
orderly and sensible (or told herself that it would be nice if he
were), she never lifted a finger to make him so. She heard her
mother and his mother and his father condemning his ways
and shaking their heads over his future, and outwardly she
agreed with them. Inwardly she thought: *Leave him alone. Of
course he's a silly ass and he ought to pull himself together, but leave
him alone . . . can't you?*

In fact, he usually saw to it that his parents, at least, did
leave him alone, taking advantage of their preoccupation with
their own problems and careers and keeping as much out of
the way as possible.

"What we're all hoping is that his National Service will be
the making of him," Lady Fairfax said, one morning when
Nell had been working at The Primula for about a month.

They were standing together by the popular table-in-the-
window, the aunt, wearing a smart new striped suit with an
immensely long waistless jacket, having swooped in upon the
niece to tell her that she 'definitely approved' of what Nell was
doing. She had known about it for some weeks, as Martin had
thought it his duty to write her a long and apologetic letter,
but she had not been able to find time, until now, to inspect
Nell in the field.

"Yes . . ."

Nell's tone was vague; her eye was flitting round the room
in search of ash-trays needing to be emptied and smears of
tea needing to be removed, but she was remembering what had
been said to her, in a frantic whisper, under the dense canopy
of a maybush in flower on the Heath two days ago—*I can't talk
about going into the Army because it makes me feel as if I were choking
and stifling and starving all at once . . . so don't* ever *mention it to me
again . . . some of my friends have nearly gone insane or become
deserters while they were in it and some of them are devoting their whole
lives to undermining it . . . I can't even say the word without
feeling sick . . . I'm like those Zulus in Rider Haggard's books who
were so terrified of the king they didn't dare say his name but called
him Elephant-That-Shakes-The-Earth . . . so now you know, Nello.
And don't ever dare to mention it to me again.*

She shook her head, in reply to a question, and a keen glance, as to whether he had ever talked about going into the Army to her?

"You wouldn't tell me if he had," Lady Fairfax picked up her sea-shell-white gloves. "Young creatures stick together." She began to move towards the door, her eye roving down the thronged and sunny High Street in search of her car, "and that's as it should be . . . "

"Was everything all right, madam?" Nell asked demurely, following.

"No, it was not. The coffee—! It's so *easy* to make good coffee, Nell."

"Not cheaply. Coffee's nearly ten shillings a pound." Nell was partisan about what they served at The Primula.

"But if you make it very strong to begin with it goes much farther. The stuff you sell here is hogwash."

"So Miss Berringer says."

"Was that your boss? The shingled one who peeped round the curtain? She looks a typical nice spinster. Why do they invariably take to keeping tea-shops?"

"I don't know," said Nell, looking wooden, and thinking about the boy-friend's car parked every night outside The Everyman, the long telephone conversations, the nighties and undies and nylons which arrived in boxes from Knightsbridge shops.

Her aunt, looking at her, wondered if Nell would keep a tea-shop one day. There were the materials for spinsterhood in those fine bones and straight hair and steady expression. On the other hand, she might become unexpectedly elegant; even attractive to men. Certainly she did not lack character, and one could never tell.

"I've left you sixpence to show you I don't disapprove," Lady Fairfax said. "You aren't a bit like me to look at, Nell, except that you've inherited my nose, but I do think you've got some of my grit. I came up the hard way, you know." She sighed. "That's why I understand your doing this. Of course, you're an ungrateful baggage, but I do understand. You don't think your father would like to come and be my social secretary when Gardis goes back in July, do you? Yes, you can laugh—I know it's funny to think of, but he ought to be earning something, you know. It would be good for his self-respect. And he wouldn't mind then so much about you."

"Well, I don't think he'd like it at all, Aunt Peggy. And I'm sure he wouldn't be any good at it, either. You know he isn't much use at talking to new people. Besides, I don't think he does mind about me as much as he did. I always give the cash to Mother, so that the idea of *tips* shan't upset him, and I think he rather likes hearing about all the dotty things," Nell casually sank her voice, "that go on here."

"You think he's better, then, since you came to Hampstead?"

"Oh, I'm sure he is."

"Dear old Marty. Bless him. (Oh, *there's* Barker. What a fool the man is.) Well . . . "

"You've got a new chauffeur." Nell halted on the threshold, ready to dart back at the summons of the unearthly bell, "What happened to Robert Nathaniel?"

She made no attempt to disentangle a coherent story from the sentences—"too big for his boots . . . hordes of black relations . . . couldn't really cope . . . " which followed, but nodded brightly when Lady Fairfax, turning back as she got into the car, called in ringing tones: "Then you're really all right and I needn't worry about *you*?" and gave the order to drive away.

Nell turned back into the tea-room. Yes, she was really all right—so far as money and an amusing job went, and as for the future, she would have her tea-shop. She already possessed ten pounds saved towards it, lodged comfortably in the Post Office, and if she were not earning anything like the majestic sum named by Benedict, she was making an average of eight pounds a week, with no deductions for food or fares because the former was supplied by The Primula, and she walked of course to her work. And she loved the job.

She desired to please. She had the one necessary characteristic for someone who must daily encounter, and satisfy, dozens of people, and Miss Berringer was congratulating herself upon Betty's replacement, for while Betty's roving eye had occasionally led to misunderstandings, Nell's eye did not rove at all, and this was only one of the new girl's desirable qualities.

"Yes, we're a *happy* ship," Miss Berringer would sing out when someone got temperamental, or something fused or stuck in the kitchen, and although the announcement sometimes had a queer note of recklessness sounding under its obvious irony, on the whole it was true: the staff of The Primula did get on well together.

Nell soon learned to beware Mary's talent for mixing malice inextricably with good-nature and to value the kindness which Tansy (whose real name was Mrs. Tanswood) concealed under a sharp manner. Mrs. Cooper, dressed in the newest fashion adopted by the Common Woman, was the gentlest, most modest creature that ever drooped cigarette from lower lip, while the evening cook was an amiable bun named Miss Cody, whom failing health had forced to give up her work as a district nurse and to take up light cooking in the evening of her days.

They all said that they liked Nell, although Mary always added, ah, what was there to *dis*like in the girl?—that question which invariably succeeds in lowering the temperature of approval. In fact, there were a temper with a low flash-point, much obstinacy and secrecy, and a strong will, but fortunately for herself Nell not only had all these traits well in hand, but found temper and obstinacy easier and easier to manage as the weeks went on, and an uncharacteristically fine summer filled The Primula, day after day, to overflowing.

To fly out of the house every morning, waving impatiently to a parent who might be looming vacantly at an upper window and perhaps be rewarded with a glimpse of John; to scramble into apron and flatties while exchanging gossip with Mary about yesterday's cream that hadn't turned after all, and what was to be done with the two snacks that were left over, and Miss B.'s new hat; to avoid, from some double delicacy of class-feeling and fellow-feeling, too jocose or intimate a reference to Miss B.'s outing last night with the boy-friend whom Nell had never seen; to sail through the morning coffees; to lay up for lunches; bolt elevenses while hearing the latest school triumph of the rock-solid little boy, Tansy's Julian; to thrust her way with laden trays expertly from table to table between the hours of twelve and two; bolt lunch; lay up for teas; do her face and her hair, listen to Miss Berringer cursing with well-bred indifference to kitchen comment, the customers streaming in from the sun-drenched Heath; to fling tips into the begging-bowl without pausing to count them while juggling during the hours from three to six with pots of tea, plates of bread and butter, pastries, scones and cakes, and jugs of hot water whose handles burnt her fingers, and little dishes of glistening watered jam; to see out of the corner of her eye the patient thirsty people wandering in through the door and resignedly or hopefully surveying the crowded room; to escort French, Spanish, Dutch, Swedish and English children to what most of them called the toilet and once to receive a strangling hug and a "What's your name? I love you", from a polite small American with whom it was a case at first sight; to feel the heat of the day beginning to decline outside and to hear Mary's evening hymn to her stomach and legs begin; to see the stream of hopeful faces begin to slacken; and the pile of dirty dishes and saucepans whisked away under Tansy's expert hand; to wonder whether, this evening, Mrs. Cooper's cigarette ash would fall at last into the bowl of trifle set ready for the suppers and, finally, to shut the door on the last pair of lingering lovers and put up the 'Closed until 7' notice; then to sweep through, wipe down, lay up for suppers and at last, in the orderly quiet of the redded room, to count her tips. This was Nell's day.

Then back through the steep streets where the evening light lay with leafy shadows on the brown brick cottages, and the red and blue roofs looked out across the rolling green masses and meadows of the Heath. Throughout the day, whenever she happened to glance up for a second from the crowds and the hurry and the rush, a glimpse of those roofs and trees reminded her of the summer streets round about; the laburnam saplings and the ancient may-bushes looking over low little fences and rosy walls, the old cobbled yards, set with the tubs and pots and boxes of a district scamped for garden-space, spilling over with rich flowers. And always, between roofs and through arches and at the end of long narrow alleys, the blue dip to London, lying far below.

"You seemed very matey with that glamorous type; was she a buddy?" enquired Miss Berringer, when Nell re-entered the kitchen's cluttered calm after the departure of Lady Fairfax, but was too busy making meringues to pay any attention to Nell's answering mutter. Nell was congratulating herself that neither Tansy nor Mary, both of whom naturally owned a telly, had taken it into her head to peep into the tea-room five minutes ago; Miss Berringer, who despised television, and did not own a set, had not recognized Lady Fairfax. Nell was not anxious to become an object of envious curiosity to The Primula's staff.

As for her aunt, although she was relieved that her own action had not been disapproved, it was a mild kind of relief, for aunts,

so far as Nell was now concerned, took their place with parents
in the back seats.

She never thought about Akkro Products nowadays, but
she had not quite finished with them yet.

On the late afternoon of Easter Saturday, when rain had
sent the crowds flocking off the Heath into every café and tea-
shop in Hampstead, and Tansy's threatened queue for the
toilet had become a reality, and Nell was pushing her way with
trays held high above the heads of the customers between the
crowded tables, trying to avoid catching any one particular eye
and to remember half-a-dozen orders, a pert voice called above
the buzz of conversation, comment and gossip—"Tea and
pastries, please, ducks. And we're not paying for them,
neither."

She looked round, with some difficulty amidst the press,
and saw the self-consciously smiling faces and fuzzy heads of
The Islanders.

She was surprisingly glad. Her heart felt really warm
towards them.

"Hullo! Hullo, Maureen—Pat—Sylvia—how nice to see you.
Isn't this ghastly? Wait a minute . . . "

She managed to get close enough, while setting tea and
scones in front of an old lady who grasped at them greedily,
to whisper—"Those people over there, in the corner, have
nearly finished . . . I'll just get their bills . . . you work your
way over there and wait by the table, and the *minute* they get
up, *sit down*. And *don't* let those two fat women by the door
see what you're doing."

When they were successfully seated, and Nell had soothed
the fat ladies and steered them off to wait for another table,
she made her way across to The Islanders with what she could
scrape together of cakes and pastries, and put it down in front
of them with a pot of tea.

"There. 'Fraid that's all I can manage. It's been a terrific
day . . . you must come again when we're not so rushed . . .
it's awfully nice to see you all . . . how are you?" ("Miss . . . "
a resigned moo from a distant table. "Coming . . . " fluted
Nell in a serious tone, without turning her head.)

"Oh . . . we was just up this way. So we thought . . . "
mumbled Maureen, ducking her head almost into the teapot
as she stirred its contents.

"Not a very large caff, is it?" said Pat, looking stonily about her. It was plain that Pat had not changed in five weeks.

"Syl's engaged!" cried Maureen, popping out of the teapot and dragging from behind its owner's back a red hand adorned with a large diamond, "Get a load of her ring."

"Do shut up, Maur. You are mean . . . "

"Smashing," Nell said admiringly. "I'll be back in a minute . . . "

"Haven't you got any creamies?" Pat was looking at the cakes with icy discontent.

"No creamies . . . sorry. They're always the first to run out on a rush-day. Is Maureen still crazy about Dicky Valentine?" Nell paused, with laden tray, and a dozen pairs of eyes fixed on her hopefully.

"She's still crackers, if that's what you mean." Sylvia regarded her friend indulgently, while Maureen crimsoned under her unhealthy skin.

Exchanging snatches of gossip as she attended to the tables in their corner of the room, she learned that The Islanders had recently deserted Akkro Products in a body and gone to a firm with premises nearby.

They were not sure what it did. Sylvia thought it was something to do with these here little machines. Except for the ring, her engagement did not seem to have progressed beyond what Nell had heard of it in the cloakroom at Lecouver Street: *I went to the pictures with 'im, 'e gave me this handbag, we was in the pictures, we was going to the pictures, 'e wanted me to go to the pictures but course I washed me hair Friday same's usual.*

Darting between tea-room and kitchen, carefully setting down the teapots with their burning-hot handles, conveying the triangular slices of bread scraped over with margarine to her patient or impatient customers, Nell found time to think that she could enjoy an engagement like that; drifting from one small pleasure to another with someone, giving affection and companionship, and receiving admiration and companionship in return.

She was beginning to have a dim, vague dread of violent love. The bed with the thin mattress and blackened brass frame in Benedict's room had impressed her. Did he lie awake on it through the long nights, when the faint lamplight was reflected in the olive-coloured canal and the little houses were black and silent, with that look of helpless love on his face? Soberly, Nell thought that it was a pity when someone got into that state. She hoped that she never would; sooner than be like that, she would prefer not to love or marry at all.

There were a good many jokes about the three twopences which The Islanders left under their plates, but in fact joking covered some confusion on their part.

Nell's own temperament, with its roots in the liberal tradition upheld at Vernon Lodge and The General's House, had combined with the shortage of labour and the decay of the class-system in England to produce a situation too complex for the privileged children of the new proletariat to grasp, and they felt only an uncomfortable mingling of embarrassment, superiority and mockery. This did not, however, prevent them from still liking Nell.

Idling tube-wards through the narrow streets under the sycamore shadows, their light thin voices dismissed her:

"You'd think she'd smarten herself up, wouldn't you? Have a Toni."

"She's got a black dress. But they have to in posh caffs."

"I like her, though."

"She ought to have a perm. I think it looks sawful."

"I couldn't stand that life, honest. I should have a nervous breakdown . . . " quavered Maureen, whose temperament was very ready to indulge in this latest refinement available to the Common Man.

"I like her, though," repeated Pat, who was the least a female, and the most a person, of the three. "She's got some guts. I bet you she does get her own caff. May take her a hundred years and we'll all look like Rip Van Winkle when she does, but I bet you she gets it."

"I should have a nervous breakdown, honest . . . "

"You!" Pat threw her a sidelong glance out of the eyes that had summed up most of the young men south of Waterloo Bridge and north of the Oval. "One day you'll stay in the sun too long and melt."

Nell was hurrying on with her work, kindly feelings towards the three lingering in her heart. She was never to see two of them again, but the star-gazers would have said triumphantly, some six months later, that undoubtedly her Destiny was Linked with that of Pat.

She hoped The Islanders had not been inspired to leave Akkro Products by her example; if they had, Mr. Riddle's comments upon her sojourn there must be black indeed, but on this point she was re-assured by a visit from Mr. Hughes himself; he dropped in to The Primula for a coffee (no biscuits) on his way by car to the north, and, although seeming rather surprised that Nell did not already own the shop, was most amiable to her and said nothing about anyone else's having left.

She had other visitors, too; sometimes, on the afternoon that he was not working in the restaurant, Benedict would bring Gardis in to drink many cups of tea thirstily, without ever glancing at food, after one of those wanderings over the Heath during which, Nell gathered, they argued about his future.

As she moved between the tables, she could not help overhearing sentences.

" . . . as a barman in Fez," he might be saying.

He had a worn shirt, not quite clean, and threadbare trousers that seemed slipping off his meagre hips, but the afternoon's sun had caught his freckled skin and given to his face a healthy colour that seemed to contradict his desolate clothes.

"You won't go to Fez as a barman. You'll go as a lecturer or something," from Gardis. "You're getting tied up to your old B.B.C. You're becoming a bourgeois. It's death to Art; *death*."

"Not necessarily, Gardis. It is possible to write poetry almost anywhere, if only you don't have to . . . grind it out in a hurry . . . and even then it has been done . . . I can imagine living in Camden Town all my life and never seeing Venice again, and still writing good poetry. Hardly anyone knows anything about writing poetry, you see. The truest things that have been said about writing it were thrown-off, almost, by poets themselves . . . but the more you think about them, the truer they are . . . I don't want to go to Fez to get fresh material for poetry, I want to go there because . . . I want to feel."

Nell put down a plate of mild little cakes in front of two schoolmistresses out for an afternoon's tramp. She was thinking that his face looked as if he had been feeling rather too much.

"Stay here and feel," Gardis said in a low tone, leaning across the table, and she smiled at him.

"Sometimes I can't feel, I don't know why . . . "

Nell was not exactly eavesdropping, but she was not shutting her ears to a conversation which she knew that she should not hear. But it was difficult to ignore Benedict's unhappiness, because she liked him.

"I shall go when I've finished this play for the Third Programme," he said. "And I want to write it. I want fame, you see. I want it very much. *Poet's food is love and fame . . .* "

"You get plenty of love," she said, with her grin.

"Do I?"

"I seem to think so—unless I'm imagining things. I can't make you out. I think you're a psycho—but then all poets are psychos, of course. . . . "

"Of course . . . " he said dejectedly, accepting the verdict of the age.

The joy which sometimes came to him while he was dreaming over the roofs and clouds visible from his window, or when the first line of a poem sprang up within him like a fountain, these, no doubt, were part of the 'psycho's' temperament; the reverse of the neurotic gloom.

Yet he did not truly, within himself, believe that they were; and while he was almost ready to accept, with poets of the past both minor and great, his share of the age-old misunderstanding of the poet's nature, something within him rebelled at being classified away into a psychoanalyst's case-book.

When the accusation had been made: when the verdict of 'morbid humours', or 'the vapours and the spleen', of 'unmanly weakness', or 'neurosis', had been passed, did not something remain, and escape? The contact of the flesh of his fingers with the petals of a quilted dahlia—was not that left behind, with all that it implied, after the poet had been classified and filed?

His temperament and talent were not nostalgic, and he felt no dislike for the broad contours of the age in which he lived, for some of its typicalities had already provided him with inspiration. He had written true poems that sprang from a reading of the works of Jung, and from the atomic explosions in the Nevada desert. But sometimes he felt that it was a great age expressing itself in an unbelievably silly, pompous and cautious jargon, and he felt it at this moment.

His irritation took the form of wishing that she would be a little sweeter to him.

"We go on like a pair of snapping turtles," he said suddenly, and got up to pay the bill. "Don't you ever wish that we could go on like a pair of turtle-doves? It's a prettier sound, anyway."

She had forgotten that her lover was a young man who worked in words, and the sharpness in his voice surprised her. She liked to be scolded, and for the rest of the evening she was almost kind to him.

CHAPTER ELEVEN

"BOHEMIA. A DESERT COUNTRY NEAR THE SEA"

"Why won't you come? Ricardo is going to be there."

"Is that any reason why I should? I've been on my feet all day and I want to sit down, not tramp for miles," Nell said.

"You won't have to tramp for miles. Oscar lives on Church Hill; it's only round the corner. And you *ought* to meet Ricardo. As a matter of fact you could have met him yesterday. He was crawling down our stairs at half-past three this morning."

"I did hear someone creeping about, but how could I know it was Ricardo? If I had I would have got up to meet him, of course."

"You can sound bloody crushing, Nello," John said approvingly. He had come to meet her from The Primula, as he sometimes did, charming the busy females, while they flitted about, with his air and his manners. "You ought to give up this ridiculous job and go and be trained at RADA. You could play acid-spinster parts."

Miss Berringer, who was swiftly putting away left-overs, threw him a protesting exclamation; Nell uttered an unoffended laugh. When one is not quite twenty—and beginning to be cautiously content with one's life—such a remark can seem amusing.

"Oh, Ricardo's terrific," John went on—"he's what Boswell would have called *retenue*. He always wears an officer's coat, perfectly pressed, in winter and summer, and underneath it he's almost naked. He's terribly attractive to women. And he's been in prison."

"Might be a good idea if he went back there," Miss Berringer said detachedly. "Nell, just smell this. Will it go another day?"

"So you'll come, won't you, Nello?" John said, when the inspection of a jug of custard was over.

"I suppose so. But I can't stay late. Who's going to be there?"

"Most of The Coffee Dish people. Eleanora, Francesca, Davina, Dominic (his real name's David but who wants to be called that?) and Adam. Adam's just back from singing in a concert party somewhere. It was terribly well-paid. But he had to give it up. The bloody man who ran it *insisted* on his turning up every day no matter *how* he felt, and he was feeling awful because Claudia (that's his woman, she's ballet) had a modelling job in London and he couldn't see her. She *had* to stick it, you see, because she's just come out of a mental home and they said she needed regular occupation."

"Or a regular swishing." This was Miss Berringer, from the depths of a cupboard. John gave her slim back view an indulgent look. Nell had noticed that he seemed to like her, as he did anyone who treated life, and himself, with firmness: it was only his parents to whom this attitude did not apply.

As she sat propped against the wall of a cellar some two hours later, she was wondering resignedly why she had not realized that any party attended by patrons of The Coffee Dish would be like this. She was by now prepared not to expect 'sandwiches or that sort of suburban bull', but even her experiences with them, and at their favourite café, during the past six weeks, had not prepared her for a floor running with pools of cider from a leaking barrel, on which people were dancing with naked feet, a fused light which gave an excuse for burning one candle in—of course—a Chianti bottle, and nothing at all to eat. Oscar lived in two cellars; one held his bed and the other the table at which he wrote short stories. He was not at the party, having early on gone out on to the Heath with his boy-friend.

Nell had accepted the boy-friend, and his delicately painted face, as she had accepted everything else encountered in London. She supposed, when she heard older people discussing such subjects, that she would one day have to make up her mind how she felt and thought about them; meanwhile, she was so busy that she had no time to think about them at all. She found herself, rather amiably, accepting everything and everybody. She supposed that she ought to be troubled about this. She supposed also that it was because of John that she was not. It was John who had detachedly and clinically explained to her about Oscar and his boy.

At this point in her reflections, while her sober eyes rested absently upon the indistinct, fantastically dressed shapes jiving all about her in the candlelight to the music of a radiogram, a voice crossly addressed her:

"Doctor Livingstone, I presume. Will you dance?"

He was a young man of medium height, distinguished from everybody else there by a lounge suit and short hair. Nell's eyes strayed to his feet: he wore shoes and socks.

"Well . . . " she said, smiling to show that she knew the Stanley joke, and standing up, "I have been but it was *so* uncomfortable . . . aren't your feet wet?"

"It doesn't come over my soles. They are wet; my shoes need mending; but I'm absolutely damned if I'll take them off . . . I say, do you *like* this sort of thing?"

He stared at her gloomily. He had a fair, snub face with what used to be called an 'open' look; he seemed about twenty-three or twenty-four years old.

"Not very much. Hardly at all, in fact."

"Why come, then? (Shall we sit down? This seems to be a place without a hole . . . do have it.)"

"I came with my cousin," Nell said, when they were rearranged on poor Oscar's decaying bergère. (Where was that cousin now? She had lost sight of him in the confusion and dimness for the last half-hour; had, indeed, been trying to find him amidst the whirling skirts, flapping ponytails, and prancing jeans and corduroys when 'Stanley' addressed her.) "But he seems to have gone off. . . . "

"Oh . . . I wonder if I know him."

"John Gaunt."

He shook his head. "And what's your name—may I know it?" he added quickly.

"Nell Sely."

"Sely. That isn't a usual name . . . mine's Robert Lyddington."

"Do you live in Hampstead?" asked Nell, who was getting along nicely with this conversation, "because my mother used to know some Lyddingtons when she was a girl. They lived in Frognal."

"My grandparents. They had a house on Vernon Hill. It's pulled down now, and my parents have never lived here.

(We've always lived in Richmond.) But I like Hampstead. I've always wanted to come back, and now I've got a room in Rosslyn Hill."

"We live in Arkwood Road."

"I know it. Looks over the Heath at one end. With your parents?" The tone was neither disapproving nor sympathetic.

"Yes."

"What do you do? Are you ballet? (You look rather ballet. Your hair's ballet, anyway.)"

"No. I'm a waitress."

Nell said it calmly. But she had to tell herself that she did not care what he thought.

"A *waitress*?" He looked quickly away from her, but she had seen his astonishment. "Oh . . . jolly good. Why not, I mean. But isn't it terribly hard work?"

"Frightfully. But it's awfully amusing and I make a lot of money."

Seeing that he was not frightened off, she began to tell him about daily life at The Primula, rather soberly, in the thin pure voice that matched the texture of her skin and the tint of her eyes, as they sat side by side against the wall (from which Robert occasionally jerked himself away with an impatient exclamation, brushing plaster off his shoulders), and surrounded by the patrons of The Coffee Dish, some of whom had spread newspaper upon the wet floor and, having collapsed upon it, were passionately arguing.

Glancing at them occasionally when a louder yelp than usual attracted her attention, Nell thought how unmistakable they were. She had first met the group of people whom John called 'we' some six weeks previously, and now felt that she would recognize a specimen anywhere.

Their long, thick, dark clothes, which they wore unchangeably in spite of weather now fairly consistently warm, and their hair sprouting copiously unbound and unshaven upon head and chin, appeared most at home in the quiet, leisurely, smoky setting of The Coffee Dish itself.

This restaurant in a little street between Berwick Market and Golden Square had been planned by its first proprietors to secure the custom of the workers in a large block of new offices facing it, and they had decorated their long room in a style which seemed original, until it was compared with that of the Espresso bars. But frescoes of space-ships and flying saucers

could not account for The Coffee Dish almost at once attracting
a type of customer who not only occupied all the tables for
hours, so that those pressed for time could never find a seat,
but also possessed faces and wore clothes which scared ordinary
customers away.

There they sat: the large, calm, dirty girls in flowing skirts
and lead jewellery, and the dreamers in drain-pipes and duffel
coats, the spinners of fantastic plans for making fortunes
brooding silently over a newspaper, with unwashed hair falling
across (in the case of the girls, who believed in living naturally)
unpowdered faces. The workers in the office block, running
downstairs to snatch their lunch in a crowded Lyons serve-
yourself-bar, looked at them rather wistfully. Who were they
all? Whence this apparently endless leisure, passed in brooding
or arguing, which could have been spent delightfully in tennis
or music or car-tinkering? And what made them all come to
The Coffee Dish; day in, day out, wet or fine, early and late, to
The Coffee Dish?

"It's their bloody parents who are responsible in most cases
for their leaving home," John had explained. "*Stifling* them
with too much safety and comfort and not giving them enough
love. (You see, Nello, one's got to be free.) One simply cannot
have parents, for example, interfering with one's work. *Never*
shall I forget the bores my papa and mamma were when I
first showed that I'm a writer. They were at me like two well-
meaning vultures. Nagging me about working regularly; trying
to show my stuff to literary giants who were as bored at the
idea of seeing it as I was furious with the idea of letting them
. . . frankly, I gave up trying to take it all. Most of the people
in this room don't have a real home any more. We've discovered, you see, that it's possible to live without food or money
if only you've somewhere to sit down indoors in the winter. In
the summer, of course, it's much better. You can eat even less.
(Most of us starve all the time, you know. That's why everybody's so white.) Sleep? Oh . . . in each other's rooms. Or at
places that stay open all night. (You can sleep quite well with
your head on your arms on a table.) Adrian, over there—"
nodding towards a long black-bearded figure in dirty jeans and
an American shirt, "hasn't slept in a bed for two years. It's
his *thing*. He sleeps on chairs and on the floor in people's rooms.
(Of course some of us do go back to our parents occasionally.
Then we get what you'd call proper food and sleep. But we

always run away again.) You see those two girls, Lavinia and Jane, yes, the one with the fair hair down to her waist, they get all their meals from men. No, they aren't tarts. The men are sorry for them. They're artists: Jane does linocuts and Lavinia is a very fine portrait painter indeed."

Nell had grown accustomed to hearing how gifted, delicately-minded, and high-principled everyone at The Coffee Dish was. Lofty ideals of courtesy prevailed. Certain virtues, but only certain ones, were much praised: romantic faithfulness in love, devotion to one's art, freedom from all control, the Spartan casting aside of any comfort and order. Tolerance was of course the master-virtue, except (Nell discovered) when it became necessary to extend it to anyone who drew a regular salary in exchange for set hours of work. Then no words were scornful enough for the poor wage-slave.

"They're about the narrowest crowd I've ever met," Benedict said to her once, when Coffee House shibboleths were under discussion one evening in the Gaunt's flat, " . . . very good, John; all right; but they are. If you aren't jobless and homeless and hungry, you're outside. That's narrowness. Call it what you please; it means the same thing."

The girls under eighteen who lived on their friends and stray meals from men; the boys who slept at home perhaps two nights out of the seven and carried always a portfolio containing photographs or poems or drawings; the youthful dancers and singers and lyric-writers who were always about to land a job at fifteen pounds a week—Nell, using her eyes as she walked on her day off about London with John, had seen them wandering as far north as Hampstead, and on the extreme limits of Soho to the south.

They were seldom seen beyond Marble Arch on the west, and their eastern boundary came down somewhat firmly at the beginning of New Oxford Street. But along Charing Cross Road and Oxford Street and in the narrow lanes of ramshackle eighteenth-century houses running between these thorough-fares, their long hair and white faces and thick, dark, shabby clothes were to be seen at almost any hour of the twenty-four, not excluding three and four in the morning. And John had told her that on the fringes of the set there were elements that were criminal.

She was interested in them because they were his friends; fearfully interested, because their influence upon him seemed to her baleful and strong, but their polite contempt for herself, her clothes ("You're the first girl who has ever worn a fitted coat at The Coffee Dish, Nello!") and her background, soon convinced her that they would never become friends of hers.

They tolerated her, because she was John's cousin, and because her job now admitted her to the ranks of those earning a living unconventionally, but they only tolerated her. Davina and Grenouille (a young woman wearing black leggings laced with bands of straw whose style was much admired) and Francesca and the rest had never forgotten that Nell had once implied criticism of the hours and hours and hours spent at The Coffee Dish in doing nothing, by taking her knitting there. They had called her—their tone did not hold the friendliness of a nickname—'Mademoiselle Defarge'.

She now found them all bores, and was glad that they could not often afford the fare out to Hampstead. As John seldom took her to The Coffee Dish nowadays, she seldom saw them. But she feared and disliked their influence over him more than ever.

She did not know—how could she?—that in one way, he was safe.

John, in fact and in truth, is the only one of them all, poets and painters, gifted or pretentious, idle or dedicated, who is safe. When—years on from this evening in early summer, while Nell and Robert Lyddington are sitting in Oscar's cellar looking at the arguers and the dancers—the door of an unspeakable room is opened; and people go in, and later on someone reluctantly, hesitatingly, opens the worn, filthy suitcase that for years, now, has been almost John's sole possession, the manuscript will be found.

It will be seamed and crossed and criss-crossed with long delicate lines of writing like flights of birds, and corrections in coloured inks; starred, blotted, patiently re-done; then re-done; and done yet again. It will look almost more like a map than a thing written; and in one sense it will be: a map of London, carved in pouring molten crystal words, that have set in massive splendour for ever. John is safe: he is with the immortals.

"If this is Bohemia, you can have it," young Lyddington said suddenly, after an interruption in their talk caused by someone bumping a large dusty behind into him and sending lukewarm cider all over his trousers, "Who was that? Do you know her? She seemed to know you," rather accusingly.

"It was Eleanora, I think—or Polly." Nell tried to disentangle the memories associated with a fat, sweet, spotty face. "I think she's going to do ballet in South Africa."

"Oh. Well, would you like to come out somewhere and have some coffee? I don't think we want any more of this, do we." It was not a question, but Nell, though welcoming the suggestion and agreeing with the verdict, hesitated.

"My partner's walked out on me, too," he added, very crossly.

"Oh. Then let's. It's a very good idea," Nell said.

While they were walking up the hill she was telling herself not to be idiotic about 'offending' John—who had behaved disgustingly rudely anyway—and listening at the same time to Robert.

He worked in a costing accountant's office in Holborn during the day, and on most evenings studied, with a correspondence college, for the examinations which he must pass in order to qualify for his costing accountancy degrees. Nell asked him casually what this was; she had never heard of it; and he seemed pleased to tell her. It appeared that he had done his National Service in the Royal Navy ("I've got an uncle in the Navy who's done rather well") and had had a wizard time; Australia, Ceylon, Straits Settlements. But friends who came home on leave *couldn't* be got to see that one must stick to one's ruddy work four evenings out of the five, or else one would fail one's exams. and then one's whole scheme would go overboard. Did Nell play tennis?

By this time they were sitting in the most expensive and glamorous restaurant in Hampstead. Nell, who had kept her love of tennis carefully hidden from the games-despising John, now joyfully admitted that she did.

"Do you play a good game?"

"I'm not too bad, I think."

"Good. We'll have some games. I'm very keen. It's about the only form of exercise I can afford nowadays—and even so I can't manage a sub. to a decent club. We'll have to play on the public courts at Parliament Hill Fields. What's your best evening?"

Nell did not like to dash the expression on a face which had now lost its gloom by telling him that all her evenings were marked by the same longing to get off her feet and sit down.

"Monday's a good evening for me. Or Tuesday's quite good," she said.

"Next Tuesday, then. All right?"

"I'd love it. I've been longing for a game."

"I'd better get along there tomorrow morning and book a court. There's a terrific run on them."

"But it's miles across the Heath . . . before you go to work."

"Miles, rubbish. I often go for a walk before breakfast. I can get the 615 trolley on down to Holborn."

It was pleasant to talk the same language again with someone. If Nell had not been wondering whether John was cross because she had left the party, she would have been enjoying the occasion even more. Robert ordered coffee and cakes with a quiet but lordly hand, and she did not protest because he seemed to like doing it.

"This is a nice place," he said, looking round at the desperate chi-chi elegance. "Dagoes, of course, but rather cheerful, don't you think? We went to a marvellous place in Hong Kong . . ."

He saw her home to Arkwood Road, and was so easy, calm and friendly, that it did not enter Nell's head that he might kiss her good night. Whether it entered his or not, he did not. He went off very quickly, with a brisk lift of the hand— "Good night, Doctor Livingstone. See you on Tuesday," and Nell went up the steps looking at the windows. They were wrapped in sulky darkness.

"So you went off with Robert Lyddington," John said to her meditatively, meeting her on the stairs a day or two later, "I expect you wondered where I was. I went out to have a drink with a girl who knew someone who might give me a job."

"Did you take it?"

Better to ignore everything else; better not to say anything reproachful; always remember to imply that he *could* have had the job if he'd wanted it.

"No . . . as a matter of fact. How did you get on with R. Lyddington? I've always thought him rather pleasant."

"Oh, do you know him?"

"Not 'know', exactly. We know some of the same people. He's a friend of Francesca's, as a matter of fact. Before she left home she used to frequent a dreadful club in Hampstead, and R. Lyddington used to frequent it too. Hence."

"Oh." Nell knew that John's 'dreadful' meant pleasant, orderly and conventional.

"How *did* you get on with him, Nello?"

"Quite well, I think. We're going to play tennis."

He would find out sooner or later, as he always found out everything, and it might . . . show him that he was not . . .

"Oh? How very healthy and energetic of you. I shall come and lie on a bench and watch, encouraging you with shrill cries. Leaping about in the heat."

But all the same Nell thought that he was not pleased.

However, what did it matter if he were not? His displeasure only meant that he liked to come first, always, with the people he called his friends. This was the first, and the last, time that she tried, ineptly enough, to arouse his jealousy.

"By the way," he said, slipping his arm round her waist and leading her downstairs, she having been on her way upstairs, "whom do you think is coming to be a waitress at your café? Chris's Nerina."

"How can she be, John?" stopping to stare at him, "Mrs. Cooper only gave us notice this morning."

"I know. What's the time?" glancing vaguely about him as though expecting to see clocks printed upon the air. "Well, even now Nerina is calling upon your Miss Berringer."

"She won't find her in. She never is in, in the evenings."

"I know that, Nello dear. I often walk the Heath at twilight, as you may have observed, and I have seen Miss Berringer and the object of her passion. (It is a passion, by the way. A real one.) But this evening Miss Berringer *will* be in. Nerina was told that she will be."

"Who told her?" demanded Nell.

"Oh . . . I helped. I know who's going away for a few days in Hampstead, and who's stopping at home . . . or rather, I know someone who knows a talkative milkman . . . I knew Mrs. Cooper was leaving The Primula, and I just set myself to find an evening when Miss Berringer would be at home . . . you see, Nerina can't call on her during the day because she's got this washing-up job in Fitzroy Street. But the open-air art exhibition is coming on soon, and Chris will be in Hampstead all day. So Nerina will want to be here in the evenings, and then he can come and meet her after work."

"Well . . . " Nell said.

Her chief feeling was regret at the departure of Mrs. Cooper.

They had all got on so well together. Was Nerina very C.D.? (Coffee Dish.) Nell now applied these initials to a certain type of young person, although she always pictured Nerina as fortyish, dark, and big. Certainly she belonged to what Margie Gaunt called the N.S.B. or No Second-name Brigade.

"You will like Nerina, Nello. She is quite enchanting."

Nell somehow did not think that she would.

CHAPTER TWELVE

IDYLL: BY GEORGE SAND

THERE was some kind of an argument or quarrel going on in Hampstead about the art exhibition. As she hurried to work every morning, looking forward to a day which grew steadily busier and more profitable in tips as the summer advanced, Nell caught glimpses of placards advertising the local paper, which spoke of Art Show disputes and controversies and deadlocks. She also heard snatches of conversation among certain jeans and beards which had begun to frequent The Primula.

"I hope this doesn't mean that our new evening piece is arty, and this is the advance guard of her pals," observed Miss Berringer, studying these portents through the slit in the curtain. "She might be, at that. But it's probably only the Exhibition, as usual."

Nell did not ask for further information. She did not want to hear about Nerina; it would be nuisance enough when she came. John's obvious liking for 'Chris's woman' had set up in his cousin a sales-resistance to the mere sound of her name.

Meanwhile a long, low, structure of steel rods and canvas began to appear along the upper part of the High Street which the new C.D. frequenters of The Primula disrespectfully nick-named The Cowshed. This, Nell supposed, would display the paintings and could shelter them if it rained. Hampstead showed increasing signs of being given over to Bohemia; the pavements echoed with flapping of sandals and the clapping of continental clogs; there were tights and striped blue-and-white jeans to be seen loitering round the Underground station, and somehow all this seemed to Nell to be linked with the expected arrival of Nerina at The Primula next Monday evening.

She did not think much about the event: she had not time: but she had an uneasy feeling. John seemed to be hovering behind it; finding out about things by underground ways, arranging, managing, intriguing. How confidently he had announced that Nerina was coming to work at The Primula! and that had been before she had actually applied for the job.

He must have taken considerable trouble, in his secretive way, to get her there. And that must mean that he liked her very much.

Nell was glad to remember that someone else was arriving on Monday evening, as well; Elizabeth Prideaux, home from her finishing school at Châteaux d'Oex, and ready to be presented at one of the Palace Garden Parties. She would be frantically busy (she wrote, on a heroic-looking postcard of the Dent Blanche), but *must* see Nell *very soon*. She would ring up the *minute* she got back. The postcard had a mysterious post-script, *Lucky you*, and Nell's pleasure in the thought of her friend's arrival was now unclouded by any fears that her own present occupation would be despised.

Lucky you to be a waitress was what was meant. Nell thought that the envy might not be shared by General and Mrs. Prideaux, but did not mind that so much as she would have three months ago.

She was not at the tea-shop on Monday, her day off. On the evening of Tuesday, being determined not to hang about a moment later than usual out of curiosity, she went back into the kitchen with her tips after emptying the begging-bowl and found it fuller of people than when she had left it; Miss Berringer, Mary lingering over a final pampering of her stomach, Miss Cody briskly changing her shoes, and someone else, who was standing in a corner slowly taking off a pale, shabby coat. She found herself addressed, in a voice possessing the quality, translated into human tones, of the silvery little bell that summoned the waitresses.

"Aren't you John Gaunt's cousin?" The intonation was social, guarded and composed, yet sweet; it was the word which always recurred when one thought of Nerina.

"Yes," was all Nell said, cross because his name made her stomach contract.

"I thought you must be. He told me to look out for you. I'm Nerina."

To look out for you . . . as if The Primula were the size of a

Lyons Corner House. Nell, making a mental note that Nerina *was* one of the N.S.B., answered pleasantly:

"Oh, you know John, don't you . . . it's nice to see you here . . . er . . . "

Her primrose hair was tied back in a tassel from a face small and white, with firm childish lips and eyes of lightest green; lovely eyes. Yet she was not pretty. Nell could imagine him admiring her immensely. He never admired people or things that were ordinary.

"Do you know Benedict Rouse?" Nell asked, beginning to roll up her own apron. She had an unfamiliar pain in her heart.

"Oh *yes*. Isn't he wonderful? So clever . . . "

"Very nice." Nell made poor Benedict sound like a cake, but she could not help it; the pain was rather dismaying.

"John's wonderful too. He's so clever too, isn't he?"

"Very," said Nell, trying not to sound grim.

There were evidently stronger reasons for his liking Nerina than her looks. Nell already knew that what *he* liked best of all from his friends was admiration. Some instinct always kept her from pretending to give it him, and she never knew whether he would have liked her more if she had. She only knew that, while she could keep certain feelings for him a secret, she could not pretend to have for him feelings which she did not.

Nerina was slowly arranging the ends of her apron strings, which went twice round her fairy's waist, into a butterfly-bow.

"How old are you?" she went on, more shyly.

"Nearly twenty. How old are you?"

"Quite ancient, aren't you? I'm nearly seventeen."

Nell, who would not have been surprised had she said nearly fifteen, thought that there would be other occasions when she could talk to Nerina. She made her farewells rather more briskly than usual, and went off.

So much for the large, dark, elderly creature of her fancy, who must have been created by John's use of the word 'woman'. Now that his liking for Nerina was more understandable it was, thought Nell irritably, more likely to be . . . a nuisance. This pain, for instance.

She dismissed the whole affair, yet at the back of her mind there was comfort. Everyone—John, Benedict, all the creatures at The Coffee Dish—agreed that Nerina was very much 'Chris's woman', and, now that Nell had seen her, she recognized (while hoping that *she* never looked like that) the dreaming, withdrawn, abstracted air of one helplessly in love which she had first noticed in Benedict.

It was surely unlikely that Nerina, thus shackled, would become interested in . . . anyone else. As Nell marched homewards she became more cheerful.

"Nell? Don't you want any supper?"

"How *can* I, mother?" she hardly paused as she was hurrying through the hall in white shorts and shirt, "I *told* you I was meeting Robert for tennis . . . leave something out for me, will you . . . or don't bother . . . I'll get something while I'm out. . . . "

"Bring him back with you, dear, if you like," Anna said calmly to the closing door.

She stood there for a moment, a large graceful figure in a cotton dress on which the pattern was faded to shadows, holding a tray laden with food more plentiful and nourishing than the Selys had been eating six months ago.

She was thinking that Nell's job could not be so tiring as it would seem to be, if she could rush off like that to play tennis at the end of the day. It was most interesting and satisfactory too, that she should have met the grandson of Mr. and Mrs. Lyddington; 'the old people' at Willow House. Anna was looking forward to meeting him and to talking about his family: she and Martin had already had two evenings of pleasurable reminiscent talk out of the event. To Anna it was nearly the most interesting thing that had happened since their coming to Hampstead.

She did not have any typical motherly thoughts about Nell's having met her first young man, because she had always taken it for granted that Nell would go out with young men when she reached the proper age for doing so. Anna herself had known many, and brusquely yet not ungracefully had rejected their attentions; and the fact that the Selys lived in the heart of the country with little money and few acquaintances had never disturbed her unconscious assumption that Nell would one day be able to make her choice. Now, seeing Nell livelier, more cheerful and apparently getting fun out of life in spite of her queer job, Anna felt pleased. She did not approve of the job; to her sister-in-law she decisively called it 'this nonsense of Nell's' and said firmly that it was only going to be very temporary; Nell must get something better; 'interesting', and

'leading somewhere'. (She had in mind some secretaryship
to the Master of a Cambridge college.) But she admitted that
the money was wonderfully useful.

And, although she did not say so to anyone, she admired
Nell for working so hard at a job which she for all her better
brain could not have tolerated for a day; 'kow-towing' to
awful people, dishing out weak tea and inferior cakes, listening
to the greasy gossip of common women (these terrible opinions,
let it be said with slavish haste, were Anna's only because she
had been born before 1914 and in *the so-called upper classes*).
Nell certainly did not get her capacity for mixing with the
masses from her mother. Anna supposed that she might get
it from Peggy, who had none of the qualities of a lady but
possessed many which were useful for living in the world of the
nineteen-fifties.

"Did you have a quiet afternoon, dear?" she asked her
husband, while they were eating their supper in the spare room.

She liked to set a tray of food down anywhere in the house
where there was a bit of sunlight or a view, and eat, and Martin
was growing to enjoy these picnics too.

Neither of them realized how irregular their ways had grown,
nor how faded, battered and chipped their always shabby
possessions had become. Anna did next to no housework;
Martin often did not dress until midday. A light veil of dust
covered the quiet, brightly painted, rather chilly rooms.
When Anna went out to shop, which she did often, she slung
on a seven-year-old knitted cap and cardigan, and sometimes
Martin, who was beginning to shuffle, went shrinkingly with
her as far as the shop where he bought his daily paper. Their
voices had grown quieter and their movements slower.

Miss Lister, who combined a sharp attention to what was
happening to other people with a perfectly splendid inability
to notice what was happening to herself, had already told the
milky-maans that they were Going Down, delivering this
verdict (she was never heard to say that anyone was Going
Up) after she had been to tea with the Selys at Anna's invitation. Another kind of observer might have said that after
thirty years spent in driving themselves and in presenting two
masks to life, they were at last becoming, so far as was now
possible, their true selves. Yet another would have said that
they were only beginning to grow old.

Martin roused himself; he had been lost in a long look out

of the open window. There it was, rising above the roofs far below the steep fall of the hill: a massive tower of pale-red brick, not of the familiar shape that, for so many months, had set him grieving and trembling, yet it must be a church.

"Quiet afternoon? Oh no, dearie. I hardly ever do, you know. The telephone went three times, and two young people came, asking for John . . . don't any of his friends have any regular work? I thought that all young people worked nowadays."

"John's friends aren't ordinary young people. Was the telephone anyone for Nell, dear?"

Nell had taken to demanding "Any telephone messages?" immediately she came home in the evenings.

"Yes . . . oh dear. I should have remembered . . . Elizabeth Prideaux. She wanted Nell to telephone her this evening; I did write down the number; I've got it somewhere here . . . yes . . . here it is."

"I'll leave it for her in the hall," Anna said, taking the paper. "You ought really to have a pad for taking all these things down."

"Yes. I could use some of my old sermon paper."

The words were spoken without any hesitation or glance towards her; his eyes were fixed upon the distant view.

"How pretty that is," Anna leant back in her chair sipping her tea, "I wish I could paint."

He did not reply. He had just realized that the sight of the church tower was not hurting him.

Nell and Robert had enjoyed their first evening's tennis so much, and found themselves so well matched, that they now played on three evenings a week, taking it in turn to manage the difficult business of booking the court. Golders Green was easier to reach for both of them than Parliament Hill Fields, so now they usually played amidst the deer, the magnificent flower gardens, and the Jewish strollers in the Park there. Nell was not quite so tired at the end of the day, now that she was growing accustomed to her work, but she would have had to be much more tired than she was to give up her tennis. She had had her racquet, which was a Slazenger and a birthday present from Lady Fairfax, restrung, and although her clothes were of the cheapest kind possible, one of the most becoming dresses in the modern world had its usual effect upon her appearance, and she was gratified to receive glances of approval.

As for her partner, slightly closer acquaintance with him (they were not getting to know one another quickly or well) was making her suspect that he might be less conventional than he seemed.

He had a way of suddenly beginning to laugh without explaining, as if his thoughts had overcome him, which she liked; he was unusually observant, often remarking later upon incidents or people which she herself had not noticed, and, as for convention, he could hardly be too outwardly conventional to please Nell, whose attitude to life during the last three months had been a struggle to make herself do, and understand, things which, in her former world, were either not done, ignored or taken for granted.

She had succeeded: for there was a side of her nature which liked to venture and to do the common-sense, rather than the orthodox, thing, but she felt it surprisingly pleasant to be once more with someone of her own kind. She knew that she and Robert *were* the same kind.

She was pleased, too, by his unselfishness in spending nearly two hours one evening chatting with the parents about Willow House, and 'the old people'; Vernon Lodge, the Misses Halliday (Aunts Eleanor and Nancy), and Anna's own parents, whom he dimly remembered. He had also actually heard legends, although the facts were well before his time, of the Vernon Lodge parrot, and this had delighted Anna who, inspired by nostalgia, pressed his memory unsuccessfully to yield up the 'arbitrary and vexatious' Miss Sullavan.

Nell and he behaved admirably; their unconscious reactions only took the form, on their release at last, of almost running down Arkwood Road and into the nearest Espresso bar while both laughing at nothing in particular.

Meanwhile, at The Primula, the only difference made by the coming of Nerina was that Nell occasionally suffered from the annoying pain, and that Nerina's Chris began to haunt the tea-shop's back premises.

He began by hanging a silent red face over the low wall of the garden, appearing the moment after Miss Berringer had gone off to meet her boy-friend, and waving to Nerina, whom he had already accompanied to the back door and left there, whenever she glanced up from her duties—which was not seldom.

Then, straying like the large rough dog which he resembled into the garden itself, he would moon round and round studying its neglected plants in what seemed to Nell an unexpectedly interested manner, always drawing nearer to the back door. When he got there, he would sit down on the step in the late sunshine and stare up at the trees in the lane, while occasionally Nerina, who seemed to have no scruples about anything if the results benefited Chris, slipped out with a hunk of bread or half a wilting lettuce which she pressed into his huge, sensitive hand; after one or two of these donations the kitchen door would remain ajar ("it's awfully hot this evening, isn't it? Miss Cody, don't you think it's awfully hot?" from Nerina) and, with the cooler air, into the kitchen drifted Chris, to sit in a corner and watch his love while he slowly masticated whatever happened to be going.

"I had a great-great-aunt in the early days in Canada who used to feed an Indian at the back door," was all Miss Berringer (whose Commonwealth connections appeared to be far-flung) observed, when she returned unexpectedly one evening and caught him.

Nell's belief that the return was unpremeditated was shaken when Tansy told her, rather triumphantly, that Lady Bottle-washer had knocked half-a-crown off of that poor kid's money this week, just to learn her not to give Chris Lady B.'s food.

Nell had to tell herself, rather firmly, that if Miss Berringer had not been a good business woman, with an eye for every detail, there would have been no successful tea-shop to provide jobs for five people, and no back doorstep for Chris to sit on; and after some reflection she persuaded herself that justice had been done.

Her dislike for the grandiose schemes and hopeless laziness of The Coffee Dishers helped her in reaching the conclusion. The job that was lost because someone preferred to sit arguing rather than go out and keep an appointment, the lofty remarks about freedom which ended in borrowing from someone in regular work, the devotion to art resulting in grubbiness, disorder and, sometimes, dishonesty—were they really better than the Berringer attitude towards money and work?

John would have said, yes. Nell never hesitated to say, no, except when she was listening to him.

Mary and Tansy both looked on Chris and Nerina with sentimental approval, Tansy referring to them as The Love-

Birds, and Mary sighing and saying it did your heart good
to see them in this old world, while neither, in discussing them,
showed any of the grim, salacious, disapproving curiosity they
had when they talked about Miss Berringer's affair.

Nell sometimes felt cross with them; their sloppiness annoyed
her. If they had known that Chris and Nerina were really
lovers, they would, she was sure, have been as cruel as they
were about Miss B. and the one John called 'her fat man'.
But it never seemed to occur to them that 'the young ones'
were anything but characters from an Anna Neagle film.

Nerina soon fitted in well with the routine and the staff,
joining in the jokes and conversation enough to make her
company pleasant, but always, Nell noticed, keeping her
reserve about her own affairs.

She was very what John's quotee Boswell would have
called *retenue*. She hardly ever said 'I'; her tastes, her past, her
views, her plans for the future, were all hidden away behind
the smooth small face framed in the severe line of primrose
hair. Only when she spoke of Chris would colour come up
there; the ethereal pink colour that stains a seashell; but she
never talked of their feelings for one another, or of their
relationship, and her only response to the sickly jokes and
smirkings of Mary and Tansy was a smile; shy, yet guarded and
slight.

"A dark filly," said Miss Berringer suddenly, at the end of
Nerina's first week there, while Nell was helping her to slice
cucumber for the evening snacks, "don't you think so? Never
be surprised at anything she might do." Nell had the impression
that Miss Berringer did not like her new Evening Girl. "As
for him," added her employer, *"he's* nothing but the gardener's
boy."

"That was discerning of the Berringer," said John to Nell,
when he had drawn from her somewhat reluctant memory,
now hampered by the presence of the tiresome pain, all the
staff comments on Nerina and Chris, "because that's exactly
what he was."

"Was he?"

It was a Monday afternoon, and they were sitting in the
garden of Fenton House. They had it to themselves; there
were a few foreign and American visitors strolling through the
rooms of the seventeenth-century place which has been given
over to a collection of china and old musical instruments,

gazing at the Saxe and the spinets, but fortunately no-one wanted to inspect the garden. Nell and John were sitting on the seat at its end which overlooks the long lawn and the back of the house.

"Yes, he was. (You're answering in questions again; don't do it. It means you're sulking about something. You *do* sulk about Nerina . . .) I would have told you about her and Chris before, only you always look so sick whenever I mention her name . . . it's a beautiful story; it's like something by George Sand. (Don't take your hand away; I like to hold it.)"

The seat felt warm and the air smelled of freshly-cut grass. Nell knew that if she opened her eyes she would see his profile, like a cameo, but with a childish charm warmer than that of any classic head, against the foliage and soft old red brick of the wall. A light wreath of flowers lay along one of the trained climbers there, and a sweet scent crept along the air. Even in this weather his fingers felt cool. Jasmine? Then the summer must be far advanced. She opened her eyes.

"Don't you want to hear about it?"

"M'm."

"Well, her people live in Surrey. (I know exactly what they're like, and they're frightful, but of course not so bad as television stars and the 'brilliant, interesting' type.) They've got a wonderful garden; it's on a hill and full of every kind of flower imaginable, it's one of those places that are open to the public for charity every summer, and Chris's father was one of the gardeners there. He lived in the nearest village. Chris was rather bright at school (I know he doesn't look it, but he was) and Nerina's father took an *interest* in him and that sort of bull: shocking cheek, and stupid, too, because Chris had made it quite clear from the start that he was going to be a painter and didn't want to go to the Royal Coll. of Hort. or wherever his papa and Nerina's were slavishly, and interferingly, planning to shove him; anyway, he often used to come up to help his father, and there was Nerina, still at school in those days, and coming home every day through the garden. She used to stop and talk to Chris, and they fell in love. Later on they simply ran away together. It *is* like George Sand, you know. Or *Paul et Virginie*."

Nell was silent, thinking about the tall bearded boy clad almost in rags whose personality did suggest, as Miss Berringer had detected, birds' nests, and paths covered in moss, and rough old trees; everything, in fact, that was the opposite of what was to be found and seen in cities.

"Were her people very upset?" she asked at last.

"I don't know about *upset*. They made a terrible *fuss*. Her mother had a kind of collapse. It got into the papers last autumn, in spite of their trying to stop it, only then there was the smog and the floods and people rather forgot about it. You see, they guessed almost at once that she must have gone with Chris, and it was rather biting-the-hand-that-fed-you. Or so *they* thought. *I* think they simply asked for it. What else did they expect? He's a painter, and Nerina is so lovely."

There it was again, the little pain. *Blow.*

"Didn't they ever try to find them?" she asked.

"Oh, just at first. In an inept kind of way. But they're the sort of people who actually *mind what the neighbours think*, so they soon dropped that. Oh, and I believe Nerina did send her mamma a card at Christmas saying that she was perfectly happy and not coming back and so forth. So there wasn't much point in putting the *disgusting* police on to them, was there? I suppose her parents still do make enquiries from time to time. But they've never found them. They've been together now for ten months, working, and eating when they can, and starving when they can't. They're utterly happy. Isn't it beautiful?"

Nell was silent again. She could believe that a certain kind of love might well make one indifferent to the feelings of those one had formerly loved best, but should the passion—which she did not call to herself a passion—be given way to?

"At least," he went on, slowly and after a pause, "I will say that it's beautiful *with reservations*. I don't think, now, that Nerina's really in her right place?"

"What do you mean?" looking at him, "At The Primula?" She tried to keep resentment out of her voice. Was Nerina, then, such a delicate piece that waitressing was not for her?

"Oh really, Nello. Of course not. (How literal you can be. But I like that, sometimes.) No. I meant that the right place for her is that garden. Petals, and the wind in the leaves, and sheltered, and yet . . . fresh and . . . anyway, that's where I like to think of her."

It's a pity she doesn't go back there. Nell's expression was her usual one of steady attention to what was going on and being said (other people besides Nerina could be *retenue*), but that was what she was thinking.

"She's so fragile, you see. She's like a wind-flower or a brook-fairy."

"She seems quite tough to me."

"Oh *no*, Nello. Now you're *tough*."

"She must be tough, to be able to lead the kind of life she does, when she's always lived at home and been taken care of."

"She can do it because she loves Chris so much. But she ought really to be taken care of all the time. He does take care of her, of course. But when . . . when he goes into the Army, which he will have to do quite soon—and he will go, because he's got all the good working-class type's fear of authority—I quite expect Nerina to collapse. Then we shall *all* have to take care of her. And I shall expect you to help."

"Won't she go back to her parents?"

"Of *course* not, Nello. How can you even suggest it? She would much rather starve. (Talking of starving, can I come back with you to tea and possibly supper? I haven't any money, and Margie is down in the country and my papa has gone galumphing off to do a lecture to an unhappy literary society in some remote part of Wales, and I do dislike opening tins. I always cut myself—did you know that someone once said, *the hands of literary people always hang down like fat white slugs?* Mine aren't like that, are they?"

"Don't fish. All right, you can come if you want to. Shall I have to get a cake on the way home?"

"Yes. How domesticated we are, aren't we? Shall I come and live with you one day?"

"No thank you," Nell said with energy.

"I meant much later on when we're both quite old . . . because I've absolutely got to have someone to look after me, you see. We shall be like Rousseau and his wife . . . she was completely uneducated and ungifted, but all the cleverest people in Europe, who came to see him, thought she was wonderful and asked her advice because, you see, she had *common-sense*. Now that's like you. *I'll* have a group of dazzling friends—and you can look after me, and they'll all think you're wonderful. (I'm fascinated by stories about groups of friends—'circles' —William Morris and his circle, Ford Madox Ford and *his* circle—I am going to have a circle instead of a wife and family. It's better, for a writer, I think, in spite of Flaubert and his

'*Ils sont dans le droit*'). Don't you think it's a good idea, my coming?"

"No I do not. I'm a tidy person and you know how you hate things being tidy. And I may have a husband and family myself."

"Yes." He slowly turned his head and fixed her with his beautiful sleepy eyes. "I quite expect you will, Nello. People will want to marry you, because you're good at looking after them. I expect R. Lyddington will. *He* isn't quite so cheerful as he makes out, you know. (I think he got a taste for having an amusing time while he was in the Navy and now he finds life rather dull.) But of course he'll *never* break away. He has *much* too much sense of duty."

"Besides, I'm going to have a tea-shop," said Nell, who rarely uttered *non-sequiturs*, but now found herself slightly confused by one or two ideas which came as a surprise.

"That's all right. I don't mind. That will be easier for me, as a way of living, than an ordinary domestic routine. You'll be used to having crowds of people about and feeding them."

"John, I'm afraid I must go. I have to telephone Elizabeth at four o'clock and arrange about a meeting. She's been so booked up, getting ready for her presentation, and my hours are so odd, that so far we haven't been able to arrange anything."

She put aside his suggestion of a mutual establishment in the distant future, refusing to let her fancy play with its sweetness. A nice, disorderly, hopeless arrangement it would be, with never a moment to write letters or do any mending and the house swarming with Coffee Dishers. No thank you.

But always there would be John; coming and asking for help, kissing good night and smiling his little boy's smile for good morning, telling her what to wear, swinging hands lightly with cool fingers, clasping close, begging for comfort . . .

She got up quickly, arranging her cardigan across her shoulders.

"Oh, must we go? It's so delightful here. Is the mint out in your garden?"

"I don't know. I never look at the garden; Mummy does it all. Why?"

"Because if it is I'll have mint-leaf sandwiches for tea. They're almost my favourite thing. When we were living at the flat, when I was small, I used to . . . "

"What?" Nell said imperiously, in a moment. His voice had died away into a murmur and he was standing still, staring at the long lawn glimmering greenly in the golden light.

"Nothing. Make mint-leaf sandwiches. Tell me about your Elizabeth," languidly, in the tone of a young Rajah commanding a slave to dance.

Nell summoned her rather limited powers of description to present her friend while they were walking towards the gates leading out from the garden, but a feeling that she was not succeeding in really interesting her hearer (whom she noticed giving an affectionate glance at the frog of green bronze who supports his bloated form upon his little curved arms near the gate) caused her to end the account with a fact about Elizabeth so unusual that it must surely catch John's attention.

"She's awfully like the portrait of one of her ancestresses in the Steyne Collection. I haven't seen it, but one of the people at school had, and they said it was really amazingly like."

"Oh? The Steyne Collection? In Castlereagh Square?" He turned to look at her, but absently, and did not sound particularly interested. "Isn't he endearing?" nodding towards the frog, "he looks exactly like a frog, and there's no nonsense about 'conveying the essentials of a frog' or 'giving you the artist's individual impression of a frog', and yet, while he's much nicer than a real frog, he's also almost as good. Very satisfying all round."

"I don't know what you mean," said Nell, after some conscientious thought.

"You're such a Philistine, Nello . . . don't rush on like that; I want to look at the house for a moment." He put his arm through hers and stood still. "There, isn't it like a house in a Dutch painting?"

"I don't know. I'm a Philistine."

"And don't be *pert*," giving her arm a sharp shake. "Go on about your Elizabeth. Is she a deb?", as they strolled onwards.

"I suppose she will be officially when she's been to the Garden Party. She knows lots of debs, and her family lives in a house in Wiltshire that they've owned for about three hundred years, and she does the deb things—hunting, and that kind of thing."

"Yes . . . has she a lovely complexion?"

"She's very fair; yes, I suppose she has."

"And not what you, no doubt, would call 'bright'?"

"I don't know . . . she wasn't, at school . . . but she likes ballet and she reads a lot of French authors. . . . I shouldn't call her at all lowbrow."

"I see."

Nell was here impelled by a feeling of mingled irritation and pain—was she going to have to worry now about his meeting Elizabeth, as well as about his feelings for Nerina?—to add rather crisply:

"Why?"

"Oh, I was just imagining her . . . she sounds a managing sort of puss."

"Yes, she is, I think. At any rate, she always managed everybody and got what she wanted at school. But I don't think you'd ever suspect that she was. She has such beautiful manners. And she's a dear."

"H'm. Thank you for the warning. You know how I detest attempts to manage *me*."

The conversation then idled off on to other matters, and as Nell bore her part in it, keeping at the same time an eye open for a cake which should supplement John's peculiar and irregular diet with something nourishing and also satisfy his finicking taste in food, she was feeling slightly better about him and Nerina.

The story he had told undoubtedly made Nerina and Chris sound completely devoted and absorbed—although that did not count for as much among semi-Coffee-Dishers as it would have in more conventional circles, for the Dishers were always dropping their heart's love without a moment's warning—and, furthermore, he seemed to have no feeling towards the young lovers but admiration for their story; as if, as he had said, it were a romance by George Sand. There had been no hint in his voice or manner of jealousy.

And neither am I jealous, thought Nell with sudden stoutness which suggested that she was pulling herself together, as they paused in front of a cake-shop window. Good heavens. And I'm sure Elizabeth wouldn't be able to stand him. She'd think he was only a little boy.

"Would that one do?" She pointed.

"The one with the Brazil nuts? Oh yes. Exotic, and gloriously expensive. Is it the most expensive one in the window? Yes. . . . Then let's have it."

Later that evening, John was drifting up the High Street in
the twilight, acknowledging and exchanging greetings with the
painters and sculptors in their ragged and brilliant clothes
who were loitering up and down the length of The Cowshed;
gossiping, arguing, scandalizing (in both senses) and pointing
out the place where, later on, they would like to see their own
particular work displayed. He paused at last by Chris, who
was squatting in front of a section of the canvas with which
The Cowshed was covered, and silently placing and replacing
against it a painstaking landscape; the colour was almost, but
some way below quite, brilliantly original.

"Hullo."

"Hullo." Chris glanced up, with his usual apple-smile and
hoarse mutter.

"That's nice." John's eyes dwelt respectfully on the landscape. A young Romantic of the eighteen-thirties in Paris,
a dandy with the loftiest sentiments hidden beneath his
superbly-fitting coat, would see nothing but genius and
unbounded promise in the work of his friends. "Is it recent?"

"Just finished. Rekkernize it?"

"It's the Canal, of course."

"That's right. I painted it through his window; he leant me
his room for three days. Good old Benedict; I like him; and
that's the truth."

"Do you happen to know where he is this evening?"

"At the caff, same as usual . . . like Nerina." Chris smiled.
"Only another hour to go, and I'll be meeting her."

"Oh yes, the caff, of course. Give her my love."

"You bet I won't," Chris ducked his shaggy head with a
Bœotian laugh.

"Er—do you know if they make a horrible fuss if one
telephones him there?"

"Depends if it's after ten, John. They pack up, then, see,
and they're all clearing up, and they don't mind if you 'phone.
Got through last week to him without no bother when we was
fixing up about me borrowing his room."

"I see. Thank you. I do like that painting, Chris, it's . . . I
must be getting along; I've got to meet someone in London
who may be giving me a job. Good night."

Chris said *bye-bye, John*, and John went on down the High
Street.

He possessed sevenpence; he was wondering whether to

spend most of it on telephoning his friend, but decided to walk
to Kingsway, where the restaurant in which Benedict worked
was situated, and hang about until he came out. He had a
plan; it had come to him earlier in the evening and now he
could not wait to begin setting it in movement.

How he enjoyed this preliminary interlocking of words and
actions, this cautious and cunning scattering of the first grains
of the powder-trail that should lead to some desired explosion,
great or small. (All his analogies were drawn from the boys'
books—*Wolf on the Trail, The Path of The King, Child of Storm*—
that he had devoured in the house at Marlow to which he had
been evacuated during the war.) This moving about of human
beings and influencing, if only in small ways, the pattern of
their lives, was what he liked doing best next to wandering, in
a dream, yet observing and hearing all that was going on about
him, through London's streets: while he was making the first
telephone call, in a box at one of the Underground stations
whose walls, of some diggable plaster substance, were gouged
with holes and scribbed over with numbers and names; or
uttering the first seemingly casual sentence while leaning back
in his chair at a table whose blotched surface was scattered with
crumbs and ash in some hot café reeking of fried food, he saw
the people whose lives he was thus gently fingering not as
living beings but as characters, even as he was a character, in
a story: and they were linked and mingled, too, in a kind of
strongly pleasurable confusion, with the manuscript, growing
ever more stained and inter-and-over corrected and crossed,
which he carried in the portfolio that hardly ever left its place
against his side.

Now, while he sauntered down through the soft grey streets
towards the deep canyons filled with dark and glowing air in
the heart, he was already savouring the pleasure with which he
would, in a short while, be saying unimportantly to Benedict:
*I want to look at the Steyne Collection in that beautiful house in Castle-
reagh Square; will you come along some time?*

She was so full of malice, so dirty and cruel. He hated her;
he wanted to see her made angry and helpless. Perhaps she
might have feelings that could be hurt, under that manner of
hers, and that would be best of all, but if he could only make
her really furious, he would be content. She was in the place
that he ought to be in, having the attention and company
which belonged naturally to him, and he hated her.

It was going to be delightful, planning to disturb her life and carrying the plan through.

Now he was lounging against the wall, in an alley of brown shadows that ran alongside the restaurant, concealed in a doorway under a dusty laurel bush, with the portfolio lying warm and worn against his side. He was completely happy, waiting there for Benedict, and mulling over his plan, and so vividly imagining the scarf of spotted silk about his neck into a stock, and his loose jacket into a fitted redingote, that if he had glanced down at them he would, perhaps, have seen what he imagined. And there was the loitering, staring, bright foreign crowd drifting past, down Kingsway on the track to the West End, and the passing faces pouring their images copiously and unendingly, with attendant fancies, into the mirror within him. At this period in his short span of time here, John Gaunt was delighting in the cries and movements of the living creatures in the world around him, and had not yet begun the agonizing struggle to crystallize them and to fix the moment, to which all that he was and had, and finally his life, were to be sacrificed.

So he was happy, and it was as well that someone should be, because none of the people who had loved him from childhood, or had learned to love him since, were ever going to be happy about him again.

CHAPTER THIRTEEN

ELIZABETH HERE

A few days later, at precisely one minute to four by the rather tortured-looking clock in the Rosa di Lima Espresso bar, Nell saw, from the bench where she had with difficulty been keeping a seat, a plump form in a bright blue linen suit leisurely making its way down the room between the pots of grey foliage and red flowers and blown-up photographs and all the rest of it. . . . She also saw, with some dismay, two debbish forms unmistakably following.

"Sely darling!" said Elizabeth, sliding into the empty seat and pushing four good-sized parcels into the side of a darkish type inoffensively reading *Le Matin* who at once whirled himself politely away to the extreme end of the bench ("Oh, *how* nice of you, thank you so much," to the type) " . . . *lovely* to

see you again. These are Penny Carleton and Cam Seton"
indicating the debbish forms, "I knew you wouldn't mind
my bringing them: they won't be with us for long because
they have to get back to their jobs. Now where can they sit?"
gazing consideringly about her. "That woman in the white
hat with the man in grey has nearly finished. You had better
go over there and wait . . . oh, have you? Well, thank you,
then," as the darkish type thrust *Le Matin* into his pocket and
smilingly indicated the seat he had vacated, "you can both
squeeze in here. What a good thing it is you are slim."

She turned to Nell, who wore a broad silent smile. "How
fetching you look, Sely. I love green and white stripes. You
don't have to diet, I expect. (I suppose I should, but I won't.
It *would* be nice to swan around the town like Fiona C.-W.,
with a waist like a sigh, but I *cannot* get through my first Season
on black coffee and lettuce leaves.) Now let us all have coffee,
and four of those things with apricots . . . yes, those are the
ones," as a quiet and beautiful girl with red hair wheeled a
trolley laden with delicious cakes to a standstill before them.

"I've only been home just over a fortnight, but already
Espresso bars are one of my things," Elizabeth went on, when
they had been served, "I've been to twelve, some of them two
or three times. My other thing is tarts. So it is Penny's and
Cam's, isn't it?" Four gentle eyes turned to Nell, sparkling
with amusement. "Are you mad about tarts, Sely?"

Nell had to admit that she was not.

"Oh, all my girl friends are . . . heavens, this coffee is good.
(I've bought four pairs of shoes this afternoon and I am
exhausted, but completely exhausted.) And Penny is also mad
about Hump Lyttleton, but she gets hardly any time to hear
him play because she's a student-nurse, poor martyr. But she
seems to like it."

"Daddy made me do it. You see, my sister is one, and
that gave him a taste for having us all do it," Penny bleated
softly.

"And Cam helps a great girl named Joanna Ponsonby run
a riding school at Richmond (but she won't be there for ever,
because the clever girl has just got herself engaged; Cam has,
that is. Not Joanna. Oh no! Joanna is the kind that has a bath
in her jods)."

"She's very nice," Camilla said suddenly.

"She's terrible," Elizabeth said firmly. "Penny and Cam

both make me feel a frivolous and worthless bubble, like Gaby
Deslys or Polaire (did you read that book of Cecil Beaton's,
The Glass of Fashion? I loved it. It's all about pre-1914 tarts,
with drawings of them in saucy hats). I'm not going to have a
job. There *was* a suggestion that I should suffer at Mrs. Dela-
warre's Secretarial hell, but we soon disposed of that. . . . No. I
shall swan around the town for a year or so, and then marry,
I think. And how about you?" (to Nell). "Are you engaged?
Walking out? Not? Me neither. I *cannot* get ready to be presented *and* be in love . . . though of course I'm absolutely
man-man. Think about nothing else," nodding joyfully.

But here she gave her chin a little pull inwards, so slight a
gesture that only someone knowing her as Nell did would have
noticed it, and went easily on—"but as most of the young men
who were my childhood friends are away, doing mysterious
courses in Cornwall or the Highlands, I haven't managed to see
many people . . . and of course I've been so busy getting ready.
. . . Penny was done last year, weren't you? and Camilla won't
be done until next year, so we are rather like The Three Bears
. . . but I *have* managed to see some plays . . . have you seen
'The Boy Friend'?" (to Nell).

Penny here put in that Mummy kept *on* seeing it; she and
Daddy had been about ten times; and, with Camilla blurting
that her's were just the same, the conversation became one
which Elizabeth deliberately did not dominate, although Nell
could see her steering it, tacking it to and fro, portioning it out
nicely between the four of them, and plainly enjoying doing so,
while her gay blue eyes laughed out of her round pearly face,
and the thick fair hair surrounding it, which was the kind the
Edwardians used to call 'fluffy' and which she refused to have
styled, glittered faintly in the pink light.

They had to hear about Nell's job, which they commented
upon by sighs of envy; and when she had made Penny and
Camilla laugh softly and Elizabeth utter the kind of snort,
well known at Claregates, as indicating satisfaction as well as
amusement, by her descriptions of Tansy and the begging-bowl,
the other two announced reluctantly that they must go because
they had to be back at their posts. So they prettily made their
farewells and went.

"Does Cam have to work in the evenings?" Nell was watching Penny's rather drooping progress down the room between
the vaguely South American women and their dapper men,

and thinking that all the girls there, except these three, looked over-excited and over-tired.

"Not really *work*. But there are always things to be done to the horses, and she lives in. . . . I was surprised to see *her* out of her jods; she hardly ever is; and as Robin, her young man, *doesn't like horses* (if you please), and much prefers her in skirts, I don't know what will happen there. But I fear me, I fear me very much. . . . " She leant forward across the table " . . . now that those worthless girls have gone, Nell, you must tell me really all about you. You've been having a nasty time. I can see it in your little face."

Nell had not realized how much she needed to talk to a listener as excellent as Elizabeth could be when inspired by affection as well as by her good manners, until she began to relate, though very briefly, the events of the past eighteen months.

But she was a little saddened by the flicking dismissal of Camilla and Penny.

She had to remind herself that, even if Elizabeth did refer to *her* 'behind her back' as *a worthy type, name of Sely*, she also did so 'to her face', and that her friend's slighting comments upon other types at Claregates had been accompanied by a steady and unfailing kindness in action, which Nell never remembered having seen departed from. She could not recall one spiteful or petty act, and countless ones of rather impatient chivalry.

Nell was thinking—while she quickly related the growing concern which she had felt about the health and welfare of her parents, and gratefully saw the understanding nod given by Elizabeth, a girl who also felt properly about her family—how much she hoped that her friend and John would never meet. Elizabeth, she felt certain, would have the lowest possible opinion—

"Hullo, Nell. May I come and sit with you?"

She stopped talking. She looked up. And there, wearing that outrageous striped blazer, and smiling down at her with his hair rather smoother than usual, was he.

"Oh . . . John," she stammered. "Yes . . . well, we were . . . oh yes, there is a seat, isn't there? . . . yes, do. You don't mind?" turning to Elizabeth, whose expression had suddenly become very polite, and who smiled and said, "Of course not."

"This is my cousin, John Gaunt . . . Elizabeth Prideaux. We were at school together."

"So I have heard you say," he said pleasantly.

He was hardly looking at Elizabeth, and Nell, amidst her confusion and annoyance—her cheeks were crimson—wondered why; he usually turned all his attention and charm upon a new acquaintance, but he was now fully engaged in trying to catch the eye of a waitress.

She did not look at Elizabeth, who was serenely surveying the room. He must have come here deliberately, she thought; he overheard me arranging things that day at home on the telephone; he can't bear to be left out of *anything*; really, he is a *trial*. . . .

He turned, smiling. He had now given his order.

"I expect you have already eaten quite a lot, haven't you? But do have another cake . . . and won't Elizabeth, too?" Now he slowly, deliberately almost, turned to her.

So he has some money today, has he? Nell thought grimly. What *is* all this? Showing-off in front of my deb-friend?

"Oh we couldn't possibly, thank you so much," said Elizabeth, with an effect as if someone had slammed a door made of sugar, "we were just going. We have to do some vital shopping."

"But I have ordered them. I can't possibly eat three great rhum babas."

"*I* thought you were going to," said Nell. The circumstances, and her feelings, had really aroused her temper.

"Oh no, Nell. You know that I eat almost nothing. But I *am* rather exhausted this afternoon, because . . . here come the babas. Yes, please . . . " to the waitress. He superintended the placing of them in front of the girls, who had waited a moment too long, and who now, without appearing ruder than Elizabeth cared to, or Nell dared to, could not get up and go.

"That looks awfully gooey and good," Elizabeth said, not even giving the impression that she was giving in gracefully. She took up the clean fork, and Nell, seething, did the same.

"They are good, aren't they? Yes . . . I'm rather exhausted, Nell, because I've been having a long talk with Benedict."

He turned to Elizabeth.

"This is a friend of mine who's a poet; I think he's a *great* poet; *the* coming great poet of the age." He turned again to Nell. "He's having a play in verse, called *Prometheus In Nevada*, broadcast on the Third Programme soon, and they've bought some of his shorter poems too, and he's very pleased because on the strength of it he can give up that appalling job.

We've been working it all out . . . I *think* I can persuade my
papa to let him have a room at home, for next to nothing, of
course, and then he can work in peace and comfort. (That
room overlooking the Canal was having a *most* unfortunate
effect on him, *I* think.) He expects the B.B.C. will offer him a
job at any time now."

"Well, you won't like that, will you?" Nell was eating her
baba very fast and crossly. "You're always saying that he ought
to write poetry for three years like mad and then die."

"Oh, I don't think I ever said that, did I, Nell? You must
have misunderstood me." His tone had just the right note of
indulgent surprise (poor Nell; rather a scatterbrain).

But Nell could feel that Elizabeth was now listening with
something more than conventional politeness; not, Nell was
both relieved and irritated to think, because she found John
an interesting type, but because she was interested in what he
was saying.

"I've been worried about Benedict, as you know, for a long
time," he went on.

"Kind of you," Nell bolted the last fragment of baba and
put down her fork. Elizabeth glanced at her with a little surprise.

"He looks so ill. It's a lot to do with that dreadful girl, of
course."

"I hope you like hearing about people you've never met,
Liz," said Nell, angrier every moment at what she thought was
an elaborate display, meant to impress Elizabeth, of gifted
friends in thrilling situations.

"It depends." Elizabeth bent forward. "Why is she a dreadful girl?"

Nell knew that she was hoping Gardis was a contemporary
version of the ladies in *The Glass of Fashion*; well, I suppose she
is, in a way, Nell thought, only I never think of her as being.

"Oh, she just is. You see, she's got him like that," extending
a big square thumb whose shape should have warned anyone
what strength of will was lodged within its owner, and planting
it on the table. "Like *that*," wriggling it about. "And she's
simply horrible to him and she's bad for his work, too."

"Really? I thought you said that they ought to be together
for twenty years of biting and clawing, because that sort of
thing 'keeps poetry alive'." This was Nell.

This time he did not trouble to answer. The fish was hooked.

But as he earnestly began to say to Elizabeth, who was leaning towards him with a look of frank curiosity, "She's an American, Gardis Randolph (yes, isn't it odd? I think it must be Old French—but, as I expect you know, they have a passion in the Deep South, where she comes from, for exotic girls' names), and at the moment she's being secretary to my mamma,"—he was making himself a promise to punish Nell. She was being *beastly* this afternoon, and why *should* she? She couldn't possibly have guessed about his plan; she was much too simple. It was just bloody-mindedness.

"If she really is such a character as you describe, it seems odd that he likes her," was Elizabeth's comment, at the end of an account of Gardis's malice, grubbiness, rudeness, secretarial ineptness and general undesirability, and he smiled and said gently that it did, didn't it, but then Benedict was a nice person, and loyal.

Having accomplished, in spite of the unexpected opposition from Nell, what he had set out that afternoon to do, he suddenly recollected that he had to meet someone who might be going to give him a job posing as a model for an advertising agency, and begged that they would excuse him; he would settle their bill on his way out; and after making charming farewells, off he went.

Nell waited with dour satisfaction to see him confronted by a bill including two cups of coffee and four cakes whose existence he did not suspect. Sure enough, there was a little confusion and explanation with the waitress, but he got through it successfully, presumably, as he was allowed to leave the place.

She saw him going away, with his deceptively slow walk that could easily cover miles of London's streets in so short a time. He might have to go without food for the rest of the day, and walk back to Hampstead. Serve him right, thought Nell. After all, he was used to it. She was seeing him, a little, as Elizabeth had presumably seen him, who was accustomed to the society of young *men*, who worked hard and played hard and had—only of course they never spoke about them—the proper ideas.

He had behaved this afternoon even worse than usual; showing off, popping in upon them uninvited and telling lies about his opinion of Benedict's affair with Gardis, and the way Benedict lived. Why? again. Nell had no idea; she usually had no idea about why he behaved as he did, but this afternoon she was very cross with him indeed.

She hoped that Elizabeth would not say anything about him.

"Come with me to Harrods?" said Elizabeth, when they were out in the street again. "I have to buy a brassière for Prideaux's Pride . . . good. It's so nice having this flat Mummy's just taken for us in Knightsbridge; you must come and see it soon; and it has a lot of domestic gadgets; of course we could never afford to have them put in at Prideaux, and Daddy wouldn't even if we could, but he loves playing with them, and he's simply glued to the television set; we can't prise him away . . . what a *blossoming* hat. Do you ever wear a hat? I do sometimes; Mummy likes me to."

They stopped to admire the hat.

"Do you see much of your cousin?" Elizabeth asked, in a rather too-creamy voice, as they went on.

"More than enough," Nell answered in a sharp and decided one.

She had made up her mind that, as Elizabeth would be much more likely to expect Sensible Old Sely to disapprove of that extraordinary little boy than expect her to be, well, *tolerant* about him, then disapprove of him Sensible Old Sely would. "He lives in the flat at the top of our house. So I have to."

She did not, however, think that Elizabeth could really be interested in someone aged about seventeen and what Nell felt about him, and sure enough, when she had given her friend the curtest possible outline of John's way of life and referred to the general hope that National Service might 'knock some sense into him', Elizabeth's "How peculiar. Perhaps he went to the wrong kind of school," was followed at once by:

"I do think that Benedict-man sounded fascinating . . . is he really like that? So clever?"

So this was the true point of interest. Nell's relief that Elizabeth was apparently going to see John, and what Nell felt about John, exactly as Nell wanted her to, was now warmed by the pleasant idea that perhaps Elizabeth might 'do' for Benedict?

Of course, one did not introduce one's friends to each other with such notions in mind, but if these two should happen to meet, naturally it would be nice if they took to one another.

Nell knew little about Benedict's work, except that she had not liked what she had read of it, or whether it would be good for *him* if he and Gardis were to separate, but she had never once seen them looking at peace when they were together; Gardis had always worn an air at once triumphant and cruel, and Benedict had looked dazed and wretched.

"Yes, he really is awfully clever," she said decidedly, "and I think he will get on, you know."

"I've got rather a taste for intellectuals just now," Elizabeth said, thoughtfully, in a moment, "I'm sure I could run a salon. ("Oh, do look at that ravishing shortie nightgown.) It all started with one of the creatures at Les Rosiér's brother; he was staying in the village (*supposed* to be painting, but really getting off with everybody under fifty, *I* think), and the girls and the staff used to get rather excited about his work and his goings-on generally. I used to talk to him rather a lot; he was good for my French."

She broke into a flow of precise yet babbling sounds that Nell had difficulty in translating. "But he had a dirty beard, and that I *could* not take," she went on, "Has Benedict a beard?"

"Not so far," Nell said cautiously, "but they do tend to grow them suddenly, you know."

"I do know one artist, but his father is a very famous painter, and that rather cramps poor Roddy's style. He paints nothing but apples. Well, I shall hope to meet your Benedict, Nell. And I mean it."

"He isn't in the least mine, Liz. He's very much Gardis's." Nell hesitated; three months of London life under the tuition of John had removed most of her inhibitions, in conversation at least, but she still hesitated occasionally. "I think they're . . ."

Elizabeth nodded mysteriously. "But *that* may be an advantage to the attacking side."

Then, as they were entering the portals of Harrods, no more about Benedict was said.

It was almost a fortnight later that John and Benedict were wandering through the lofty air-conditioned rooms of the mansion in Castlereagh Square where the Steyne Collection is displayed; pausing before gilt and inlaid furniture, and pointing out to one another—that is, John pointed out, while Benedict apathetically stared—china figures of fairy delicacy, and miniatures glowing with the ethereal, yet intense, blues

and greys and rose-colour which seem to belong to this art
alone; while the fact that they were almost the only visitors
made each object appear to display its peculiar beauty with an
added, concentrated, silent force. Chandeliers flashed stilly
in the sunrays, the deep browns and purples gleamed along
the lustrous wood of Empire desks and tables; and on the walls
Guardi and Canaletto displayed the stately splendours of
Venice above stretch after stretch of water, crisped into stiff
grey wavelets or green and flowing, yet never presenting the
disturbing quality of life. Always the scene was blessedly
removed; into that realm where it can charm, delight and
console the poor human eyes that behold it.

John would have been rather bored with these beautiful
things, had he been required to give them his full attention,
for he preferred living objects and more fluid scenes, but he
was seeing and using them as part of the plan which he was
this afternoon zestfully executing.

At the moment, he was neither speaking nor apparently
moving in any particular direction, but dawdling through the
rooms with a vague gaze, while Benedict, whose face was
greenish following on a night of heavy drinking, was silently
wavering after him. John had what he used to call, when he was
a little boy, *butterflies in his stomach* as he loitered through a
doorway which he had carefully noted during a visit made
alone, some days previously.

Benedict was feeling sick. He was also wondering, in a
dazed and confused fashion, whether his creative power and
technical ability was of the kind that would benefit from being
compelled to apply itself, industriously, copiously and almost
unremittingly. Could his gift be forced, in short? If it were big
enough it could respond without being damaged, but was it big
enough?

He was almost satisfied with *Prometheus In Nevada*, and that
had been a commissioned work, of which not a line had been
set down on paper until he had been told by the Third Programme people that if he would write it they would use it.
And now it was written, and it was true poetry; even those
damned 'bridge passages' that were always such brutes to do,
were plain and light, supporting the gorgeous or the horrific
. . . It was tempting to believe his gift *could* stand being driven.
But then there was Wordsworth, poor old man, outwriting
himself so pitifully . . . and some contemporary examples he

could think of . . . and Keats's fatal remark—or so Benedict thought—about *loading every rift with ore*, so that the lines hampered the imagination like a voluminous, over-rich (or over-dry, for that matter) trailing fancy dress. . . .

"That's rather nice."

It cost John an effort not to speak sharply, for he had set his heart on having ·Benedict's eye fall naturally upon the portrait while they were animatedly surveying the contents of the room, and now he had twice to draw attention to it, so absent and dopey was his friend this afternoon.

Benedict loitered to a stop in front of the oval frame whose richly tarnished gilt proclaimed that it was old, and stood there, vacantly looking. John stood quietly at his side, also looking, and compelling himself to wear an expression in which critical appreciation was nicely blent with admiration. Inwardly he was dancing with impatience. Was his miserable friend, who this morning looked more desolate and lost than ever he recollected seeing him, merely going to say "That's lovely," and stroll on?

But suddenly his machinations were crowned with triumph. Benedict actually made an affectionate mutter.

"What a poppet," he said.

She had a pearly round face, with fair hair drawn up beneath a turban of gauze. Her plump shoulders, set off by one glowing rose, came up out of a bodice of softly gleaming satin, but for most beholders, all those beauties would be subordinate to the charm of the smiling young woman, leaning slightly forward as if to bow a gay retort to a compliment.

"Isn't it a delightful colour-scheme, and *masterly* simple, just yellow and white and salmon-pink," John said. "It's so *clever*. And of course, so civilized." Her best friend, if she had any friends, could not have called Gardis civilized. There could hardly have occurred a better opportunity for implanting the idea of contrast.

"I suppose we ought to have bought a catalogue." His tone was innocence double-distilled.

Benedict shook his head. He was still looking at the portrait.

"They're half-a-crown and you tend to look at them instead of at the pictures. It says here who she is, doesn't it?" He bent closer; his sight was bad today. "She is—or was—the Honourable Georgiana Prideaux." He paused. "She could be lovely to kiss," he said.

John's emphatic nod concealed the opinion that the pleasure thus obtained would be heavily paid for by submitting to the will shown in that round, firm, Regency chin. "If I were a horrible old aunt, or someone of that sort, I should say it's so alive it might walk out of the frame."

"If that's what you really feel, why pretend you're a horrible old aunt? God knows the last thing one wants contemporary portraits of girls to do is to walk out of the frame, and then have to kiss them."

"No indeed. But such ideas about art are rather low, you know. Shall we be moving?" for John did not want to linger in front of the portrait until Benedict suspected that he was up to something; his friend had a disconcerting habit of suddenly emerging from the daze caused by hangover and amorous suffering and turning a very keen eye upon the surrounding landscape with figures.

Benedict slowly followed, blinking slightly with the pain of a headache which the brilliant shafts of sunlight striking upon the glittering and gleaming objects all about him seemed to intensify, and wincing as the thought returned on him, acute as toothache and harder to endure than his headache, that in less than a month Gardis would be flying home to America.

She was refusing to admit feeling any sorrow at leaving him, merely reminding him, when reproached, that she had only meant to stay in this dump for six months anyway, and what was there to stay for, now that she had learnt all that they had to teach her at the Art School, and a certain master there had left?

"Hadn't you better have some lunch?" John said rather irritably, turning at a slight sound which had been wrung from Benedict by an unbearable jab of physical jealousy; he was going to see to it that no young woman ever wrung groans out of him, "you look quite alarmingly green."

Benedict agreed with a rather unexpected docility, and they went to an open-air place in a park where he paid for five tomato sandwiches and two glasses of milk for John while himself eating nothing.

John ate and drank with a conscience as good as his appetite, for it seemed to him that this afternoon he had not only started to score off Gardis but had laid the foundations of Benedict's future prosperity and happiness.

As for his poetry, that must take its chance.

He himself believed that Benedict had taken the first steps towards destroying his talent when he had accepted a commission, and if he were going to develop into the sort of poet who could, before he was forty, invite the Douglas Fairbankses to breakfast, he would do so whether John steered him towards Elizabeth Prideaux, and her way of living and her managing temperament, or not. John felt that he might go on with his plan, and take and enjoy his revenge without seriously troubling himself about his duty towards the Arts.

CHAPTER FOURTEEN

NO-MAN'S-LAND

On the wall of his father's study in the old house at Eltham, Martin could remember, there had hung a large brown photograph of the youths and bearers of libations who wreathe eternally around the frieze adorning the Parthenon.

There had been a fashion for such earnest reproductions in the days of the old man's prime, even as now, according to descriptions brought home by Nell, there was a fashion for putting blown-up photographs of foreign buildings in these new coffee-bars.

The days when Martin had looked up at the picture with a reverent admiration, absent-minded only because his own vigorous young life was full and so all-absorbing, now not only seemed far away; they were far away: in time; in place; in spirit. For they belonged within the region of Nevermore.

Yet lately, with a fancifulness not usual in him, he had been thinking about that frieze and its youths, because it had occurred to him that the continual coming and going of young people up and down the stairs of the house, which was so quiet when he and Anna were alone in it, was like the young procession winding along the sober walls of his father's 'den'. He did not resent their presence, nor the having to open the front door to them and answer them on the telephone half-a-dozen times a day, although he realized that five years ago he would have been as annoyed by the constant interruptions as he would have been disapproving of the disorderly and planless lives which apparently they all led. Even judging them by the slacker and weaker standards that he had begun to form since his misery had fallen upon him, there was plenty to justify disapproval.

The glimpses of their activities which he from time to time obtained had been what he described to Anna as an eye-opener.

He had of course known that most youngsters nowadays had jobs, although he had never thought it necessary for a girl to have one if she had a father to keep her until she married, and a home in which she could be a companion to her mother, but when he had succeeded in accepting the idea that nowa-days *everybody* worked, he discovered a whole set that did not work at all, appearing to spend their days and their nights in talk (gossip, probably, dressed up as highbrow nonsense) and coffee-drinking and dashing off here and there meeting people who might be able to employ them for sums of money which seemed astronomical to Martin, until he observed that he was continually hearing in a roundabout fashion that, somehow, these jobs invariably failed to be given and paid for.

Then he began to feel pity for these young people, none the less because when he held a conversation with one of them that lasted for more than a few sentences, he met a front of such impregnable self-satisfaction that he positively quailed before it. He had been like that once; in the land of Nevermore —which, now that he came in these days of midsummer while he was watching the distant spire, to think about it—neither hurt him so much to remember nor seemed so desirable to return to as it had formerly.

He was in a country of the mind and feelings like the scored-up fields between the trenches which the chaps in the Great War had called No-Man's-Land; neither longing to return to where he had come from, nor acutely anxious to press on, and if another comparison once occurred to him, seeing Anna sitting upright with *The Pilgrim's Progress* held in front of her and her spectacles on the extreme edge of her nose, he dismissed it with a kind of jeering shame.

He, Christian! What infinitely petty moods and fusses and vague feelings *he* had had to endure, in comparison with the Giant Despair and the fearful Apollyon. Yet, thinking after-wards while he was out on one of those strolls through the unalarming back streets to which Anna had recently persuaded him, he had to confess that, if he were honest with himself, he *had* looked the Giant in the eyes . . . ah, and had fallen down flat before him too; on his face; in the dust; in the bitter choking dust.

Why?

He could no more answer that question now than he could have answered it on the morning two years ago when the Spirit had been withdrawn from him, but could say now that he was no longer miserable. He pottered about, and he enjoyed his potterings, and he liked being nobody in particular and having nothing much to do; and one afternoon in the middle of August, while he was making his way cautiously down that precipitous flight of steps which leads from Christchurch to New End, having glanced without a pang or a thought as he passed it at the church itself and thinking at that moment, as it happened, of what Anna might possibly have provided for their tea, he was filled again with the Spirit; there without glory, or solemnity, or vision or sense of dedication or even of bestowal; just a sweetness, and an intensification of everything round about him. That was—and afterwards when he was alone again and thinking about it he smiled at the inadequacy of the word—all.

The sweetness was such that it could be imagined a human creature would sacrifice, for the having of it again, and more especially if that intensification of the ordinary scene *were to increase and go on*, everything here that was loved and possessed; yet, even while he was thinking this, he knew that he would sacrifice nothing.

There was no need to. He had done, or been tried, enough; and now his immediate business was to get himself safely down these steps and home to tea, because Anna would have it ready and perhaps be wondering where he had got to, and he wanted a cup. And, in some way that appeared to be un-connected with time, the surrounding landscape and what was within himself became ordinary once more.

He went on cautiously climbing down, an ageing man with a red face in nondescript shabby clothes, mild and common-place as one of the myriad harmless insects darting and hovering in the sunlight: an untroubled speck; safe, and tempered, and beloved.

When, on an afternoon some days later, he began to make his way downhill through the streets due east towards where his

countryman's sense of direction told him that the church with
the tower of red brick must stand, he was only doing so because
this was what for some time now he had wanted to do, not
because he felt it was his duty, although he supposed that it
was that as well, now that he was healed.

He pottered along briskly, and the hasty absent gesture with
which he acknowledged a smile and bow of gracious condescension from a passing very small lady muffled against the
July sunlight in a fur tippet, set up yet another black mark in
Miss Lister's private score book against the Church, although
you would naturally expect anyone wicked enough to become
an atheist to be rude to ladies as well.

However, good came out of evil in that she spent a dramatic
session marching in and out of the dozen or so small shops in
Archers Lane and relating an account of her amiability and
his stuck-up-ness to Mrs. Bodger, Mr. Watfill, that nice girl
in Parke's and the others.

Martin, some half-an-hour later, found himself staring up
at the tower for which he had been searching. The streets were
full of children loitering and calling on their way home from
school; the day had clouded over, but pleasantly, and pigeons
and starlings were floating about the windows and orifices
with which the tower was pierced. The grey light was clear and
warm. Some workmen were sitting over their tea in the small
churchyard littered with buckets and mounds of cement and
beams, and he went up to them.

"Saint Saviour's, sorr." The voice was Irish and so was the
colour and shadowing of the eyes. "Yes, we've been refacing
the tower. It was bombed, and the church has been closed for
nearly twelve years."

"Opened last Sunday fortnight," said another man, "and
it was too much for the verger, it was. The excitement took
'im off. He's dead." There were lurking grins on the gay hard
young faces, which did not belong to what Martin would have
called decent working men. He was turning away, thinking
that he would just go in for a moment and find out if his prayers
felt any different when uttered *there*, as well, when the Irishman
said that the Vicar was just inside taking a look around, if the
gentleman wanted to see the church.

Inside it was dim, lofty, dusty and silent. There were dark
old pictures, and a strong smell of plaster, and the eagle on
the lectern glittered like fire. The altar was covered with a dust-

sheet, but the Lady Chapel was a bower of roses. A middle-aged man was coming slowly down the nave with his hands linked behind the back of his cassock. When he saw Martin, he smiled.

The smile did not become less when he heard Martin, after some remarks about the re-facing of the tower which were unconsciously touched with a recent professionalism, saying eagerly that he understood they had recently suffered a loss in the death of their verger and would the Vicar be prepared to consider himself as a candidate for the vacant post; in fact, it showed what on a lay countenance would have been greedy surprise, but when, realizing with strong satisfaction, while wondering what on earth Anna was going to say, that he was going to be accepted, Martin hurried on with—"Perhaps I ought to tell you before you come to any decision that I was in Orders myself until two years ago," it vanished, and the Vicar said "Oh."

"I suppose that makes a difference?"

Martin told himself that he did not mind if he were turned down. But how he was longing to get to work in a church again! The mere plastery, chill smell in here had made him anxious to begin.

"Well . . . you see, the trouble is that it might be . . . but shall we have a chat about it? Let's go into the vestry; it gets the sun about this time in the afternoon."

When Martin came out settling his hat on to his head three-quarters of an hour later, he could congratulate himself on nothing more than having brought back to the Reverend Denis Mollison's face the smile which anticipation of hearing a sordid story had banished. The lamb within the fold and the one outside had parted cordially enough, but Martin had had it firmly explained to him that the presence among the tiny congregation at Saint Saviour's of a verger who had formerly been a priest could be embarrassing.

They were simple people; practical, everyday Christians to whom theological speculation and the niceties of spiritual crisis were likely—Mr. Mollison did not think that any of them had so far come up against either—to prove very suspect in-deed. It often required, unfortunately, a certain worldly experience to make people tolerant of misfortune, unless its crushingly undeserved quality was clear and plain. Mr. Molli-son hesitated. Then he said with increased gentleness that he

feared most of them would take the point of view that Mr. Sely's
own Bishop had 'thought it right' to advise him to leave the
Church. That would prejudice the older ones among them
against their new verger; while the very few youngsters who
worshipped there might—he smiled—welcome 'a—a relish
with their tea.'

Martin smiled too, although something more than dislike
of being described as a tea-time relish prevented him from quite
seeing the joke. He got up, dusting the fine film of plaster from
his clothes. Mr. Mollison, escorting him to the little door opening on to the yard where a new crucifix of yellow wood cast its
shadow on the dust, promised to write to him giving his final
decision when he had thought things over.

As Martin climbed back through the crowded streets of old
white houses marred by the glaring smiles of advertisements to
Hampstead, he was telling himself that he did not care what
that decision might be, because now he was healed and filled
again, although nothing remained of his earlier experience
except the memory of it. But he did know how far he had come
from the misery of two years ago.

It looked as though God intended to manifest Himself to
Martin Sely by the sense of His Absence. Well, that had been
experienced by other people (Martin had done a little casual
dipping into the Theology section at the Public Library which
had not helped much), and if that was God's Will it must be
accepted. And it looked—the thought was cautious and
tentative but it was thankful—as though Martin Sely were
going to be able to accept God's Will with more than patience;
there was the possibility of joy.

He paused at the top of a hilly street, panting slightly, to
rest for a moment. He wanted to be the Verger at Saint
Saviour's, but if God did not want him to be, then he would
be happy in giving up his own wanting for God's.

The man, full of grace, went slowly on up the hill.

CHAPTER FIFTEEN

"SO ALL DAY LONG THE NOISE OF BATTLE ROLL'D"

"But I'm liking it, truly, Nell. It's lovely here; look at those poppets of ducks. What did you say this little park is called?"

"Waterlow Park. It was given to Highgate by Sir William Waterlow (that's him, over there, in the frock-coat and the beard). He was Mayor of London at one time."

Elizabeth glanced at the statue which Nell had indicated, and remarked that it was being an afternoon for statues, wasn't it?

The occasion was a party of pleasure, arranged to take place some days after the events just recorded, by John, who had shown throughout his discussion of the plans with Nell a casualness that had aroused her suspicions.

The participators in the excursion to Kenwood House, with the object of viewing the paintings of Angelica Kauffmann there displayed, were to be Nell, Elizabeth, Benedict and the impresario himself: and he had concluded his instructions by telling Nell that she must first take Elizabeth to see a statue lying forgotten in a ruined conservatory at Waterlow Park, which he called the White Nymph.

"But Highgate's miles out of our way, if Liz is coming to lunch with us first."

"Don't be so lazy, Nello. I *want* you to see the White Nymph. They have pulled down my old conservatory and are building something in mud-coloured bricks on the site which may be either kraals for the Jamaicans or a comfort station; it is too early to tell; but I love the White Nymph and I want you to see her before they take her away. You can walk over there after lunch and take the little 210 bus to Kenwood House."

So Elizabeth and Nell, having descended a dry secluded path shaded by trees and embowered in shrubs, and peered wonderingly in through a broken window at the fair spray-white sea-maiden lying on a marble plinth amidst ferns sprouting from the cracked floor, with the airy frame of the glassless conservatory for her roof, were now on their way to catch the single-decker which runs along Hampstead Lane to Kenwood House.

Elizabeth's doubts as to whether the work which she had just seen was really Art were pleasantly mingled with looking forward to meeting a clever poet, whom she already pitied because he was suffering in the power of an appalling girl.

The bus bounded along the wide, leafy 'select' road, whence blue glimpses of distant Hertfordshire patched with the pink of building estates could be seen between the mansions of rich Jewish families, and then it bounced to a standstill outside the lodge of Kenwood House. A few passengers alighted, and John, wearing clothes less noticeable than was customary with him, advanced leisurely to meet the girls out of the shade of Kenwood's great trees.

"Hasn't Benedict come?" Nell demanded, when the greetings were over. Her suspicions were increasing.

"He's wandering about inside," was the soothing reply, "let's go in, shall we? Well," to Elizabeth, "did you like my White Nymph?"

"I thought she was charming, but of course you can't call the poor poppet a work of art, can you? and as for that peculiar seagull hovering over her on a sort of marble stick . . . "

"No more peculiar, surely, than the birds executed (what an appropriate word) by Picasso?"

"Picasso is tremendous." Elizabeth's tone was light but final, and before John quite realized what was happening the conversation was running smoothly along quite other lines.

He was gratified to have his estimate of 'the managing puss' confirmed, but it settled him in his dislike of her; it seemed, if the plan were to succeed, that Benedict would be in a position to estimate the respective advantages of frying-pan and fire. But that had ceased to trouble John.

As they passed through the shrubberies which mask the great front and forecourt of the house, he was enlarging on his good fortune at collecting all his party together when some of them (a dig at Nell, who was still being unco-operative) worked at such uncivilized hours, and for once his elaborate air concealed something more than detached interest in the behaviour of those who were with him; he was excited. He kept his expression as serene as he could, but a distinct impression that the cat had got at the cream nevertheless seeped through. Nell had glanced at him more than once as she wondered why, and the next moment she knew.

He went ahead of them through the door into the long, low and spacious hall which begins the mansion. There, standing in silence under the ceiling gaily circled with painted blossoms and vines, was Benedict—and with him Gardis.

She was very much with him; she was standing so close to him that her ragged sweater and closely-fitting jeans of tartan cloth almost touched his side, and, while agitation hovered above the pair almost visibly, Benedict's passion was wretchedness as plainly as Gardis's was anger. Both were so lost in what was happening to them that when John addressed them they did turn round, but only to look at him for a moment without answering.

Benedict's face was a greenish-white colour. Elizabeth, looking into it with the calm courtesy of a girl awaiting the presentation of a young man, thought: *Gosh. Poor him. Hounds are pretty nearly up with the fox.*

"Hullo. Here we are" (Nell, furious at this totally unexpected addition to the party, thought that John was sounding fatuous on purpose), "and Nell's brought Elizabeth . . . you don't know each other, do you?" to Benedict, who turned slowly and looked at her, "Gardis Randolph . . . " he continued, "and that completes us." He continued to keep exultation out of his voice by remembering that only the first stage of the plan had been brought off.

When the usual murmurs had been uttered, and at John's suggestion and under his leadership they were all silently mounting the stairs to the upper rooms where Angelica Kauffman's paintings were displayed, Nell saw Gardis suddenly put hands up to her head, then give it a backward shake.

Down fell the hair. It was exactly the cry 'Seconds out of the ring!' translated into a gesture, and Nell noticed that John saw it too, for he just flickered a glance at Gardis while he was brightly drawing the company's attention to a self-portrait of Angelica hanging at the top of the stairs.

Elizabeth was also regarding the loosened locks, with no more than well-bred interest, but Nell hoped that her own wish for a warm relationship to grow up between Liz and Ben, which she now felt free to indulge because their meeting had not been brought about by herself, might not be spoiled by any liking of Elizabeth's for Gardis. Tart-ery, shared at second-hand, might be the fascination there, and, if she liked Gardis, Liz would not poach on a friend's preserves.

Or would she not?

Nell glanced at her, but the fair round face was giving nothing away.

While she made her first conscientious inspection of a canvas whose maiden in classic draperies with hair of a distinctive golden-brown displayed most of the qualities pertaining to the maidens and maidenly-looking youths in the other paintings, she was beginning to think that something serious must be afoot; otherwise John would not have laid out a shilling upon the catalogue which he was showing to Elizabeth. In a moment she saw him, out of the corner of her eye, distract Benedict from a pitiful attempt to look with interest at the paintings by asking his opinion about something, while Elizabeth offered her's from the other side. Then they all, even Benedict, laughed, and moved on together.

So that was it. Match-making, now.

Oh, well. At least he was not after Elizabeth for himself. And—except that he did so love plotting and running other people's affairs—it showed a kind thought for his friend.

The shining narrow boards of the floor creaked behind her, and she turned to see Gardis crossing the room. The clouded light poured down on the darkness of her face and hair and clothes; and probably it had never, since the house was built in the eighteenth century, shone through those windows on so fierce a version of the young *Incroyable* who always follows, with desperate steps, on the wreckage left by any revolution.

"How are we doing?" Gardis said.

Nell had an odd fleeting impression that she was being asked for help. She did not feel like giving any.

"The pictures? I think they're rather pretty."

"You've put your finger right on the trouble." The voice was almost a croak. "This gal certainly paints clear out of her sub-conscious." She paused.

"I didn't know you were bringing a deb along with you."

Nell said nothing.

"Maybe you didn't know that Ben was bringing *me*, either?", Gardis continued.

"Well ... as a matter of fact, I didn't." The answer was more amiable than Nell felt.

"I see."

Gardis swung round, and stared at the corner where Benedict and Elizabeth were looking at a small picture hanging high on the wall. The fresh, amused, decided sound of Elizabeth's voice came distinctly across the twenty feet or so between the two and Gardis, and Benedict was smiling. John had his nose almost touching a painting at some distance away, but Nell thought that the very back of his head looked smug.

She had never before seen Gardis look undecided, but she saw it now. It served her right, of course: the biter bit, tit for tat, and so forth, but the repeating of these smug yet sombre proverbs did not prevent one from feeling sorry for her.

"Don't you like any of them?" Nell enquired, indicating the nearest pictures; she felt a nervous impulse to say something conventional and forestall a possible outburst.

"Jeez no. Who could? Never saw so much cheesecake in my life. But I'd like a look at the catalogue. There's a gal here all canned up in armour. . . . I never saw a painting of a masculine protest before. . . . "

She turned round again, so vigorously that her hair swung with her. Nell saw that her hands were clenched into fists.

"Ben!" she called, "I want to look at your catalogue."

He turned, and came slowly over to her, holding it out, and there was no mistaking the reluctance with which he came. She stood still, not advancing an inch to meet him. It was the pose of the master awaiting the crawling return of the penitent dog, and although the mere sight of her was painful to him as a touch on an open wound, he had not emerged far enough out of his stupor of suffering to draw the comparison, for which John had hoped, with the face into which he had just been looking.

"Thanks loads."

She took the catalogue without glancing at him, and was going across to the picture which she wanted to identify, when Elizabeth, who saw quite well what was going on and was rather amused than otherwise, apart from much sympathy for 'Ben', came up to her saying: "Do come and look at this little picture of 'Poor Maria'; the others are pretty awful but this one really is rather sweet." However peculiarly other people might behave, Elizabeth at least was not going to forget her manners.

Gardis smiled at her.

It was the smile that she had given Nell when they were alone before the mirror in the house by the olive-coloured canal, when she had asked what Nell thought of Benedict and

John. We are women, aren't we, said the smile, and men are fools and beasts and rather rough, don't you agree? It was a false smile, yet it was like a distorting mirror in that it reflected something that was not false.

The smile which Elizabeth gave in return would have graced that Garden Party which she was shortly to grace herself; she was wondering how Gardis would look if she were properly dressed.

Gardis turned away. A wretched expression replaced the smile; this girl could not be more than nineteen at the most, and every month of Gardis's twenty-four years seemed hanging heavily upon her, and in Elizabeth's answering smile there had been no kindness or mercy at all. Gardis was in fact unaware that she had asked for any, but she stared up at the small painting in its unimportant corner without seeing it.

It was that son-of-a-something, John, who had planned the whole set-up, of course.

"'Poor Maria', who's she?" Her voice sounded rough and dull.

"She comes in 'Tristram Shandy'," Elizabeth was consulting the catalogue, "she was crossed in love, and she used to wander about the country with a pet dog or a kid on a string. It's a little dog in this picture. It was a favourite subject for painting on cups and tea-trays and things in the late eighteenth century, it says here."

"She looks singularly dotty," observed John, "but you're right, Elizabeth; it is a charming picture. She's being broken-hearted *so* comfortably."

(So it was Elizabeth already. Well, you didn't expect him to call her Miss Prideaux, did you?

I don't know what I expected. Damn.)

"I love those idyllic blue mountains. I shall see some Blue Mountains in the autumn. In Jamaica, where I'm going to stay with an uncle," Elizabeth said.

"How *love-lee.*" Gardis's coo might have been the usual American enthusiasm or it might have been mockery; no-one cared to decide. "I've got relations down there too. Where exactly are you staying?"

They moved on, talking as they went, and now finding the unspoken thoughts and passions and pains animating their own group so much more absorbing than the graceful classic scenes and figures on the canvases, that they gave the latter only perfunctory attention.

Nell had been wondering if she were crossed in love?

Oh no; to be that, you had to be first *wooed* and then deceived, and, except for his sneakiness about getting the key of the flat on that first evening, he had made no attempt to deceive her at all, while as for *wooing* . . . well, admittedly there had been a certain amount of what some people might call wooing, except that it had not seemed to have any object in view . . . she thought that it was no wonder Maria never got any better, wandering all over the place in those uncomfortable clothes with her hair down and a goat on a string and sitting down at intervals to lament . . . she should have done a day's work at The Primula, that would have soon set her on the road to recovery. . . .

Recovery from what? Of course I am not crossed in love.

"I think we've seen enough of this, haven't we? "It was his voice. "How about some tea? You can get tea here, in what used to be the stables when it was a private house."

When they were seated at two tables, pulled together under his supervision and arranged in the pleasantest part of the colonnade outside the stables, and he and Benedict had returned from the cafeteria with two laden trays, he drank some milk, and then observed to Nell that it must make a nice change to be waited on.

"It does. But actually the service isn't awfully good; you've spilt tea in my saucer," his cousin answered, aware of spite beneath his remark.

"I'm *so* sorry," he said, amidst laughter from some of the party, "but I haven't a waiter's temperament . . . one has to be born to waiting, I suppose."

"I probably was. I like it, anyway."

"Do you? Really?" Benedict roused himself to look at her. "God, I didn't. I loathed every minute of it. What in heaven's name do you *like* about it?"

"Well, there's always something happening. And I like seeing people cheer up when they get their food."

"Nice Nell," John said, with an acidly affectionate smile which set yet another black mark on his sadly ebon page in Elizabeth's private register.

"Well, I do. I'm going to have a tea-shop of my own. I've got forty pounds towards it already."

"Sely, what a *perfectly* extraordinary thing?" Elizabeth leant forward across the table, fixing the attention of the entire party upon herself and even arousing Gardis from her unseeing, jerky casting of cake crumbs towards a hopping horde of sparrows, "so have I! I'm going to have one, too."

"I don't think it's so extraordinary. Hundreds of people must have the same idea."

"But not two—" Elizabeth tucked in her chin and swallowed the word *virgins*, which had been coming out in the bell-like and uninhibited voice already attracting attention from the few weekday visitors at other tables—"two people educated at the same appalling school *and* having precisely the same amount saved. Now that is odd, you must admit. We ought to have one together."

"So we ought." Nell's eye gleamed.

"Only mine's going to be a coffee-bar."

"Ben, I want some more tea." Gardis thrust out her cup. But he was looking at Elizabeth, who was leaning forward across the table and laughing at Nell. The yellow rose pinned on her shoulder was drooping a little, from the double warmth of the day and of its resting-place.

"Did you say Prideaux?" Benedict asked her.

"Yes. Why? Do you know any of us?" She was still leaning forward and smiling, as if in gay retort to a compliment.

"That's it," he said, with a note of enlightenment and satisfaction. "It's the portrait, of course. I couldn't think where I had seen you before."

"Great-great-great Aunt Georgiana? Yes, we are alike, aren't we? I went to that worthless girl Prue Cunningham's coming-out dance as her, in an exact copy of her dress (everybody had to go as an ancestor *and poor Billy hadn't any*) . . . by the way, this," touching the rose, "is a descendant of the one in the portrait; we still have some bushes grown from the cuttings of the first one, at Prideaux." She smiled into his eyes. "I thought you might like that, you know . . . being a poet. A box came up this morning; Daddy won a First with them at the Morley show . . . isn't it amusing, our both being descendants?"

"And so resembling each other," Benedict said.

Her little bow and her laugh were as if the portrait had completed the gesture whose first stage the painter had caught upon the canvas, and the fascination with which Benedict was staring at her was plain enough to cause strong and varied emotions in those who were watching.

"John, Gardis wants some more tea. You'd never last a day at The Primula, you know." Nell's sharpness of tone was due to an increase in the cat-and-cream expression; he was positively *gloating*.

"I would not want to." He took the cup and twisted his way deftly between the tables, then paused. Occupants of the nearest one leaned stiffly away to escape a possible shower of tea-dregs as he gestured. "I know that nowadays educated people can earn large incomes by working with their hands; there are too many white-collar workers, you see, both here *and* in India . . . (you're only a social symbol, really, you know, Nell; a kind of *pointer*). . . . Irish dockers over here can earn fifteen pounds a week and in Australia they get thirty (pounds Australian, of course), you see, while the masses are waiting for atomic energy to set them free *altogether*. . . . "

"Do I get my tea?" called Gardis, and amidst advice from Benedict to confine himself to discussing subjects about which he knew something, John made off.

He was so anxious both not to miss any detail of the battle which was beginning, and not to betray his interest in it, that he returned with the full cup at a kind of leisurely lope which caused more rearrangements of posture at the tables as he passed.

He set the tea down in front of Gardis in a general silence which was eloquent. Something had been done, or said. And he had missed it. Damn Gardis; it was her fault; he hoped that whatever it was had been a reverse for her.

Elizabeth was now throwing crumbs to the sparrows. Nell was pink. Gardis was whiter than usual, Benedict was again pale green. No-one was looking at anyone else.

"How are we going to spend this evening?" John began, sitting down and beginning to sip the remains of his milk. "Elizabeth, I somehow feel sure that you have never heard Humphrey Lyttleton play, and I think that you ought to, and you would like to. It's a club, but I daresay I could find someone who could get us in."

"I'm playing tennis," said Nell firmly.

"I've got a life-class," mumbled Gardis, not looking up.

"That would be wonderful. Will you all come back to the flat for supper before we go?" Elizabeth said. She turned to Gardis. "Do come. Can't you cut your class for once?"

Gardis's lips were always painted the red of a pomegranate-seed. Now Nell, before she looked quickly away again, saw them set.

"All right. I suppose I can, for once." Gardis looked up, and at Elizabeth. "But I'll go home and change first, I think."

"Those clothes are perfectly all right for jiving, Gardis." This piece of information came from John, who did not want to see Gardis reappear in yellow silk and ropes of coral.

"Oh . . . well, guess I won't then. All right; thanks loads." She nodded and smiled at Elizabeth; nevertheless, everyone knew that a weapon had been most skilfully knocked from her hand. The effect upon the ringside seats was again varied; in the case of *one* it was not what might have been expected.

John now turned his attention to the cousin for whose observant and non-co-operative presence that evening he had no wish.

"I suppose *you* can't disappoint R. Lyddington?"

"It isn't Robert," Nell said, unmoved by this dig. "It's a girl I met at The Primula."

"Then put her off," Elizabeth said. "Or bring her along. Is she nice?"

"Yes. I don't know. She's Hungarian."

"Then you mustn't stand her up, Nello. She will get a bad impression of English manners."

"Who is R. Lyddington?" Elizabeth asked idly. "Do come, Nell."

John turned to her. "He is a worthy young man whom I call R. Lyddington because it's the kind of name you see under photographs of cricket teams, and that's what he's like."

"He might like to come with us." Nell stood up. "You don't mind, do you?" to Elizabeth. "I'll go and do some telephoning."

She marched off before he could speak, leaving John with his mouth open.

"What happened?" he murmured to her, while the five were waiting for the bus outside Kenwood House when the arrangements had all been made; in a group of two and a carefully animated three, separated by a safe distance.

It was typical of their relationship that he should forget all his annoyance with her, and his digs, and his spite, and assume that she would immediately tell him what he longed to know.

"What *are* you up to?"

"Shut up. They'll hear."

"What's it all *about*?"

"'Just trust me'."

"That's the last thing I feel like doing. . . . I suppose you're trying to push B. on to . . . someone else."

"He won't take much pushing. I say, isn't it exciting? I'm having buzzles down my back, aren't you?"

Nell turned that neat quarter upon him in pretence of looking up the road for the bus, but he gently swung her round again.

"Don't force me to *lay hands* on you, Nello. What happened?"

"Liz really started it. It was naughty of her. We were talking about having our tea-shop—and I really think she means it, that *is* exciting, now—suddenly she asked G., who was looking awfully sick, if *she* wrote poetry too, and G. said she didn't, and poetry stank, and *he* said that she didn't have to write it because (let's walk a little way on, shall we?) she practically was a poem herself. By—Rimbaud—I think—"

"Now perhaps you wish you weren't such a Philistine, Nello. Go on."

"I have heard of Rimbaud, John. It was something about G. being the original 'slum-child sailing its paper boat in the gutter'. S'sh!" as he uttered a low delighted whistle.

"G. went a most peculiar colour and stared at the table, and soon after that you came back."

"Thank you, Nello. In spite of being livid with me for being 'up to' something, I notice that *you* seem to have kept your beady eye pretty closely on the proceedings. You must admit that it's exciting."

Yes, but in a horrid way, Nell was thinking, as the bus bounced them back to Hampstead between the masses of July foliage arising from the valleys on either side of The Spaniard's Walk. She sat beside Elizabeth, aware, in spite of the absorbing nature of their conversation, of Gardis silent somewhere at the rear and Benedict silent somewhere up at the front.

Elizabeth suddenly interrupted herself in her speculations about the respective attractiveness of spotted or striped aprons for waitresses in Espresso bars.

"Sely. Am I being a cad?"

The tone, though subdued, was judicial rather than emotional, and her blue eyes looking straight ahead were calm.

"Say so, if you think so," as Nell said nothing.

"Not really, I think, Liz," at last.

"But not *quite* cricket, no?"

"Well, I never see why things can't go on as they are; unless of course they happen naturally."

"Not go out to get something if you want it?"

"Oh yes, of course. If it's a *thing*. But not a person."

"Then you've never wanted a person."

Haven't I? The reply which Nell suppressed suggested a more abject state than she believed herself to be in, and she dismissed it with a frown.

"I'm sorry for . . . someone, you know . . . but then I'm sorry for someone else too," she said.

Elizabeth's shake of the head was quite untouched by any shade of doubt. The chivalrous tradition in her family had imperceptibly, throughout the passing of four hundred years, assumed the shape of fair play, but it was significant that its definition still included the ancient *fair*, one of the master-words of the past.

However, at nineteen she was more of a woman than many a woman among her mother's contemporaries: and she did not extend the chivalrous family tradition to snakes, a category in which her observations during the afternoon had convinced her that Miss Randolph belonged.

"Do you want *someone*?" Nell asked, smiling.

"A little. It's very cuddley and so clever! (It's read simply masses.) And of course I like the way it fancies me. Someone else will just have to take its chance; it really deserves it, for wearing those clothes; and although I don't mind men being dirty, I really do dislike girls being; men hate it, you know."

Nell made no comment; she already knew that some men did not mind it at all but rather liked it. This dolorous information she had picked up, as usual, from her own particular Virgil who was guiding her through London; he might have said with another Latin poet: *Nothing human is disgusting to me*. She did not think that Elizabeth would learn the fact; if it ever confronted her, she would deny it.

"What is R. Lyddington like?" Elizabeth glanced at her. "Nice?"

"Very."

Nell did think of Robert, amidst all this plotting and planning and suffering, as being very nice, and wished that he had suggested playing tennis that evening with herself and her

Hungarian friend, instead of agreeing rather eagerly over the telephone to go to Elizabeth's flat for supper and then on to Hump Lyttleton's.

Perhaps John was right, and Robert did find his life rather dull.

She ventured a glance across the crowded bus, where her cousin sat beside an old woman whose superior proportions had not prevented him from typically securing most of the seat ... she knew quite well that *he* thought *Robert* dull: he had often hinted as much: and as it was an attitude he never assumed towards anyone but his parents, saying that a writer should be capable of finding interest in *anyone*, she could only assume that he was, after all, just a very little jealous.

It hardly gratified her: there was never any comfort; the situation between them was irritating and degrading and yet necessary; like smoking too much. Perhaps when he went into the Army ...

The pang was quite alarming.

She was pleased to see Robert waiting in the hall of the new blocks of flats where the Prideaux's apartment was situated, hatless and wearing a waterproof which contrived, like all his clothes, to look vaguely Naval.

The short walk from the bus stop had been embarrassed because of something John had said; and although Elizabeth's gift for controlling situations was successfully preventing the party from sinking into a failure, and although Benedict was now out of his earlier black mood and chattering and laughing with his hostess, Nell was always aware of Gardis slouching along with a white and sulky face. Nell's pity for her was now modified, however, by contempt; really, she was behaving like someone aged about eight who had had a toy, which in any case she did not much like, taken away from her and given to a nicer child.

"I'm so sorry you were here first, we got into a traffic jam," Elizabeth said to Robert, when the introductions had been made and they were all sailing upwards in the lift which he, mistrusting the capabilities of Benedict and John, had casually taken over, and was now operating, "but I am going to give you my wonderful spaghetti, to make up. My family are still in the country and so I can get at all Mummy's emergency stores ... we have a kitchen so full of gadgets that you can hardly get into it; you must see it." She turned to Benedict; the lift was small, but that was not altogether why she did not have to turn far. "Can you cook? I expect you can."

"Artists can always cook," John said grandly.

"I can't," said Gardis. "I don't have to. At home we've got a Philippino couple, as well as a waitress and a man, and the woman cooks."

"It must be wonderful to have regular domestic help. We have to rely on Manley, who's seventy-eight, and people from the village who don't always come," Elizabeth said.

"There's a lot of space to be covered back home. Fifteen bedrooms take some keeping tidy, and when you entertain as much as my mother does. . . . The house is always full—and the swimming pool."

Elizabeth's bright silence, with eyes fixed upon the door of the lift, was beautifully timed. She let Gardis's words linger just long enough for everyone to digest them, then said something graceful about the delights of having a swimming-pool, serene in the assurance that the thirty bedrooms at Prideaux would still be there, as they had been for four hundred years, if she ever should want to show them to someone. . . .

"Robert's getting his tennis after all," John said innocently to Nell, when they had all been made free of the flat and inspected its devices for ameliorating the misery of life in a great city. Robert was seated, on the cordial suggestion of his hostess, in front of the television set with his eyes fixed upon the last match of that day on the Centre Court at Wimbledon, and the living-room was almost in darkness. Nell had been sitting down to rest her feet, which ached even on her day off, but the almost complete silence from the kitchen, where the other three were now cooking supper, had convinced her that she could be useful there.

"What are you getting at now?" she said very quietly, stopping by John's chair.

"Well . . . he is, isn't he? Two kinds: Wimbledon Centre Court and another kind 'right here'. Whang! and into the net. Whang! Missed it again. Whang! Love, game and set, or however the jargon goes."

Nell was seeking for a reply which should convey both bewilderment and disapproval when Robert, without turning his head, said quickly, "Nell, you *mustn't* miss this, it's the most marvellous men's double—oh, wizard serve!" and she changed her mind about going to the kitchen and went to sit beside him.

In a moment she was a little surprised to find her hand being firmly held. If there had not been the long silent figure lying back in the chair behind her in the half darkness, no doubt sarcastically taking everything in, her sensations would have been all pleasant: and even as it was, satisfaction predominated. Let him see; it would show him that other people could like her. And there was a great deal going on this evening in which Nell herself was not actively engaged, but drearhood certainly had been left definitely behind; drears did not get their hand held in the dark.

Robert, with Nell's hand in his and first-class tennis going on before his eyes, had at the moment nothing left to wish for.

He had been considerably cheered, after a hard and dull day, to see someone like Elizabeth, and he was rather amused than otherwise by the three crazy Bohemian types, but for him Nell was, already, *Nell*; not like anyone else, sensible as a man, yet never suggesting any qualities but the desirable feminine ones.

He summed her up by the thought that she would never let you down.

In the kitchen, the spaghetti was drained and waiting for the sauce which Benedict was making, while Elizabeth flitted about in a blue apron and Gardis leant with folded arms against the wall, watching.

Her darkness of hair and clothes and eye, and much more her savage air, looked exceedingly out of place there. She belonged to the nation which had invented the white bulky devices for mechanizing housework by which she now stood surrounded, and she looked like a squaw from the forests who cooked in woodsmoke and ashes.

Benedict was scarcely conscious any more of her presence, for Elizabeth, when serving drinks, had given him the freedom of a bottle of General Prideaux's excellent whisky—not without pleasurable qualms as to what might happen—and he had had enough of it to blunt his pains. He felt warm and blissful; the mere absence of pain was blissful, and gone too was the sick pain in the pit of his stomach which had afflicted him since that moment earlier in the afternoon when he had called her *the original slum-child sailing its paper boat in the gutter.*

It was the first time that one of the insults with which in private he relieved upon her his sufferings had been uttered in public, and how she was going to make *him* suffer! He had absolutely quailed when he imagined it. But now, while the warmth of the whisky glowed within, and he was drawn into the warm sunny *ambiance* of the personality of Elizabeth without, he was not any more afraid or suffering, and if *she* were suffering he neither knew nor cared; he had come to the stage when he hardly believed that she could suffer. All he wanted was to go on feeling warm; and to hear his own voice saying silly, pretty things to Elizabeth.

"Your voice is delicious," he said suddenly, and the effortlessness with which the last word came out would have told a more experienced girl that he was used to saying difficult words while rather drunk, "it's like a syllabub."

He did not have to explain to her what that was; there was an ancient book of recipes at Prideaux . . . wine and cream . . . creamy roses . . . at Prideaux . . . Prideaux . . . and how many bedrooms are there at Prideaux, Elizabeth? Thirty. *Four-and-twenty bathrooms, a ghost on every floor* . . . that's from *Tantivy Towers*. Written before you were born. And have you a ghost at Prideaux, Elizabeth? Two? Tell me about them . . . the White Lady and the dog that barks, when no dog is there, to herald a disaster . . . but we do have dogs there, two darling ones, Rosa and Useless. . . . Tell me about them, Elizabeth.

Gardis stood with bent head and folded arms, listening. What were she and Ben doing here? with these kids; who didn't know anything about anything; virgins, starry-eyed; dumb.

The bitter inward colloquy becomes obscene.

She was very conscious of her dirty and ragged clothes, cursing the little son-of-a——, John, who had cut in with that crack about their being all right for jive, and stopped her going home to put on the new yellow number. She saw herself in it, with her hair coiled and smooth, patronizing the smug child who was taking Ben away from her.

"I'm so hungry——" she said suddenly and hoarsely.

"It's done, I think," Elizabeth said gaily. She looked at Gardis. "Shall we go and powder our noses? Robert can help dish up, if the tennis is over."

Gardis shook her head, then changed her mind.

She had intended to linger behind, and say something to him, but now thought that she must leave him alone for a while; she had never seen him like this before, and she had a sensation as if he were a thousand miles away from her.

She smiled, or her face did, and she followed Elizabeth.

Her raging nerves had set her heart hammering at the prospect of being alone with the rival whom she hated with a neurotic's intensity. She was swearing to herself that she would say nothing; nothing. Or no . . . she would spit something vile at her. . . .

"Robert, will you be sweet and help them dish up?" Elizabeth said, as they went through the living-room, "oh, the tennis *is* over; good. Keep an eye on them, will you? They don't seem awfully able to cope, although Benedict is a wonderful cook," smiling as he scrambled up from the floor.

To the relief of Elizabeth, and perhaps to that of Gardis also, Nell was in the bedroom soberly powdering her own rather longish nose before the mirror.

"I hope you didn't mind, Liz?" indicating an open box on the dressing table.

"Don't be a formal ass, my girl. (There's some rather glam scent there; do try it, it's just called *Ruby*. Very telling, no?) Well, I suppose I must change. (Do take anything you want"; to Gardis, "I think everything is there.) How about you, Sely? The loo? No? Well, well, things have changed since the Old Claregates Days, haven't they?"

They explained to Gardis, laughing and talking both at once, that their schooldays had been brightened by a booklet about the past years of the school called *Old Claregates Days*, with wonderful photographs of former staff in boaters and collars and ties.

"We were all given a copy of it the day we arrived, and told to read it, but there was a sort of tradition that you only read it in the loo. You kept it in your desk and whenever you saw someone with it you knew they were bound for *there*," said Elizabeth.

Very funny. Gardis, smiling, capped the story with one that made them both smile bravely too, with scarlet faces.

Then, her suffering slightly relieved, she sat down at the mirror and took out her lipstick of pale pomegranate pink. In the room there was now silence.

But they came brightly enough back into the living-room where John and Robert were putting the large platter of spaghetti on the table, and Benedict was lying back in an arm-chair nursing a glass of whisky with his eyes shut.

It was just seven o'clock.

It seemed to at least two members of the party that the day had already lasted some fifty-six hours.

Conversation for the next half-hour skated successfully along, only once avoiding a nasty corner when Elizabeth was telling how the Mrs. MacBridemont from whom her parents had rented the flat had come down on a short visit to Prideaux —which she had loved, dogs and Manley-who-used-to-be-odd-job-boy and everything; except that when she heard that Daddy sometimes read the lessons in church she talked about the *Christian Myth*—but then of course she was American.

In a breath-holding pause, Gardis asked dryly if that meant she just didn't know any better, and everyone was relieved to laugh.

Gardis felt drearily that for once she had almost been her age; it had been better to take it like that; and now the smug kid was red in the face; not because she'd been scored off, but because she'd been *rude*. Christ, the British. But undoubtedly it had been Gardis's point.

It was the only one she scored throughout the rest of the endless evening. In the taxi into which they crowded to be taken to Humphrey Lyttleton's club-room in Oxford Street, Benedict sat beside Elizabeth, and when they stepped out into the street almost empty of traffic and filled with crowds drifting slowly along in the ruddy glare of the chemical-burning lamps, he and she wandered, together, ignoring everyone else, down the unimpressive stairs leading to the basement. Gardis saw the backs of their heads, disappearing in the groups hurrying downwards, and it was one thing to know that he must sometimes go about with other women and quite another to see him doing it. For a moment she thought that she would go off and leave them; she couldn't stand it; it wasn't, she told herself, that she cared about him so much but there was this . . . again her thought became obscene . . . feeling . . . of having something taken away, and being lost, and let down, and drowning because it was going . . .

She ground her teeth together, hurting herself, and decided to stick it out. The evening could not last for ever; she would get him away after it was over; they would go off somewhere and she could give him the works; he and she could look into one another's eyes and smile then, as they sometimes did, not caring for anything in the whole bloody set-up. It was the thing that she liked best, of all the things they did. And that was crazy, too. Considering the things they did.

John was fussing authoritatively with tickets, and then they all made their way into one of those long, low and dimly lit rooms in which contemporary youth takes its austere pleasures; austere in the sense that no concession is made to the minor senses, but satisfaction is direct between audience and performer. The drab, worn colours, the dusty, smoky air and dim light and the sweet yet stinging flavour of soft drinks, the only beverages sold there, would have seemed dreary indeed to, say, Herrick, could he have compared them with the ravishing smells and heady root-brews and sweet sounds and clear air of a day spent pleasuring with his girls and hinds in the fields.

All around the walls people were already leaning. The rows of tables beyond these loungers were filling up. The two small bars were serving out lime-green and orange fluids as fast as they could get them over the counter, and every moment more and more young people came crowding in.

The party of pleasure which included Gardis and Benedict had seated itself at two tables near the band, which now, in jeans and shirtsleeves and with cigarettes hanging from lip, began to saunter onto the low platform at one end of the room; their instruments gleamed softly in the smoky dimness. They sat, blowing shortly and casually into their horns or tapping desultorily on their drums; pale, youngish men. They were a type, yet it was difficult to say in what the typicalness lay. Presently, when the room was almost full, one of them began to beat softly with a foot on the floor, and soon there was a deliberately hesitant yet decided theme wavering up into the air. No-one was dancing. The young men, greatly outnumbering the girls, stood watching, with a serious, listening expression. John turned from a conversation with Robert, to Elizabeth at the next table.

"Liz, will you dance?"

(Liz, now. Oh well. He is sure to get snubbed presently; he can't have any idea how crushing she can be when she likes.) Nell watched while he led her friend out on to the floor and began to jive with her in not too striking a manner, and giving her occasional advice (ha! she won't like that! nor will she like his making allowances for her not being very good at it in that condescending way. . . .)

She was surprised to have her reflections interrupted by a

request from Robert that he might lead her out; she had not even known that he could jive. John, so that she should not disgrace him, had given her some instruction in the style before he had brought her here some weeks previously, but Robert jived much better than John, putting into his movements all the energy bottled up during the day by costing accountancy, and giving his full attention to what he was doing, while John always, amidst his wildest and most graceful gyrations, kept in mind a possible audience.

As soon as they were all four well out on the floor, bumping and swinging between the flying forms and soon becoming indistinguishable amidst them, Gardis said to Benedict as if nothing had happened:

"Haven't we had enough of this? Let's go."

Without turning round, he shook his head.

"Oh, come on."

There was a pause. He kept his eyes, that burned and stung, fixed on the down-gazing face of a very young boy sitting at a nearby table; it was a thin and strangely pathetic face, lost in a dream.

"Let's go back to the flat," Gardis said.

This time Benedict heard the sound of the words: and their sound was ugly.

> *Retire we then, my may, to a greene bowre . . .*
> *Away, the moors are dark beneath the moon,*
> *We'll go together to my house in Padua . . .*

Let's go to the flat.

To the flat no more; we'll to the flat no more; the laurels are not only cut down but their dying scent is unendurably stale; yet, no more than three weeks ago, the most ordinary words spoken by Gardis had sounded with the romantic chime, and the ugliest places in which he and she had made love had shone in the romantic light. And he knew that if he were unwise enough to turn round now, and see her face, there would instantly rise up to hover between them the false cruel ghost, crueller than any torture inspired by true love, who haunts lovers when love is dying: the ghost born of memory and regret and the longing to be once more enslaved.

"*Ben.*" The voice was a croak.

But the number was concluded, and amidst the whistling

and applause the dancers were wandering off the floor and taking their seats once more at the tables, and he was rising to make room for Elizabeth. She was saying that she was terribly thirsty.

"I'll get you some orange juice." He began to walk rather carefully towards the direction where he thought the bar might be: you did not drink whisky out of the bottle in your pocket in front of a deb, but there was no reason in hell—or was there?—why you should not drink it behind her back.

But someone said decidedly, "I'll come with you," and the next moment he felt a firm warm hand slipped into his. His "Oh, but . . ." was effectively silenced with a pressure by no means experimental, which he returned with violence, feeling Gardis's eyes locked on the two locked hands, and they went off.

"Dear me, what warm work jiving is."

John had sat down, apparently absently, in Benedict's vacant place. He now gently pressed his forehead with an exceedingly grimy handkerchief and surveyed Gardis, who was sitting upright with hands clasped on her trousered knees, staring stonily at the floor. What he saw almost satisfied him, and he said genially:

"Poor dear, I'm afraid you're having rather a dull time. We ought to have got you an extra man. (Don't growl like that— I only mean that one provides men for you as automatically as one does meat for a lion . . . but your growl was quite natural, I suppose, in the circumstances . . . long past feeding-time) . . . *really*, Gardis!" as her head jerked up and she said something.

He glanced quickly at Robert and Nell; their cheerful conversation appeared undisturbed, but he was amused to notice that the small ear he could just see on Nell's averted face was deep crimson. She had heard. She had also understood, which was more than she would have done four months ago. His education of her had been in some ways very successful.

But only in some ways. He had to admit that. She still did not hesitate to show disapproval. One day soon he would have to test her and cure her of that.

The silence that now lay between Gardis and himself was something more than the stillness lying over the entire room, but the room was very still, because Humphrey Lyttleton was playing a solo.

He stood with the familiar sideways stance, blowing and warbling like some leviathan riding in its own element, and the powerful noise bewitched the room. Benedict stood with Elizabeth near the wall, unable to resume progress with their drinks, but held there, both by the attentive hush and by the force of the figure and its playing.

When they got back to their table, and the soft drinks were being consumed, it did not occur to anyone, even those suffering most, to suggest in the midst of the discussion about where they should go next—that they might break up the party and go home. Nell and Robert could have offered the excuse of having to keep early hours in order to keep regular jobs, but never once thought of doing so.

Elizabeth was telling herself that she had now got her back up and her teeth in, and meant to be in at the death, although the pearly face which became calmer and gayer as the evening wore on did not permit these sporting resolutions to appear thereon in changes of expression.

John was quietly gloating; Benedict had begun to wish that he were dead; Gardis was in the state of one who bites on the aching tooth.

Nevertheless, the discussion as to whether Bunjie's was 'better' than The Nucleus, or The Rosa di Lima could offer more than The Schubert Lounge, went on; while the dancers dipped and bumped in a ragtime number, and when the jam session broke up, at eleven o'clock, and the audience drifted out into the street, the party was still undecided.

They stood about, arguing. The young crowd eddied round them on pavements dim with summer dust: a girl stood on one leg, while she inspected a foot that had got a splinter during the bare-footed dancing; the glow and murmur and red darkness of the West End at night gave to the advertisements and the traffic, and the avid, lost, or empty faces wandering past, the quality of a scene on the stage.

At last John said decidedly that if they all went back to Hampstead to the flat, they could eat a large haddock that he had seen there in the refrigerator and drink some of the hock given to his father by a wine firm; one should drink hock with fish: and although this was regarded as an anti-climax to the evening's pleasures by everybody except Benedict, who had some whisky at home, that was what they did.

All the way in the taxi up the long hill leading to the sweeter-smelling, darker air of the village, Gardis was quiet. Nell would have thought her asleep, but that sometimes a passing light gleamed in the black depth of her eyes. Her expression was very sad, and for the first time Nell wondered at how old she could look for someone aged nineteen. Elizabeth kept her stubby, distinguished profile turned to the passing roads with a rather resolutely serene expression; and Benedict was humming a silly little Swiss tune over and over again in a manner undeniably suggesting drunkenness rather than gaiety.

Some confusion was added to the situation by the encountering, as Nell cautiously unlocked the front door, of Anna and Martin on their slippered and pottering way up to bed; unprecedentedly late, surely, and so absorbed in some discussion about vergers and a Mr. Mollison and a letter which had apparently just been posted, that they gave the party crowding in through the front door not much more than absent smiles and wavings ahead up the stairs.

"You're awfully late, Mother; is everything all right?" Nell paused a moment half-way up the flight, looking down at the two reddish, sleepy faces. Four months ago she would naturally have said: "Is anything wrong?"

"No, dear. Daddy has accepted a job, that's all."

"Oh, *not* with Aunt Peggy?" It was the first thought.

"Of course not: that was a very silly idea of your aunt's. He is going to be verger at Saint Saviour's in Kentish Town."

"*Verger?*"

"Yes. We heard from the Vicar by the four o'clock post. It's going to be great fun."

Anna's face showed not the faintest shade of warning and her tone was the usual brusque calm one, yet Nell took the cue so quickly that her father's half-irritable, half-jocular, "Have you any objections?" was lost in the hearty "I *am* glad! Tell me all about it tomorrow," which she sent back over her shoulder as she darted up the stairs.

But she was sufficiently disturbed by the news to forget prudence and announce it to John, whom she found lingering half-way up to the top flat; he was only inquisitive, she knew, to hear if 'everything' was 'all right', but she had to tell someone.

"Well, I suppose *you're* very pleased," was his comment.

"Why should I be?"

"Because you're always wanting people to have regular

jobs and *pull themselves together* and that sort of bull, aren't
you?"

"Yes, I am." Nell saw no reason for sounding apologetic.
"But I'm not sure that Daddy will like this. It may upset him
again, just as he was getting better."

"Such a poor, creeping, *humble* little job . . . yes," musingly.
"I can understand why you feel worried. *Poor* Nello. There's
always something, isn't there? But you should be like me: I
never worry."

"Never?" Nell said.

They were talking almost in whispers, standing close to one
another on the landing in the dim light reflected from a street-
lamp outside, and suddenly, with a furious change of expression
that distorted his face with grief and pride, he snatched at her
and began violently to kiss her. Nell struggled silently: there
had never been anything quite like this before and she did not
like it, and in a moment he released her.

"What on earth's the *matter* with you?" she whispered
angrily, straightening her hair and coat, "do let's go in to the
others, they'll be—"

She did not quite know what she was saying: she was trembling.

He turned away; she thought that she heard a mutter about
something being 'a bloody nuisance', but what he meant,
whether he was apologizing for being one himself or whether
he meant her own behaviour, she had no idea, and the next
moment he had opened the door of the flat and gone in,
shutting it behind him.

Nell thought that she owed it to herself to go down to her
bedroom and repair her face. The small amount of paint which
she habitually used upon it had been rubbed off by his on-
slaught. When she got there, she found that she could prevent
herself from sitting down on the bed and indulging her own
trembling only by thinking about her father's news, so that
was what she did, and learnt that her dismay was largely selfish. She did not want to come home, later on, to long discussions and longer faces. What would Aunt Peggy say? Would
her father become silent and glum again?

She scolded herself, painting her lips upon which John's
kisses were still stinging, while the trembling subsided. Her
father had made surprisingly little fuss when she had become
a waitress, and now it was 'up to her' (an Edwardian girl would

have said it was her duty) to make no fuss now that he proposed to be a verger. Suddenly she saw the red, sad, empty face; so vividly that she no longer saw her own reflection in the mirror. Poor Daddy; he had had such a miserable time; she ought to be pleased that he had found a way to creep back into the Church. . . .

"Nell?" It was Benedict's voice coming down the stairs. "Can you come and deal with this blasted haddock? No-one knows what bits to cut off."

It occurred to Nell to reply that *surely* their know-all host was not being baffled by such a small point? but she suppressed the retort and, after a final glance at herself, darted back to the Gaunts' flat.

The company was sitting rather languidly all over the kitchen.

"Oh *there* you are, Nell. Where on earth have you been? Do come and deal with this horrible haddock while I do the hock."

Not a glance; not the shade of a shade of a conspiratory look, thank goodness. But this was something new; she had not felt conscious in this way with him before; and she disliked it exceedingly. If . . . that . . . ever happened again, very firm steps would be taken.

"I'll make a haddock soufflé," she said.

"Competent Nello. But won't that take ages?"

"About three quarters of an hour. Are there any eggs? (Robert, look in the cupboard, will you—oh, good.) And I shall want milk and butter and pepper and salt and a whisk."

"*Competent* Nello. But I thought that was a sort of card game."

"No you didn't; you know perfectly well what a whisk is; don't pose," in an undertone, while the others were darting about finding things, "now you can cut off the ears."

"Cut off the *ears*? How perfectly horrible. Indeed I shan't."

"It's those flat pieces at the side. Hurry up; and I want a piedish and a basin."

"I hate touching damp things. I hate your hands when you've been washing up."

He went to the table and sulkily began to trim the fish. Nell was so angry and hurt that she could not trust herself to look up, although it was a little comfort, if only a bitter one, to know that he was furious because of what had happened on the landing.

"Now put it in water—just enough to cover it," she said.

Gardis had somewhere found time to coil up her hair, and her expression was now lively and gay as that of a very young cat, and Elizabeth's eyes darted commandingly here and there while she organized everything. The slight touch of *resolution* in her serene expression had vanished; perhaps because the familiar prospect of a breakfast dish eaten in the small hours had made her feel upon her home ground: or perhaps she was recalling the scene of a little while ago.

The window had been opened, letting in the soft black summer night and its wandering moths, and Benedict and she stood side by side, looking down at the quiet lamplit road and unmoving trees and ignoring the silent figure crouching before a bookshelf with its back to them. Their voices were soft; they did not look at one another as they spoke, and Elizabeth was smiling.

"Oh . . . in my bag. I hate wearing dead flowers."

"It can't be quite dead. Just tired at the end of a long day. It must still smell sweet."

"They do have a delicious smell—that kind."

"What *is* its name? The Honourable Georgiana Prideaux?"

Elizabeth laughed, "We've never bothered to give it a name. It's just that-big-bush-on-the-right-by-the-door-into-the-kitchen-garden."

"Well, you must give it to me."

"Wouldn't that be rather corny?"

"Only by the standards of this painfully impoverished generation. Please."

She hesitated. "I'll get it presently. But won't everyone ... ?"

He only shook his head, which he had slowly turned towards her, and they smiled at one another.

Now the rose hung limp and sweet in his button-hole, the object of much careful avoidance of glances on the part of everyone, and Gardis's manner was gayer than ever; so gay that the meal which followed quickly grew rowdy as the others became affected by her loud laughter and her chuckling voice; the talk sparkled and was quick and it included everybody and touched on all kinds of subjects, but usually ended in threatening an angry argument, which Elizabeth again and again deftly and unobtrusively averted.

Benedict was amused to notice this and fascinated by it: he could fancy that the blood of her ancestors was constantly showing itself in her actions, not least in her impatience with any lack of urbanity threatening the smoothness of the social surface. She seemed to him quite enchanting.

He could now look at Gardis with the memory of pain rather than pain itself, so far had his cure advanced since the first moment of his seeing Elizabeth early that afternoon, but he thought, even while his eyes rested on Gardis's face, that he must already have been well on towards his release from enslavement without realizing it, and what struck him now was the fact of her gaiety being unmistakably that of an older girl. He wondered that the others did not perceive this. Elizabeth's poise came from training and tradition. Gardis's came, when she chose to display it, from having been 'in circulation', or knocking about, for some six years longer than Elizabeth, and, when she dropped her baby girl-goblin manner, this was clear to see.

As for Nell—and he looked across the table for a moment at that longish-nosed face which was certainly not plain, yet which instantly suggested the word and for which it was difficult to find the precise adjective—*her* poise, and she had plenty, came from character, and she would be all right.

When men decide that a woman has character and will be all right, they usually also decide that there is no need to worry about her feelings; Benedict, without knowing it, felt grateful to Nell (who this evening was full of feelings and all of them disagreeable) for not demanding from him pity or love or admiration or anything else.

After they had finished poor Charles-for-god's-sake's three bottles of hock (John was dissuaded from leaving a note saying 'Not too bad; thank you', with the empties) they sat on the floor and drank those quarts of tea which everyone since the war drinks as avidly as the pre-Revolutionary Russians did. Time was wearing on towards half-past two. All was hushed and still, yet mild, and gentle, in the road outside under its full summer foliage, and in all the roads leading, winding, and falling down the broad hillsides of Hampstead into the city. John was leaning out of his bedroom window at the back of the house into the soft dark: he had been there for some time, with the doors open so that he could hear what was going on in the living-room, and he suddenly called out that there were now only a few stars shining in the hair of his old love.

"What *are* you talking about?" Elizabeth turned round from

her place near Benedict on the floor, "Who is your old love?"

The silence which suddenly fell upon the company was not entirely due to a wish not to miss the answer; in the circumstances the words *old love* suggested the heartless proverb.

The answer came in a dreamy, absent tone.

"London. She is my old love—in the sense of being ancient, I mean, not in the sense of my having loved her once and now loving something else—I don't want anything else—and the lights down there are the stars in her hair. What a whimsy idea," he added, as if surprised rather than pained at his own lapse, "but all kinds of people who were first-raters began by being whimsy. . . . Keats was actually *vulgar*, with his 'slippery blisses', and so was Coleridge."

"Those were poets. Feet off my territory, please," from Benedict.

"I thought it was robins who had territory, not poets." John strolled back into the room, glancing from face to face to learn if any fresh moves had taken place during his absence. "And talking of territory, isn't it time that you all went home? I'm horribly tired and so is Nell."

Nell said indignantly that she was not; she did not add that he wasn't either, but she knew it; he could stay up all night, as she also knew to her cost, without consciously feeling fatigue, and must have some other reason for saying what he had.

"And Robert, I am sure, wants to be on time for work in the morning," he went on, ignoring her.

"It would be as well." Robert was unmoved: he did not like Nell's cousin, whom he looked upon as an unwholesome ass, but neither did he respond to small digs.

"So we had better see about taxis." John glanced again round the circle of tea-flushed faces. "Now: where does everybody live?" and he crossed to the telephone.

If the tone was a shade too innocently businesslike, it was only a shade. Nevertheless, there absolutely sprang into everybody's mind the question: *Who will be seen home by Benedict?* Benedict said irritably:

"You know where everybody lives, except Robert. You'll have to lend me some money; I'm seeing Elizabeth home. Robert can share Gardis's taxi as far as Swiss Cottage, if he goes on beyond that; if not, she can drop him."

John was already at the telephone, dialling the nearest radio-taxi rank. Elizabeth, for once, had nothing to say. Into *her* mind had sprung the possibility of being kissed by this thin, charming, haunted-looking man—she did not think of him as a *young* man—who smelt of whisky, on the way home in the taxi. Gardis too was quiet, looking at the floor. Benedict said again, with increased irritation:

"John, you'll have to lend me some *money.*"

Nell saw Elizabeth make a tiny movement; then tuck in her chin and relax. Clever Elizabeth; she knew that she was inclined to be bossy and that men hated it. Gardis looked up suddenly.

"I've got some. That is, I've got about ten shillings. Will that be enough?"

We are friends. We are such close friends that I can offer you money in public, as if you were another girl or I were a man, and it doesn't matter that you are seeing someone else home or who hears me do it, because we've known one another so long and so well. Clever Gardis.

But John was saying smoothly, holding onto the receiver, listening as he spoke, not looking at anyone:

"I've got a pound. You're welcome to it, provided that you can let me have it back tomorrow. I need all the money I can collect, just now. . . . Oh . . . thank you," into the receiver. "One will be here in ten minutes," he said, turning to the room, "and they'll ring us back when they get another."

"Thanks; it's all right," Benedict told Gardis, who had got up from the floor and was painting her mouth. She slid her eyes sideways to smile at Robert, who in fact was not entranced by the idea of sharing Gardis's taxi as far as anywhere.

"You can have your taxi to yourself," she said. "I'm walking."

"Oh, but . . . then we can go together. I've been *trying* to say that I live only about twenty minutes away for the last ten minutes." Robert's tone was as irritable as Benedict's had been. "If you want to walk we can go together. Do you mind calling the second one off?" to John.

Gardis shook her head, smiling as she widened her lips to paint them and thus gave to her face a grotesque twist, but she did not answer. She had just suffered her final defeat of the long embattled day.

They sat about in silence broken only by John's elaborately courteous apologies to radiocabs for cancelling the second taxi, and everyone was relieved when they heard one coming along the street below. They trooped down the stairs in silence.

In the farewells and thanks and expressions of gratitude to John for having arranged the delightful day, Gardis's slow wandering away, with bent head and hands in her pockets, was not observed. She said good night to no-one, and when Robert turned to look for her, having disengaged himself from the party and recalling after he had made twenty smart paces down the road that he had suggested he should accompany her and feeling that the unwelcome duty must be done, he could not see her.

He stood still for a moment. The night was warm, and very dark because dawn was at hand, but it was not quite silent; some voices in the distance, filled with a kind of weary bravado, floated over the silent houses and stilly-hanging trees. Robert looked about him; he heard the light step of retreating feet and ran after the sound.

"Hullo—I'm sorry—" he said, when he caught up with her, "where do you live—Swiss Cottage, isn't it? That's rather a walk for you—perhaps we may pick up a taxi. I wish you'd let John—"

She shook her head. "It's all right."

"Oh, then we go straight down Fitzjohn's Avenue."

"I don't want you to come." She whirled round, and her grin startled him. "I *told* you I didn't want anybody."

"You can't walk home alone at this time of night. You'll get—annoyed." Oh really (as Nell would have said), was the girl a half-wit?

"Perhaps I like being annoyed—how do you know? Perhaps I'll pick someone up; a black man. But right now all I want you to do is to go off and leave me alone and stop—and stop running me ragged, can't you?" She was keeping her face turned away from him. "If you don't"—in a choked voice, "I'll yell to the first policeman we meet."

This did intimidate Robert: three years in the Navy had not diminished his Englishman's horror of being involved in a scene, and she looked wild enough, striding along with floating hair and in those clothes, to let him in for anything. His tone was short indeed.

"Oh all right, but I think you're very silly and I only hope nothing happens to you. Good night." And he struck quickly away down Christchurch Hill. Something was plainly the matter with her, but then there probably always was.

She forgot him at once. She walked on, almost skimming

over the dew-wet pavements as if the speed of her motion in
some way relieved her inward writhing. The night was all
about her, with the unmocking sense of promise, of breathless
waiting, that summer nights have, and in the wide silent
streets and the city lying below in uneasy sleep she had not
one friend. She began to cry as she walked, the little girl alone
in the night whose toy had been taken away from her and
given to a nicer child.

CHAPTER SIXTEEN

"AND WHEN SHE WAS GOOD . . . "

"Was that your dad in New End I saw you with the Monday
at the paper shop, Nell? He's a fine lookin' man. It isn't ill he's
lookin' now, no matter how ill he may have been before. And
what work does he do, now that he's better?"

Mary's slow lamenting voice made these remarks one morning almost a week later, while she and Nell were busy in the
kitchen at The Primula. Tansy had not yet arrived; Miss
Berringer was at the table rapidly slicing tomatoes for the
luncheon salads.

Nell had been glad to return to the teashop's bracing
atmosphere after the events—and their continuing effects—of
last Monday, but had almost immediately perceived that Mary
must have heard something.

It had begun with vague references to the road where Nell
lived; had gone on to the kinds of houses there and thence to
Nell's dear mother and unfortunate lack of brothers and sisters.
This brought the campaign up to Thursday evening; now, on
Friday morning, Mary was in sight of her objective, which was
to hear from Nell the whole story of Nell's father.

Nell was irritated by all this. She was ashamed of her own
shame about Daddy's new job and she wanted to put the entire
subject, even the off-hand prayer which she had snapped at the
Almighty on Monday evening, out of her mind. Blow Mary
and her Irish feeling for drama.

"Yes, that was my father. He had pneumonia two years ago
after he'd had a lot of worry about making up his mind to leave
the Church, and it took him a long time to recover but he's

quite well again now and he's verger at a church in Kentish
Town; he started last Wednesday." Nell ended her gabble and
quickly but gently set down two clean cups on a tray.

"Ah, is he indeed, God love him. Lost his faith, did he?
Isn't that a terrible thing to happen to a priest?"

Nell muttered something, and Mary went on:

"Is it thim little old gentlemen that shows the seats for you
in your churches? (Av course, I've never been in a Protestant
place; Father Molloy would skin me alive if I was to confess
so much as the thought) and a terrible come-down for him,
wouldn't it be? him havin' been a priest. (Give me over the
baking-powder, will you, Nell.) Showin' the seats to thim that
two years gone he was showin' the way to Hivin to. And your
poor mother—takin' on about it?"

"Oh do shut up, Mary!" Miss Berringer did not turn round
but her tone had a startling note of suddenly snapping nerves.
There was silence for a minute. Mary's face wonderfully
expressed majestic indignation, holy innocence, bewilderment,
and, underneath it all, gratification that Lady Bottlewasher
had for once come off her pedestal.

"Nell, get those things in, time's nearly up," Miss Berringer
said, going quickly out of the room. Nell, happening to glance
at her as she went by, noticed how thickly rouged this morning
were her plumper cheeks; lately she had begun to put on weight
and it did not suit her.

She picked up her tray to carry it into the next room. Miss
Berringer darted back, almost knocking into her.

"Isn't there something about it's being 'better to be a doorkeeper in the house of my God', Nell?" she said, laughing.
"I've been feeling like a doorkeeper myself lately—I never
want to see a human face again. Never mind—six more weeks
of it and then Westward Ho! A month in Cornwall." She
disappeared again.

Mary was heard muttering in a scandalized tone—"niver
wants to see a humin face again, God forgive her," as Nell
went out to the tea-room.

She was thinking that a holiday would be agreeable for
herself.

It was almost four months since she had started at The
Primula, and although every moment of the time had been
enjoyable, the pressure upon feet, memory, attention and
temper had been unremitting. She was inclined to be snappy,

and to twist herself into knots in the chair when she sat down, and she was not sleeping well. She had almost forty pounds in the Post Office. A month, or even ten days, in Cornwall or anywhere else sounded very desirable, but she was not going to indulge herself; she would spend her holiday, when the tea-shop closed during October, sitting in the late sunlight (if any) on the Heath, and then, perhaps, looking for a job in London with higher wages and tips.

She would be sorry to leave The Primula, and Tansy and Miss Berringer and Miss Cody and Nerina (whom she liked in spite of the slight pain always associated with her presence) and even Mary, but she meant to have her own tea-shop before she was twenty-three. She was already past twenty, there was no money to be spent on holidays.

And although she was still happy at The Primula, she was beginning to feel the atmosphere there as less carefree than formerly; only a little less; only because of the slight touch of genuine irritation in Miss Berringer's manner, and the pensive shade cast upon her fellow-workers by Nerina, drooping as the day of Chris's going into the Army drew near, but the difference was there. Nell already looked back on the early weeks of summer as the Golden Age.

But at home the atmosphere was—livelier. It was already so, although her father had been working at Saint Saviour's for only three days. Someone else had to be got off to a job, besides Nell, and now it was the nominal head of the house, and this was healthy. Like Nell, he got himself off; perhaps the humble nature of the employment made him more willing to slip away almost before Anna was aware that he was going. But she was determined to support and encourage him in every possible way in doing his new work, and she soon learned the hours at which he left on different days, and was there in the hall to say good-bye to him and 'wave him off'. She did much more; in spite of a distaste for churchgoing and church ceremonies which almost thirty years of being a parson's wife had only repressed, not cured, she took to going to Saint Saviour's, resuming the habits which she had thankfully dropped when Martin left the Church.

She was depressed by the dim Victorian Gothic interior—which John Betjeman might have, for all she cared; the feeble singing irritated her, and she found Mr. Mollison's manner too pontifical when he was being a parson and too hearty when he was being a fellow-creature. She never ceased to dislike the long walk down through the dreary streets of Kentish Town, and to be irked and bored by the entire business. But, when all this was candidly admitted, there remained the two facts that she was intellectually, if not emotionally and spiritually, convinced of the existence of God, and that it was her duty to support her husband. They were quite enough to send her regularly, if not often, to Saint Saviour's.

Nell continued to scurry secretively at intervals into the church at the end of Arkwood Road. She was really too busy nowadays to think much about Faith; Works, of a rather worldly and pleasant kind, had to serve instead.

Anna also took it upon herself to tell Lady Fairfax about Martin's new work, proposing herself for tea one afternoon at Odessa Place in order to break the news.

Tea, said her sister-in-law; she never had tea; but wouldn't Anna come in for a drink about six?

When the news had been broken and Lady Fairfax had made her surprised comments, they sat in silence for a moment. The smart dark walls of the drawing-room glowed in the soft light of early evening, and the fragile glass statuettes and chandelier-candlesticks glittered on the mantelshelf.

"I'm just wondering," Lady Fairfax said suddenly, "if something couldn't be got out of this for T.V."

"Out of what?"

Anna, dressed in a fifteen-year-old skirt and a jacket bought, Lady Fairfax surmised, at some Sale of Work, was enjoying a very dry Martini and thinking that she did not dislike Peggy as much as she used to. One might never see eye to eye with her, but it was very possible to respect her, and Anna had also discovered, to her surprise, that Peggy silently acknowledged their mutual dislike and—more surprisingly—found it amusing.

"His going back into the Church by the vestry door," she said. "You know, people are *interested* in religion nowadays. (Of course, they won't stand for dogma—don't you call it dogma?—laying down the law, I mean, or anything of that sort.) But look at the huge success Billy Graham had. And there's Wilfred Pickles. And of course those songs of Johnny Ray's—though that really *is* going a bit far . . . *do* you think Marty would agree to do something about it?"

"Good heavens, why should he?" Anna's tone had the

irritating casualness which dismisses the inconceivable. "He hasn't done anything exciting."

"It doesn't have to be exciting." (Really, what *right* had a woman wearing those clothes to look both handsome *and* clever, but nowadays it was not possible, really to dislike tiresome, highbrow, snobbish Anna.) "Naturally, the story would have to be knocked into shape," Lady Fairfax said.

"There isn't any story."

"But of course there is, Anna. His loss of faith—"

"It wasn't quite that, you know."

"Well—that's near enough. And then the long months in the wilderness—I *know* that sounds rather corny," sharply, as Anna laughed, "but it needn't necessarily be put in those words, so long as viewers get the idea . . . and then the gradual return to the Church through the vestry door. Through the Vestry Door! It might make a series. There's so much *feeling* about the Church since the Townsend affair. . . ."

Anna finished her Martini. It occurred to her that another would be agreeable, but really, if Peggy continued in this style it might be her, Anna's, duty to refuse another, rather as an Arab would refuse the salt of a host whom he disagreed with or disapproved of.

"I'm quite sure he wouldn't hear of it," was all she said, looking out of the window.

"He might be able to help someone, Anna," Lady Fairfax said gravely.

"By painting his face and showing off to millions of people? Poor old Marty, I doubt it."

Lady Fairfax decided to drop the subject. It was a little irritating that Martin had refused to remain *completely* passive in the backwater into which she had steered him, but perhaps that had been rather a lot to expect; it must have been excruciatingly dull, pottering round the Arkwood Road house on pocket-money supplied by Nell, and Marty was not yet quite sixty. Her feelings towards him warmed. Poor old boy, it was nice that he had found himself a job that he liked, and felt himself capable of doing.

Her reflections were interrupted by the entrance of Gardis, in outdoor clothes.

"Dead on time again: are you doing a last-minute reform so that I'll give you a good reference?" Lady Fairfax got up and took some letters from the mantelpiece. "These came this

afternoon; I have scribbled on them what I want said, and
will you ring up . . . "

"That child looks ill," Anna observed, when Gardis had
left the room.

"I'm not surprised. She hasn't been in bed before three in
the morning since she got here—except lately; she's been earlier
these last few days; and she's *also* stopped wearing those disgusting clothes. I think something must be up. I can't imagine
what, of course; she's never told me anything and heaven knows
I haven't wanted her to, although I have *wondered*. . . . (I'm
pretty sure there was something going on with a beard at the
Art School. But he's left.) And just lately she *has* been different.
Of course she's just a poor little psychopath, and if you knew
her background you wouldn't wonder: *I* only wonder she isn't
worse. I'm actually rather sorry she's going home. I never
thought I would be. She grows on one, in an odd sort of way.
(Of course, she's fascinating. But then I haven't much use for
fascinators—being one myself and earning my living by it.)"

Anna did not trouble to smile at this: she glanced at the
clock and remarked civilly that she must go.

After she had seen her out, Lady Fairfax ran upstairs, a thing
which she only did when raging irritation insisted upon a
physical outlet, and burst in upon her secretary.

"Gardis—drop everything and get on to Harrods (they'll
still just be open). Tell them to send the biggest and best
television set they've got to Mrs. Martin Sely at Twenty-five
Arkwood Road, Hampstead, N.W.3, with a card with my
name and my best love. I will *not* let her get away with this—
this smug high-minded attitude about T.V."

Gardis looked at her, with amusement in the black eyes
ringed with black, and said: "Squared away, Lady F.," as
she began to dial Harrods' number.

When her employer had signed her letters and gone, she
sat still for a moment, looking down at the immaculate pink
nails resting on the pink typewriter.

She could hear, through the quietness of the room and the
luxurious hush cossetting the house, the far-off hellish drone of
traffic battling its way homeward to the suburbs. She was
struggling with the wish to destroy the harmony in yellow and
pink which she had carefully arranged upon herself in clothes
and jewels; it was not honest: she felt herself as a walking lie:
she had *tried*, during the past week, 'to be her age' and to look

as if she were living graciously and possessed an integrated personality, and she hated every minute of it. The pain within her clamoured for expression in outward grime, and her poverty of heart wanted to show itself in rags. She was empty and yearning and raging as an addict kept without his 'shot'. Yet this passion was not love: it was stronger, and deeper, and—worse.

And now she had done something . . . she had been such a fool . . . after getting herself organized a little, with enormous effort, towards what she supposed that she ought to be . . . she had spoilt everything . . . and John, she had asked John for help . . . and he would go straight to Ben and tell him . . . she must have been crazy.

She knew what John was. He could be trusted about as much as she could herself. Only, there had been this awful burning feeling that she must hurt Elizabeth somehow, and there hadn't seemed any way of getting at her . . . she had that British-deb manner that wouldn't show anything even if she were half-killed . . . and then her going away to Paris for the week-end gave one a kind of chance . . . to do something . . . those two had been together almost every minute of the day and a lot of the night too for the past week . . . oh, it was a case all right, a bad case . . . and if they hadn't been together all of the night yet, they soon would . . . of course, marriage . . . you could always get someone away . . . marriage didn't mean a thing nowadays . . . but it was this thing that John had done for her . . . her idea . . . everything . . . and now she must wait and wait and wait, without moving, until Ben showed that he knew.

About half-past one on the previous day, Mrs. Prideaux had been at home in the Knightsbridge flat after passing a profitable morning doing some necessary shopping, in an atmosphere quieter than it would have been in her daughter's delightful but masterful company. Elizabeth had taken a morning plane for Paris where she was to spend a long week-end with friends.

As Mrs. Prideaux came through the hall the telephone bell rang.

"May I speak to Mrs. Prideaux, please?" It was a man's voice, young and guarded and grave.

"This is Mrs. Prideaux. What is it, please?"

"This is British Overseas Airways Company. I am afraid

. . . there is some very serious news I have to give you, I am afraid, Mrs. Prideaux."

There was a pause; a questioning pause. The General came pottering out, swishing discontentedly with *The Times* at the Corgi, Useless, who had also strayed into the hall; then paused, for his wife had held up a warning finger.

"What's the matter, Mag?" he demanded loudly. "You're ratty about something. You've turned pink."

"Mrs. Prideaux? Are you there? Are you all right?"

"I'm perfectly all right, thank you," Mrs. Prideaux said steadily, with the pink deepening ("do be quiet, Reggie). Go on, please."

"It's . . . your daughter, Miss Prideaux, I'm afraid. There has been an accident . . . I am very sorry to have to inform you . . ."

"There may have been an accident," Mrs. Prideaux interrupted, "but it hasn't affected my daughter because I was talking to her in Paris ten minutes ago. Whoever you are, I hope—"

She checked herself, hesitated; then quickly replaced the receiver.

"Some lunatic, no doubt," said the General in a moment, looking at her uneasily. She had sat down on a chair and was gently lifting the string of pearls lying on the neck of her jersey.

"Of course. All the same, dear, I think I will have some brandy."

"I'll get it," said he, and bustled off muttering.

Mrs. Prideaux was now stroking the head of the Corgi pushed against her knee. She was feeling thankful that Elizabeth had always been so understanding about the nervousness afflicting her mother since the latter had started the C. of L. If she had not been, and had not taken it for granted that she should always telephone her mother on arriving at the end of any journey, the cardiac weakness that Mrs. Prideaux had had from her girlhood might today have . . . done something tiresomely dramatic.

As may be imagined, the General caused enquiries to be made about this incident, but the caller was never traced.

Gardis stirred at last and looked at the clock. It was almost eight. Lady Fairfax was going with her husband to dine at a house whence the company's table-talk would be televised, and had long since left; the various foreign servants were out roaming the streets of the West End; she was alone. She was not often so, except occasionally when hurrying from one party to another, and she loathed her own company; particularly now, on a sad evening in late summer when the stillness in the room seemed an accusing presence, compelling her again and again to turn and look into what she, and her life, had become. She looked, at last, for she was tired, and no longer a young girl, and she was sick of holding out against the insistent silence.

And what she saw was unbearable.

She sprang up; she was supposed to go to a party somewhere, but she had now forgotten even having said that she would be there. She ran to the telephone; it was three days since she had spoken to him, threatening him with hatred if he dared to accept Elizabeth's invitation to go with her for the following week-end to Prideaux.

She had had to bite her tongue until it bled to keep herself from gasping out—was he going to marry Liz?

But now she could bear it no longer. It wasn't love or the other thing, it was like being terribly hungry. Since he had left her, she had felt nothing but darkness and bitter cold.

She was broken; she muttered the words over and over to herself while she dialled the number of the Hampstead flat: "I'm broken up, I'm all broken up, I can't even get warm, I've been like ice for days, you must . . . you *must* . . . "

The bell rang in the rather sad silence of Charles Gaunt's rooms. Benedict, who was just running downstairs on his way out, turned back only because he thought that it might be Elizabeth.

When he heard the familiar harsh voice all the muscles in his stomach contracted in the awful familiar clutch.

"Please may I come and see you, Ben? I've got to bring back . . . that book of Picasso drawings. . . . I just thought I'd like to see you again, as I'm off the day after tomorrow."

A pause. He stood holding the receiver, not thinking or seeing. The low dark sound washed over him like the waves of a twilit lake.

"I'm quite all right now. I'm . . . I won't . . . "

But he knew that she was not all right. He knew her voices so well; the mocking note and the hysterical note and the self-pitying note, and the note of hate and that of desire; and as he listened he heard the note he dreaded more than all the others.

It was the bad little girl talking to him; the lost one who had run away from the grown-ups to walk alone on the shores of a twilit lake and let the wind blow through the curl on her forehead. She was crying for her lost toy, rubbing her knuckles into her eyes and gulping as she stumbled along, and it was getting dark.

He did not love her any more but his heart was wrung.

"I'll come over, shall I?"

He did not answer. He was going into London to see Elizabeth.

"*Ben* . . . ?"

"Yes, all right then. All right. Where are you?"

"At home. Be with you in ten minutes."

When the room was again quiet he walked over to the door. He stood there a moment; then went back to the telephone. But it so happened that he was not meeting Elizabeth alone that evening, but was going to the flat to meet some of her friends and had not to be there until about nine; there was no real necessity to telephone her and warn her that he might be detained.

He turned away from the telephone; then hesitated. At this moment he felt a strong desire to hear the confident delicious voice saying *Elizabeth here*. It meant to him sweetness and gaiety and joy.

But almost at once, it seemed, the front door bell was ringing through the quiet house.

"I was lucky; got a taxi right away." She spoke breathlessly as she looked at him, and her eyes were frightened, but she was a perfectly groomed and dressed young woman, standing upright with gloved hands clasping an elegant bag. "I . . . you were just going out, weren't you?"

"Yes, but there's no great hurry. Will you . . . " he hesitated; the book of Picasso's drawings was under her arm. But she was stepping into the hall.

"Oh, I'll come up. Just for a minute."

Now she was all right. Now the darkness had lifted and the bitter cold was thawing and the lonely sense of deprivation was going away. She followed him, almost gasping with relief.

Benedict, too, was relieved. The bad little girl had spoken to him over the telephone, but Miss Randolph of Wide-meadows, Long Island, was coming after him up the stairs, and although he had not often met this young lady he knew

that she was easier to deal with than any of the other mani-
festations of Gardis. He could hardly believe that it was she
who had called; because it seemed too good to be true.

When they were in the living-room, she put the book of
Picasso drawings carefully down on a chair, then took off her
coat. A pink dress was revealed, and loops of yellow crystal,
and yellow crystals were swinging from her ears. But her lipstick was the wrong pink. It was a flaw in her appearance, and
for some reason when he saw it his sense of relief began to grow
less. He stood, watching her.

She did not say anything for a moment, but sat down rather
carefully, looking at the carpet, and shook her head at an
offered cigarette-packet. In fact she was trying to throw off
the trance induced by momentary relief from pain, but, as
well, she could not think of anything to say. He and she had
never been great talkers when they were together, and this
was probably the last time that she would ever see him.

"'Came to say good-bye, really," she said suddenly, looking up.

"The day after tomorrow?" he said, and she nodded.

"I'll just stay for a minute," as he did not speak, "if—you
won't mind?"

"Oh, for God's sake. If I won't mind."

"Well, we haven't seen each other for quite a while, that
makes—anyone—feel queer."

Benedict did not answer; he was frighteningly touched by
the carefulness of her grooming and her dress. The wonderfully exotic charm of her appearance moved him not at all,
but the signs that she was trying to pull herself together did.

Gardis was frightened too. She had come because she was
starving for the comfort which she had learned during the last
three days that only he could give, but she was beginning to
feel desperate again: in two days she would be at home: in
the States: and he would be more than a thousand miles
away.

She looked up and fixed her eyes on him, within them the
hate which she felt for all men. She hated them, indeed, but
she could not do without them, and this one she knew she
could never learn now to do without, because she had never
felt thus about anyone before.

"I must go," he said, looking away from her.

The thought of Elizabeth, and his wish to be with her,
were very strong; their mere presence within him was like an

escape from the atmosphere in the room of tension and pity.

"Come along," he said gently. "I had some more money this morning. I'll get us a taxi."

Gardis slowly stood up. She had not come here meaning to weep, or rave; she had only put on her best clothes to make herself feel better, and come because she had to see him. She had not meant to plead. She hated him. But she looked down at the floor, and all at once the uncontrollable and welcome despair came welling up, with the hard and difficult tears. No need now to try any more.

"I hate you. You hurt me," she croaked, in a tone so low that the words were deformed as they came out through her trembling lips. She began to sob, in her aching throat, "Why . . . ? I hate you . . . why do you . . . so mean to me? You're my friend. We're friends, I never had a man friend before and you've *got* to stick by me." She sank to the floor and sat there rigidly, beating with one hand on the carpet, with her dark shining head sunk far down on her breast. The long hysterical moans began, while he stood looking down at her. "You've got to stay with me. I haven't got anyone but you."

Benedict stood still for a moment. Distinctly, in the eye of his mind, where the poet's bright or terrible images perpetually floated, he saw the face of Elizabeth and heard the gay clear ring of her voice, which, already, after two weeks, was beginning to sound within his own body when he heard it, as a beloved voice will. Oh, but now the lost little girl was rubbing her eyes with her fists.

An unbearable pang of pity shook him. He knelt quickly beside her and gathered her into his arms. The musky scent of her hair sickened him for a moment.

"Darling, there. There." He rocked her to and fro. "I am your friend. I am, truly."

"Don't want you to love me or promise or . . . just be my friend for ever."

"But I do promise."

"Truly?" The reddened, drowned eyes looked up.

"Truly. Now . . . oh Gardis." He held her closer, looking vaguely round the room, then gently kissed the fall of her tumbling hair.

He would never get away now. The bad little girl had got him and they would serve a life-sentence together. The pity,

welling remorselessly within him, was almost strong enough
to prevent his realizing the fact.

"I say, you do look green. Is something the matter?"

Camilla Seton, with the lightest of touches on the reins,
kept her horse moving at Elizabeth's side. It was the next
afternoon, and the two were under the trees of Richmond
Park. Camilla spoke with the bluntness which sometimes
broke through her characteristic silence.

"No. Well—yes." Elizabeth screwed the letter, which had
arrived as she left the house, into an extremely small ball and
shied it into a bush. "I've been stood up and given the brush
off, if you care to know."

"*Not* your poet?" Camilla's tone was actually awed: really,
one couldn't rely on *anyone*; absolutely *no-one* was safe. Even
Robin, perhaps . . . Her eyes widened and she quickly shook
her head, as if to dodge an alarming fly.

Elizabeth nodded. Her face looked very like that of the Hon.
Georgiana, and the lines in which it was set brought out the
shape of her chin. She did not, however, relax the hand and eye
she was keeping on a rather temperamental mare. After a
pause during which they walked the horses some hundred
yards under the yellowing oaks, Camilla observed that it
was hard luck.

"No; it's my own fault," Elizabeth answered calmly. "You
see, it's the first affair I've ever had with someone middle-
class, and I ought to have known what would happen."

"Poor Penny got the brush-off from George Charteris, and
he isn't middle-class."

"I know, but he didn't not turn up to a party, and not
telephone, and then write to her to say he'd gone off to Spain
with a girl who doesn't wash, and not one word of apology."

Camilla reflected for some four minutes. "Perhaps he minds
so much he *can't* apologize," she sagely observed at last.

"Perhaps. But I don't mind. I *could* mind." She looked calmly
into the blue distance at the end of the turf ride. "But I shan't
let myself. I shall concentrate on getting my tea-shop with
Sely. ('Don't like her friends but the girl herself is all right.)
Now let's gallop."

The horses romped away under the yellow leaves through
the sweet damp-scented air, and soon the riders were lost in the
promising distance.

CHAPTER SEVENTEEN

THE VOICE OF MY OLD LOVE

NELL had been the second person to hear the news of Gardis and Benedict's flight, because Elizabeth had told her a few hours after she had read Benedict's letter.

The two were engaged to see *The Beach* together, and while they had been watching Martine Carol sympathetically interpreting that type so interesting to Elizabeth, Nell had been surprised to hear a sniff. Cautiously, barely moving her head, she glanced sideways. The glare from the screen was reflected in a ribbon of wet on Elizabeth's cheek.

"I'm sorry I was silly in there," Elizabeth said later, when they were sitting in an Espresso bar.

"Don't you usually cry at films? Lots of people do," said Nell, who never did. She was not surprised at Elizabeth's remark, having suspected since the sniffing that something more was wrong than sympathy with the poor little tart in the film.

"Oh heavens, no." Elizabeth seemed reluctant, yet wanting, to talk.

"But it was very moving, wasn't it?"

"Oh yes—poor poppet. What ticks they were. But it was really that Existentialist girl in the film that set me off. She was so *exactly* like Gardis."

Nell only nodded, with emphasis. She had been wondering why this comment had not been made before, and had deduced that the battle must still be rolling underground—although Elizabeth was apparently victor in the field.

"You-see-they've-gone-off-to-Morocco-together." The sentence came out in a rush.

"Gardis and *Benedict* have?"

Elizabeth nodded.

Nell looked down at her coffee cup. She was still trying to think what to say, when Elizabeth went on very decidedly:

"But don't let's talk about it, please. And don't go blaming yourself all around the town for having introduced us, Sely, because it was good while it lasted and it's been a useful lesson and in a few days I shan't care a bit."

But Nell for the rest of the evening wore two red spots of anger in her face and her lips were compressed.

"*Record one lost soul more!*" Another faithless male, another girl given the brush off, another blow at those foundations of faith and trust which were always, after repeated shatterings, trying to rear themselves in the average female heart. Even Elizabeth, the managing puss, was not safe. It was at this point in her sentimental education that Nell began to think: *I don't think I shall marry if I'm asked. There's too much occupational risk.*

It was not perhaps surprising that her indignation should have concentrated itself upon her cousin John.

She went home that evening determined to seek him out and demand his opinion of what had happened, and ask him if he wasn't pleased with the results of his plotting (because she was absolutely certain that he had been plotting).

But he was not to be found, and no-one had seen him all that day. Nell went to bed, still in a fine fury, without having told the news to her parents; after all, it affected them only indirectly, and she did not want to become drawn into a discussion about John's friends and then, inevitably, John.

And the next morning something happened which put the flight of Gardis and Benedict out of her mind.

The television set ordered by Lady Fairfax came, before Nell left for her work, and Anna, making no pretence of being anything but rather annoyed at the arrival of the great moon-stone-faced thing, telephoned to her sister-in-law to thank her for it. Nell was whisking a broom through the hall, removing the traces of the television men's presence.

Her mother tendered some rather exasperated, though also amused, thanks for the magnificent present, and assured Lady Fairfax that they would be able to use the set that afternoon: yes, the men had simply reconnected everything; Peggy would remember that the Palmer-Groves had had one? and of course the Gaunts had one upstairs . . . Then Nell heard her say:

"Oh, have they? Well, you were expecting them about now, weren't you? All right; I'll tell her."

She turned to Nell.

"John's papers for his Medical have come. They're being forwarded on here today from Odessa Place and your Aunt Peggy wants *you* to make sure that he gets them safely. (She says *you* know what he is.) What?"

She turned again to the receiver, while Nell, nodding, continued to sweep energetically and to play with and then dismiss, a silly idea of losing the papers and thus gaining for him a short time of further freedom. "I didn't know anything about it," Anna said. "How tiresome for you. (Nell, that American girl has run off with John's friend Benedict.) But I expect it's really rather a relief, isn't it? Now you can get somebody efficient. Oh, have you? Already? I hope she's better than the last one. Well, thank you again . . . "

Nell was just going out of the door when Anna hung up the receiver. At the same moment Martin Sely came pottering out into the hall to begin the ceremony of coat-brushing, hat-handing, and seeing-off which he and Anna had lately fallen into the habit of performing every time he left for Saint Saviour's, but Nell scarcely heard the discussion about Gardis and Benedict which followed; she could think of nothing but the fact that John was going away. Impatiently she struggled with the pain which was gripping her.

"How large it looks." She came back to the hall, and duty, and the affairs of the day, to find her father wonderingly surveying the Face staring out through the drawing-room door. "But I suppose we shall get used to it. Now remember, Nan, you've promised faithfully not to 'look in' until I get back this afternoon. No cheating."

Anna said indignantly that she never cheated, and shut the door on them.

"Daddy, do you mind if I fly ahead?" Nell said. "I walk so much faster than you do—and I've masses to do this morning."

"Can't you just walk with me to the end of the road, Helen? We never see one another nowadays, and I want to talk to you."

"Of course, Daddy, I'm sorry."

The papers will be there when I get home this evening. I wish she hadn't asked me to give them to him, he'll be beastly about it. . . .

"Yes? I'm sorry. What did you say, Daddy?"

She had seemed to hear something about "all these young people . . . can't something be done . . . "

"It doesn't matter. You don't seem able to give me your attention this morning."

They were already near the turning where he must turn aside to make his way down into Kentish Town.

"I'm sorry, Daddy. I really do have so much to think about ... I didn't mean to be rude."

"It's all right. It doesn't matter. I'll talk to you about it some other time. Good-bye."

They parted with absent, and slightly ruffled, smiles.

Poor Daddy—(Nell's thoughts stayed with him for a moment as she darted off into the High Street) he does begin to stoop. But he doesn't look so lost, now, as he did, so he must like his vergering, and it must be good for him, and that's a good thing. . . .

It also gave her an excuse not to feel guilty at now forgetting him completely.

But as he went on down the hill into the wide streets of shabby, pale grey houses in Kentish Town, where in the main roads the buildings seem almost visibly flaking and shaking down under the merciless, hollowing noise of the passing traffic even as the banks and bed of a river are visibly worn down beneath the rush of it in spate, and to be dumbly entreating a respite in which to be silent, to be clean, to be themselves, he was still thinking about that American girl and the boy.

All these young people whom he saw, from his silence in the background, coming and going in the house—with their proud movements and strong bodies, were often in his thoughts; and if, this morning, his growing concern for them all was mixed with pleasurable anticipations of going on with his polishing of the pews (he meant by degrees to do the woodwork throughout the church) and with thoughts about tea that afternoon, at which he and Anna would enjoy the cakes brought home for them by Nell, and the novelty of seeing 'the thing' at work, this mixture of the important with the trivial was only what had been going on in his life—and his mind—ever since he had known that his misery had left him.

It had seemed, right at the end, when he had felt the touch of the Spirit while he was descending the steps near Christchurch, that the entire experience might be going to lead on into something important and big, but that had not happened. It had been humbling to realize it, but then the whole business had been humbling . . . he supposed. He did not really feel it so. He seldom thought about it nowadays.

But these young people . . . there seemed no way of getting at them. They were immovably encased in their own complacency. The very thought of 'tackling' one of them made his stomach quail. It was strange to remember how confidently he used to lecture the mildly erring young (such harmless adolescents!) at Morley Magna two years ago.

He paused for a moment to rest, standing with the duster crumpled up in one hand while he looked critically at the pew. It would take months, of course, to get it looking as it ought to look. The cavernous, dim, lofty spaces of the church soared above him while he stood there, a big silent man absorbed in what he was looking at, forgetful for the moment of the young people and their peril. A voice suddenly said casually within him, *You could always pray for them*, and at once, without hesitating, he knelt down and followed the suggestion.

It was a long, rather fierce prayer that he made, although all the time that he was praying he had a picture before him of the young stony faces and the young self-loving eyes that was positively daunting: it absolutely ignored the prayer and was impermeable to it, as a column of granite might seem to ignore and be impermeable to a wreath of mist. The prayer belonged in another dimension to those young figures, and there could not conceivably be any interlocking between them, or any communication.

He got up from his knees and dusted himself.

Not an encouraging experience. But then perhaps he was not meant to feel encouraged, and, in any case, what did his feeling of encouragement or discouragement matter, what did it matter whether he felt his prayer had been a good one or a bad one or a lukewarm one, so long as he ignored all his feelings and went on, every day, doggedly and faithfully and importunately praying?

"That poor kid never come in last night," said Tansy, as soon as Nell entered the kitchen.

"Nerina? Good heavens. What did you do?" Nell paused with a shoe suspended half-way to her foot; this was disturbing; it might affect her own plans for leaving very punctually to-night in order to pick up the letter with the Medical papers in it, arriving from Odessa Place.

"Lady B. carried on. Tearing strips off us left, right and centre. Well . . . stands to reason. Had to stand-up the boy friend."

Nell contented herself with a whistle.

"Not but what that hasn't been happening more than once lately," Tansy continued mysteriously, while rapidly peeling potatoes. "Everything in the garden's very far from lovely there nowadays, if you ask me."

"Did Nerina telephone or anything?" Nell never encouraged kitchen gossip about Miss Berringer's private life, and now was anxious to find out exactly how matters stood with the Evening Girl.

"Not a word so far," Tansy said.

"'Tis all these party transformations she's going after," Mary, sitting at the table, spoke for the first time, "and who would blame her, cheering herself up now that her boy's been taken by the Army?"

Nell thought it extremely unlikely that Nerina was consoling herself for the absence of Chris by going to parties. Since his departure for a camp in the north almost a week ago, she had gone about her work wearing a smile like a sweet cold mask, answering sympathetic questions with an airy politeness. Tansy and Mary were rather shocked by her attitude, but Nell had been half expecting that one day she would simply fail to come in. She almost knew what Nerina was enduring.

"Does anyone know her address?" she asked.

They said that Lady Bottlewasher would be sure to have it.

But that evening, to her raging impatience, Nell was asked to stay until eight o'clock, with the promise of an extra half-crown, because again Nerina had not turned up.

Miss Berringer admitted in a sharp tone that she had no idea where her Evening Girl lived.

"I wish I had; I'd get one of you to go round and see what on earth she's playing at. It's most unlike her."

Nell nodded. She was flying through the process of laying up for suppers with a very flushed face.

"I don't think she's been late or away once since she's been here, has she?" Miss Berringer went on.

"Indeed, and she has not," Mary chanted, solemnly wagging her head.

"She's worried about Chris," Tansy said.

"*Worried* about him? A thing that size? All she needs to worry about is whether the British Army can meet his appetite. Well, Nell, you'll be here until eight. I suppose you can't possibly do the entire evening for me?"

Nell shook her head. "I'm going out. I'm sorry," but as she

spoke she was thinking that policy would recommend her
staying: Miss Berringer might later on be a useful person to
know.

"Oh. Well, I shall just have to . . . " and her employer left
the kitchen muttering.

The instant she got into the hall, Nell's eye went to the chest
where the day's letters were always arranged. Nothing but a
circular for Margie. He must have come in earlier, and taken
the letter away. Or perhaps it had not come?

"Mother?" Hearing muffled voices from the drawing-room,
she half-opened the door, only to be received with cries of
"S'sh!" and "Do go away—this is so interesting," while in
half-darkness a bluish-white square glowed and changed.
Really—! "Mother, did that medical call-up letter come for
John?" she asked.

"Yes . . . " droned Anna, eyes fixed hypnotically upon the
screen.

"Oh. Well, it isn't there now."

"Then I expect he's taken it. How late you are. You can get
yourself something, can't you, Daddy and I don't want to
miss this."

Nell withdrew, a little shocked amidst all her disturbed
thoughts and feelings by the sight of her mother, the reader,
absorbed by a toy.

She did not want any supper. She did just snatch up an apple
as she looked into the dining-room, with the silly hope that he
might be sulking there; then she ran upstairs eating it. She was
half-hoping that he wasn't in the house; if he had the papers
he would be furious, and striking out at everything and everybody, more especially Nello, like a . . . like a snake, and then
again, he might pretend that he had not had them, and lie
about it, and she wouldn't know if he had had them or not . . .
except that in a few days, of course, someone would begin
asking questions.

She opened her bedroom door.

"Hullo, Nello." The low, lazy, darling voice. "Do you mind
my being here? My bedroom is so dusty."

He was sitting on the old chintz-covered sofa in front of
her window, and as she came in he slowly turned his head
away from the leaves of the sycamore and their shadows, and
gave her his charmer's smile.

"I like you being here," Nell said.

It was the kind of confession she almost never made, but she knew from the first glimpse of him that this was one of the rare times when something like that could be said. It would be accepted exactly as it had been spoken; with a kind of light sweetness and calm: she knew exactly the mood he was in, and it was the one she liked best. Obediently, she turned to meet it.

"Doesn't Mrs. Holdsworth dust your bedroom?"

She seated herself beside him, lying one arm along the sofa rail, and looked at him. It seemed a pity that all her cross and painful learning of his moods would be wasted because they were never going to live together over her tea-shop—but Nell quietly dismissed the sting. Here were peace, and fading sunset, and the shadows of leaves: let her make the most of them.

"Oh, I suppose so. It isn't real dust, it's a kind of dusty light . . . it's nicer here, anyway. Well, Nello, I expect you know The Papers have come. They sound like something in a before-1914 spy story, don't they?"

"Oh . . . have you got them?" was all that she could say.

"I have," he tapped his pocket with a touch of drama. "And I go for my Medical on the tenth."

"But that's only a week from today!"

"I know. It *is* almost upon us, isn't it? Don't look so startled, Nello. I am feeling quite differently about my National Service now. I shall look on it as 'experience' (I dislike the word 'copy'; it's inexpressive and cheap) and submit myself to it without protest." The drowsy grey eyes were fixed smilingly upon her own.

"You may not pass the Medical," Nell said.

But he shook his head. "I don't think we should count on that. I've always been very strong; I never remember being ill in my life. I see no reason why *They* should find anything wrong with me. Besides," turning round animatedly, "why are we talking like this anyway? It will be too *long* an experience, two whole years of it, but I'm going through with it. There must be something fresh to say about Service life; I shall be the one to say it. Or perhaps I shall re-say the things that have always been true about soldiers, in a fresh way."

"Why soldiers? Have you always thought of going into the Army? I should have thought . . ."

"Now what, Nello darling? What would you have thought?" taking her hand and moving it up and down.

"That the Air Force or the Navy would be more interesting to a writer."

He dropped her hand. "Everything's interesting to a writer ... have you never wondered why I didn't try to get deferred? You see," as she nodded, "that—not trying to—was a kind of sacrifice to my writing, as well. If I'd got myself to a University —and I *could* have, you know, Nello; I'm clever; I'm 'a great passer of examinations', as someone—Aldington, was it? said of that ass D. H. Lawrence—and started off on a promising career, I expect I could have got deferment. But *that* would have meant being tied down; not being completely free to wander about and do what I want to and go where I choose. And these two years have been ..." He stopped, and turned slowly, to look at the sycamore tree where the low dusty rays lingered. "Very useful," he ended.

"Of course, no-one could get deferment on the grounds that they were training themselves as a writer," he added, after a silence, "or everyone would be doing it. So I've had to arrange my affairs to fit in with *Theirs*. And really, you know, it hasn't turned out too badly." He smiled at her. "I'm resigned to doing my best, Nello. I expect you will soon be getting letters from me telling you how 'grand' it all is and that I'm 'mad keen'."

Nell sat looking at him, with thankfulness flowing into her heart. This change of attitude might lead on to anything: might make him into a sensible, open-air-loving boy, who liked plenty of sleep and regular meals, and hated dishonesty and always told the truth, and then she would be able to concentrate all her energy upon getting her tea-shop, because she need not worry any more about John.

"I'm awfully glad," she said.

"I thought you might be. I've always told you, haven't I? that you need not worry about me. Well now," his voice slid on without change of expression, "what do you think about silly Benedict and dear little Gardis? Wasn't it a *fatal* thing to do? Ben was just beginning to get a foot in with his poetry. This will set him back *years*."

"Oh ... yes ... well. ... " Her sudden recollection of having been very angry with him for his supposed hand in that affair was unwelcome; she did not want to spoil the peace, and her thankfulness. She took a weak refuge in silence.

" ... of course people will take any amount of that 'wild

one' pose from poets nowadays; they're all expected to be 'wild' just as all doctors are expected to provide the raw material for future hagiographers. . . ."

"What is a hagiographer?" She felt that she ought at least to interrupt occasionally, not just sit there implying approval of his verdict on this affair which had, she was certain, not ended as he had planned.

"Someone who writes about saints," kindly, " . . . but it's fatal to start being 'wild' before anyone has heard of you . . . it's much better to get yourself well known first and *then* be wild; drink too much; womanize like mad; even be a pervert, if you can stomach it . . . or get into debt on an impressive scale. But dropping all your contacts and running off to Spanish Morocco with a little bitch of whom nobody's ever heard . . . that was *very* silly of Ben." His voice was gentle, but he glanced away as he spoke, and she could tell that he was remembering that day at Kenwood House, and his shifting plots and plans during the fortnight that followed, with cold anger.

She murmured yes, it was silly, and left it at that: she was pleased that his scheming had failed and yet sorry for his disappointment. The unexpected thought came to her that she would be *relieved* when he had gone away into the Army. It was uncomfortable to have her feelings for him and her opinion of him so much at variance.

"Is Aunt Peggy furious?" she asked, for something to say.

"No, I don't think so (I don't think of her as an aunt, of course; aunts were put here to get furious). I think she's relieved, on the whole. And so am I. Those two were getting tedious. They were so much older than most of us, you see. Of course in theory I believe that age should make no difference in friendships, but it does, you know. It does."

"Gardis was only nineteen."

"Twenty-four," smiling.

"*Was* she?"

"You're so endearingly 'green' Nello dear. 'Pushing' twenty-five."

"I should never have thought it," said Nell, pondering.

"Oh yes. And getting rather desperate about it, I think. *So* silly. (Only women and perverts get desperate about becoming older.) My real regret is Elizabeth."

"Why? Do you . . . ?" Nell suppressed the words *like her so much*?

"She will think I introduced her to some very ill-bred people. She may even think I'm ill-bred too."

Nell was not anxious to be led into a discussion of Elizabeth's opinion of him, because he always became so angry when people did not like and admire him, and so she only made a soothing sound. Then she looked at her watch.

"Don't do that," he said instantly.

She laughed; she had only done it at the prompting of that instinct which always warned her, when in his company, to be the first to suggest making a move.

"Why must you wear one of those horrible things?" he went on.

"I couldn't do without one, now. I'm used to it."

"Yes; in other words you're a slave; a slave to Time. Don't you like just being here with me? Where have you got to go rushing *off* to? You're so *active*, Nello."

"Nowhere, actually. But I was . . . we've got someone on at The Primula this evening in place of Nerina, and I was just wondering how they're all getting on." (Too well she liked just sitting there with him . . . the useless, hopeless, 'fruitless'— in the pet word of her headmistress at Claregates—pastime that led nowhere, and achieved only a little temporary happiness) . . . "she's awfully ancient; Miss B. dug her up from somewhere in one of the back courts . . . we were all rather afraid she would collapse."

"In place of Nerina? Miss Berringer hasn't sacked her, has she?"

"Oh no. But she didn't come in yesterday evening or this evening. We're wondering if she's ill." She hesitated; she had meant from the beginning of their talk to ask him if he knew Nerina's address, but had put off mentioning it because of the annoying little pain. "Do you happen to know where she lives?" she said.

"It's somewhere at the back of Kentish Town Road, I think. But why are you wondering if she's ill? Did she look ill the last time you saw her?"

"Not *ill*, exactly, but I do think she's missing Chris very much."

"The bloody Army," he said, but mildly. "Well, I suppose I must get to work." He stood up, as if he had abruptly come to a decision, and the quick movement almost audibly dispersed the peace in the room. "I've been meaning to . . . only this business with Benedict rather got in the way. Thank you for your sweet company, Nello." He paused; Nell had gone to the dressing table. "Are you going to brush your hair? If you are, I'll stay."

She shook her head. "Only comb it." But he lingered at the door, watching.

"I shouldn't take your parents' passion for television too seriously," he said, turning away as she put down the comb. "You must make allowances for novelty with elderly people, you know. By the way, will you make arrangements to be at home tomorrow evening, please."

"I'm going to a film with Robert."

"Oh, you must put him off. I may need you."

Nell just smiled, sitting at the dressing table and beginning to paint her nails.

"I mean it, Nello. You may be able to be of real use to someone in a serious hole if you arrange to stay in."

"Do run along, John, if you have work to do. I have; masses."

"I shall expect you to be here."

He shut the door behind him with distinct annoyance. Such rubbish; as if I should put off Robert, Nell thought.

In a moment she got up and turned on the light; the shadows in the room had lost their tender bloom and become merely inconvenient, and she was remembering the expression which had come into his face when he had heard that Nerina was perhaps ill.

Was the 'someone in a serious hole' Nerina?

The next day, to John's great pleasure, was very hot.

He passed its earlier hours in his favourite place, lying half-asleep on the sofa and watching the shaft of sunlight imperceptibly moving round the room while its clear morning gold changed to the heavier beam of afternoon. The old woman shuffled in and out, silently setting before the boy and the huge cat dozing on his chest a scrap of fish or a steaming drink; the two scarcely spoke to one another throughout the unnoticed gliding by of the hours. It was one of the days when Miss Lister appeared lost in the past.

Late in the morning he suddenly began to feel charged with energy. He gently lifted the warm limp weight from his chest and set it on the floor, laughing at its outraged expression, then sprang up and stretched himself and went into the kitchen.

Miss Lister sat there with *The Sketch*, before the open window.

"I wasn't asleep," she said instantly.

"I know, auntie. I'm going out now. Thank you for a lovely time."

"That's all right, dear. It's cosy, just you and me, isn't it? Will you be back tonight?"

"I don't know. . . . I don't think so."

"Sorry you had such a business waking me up last night. Getting old and deaf."

"Nonsense. You'll never be old." He dropped a kiss on the tiny claw, covered with brown patches, resting on the table; it was the first distasteful moment of the day, "I do wish you would let me have a key."

She shook her head. "Can't do that, dear. You'd lose it."

"I would be so careful, truly."

"No, dear. I'm not afraid of burglars (I once told one he ought to be ashamed of himself and go home, when I found him in the kitchen; I wasn't much older than you; I'm not afraid of the brutes). But I can't have strangers wandering in."

"They wouldn't have the chance to. But I won't worry you. Good-bye."

He left her humming 'Dolly Gray' to herself, apparently moved to memory by some photographs of marching soldiers in the paper, and slipped out through the stiffly opening, seldom-used front door and into the street.

It was asleep in the lunch-time hush. All the little shops were closed; children were indoors at their meal or taking it at school; lemons and carrots in the greengrocers' glowed through the warm shadows. He went down the steep narrow hill, past Well Walk and its large now-fading elms beneath which Keats once strolled, to the East Heath Road, and there was the Heath outspread. The rains of summer had left its grass still green, but already the chestnut leaves, first to bud and first to wither, were shaded with gold, and the still air cast a veil over the sky that made its blue faint and pale. A distant figure in black, walking slowly under the motionless trees accompanied by a dog, might have been either man or woman; it was only a human figure, acceptably unobtrusive, and just warding off from the scene that hint of mystery, which some find sorrowful, that haunts an empty landscape.

But Nature did not please John best of all; he preferred people and houses, because to watch people, and to reflect their

actions back in words, was his purpose in life; and now as he
went down the avenue of lime trees casting a shade green as
emeralds and making the fields beyond their cool gloom appear
dazzlingly bright, he was looking towards the Viaduct, the
massive brick erection spanning the Heath's darkest and
deepest pond.

They were not visible from the lime-tree walk, but in fancy
he could see the two black archways set one at either side of
the towers supporting the bridge, and he was recalling the
story, told to him by one of those women whom his mother had
paid to take him out, when he was a little boy.

He remembered Mrs. Russell well; and now he knew what
she had been; a near-lady fallen on hard days, with a fondness
for beads and scent, and a liking for chatting with the fine big
outdoor men who were the keepers of the Heath. John could
hear her excited laugh now. The noise had strangely repelled
him even when he was six years old: he had never liked loud
talk and rough greedy behaviour; the silent, the soft, and gentle,
and orderly, and getting what he wanted by secret ways, had,
ever since he could remember, been what had drawn him
towards itself.

One of the keepers had told Mrs. Russell the story.

This had been before the Great War, before 1914. There
had been a young girl who had 'fallen into some kind of
trouble', and she had run away. She had gone to live in one
of the cold, dark, lofty cells hollowed in the bricks of the
Viaduct, hiding there by day (not so many people used to
come up to the Heath in those days; people worked longer
hours and there wasn't so much money about for making
excursions) and coming out at night to buy her food—in those
days, too, the shops in Kentish and Camden Town stayed
open very late. But presently, the man had said, *she began to
smell*, and the keepers, about their business of guarding and
tidying the Heath, noticed this animal odour coming out of the
dark hole and went in and found her, and brought her out.
After that, the bars of iron had been placed across the archways.

The story had enthralled the little John, standing silently
beside Mrs. Russell and hearing the deep voice sounding far
above his head, punctuated by her exclamations of wonder and
disgust.

What had become of the girl? Had the keepers sent her to

prison? What had been *the trouble* into which she had *fallen*?
And what had she done all day, hiding in the dark hole from
which she could look out, and downward, at the wide sleepy
faces of the water-lilies gazing up at the bright sky? He had
once smelled a water-lily; an older boy, a member of a gang
of rough, determined children sleeping in air-raid shelters and
eating when and where they could, with whom he had for a
few days played by the pond, had given up a whole morning
to securing the flower with the help of sticks, and string, and
wadings into frighteningly deep mud.

John had never forgotten the feeling of the thick, wet, heavy
petals thrust against his face by the triumphant picker. The
faint, dirty smell of the boy's hand had been overcome at once
by the astonishingly powerful scent of the flower; a scent that
went too far, like a banquet which will at any moment collapse
into riot as the water-nymphs undulate into the hall.

Soon afterwards, these children had been found by their
friends and relations and the authorities, and had left the Heath.
He never saw them again, but the flavour of their lawless life
had lingered on, holding for him a wonderful charm that had
persisted until now, almost into his manhood. This memory,
so strong as almost to deserve another name which should
embody its power over him, had formed his present way of
living. It returned upon him, whenever he crossed this part of
the Heath; shutting all other thoughts and feelings away; and
of course when there returned at the same time the awful
sentence *she began to smell*, what he breathed, almost before the
horror had time to get upon him, was the scent of the water-
lily.

Now these memories gradually receded, and he looked
vacantly about him. He was crossing those wide upland slopes
stretching between Kenwood and Highgate Village which
must surely, as the months of summer which see them covered
in red sorrel and silver grasses suggest, have formerly been
grazing meadows. But he was bored by now, and as he walked
quickly onward over the grass bleached to pale gold, his
eager expression was already welcoming those streets of
houses yet unseen where he was going to look for Nerina. They
would make no demands upon his pity or his kindness; they
would only hold up their mysterious squalid beauty to the
mirror of his senses; and he longed to be among them.

Half an hour later, he was; his long legs carried him swiftly through the cheerful commercial ugliness of the main roads, and now the beauty of private life, expressed in houses shabby and quiet, was opening before him again.

The streets were a maze without an ending beneath a silent, hot, blue afternoon sky; façades of pale brown brick trimmed with white stone looked out forlornly on trampled gardens where the white privet, flower of the back streets, bloomed. He began to wander, lost in delight. The languor of mid-afternoon hushed the long empty roads; there was hardly anyone about; late August heat beat upwards from pale pavements, and every now and then he passed a bush covered in black berries that looked at him with a glinting stare: children of the elderflowers that had been white there in early summer; witch-potion berries; country cousins to the drugs and nostrums sold in the furtive little chemists' shops in the main roads . . . and he had forgotten that he was looking for Nerina. He was wandering, moving always more dreamily and slowly, farther and farther into the maze of back streets.

But when he had drifted at last to a standstill, and, everything now forgotten, was sitting on a low balustrade of weathered grey limestone that had once held a row of iron railings and now had only the sockets, with the flowers of a privet bush falling on his shoulders, he saw a girl with fair hair go by at the end of the road: like someone in a painting; beautiful; and she made him think of Nerina.

He sighed, and got up from the balustrade. Human beings: except inasmuch as they provided material for writers, what a bloody nuisance they were.

There came a puff of breeze and the innocent smell of the privet blossoms blew over him. Then, floating across the roofs from two or three roads away, there came a hoarse, hollow, quavering cry.

It was the voice of the rag-and-bone man, walking slowly down some street hidden by the brown houses under their roofs of warm grey slate; moving along beside his small cart loaded with iron bedsteads and pickle jars and old mattresses, and drawn by a plump elderly pony:

"A—a   ra'—a—a   a' bo-a—a—,
A—a   ra'—a—a   a' bo-a—a—,"

and as the call floated down through the dreaming air, a flock of pigeons went up; grey and white in the hot, still blue, and their shadows skimmed across the road.

That was the voice of London, my old love, John thought; the voice of my wicked old love; and, looking about him and realizing that a turning far on to the left of this street would bring him out near Landseer Circus, he began to move more quickly towards it.

Now a slope covered with tall, white, ruinous houses was bringing him out onto one of the many gentle ridges of North London; gradually lifting its burden of very poor houses up into the sunlight of a crescent where grew huge, ancient, shabby trees. Attic windows here glared darkly at the sky, and their bleached, askew frames were sinking sideways into their roofs. They sent down a breath from Mayhew's London— and older yet: Hogarth's procuresses, and country innocence blasted and betrayed. And here, glancing upwards, he saw at one of these terrible windows a turbanned head; this was where Africa could afford to live, and Africa had found it.

Front doors stood open; a stench of stale fat or a cold catty breath came out of dark entries as he went by. The oval expanse of grass was trampled almost bare; the trunks of the big noble sycamores were scored deeply with names and initials and linked hearts; all round the crescent was a curve of huge, decaying, massive dark grey mansions; with attics high, high in the sky of summer, and appearing as if sealed for ever against its warmth and light. The dusty masses of leaves and the dirty masses of plaster and brick enclosed the air here, making it smell stale. John, disliking nothing that he saw, sat down on one of the remaining patches of grass and smoked: this was Landseer Circus, and if Nerina lived here she would be easy to find, for he saw people going in and out of each other's houses continually; they must all know one another; while the place was becoming crowded with children beginning to swarm home from school. Someone would be sure to know Nerina, if she lived here.

Presently a shadow fell upon him.

He looked up; an African girl of about twelve years old was slowly pushing a perambulator across the grass, with an African baby in it, gazing into the distance with a grave expression that somehow matched her neat clean dress and her polished shoes.

"Good afternoon," said John.

She just nodded; she did not turn to look at him.

"I wonder if you can help me," he went on. "I expect your

mother has told you never to talk to strangers and she is quite right. There are some very wicked people about. But I am only trying to find a friend, whom I think lives in the Crescent. Her name is Nerina. Do you know her?"

Now she did turn to look at him.

"Chris's Nerina?"

"That's exactly what she is. Do you know her, then?"

"Not so well as what I do him. He painted my photo. In my Guides uniform, I am." The voice, gentle as his own, had a cooing undertone that suggested—to John, at least—generations of forefathers who had come running in haste at the master's summons; timid, yet anxious also to please; but her liquid black pupils set in yellowish whites looked at him without a trace of anxiety or suspicion.

"Can you show me the house where she lives?"

The girl nodded and pointed. "It's the one with the red curtains. But she don't live there no more now; she's gone away," and the voice dropped to a doleful note.

"Oh dear. Far away?"

Again a shake of her head. But a glimmer of laughter was in the black eyes.

"How far?" he asked, beginning to smile too.

"Just down there in Padstow Street," pointing to a turning visible from where they stood, "that's the house, with the *blue* curtains." They both burst out laughing; a crowd of little boys rushed shouting past the perambulator accompanied by three dogs seeming well able to support the prevailing spirit of the group, and the African baby began to cry.

"There, s'sh; there," she said, rocking it.

"Will you tell me your name, please?"

"Grace. What's *your* name, please?" The glint of laughter, which the baby's distress had banished, returned.

"John Gaunt. Do you like it?" Admiration he must have, if only from a little African girl.

She shook her head, laughing still.

"Oh, well, I like yours. It's charming. And now will you come with me to the house where Nerina is?"

"Go on; you can get there easy yourself; it's that one with the blue curtains; I showed you."

"I know, but I want you to come too; I like your company."

"Mammy says I'm not to go there and I don't want to neither," she answered calmly. "That Angie is a bad woman who drinks. She drinks all her pension away. I wouldn't even take our baby the side of the road where her house is; he might catch something. But tell you what I will do, John, I'll come to the end of the patch with you and across the road to ours."

"That's very kind of you, Grace. Thank you."

They strolled together across the stale, trampled grass where sheets of faded newspaper were lying; between the children, playing busily in the dust. The eyes of the baby, liquid and grey as those of a very young kitten, rested fixedly upon John, and Grace said that he had taken to him; John looked at the two dark faces into whose shining skins the sky seemed to have reflected some of its intense, its almost African, blue; and lingered long enough by the open door of Grace's house to catch a glimpse at the end of a dimly-lit passage covered in well-polished oilcloth, of a low, glowing red fire. He could catch a soft high babble of voices; a leisured, lazy, cosy feeling floated out from that dimness, alluring as a savoury smell.

"I wish you'd ask me to tea," he said.

"I can't, John. I've got me homework to do, and then there's our baby to put to bed, our Lily does it most days but this week she's on night-shift, and then there's me Guides."

"Who is your Lily?"

"My sister. And Mammy says never to ask anyone to ask you in to theirs without they say it first."

"Give Lily my love. Tell her that John Gaunt, the writer, sends her his love. I hope you'll have a nice time at your Guides. *I am a Girl Guide dressed in blue, These are the things I have to do*—that's what you say, isn't it?—and thank you for telling me where Nerina lives, and thank you for your company, Grace dear. Perhaps we'll see one another again one day. Good-bye."

She said "Bye-bye, John. Be seeing you." Well, one could not expect everything, even from someone who looked as if she could have been niece to Jupiter in "The Gold Bug". As he crossed the street and went up the steep, filthy broken steps of the forlorn house where Nerina lived, his head was filled with parrakeets, and sugar cane, and voodoo, and an African waterlily.

CHAPTER EIGHTEEN

ACT THREE:
THE GARDEN IN SURREY AGAIN

NERINA was lying on the bed looking at those marks on the door.

It was one of the broad, thick doors found in London whose presence means that a house is very old, and it had the slightly clumsy cast that such doors always have; a disturbing look; a too-old look, if you are someone who likes straight lines and finds comfort in firm, stately controlled proportions. The whole attic, filled with late sunshine, papered in ragged, peeling blue, looked as if it had been built by twisted, evil people.

The marks were the worst thing. The lock had been taken off the door, leaving a white square, but it had been *wrenched* off; there were the savage gouges, deep in the wood. Why? She lay still, staring at the marks between eyelids stiff and sore with crying. In fancy she heard the shouts of rage, and feet rushing up the stairs. Then, afterwards, when it was quiet, somebody had taken the lock off the door, tearing it away, muttering while they worked on it in remembered fury, so that someone else should never again be able to lock themselves into the room, and feel safe.

Nerina had put the broken armchair against the door, but Angie had pushed her way in and sat on the bed, talking, for nearly an hour. She had just gone. The room still smelled of the powder she used, and Nerina could still hear her deep, slurred, old voice saying kind things that made Nerina feel sick.

Suddenly her calm face twisted. She rolled over on the filthy flock pillow, buried her face in her hands and her dulled yellow hair, and began to cry again. The tears poured down her burning face, onto Chris's first letter lying beneath her cheek. She was dirty; she had felt too ill to go to the public baths or take her clothes to the laundrette, as usual, yesterday, and besides there was the money . . . she only had half-a-crown left, now that she had paid Angie a week's rent in advance, and although it would be all right when she went back to The

Primula, they would probably pay her . . . but she wasn't
sure . . . Miss Berringer was not generous about money and was
very down on slackness. . . .

She kissed the letter weakly. It had been all right; for hunger
and exhaustion and even dirt had not mattered while Chris
was there, but now he had been gone only a week, and it was
two years before they would be really together again, safely
together and free. Two *years*.

He had never been in this room; she could not think, *that's
where he used to stand to take off his sweater, here is the mark of his
head on the pillow* (she would leave a pillow unshaken for days
because it bore the impression of his head). There were only
his precious painting materials to remind her of him, arranged
carefully on a clean piece of sacking in the middle of the black
rag that had once been a carpet. Whatever happened to her,
those must be waiting for him, complete and unharmed, when
he came back.

She lay still for a while, occasionally giving a hiccoughing sob.
There was no abandonment in her crying; it kept some appearance of control and reluctance, like the crying of a well-
brought-up child; she would not have been crying at all—she
told herself—if only all her will-power and her energy and her
sensibleness had not suddenly gone. It was disloyal to Chris
to cry. She had been all right up to three days ago. It was
Chris going away, and this queer feeling-ill, and having the
money stolen.

Four whole pounds. She moaned again, softly, with a note
of exasperation rather than of despair. It was a nice house in
the Circus, where she and Chris had had their room; they were
nice people in that house, truly, it wasn't like this dreadful
house, but Rosina, in the top front room—she was a dear but
she did have men in. One of them must have stolen the money
from behind the picture called *Excelsior*, with that ridiculous
St. Bernard rescuing the traveller, which she and Chris had
always laughed at, where Nerina had hidden it.

Four pounds. Oh . . . h . . . h . . . Chris had saved it for her,
eating apples and oatmeal; going hungry, so that she might
have a little secret hoard to fall back on if anything awful
happened. And she had hidden it behind the picture that they
had so often laughed at together, and someone had stolen it.
She had nothing but half-a-crown in the world, and she was
dirty and hungry and feeling ill.

She was half-kneeling on the broken bed now. The intense gold of fading sunrays stained her scanty petticoat and turned the damp strings of her hair to pallid fire. She was looking straight into the glare beyond the dim, sunken window panes, pressing her lips together to keep back the tears, when there came a sharp rapping on that awful door. Angie!

"No! No, you can't come in," Nerina called, in a tone from which the silvery note had gone. She stared at the door with drowned, dilated eyes, keeping quite still. If she came in again, reeking of scent, with her wrinkled naked neck rising out of that dirty lace blouse . . . But—

"It's John Gaunt, Nerina," and at the mere sound of a voice she knew, terror and loneliness seemed to lift.

"Oh yes—John . . . come in. I'm sorry," she gasped.

She was drawing the dirty coverlet up to her chin while she felt beneath the pillow for a tortoiseshell ring, and when he did come in, having given her a moment's grace, on hearing the fear and the tears in her voice, she had drawn her hair back into its accustomed tassel.

She knelt on the bed, holding the quilt high in her two hands and looking full at him above its limp folds.

"Dear Nerina. How glad I am to have found you," he said, smiling. "I've been hunting for you all day, all over Camden Town and Kentish Town and Highgate, and I shouldn't have found you now if I hadn't met a delightful little African girl named Grace."

He leaned with folded arms against the door, and even as his long graceful body concealed the chisel marks, so his calm expression and gentle voice seemed to cause the tension in the hot, quiet, dirty room to become less, to subside into ordinary unhappiness.

"Grace Ajuna? Oh yes—Chris painted her. She's a darling . . . it's nice to see you, John." She tried to give him her sweet masklike smile. "Did—have you just come to see me yourself? Or—I expect they're wondering what on earth's happened to me at The Primula, aren't they?"

Already she was feeling better. The world was becoming real again. She would not be so afraid of Angie if John could be here when she came back. . . .

"I believe they *are* rather agitated. But they've managed to get in some old person temporarily, I believe. Or so Nell says." He glanced round the room. "May I sit down?"

"There's only the bed, I'm afraid . . . this is a horrid place; I'm sorry. . . ."

"I thought you lived in Landseer Circus?" he said gently, when he was seated at the end of the bed, then, without waiting for her answer, "no, this is a social visit. No one sent me. The fact is, I thought you might be feeling rather low, with Chris in the Army, and would enjoy some company."

"It was nice of you." She glanced restlessly away; then controlled herself, straightening her limbs beneath the quilt, and went on, "but I'm all right really, you know. I'm just missing Chris and feeling rather tired. I was going back to work tomorrow—back to The Primula, that is. I've lost my job at Maretti's."

Suddenly she gave an hysterical chuckle.

"Oh . . . you know, I thought I was safe for ever, there, but it was the chef."

"The one Chris wanted to bash, and Benedict and I restrained him?"

"Emilio, yes. You knew he always pinches people, and we have to put up with it because the whole place depends on his cooking . . . I always hated it but I couldn't say anything . . . and then Chris went . . . and somehow I felt much worse about the pinching. I was *angry*. I belong . . . " She stopped; the sea-shell pink came slowly up. "So I pushed him. He fell into a pan of batter," she ended gravely.

Neither laughed. John smiled faintly and inspected the tip of his shoe; Nerina drew a long quivering sigh.

"And then our money was stolen," she said.

He looked up. "All this in three days?" and she nodded.

"What a bloody silly place to hide anything," was his mild comment when the story had been told. "Have you let Chris know?"

She quietly shook her head.

"I think you ought to, you know. He'll be much angrier if he finds out you've been having a horrible time without telling him."

She reared up her slim, long white neck, looking dignified for all her not-quite-clean petticoat and reddened eyes, and he was filled with admiration. Love must be a powerful agent indeed; he wondered for an instant what it must be like to lie helpless under that spell. . . .

"I can manage," she said. "I expect they'll have me back at

The Primula—Miss Berringer's always telling me what a good waitress I am—and if they won't, washing-up jobs are very easy to get. I should have gone job-hunting today, if I hadn't been feeling rather ill. Most unlike me. Very odd."

He had been watching her. Now, with a muttered apology, he leant over and held out his cigarette case.

"Oh *no*—thank you." There was a note of uncontrollable repugnance, and he looked at her for a moment before he put the case away.

"You know, Nerina . . . " he was examining a shoelace with a dissatisfied expression, "you must listen carefully to me. Because something has got to be done about you. And—"

"I can manage, John," she repeated rather haughtily. "I'm perfectly all right. I know this is an awful room but I shan't stay here. I only moved into it because I got rather fussed about having our money stolen, and I hadn't enough for the next week's rent of our old room. I didn't *want* to leave there." She looked quickly round the attic. "I think it's horrible here." Suddenly she gave a violent shudder, "And Angie. . . . " She looked at him. "Have you seen her?"

He nodded. "She opened the door to me."

"Isn't she . . . I think she's frightening."

"Oh, do you? Well, perhaps—to someone like you. She doesn't frighten me."

"Oh, doesn't she? Why not, John?"

"Because I could manage her," he said. "Any man could; she's like that."

"Oh," Nerina said. She did not seem to be listening. "Well," looking down at the quilt and smoothing it, "so you see I'm getting out of here just as soon as I can. Tomorrow, I hope. Only . . . " she began to speak more quickly, "I got rather fussed about everything, the money and missing Chris and feeling rather peculiar, and when I tried to get up . . . tried . . . to see if there . . . go to our old room to see if there was a letter . . . I couldn't . . . sick . . . so sick . . . I . . . can't even . . . a *letter*. . . . "

He had moved over to her and was stroking her shoulder as she lay shaking on the bed.

"There, there, Nino. *Do* cry, if it makes you feel better. Don't you like being stroked? Sorry: I'll hold your hand then, instead. In a brotherly clasp. (You've got quite a grip, haven't you?) You see, Nino darling, something has *got* to be done about you now. Why you feel peculiar is because you're going to have a baby."

She had been wringing his hand in a sort of distraction. Now she suddenly became still. He did not move, but kept a gentle clasp round the long limp little hand lying in his own, looking down at the yellow head. Presently it jerked feebly; hardly a movement from side to side; just a weak movement implying negation.

"I think you are, Nino. People are always sick when they're going to have babies. (I don't wonder at it. The prospect is enough to make anyone sick.) And your eyes look *most* odd: just like Harry Miles's girl's eyes did when *she* was going to." He paused: the head stayed still. "You were thinking it was hunger-sickness, weren't you? But I'm sure it's not."

Again she slightly moved the tassel of primrose hair.

"Don't keep on like some charming little parrot. I say you *are*. You think, for a moment."

Apparently she did, for soon she surprised him by sitting up, and composedly putting a very clean handkerchief to her stained and swollen face.

"I did think. But I thought . . . I didn't think for a minute . . . "

He was not certain if that was what the murmur was.

"I'm sure of it," he said with his air of authority. "You must go to the doctor tomorrow."

"I simply . . . can't believe . . . "

"You will when you've had some dinner. I don't want to hurry you, because you've just had a perfectly horrible shock, but shall we be making a move? We can talk about what you're going to do while we're dining."

For the next twenty minutes he enjoyed one of those 'times', more frequent with him than with most people, when he was completely happy. Nerina was responding to his instructions like an automaton; he moved her from the bed to the washstand with a stained marble top where her comb and brush were arranged; he made her smooth her hair and powder her face; then sent her back to the bed ("—put your feet up. You see, I do know something about it") to wait while he quickly assembled her possessions.

All expression had left her small face. She looked completely peaceful and passive, and he moved her round the attic as if it were a chessboard and she the Ivory Queen which she now rather resembled.

"There," he said at last. He looked with satisfaction at the two shabby cases, fastened with that thick string which the postal authorities tie round bundles of letters and which postmen drop in the streets as they make their rounds. "Now you wait here for five minutes. I'm going to run these downstairs and soothe down Angie. When I'm ready I'll call you. And mind you come down at *once*, Nino dear."

He caught up the luggage and swung out of the room, mastery and enjoyment expressed in every movement.

Left alone, Nerina at once shut her eyes. She did not want to perhaps harm the baby by looking at this ugly, frightening place, and she at once filled her mind's eye with the image of Chris. She was now certain that she was going to have the baby, but she was so tired that she had no thoughts.

Presently she heard John's voice. The strong, commanding sound rang up easily through the house, penetrating the tainted air that lingered in black damp passages and lay thick in quiet rooms muffled with dusty curtains and dirty furniture.

"Nino! Everything's ready. Come down, please."

It seemed already on its way, that voice; moving off; leaving everything in this evil, frightening house behind it.

"Nino! Come down, please!"

Obediently, she got up off the bed and went out of the attic and down the stairs without once looking around her or giving a backward glance.

In the hall, John was standing with Angie, and the cases were being taken out of the front door by a taxi driver. John and Angie moved apart as Nerina came down; it looked as if he had had his arm around her; but Nerina's mind was still empty of thoughts; and she did not look at the woman after the first sight of her, which she could not avoid. She went straight out of the house and down the steps to the taxi, and when the driver saw her, in her pale shabby coat with her head held high, he first looked surprised, and then he opened the door of the taxi for her, calling her 'miss'. No-one would ever believe it of Nerina that she was one of the rare ones who will throw away safety and shelter and peace and virginity, and run a knife into their parents, for love; she would always be looked at with respect and called 'miss'.

She settled herself into a corner seat, looking ahead at nothing.

" . . . know you won't believe me, to look at it now, but it was exactly that colour," Angie was saying to John. She patted the dyed frizz of tow on her forehead. "I was as blonde as a chicken. That's why I took to her . . . don't you hurt her! I know your sort, I knew the sort you are the minute I saw you . . . there, now I'm crying and you've made my mascara run. . . . "

He got away from her somehow and ran down the steps.

"Don't you hope you won't ever get old?" he said, suddenly, when the taxi had been travelling for some moments, "I'd much rather die at thirty-five than live to be like that. Of course, if one could have clean silver hair and no stomach and be the greatest writer in the world . . . "

Nerina smiled vaguely without answering, and he leaned back and was quiet for a little while. He now looked rather cross. Suddenly she turned to him, exclaiming:

"Oh! Chris's painting things!"

"It's all right." He pointed to a bundle wrapped in newspaper at her feet. "They're all there, everything. Quite safe."

"Oh, John. You are kind. Thanks most *frightfully*."

For the first time since he had come into the attic, she appeared to be moved by what he was doing for her. She put out her hand and gave his a quick pressure. But she added at once: "I'd *forgotten* them. Imagine: Chris's painting things. That was *frightful* of me."

"You had something more interesting (I don't say more important) to think about," he said tolerantly. "Motherhood is always said to be the most important experience in a woman's whole life. As for being kind . . . " his expression did not change and his voice went on smoothly, "never mind that . . . now. We can talk about it when we've had dinner."

In a moment, as she said nothing, he added hastily in what Nell, and Nell alone, would have recognized as the youngest of his voices, "I say, please don't get the wrong impression, Nino; I may have sounded like some horrible little stockbroker; I'm not at all in love with you; as a matter of fact, I'm terribly in love with someone very grand; older than I am, and quite hopelessly out of reach, who's just had a tragic affair herself with the most frightful vulgar publicity attached —so you needn't be at all alarmed; so far as you are concerned I'm just *brotherly*."

She did not answer. In a moment, not knowing, in spite of

his boast, much about pregnancy, he leant forward and peered in alarm at her pale face. She was peacefully asleep. He smiled, and drew her into the shelter of his arm so that her head rested on his shoulder, and thus they rode on up to Hampstead.

About eight o'clock, as Nell was letting herself into the house after an unusually tiring day at the tea-shop which had ended in an unsatisfactory hour with a mysteriously gloomy Robert in an Espresso bar—(don't want to go to a movie—what's the matter?—I should think it was obvious—well, it isn't—oh well, then—what on earth *is* the matter, Robert?—oh well, this doesn't seem to be getting us anywhere—I'm going home, I'm tired—oh very well then, I'm sorry to have been so *boring*—) she heard herself imperiously hailed. She turned quickly, to see John assisting Nerina to alight from a taxi.

"Assisting her to alight" was precisely what he was going; "helping her to get out" gave a quite inadequate impression of his manner.

Nell came leisurely down the steps in response to his urgent beckoning.

"Hullo. Hullo, Nerina. Have you been to a party?" she said, giving the little pain a little dismissing slap.

"Yes, and no," said John. Nerina, standing as if in a dream at the foot of the steps while he paid the taximan, gave a vague smile in no direction which, Nell supposed, she might take for herself, if she wanted it. They were surrounded by cases and bundles.

"Now don't rush *off*, Nello." John began to sweep up the luggage into his long arms. "I'm glad you stayed in; I shall want you. Will you please go up to the flat and make some coffee? (We have dined, but there was no time for coffee.) We've got some telephoning to do, and we can't do it in a booth, with morons bellowing for their turn . . . go on, Nino, darling; you know the way." As they entered the hall and Nell shut the door, he added, "Is my papa at home, do you know?"

Nell shook her head. "I haven't the faintest idea."

She was annoyed; first Robert, going on like Marlon Brando, and now John, taking it for granted in spite of having *seen* her just *going* into the house that she had been quietly sitting at home waiting for him all the evening. Really, it would be a relief when she was peacefully sharing her life and work with Elizabeth. . . .

"I must just let the parents know I'm in," she said.

"Oh, all right. But don't hang about."

Nerina had gone on ahead, drifting up the stairs with her spoiled ballet-dancer's walk. As Nell was going towards the drawing-room door, John stopped her.

"She's going back to her people," he said so quietly that she barely heard, "she's going to have a baby."

"Oh? Is it Chris's?" Nell asked.

It was a shocking thing to say; she knew, as she said it, that of course the baby was Chris's. Whatever else one might feel about Nerina, where her love was concerned she was 'as chaste as ice and as pure as snow'. But the little pain, long endured and now, thank goodness, presumably to be endured no longer, would have its little revenge on its cause.

He drew quickly away from her and straightened his shoulders.

"*Nell!* I knew you could be a Philistine and smug and narrow. But I didn't know that you could be . . . *base.*" He went grandly up the stairs after his protegée.

"Oh phooey," muttered Nell, as she opened the drawing-room door. She was greeted with the usual half-darkness, changing square of greyish light, and sound of playful voices. She withdrew at once, to the sound of impatient murmurs from the rapt audience.

She was thinking more about Robert, and wondering how he was spending what remained of this ruined evening, than about Nerina or John. They had parted with a half-promise from him to telephone her; she was not concerned lest any silly final break had occurred; it was only that she did not like him to go in for sulky mystery; she had quite enough of that with someone else.

The door of the Gaunts' flat stood open and the lights were on. As she came up the dark stairs she could see John and Nerina sitting together on the big sofa which had sometimes held him and herself. He was fondly surveying his Work in Progress.

"Aren't you still a little drunk? You look rather glassy, you know."

"I don't think so. Not now. But I feel much better . . . oh! You don't think being a little drunk could be bad for the baby, do you?" The silvery note was returning to Nerina's voice.

"I shouldn't think so. It can't be much of a type if a drop of

Sauterne upsets it. Nell," turning to her as she came into the room, "will you make the coffee, please? We can begin tele- phoning as soon as Papa has taken off."

Nell went into the kitchen and began clattering saucepans about, but however loudly she clattered, she could hear the conversation on the sofa. She could also hear, from behind Charles Gaunt's closed bedroom door, the sound of an electric razor.

" . . . if you're really sure, Nino darling, that they *will* have you back," John was saying.

"Oh yes." Nearly seventeen years of unshaken security and love sounded their calm chimes in the silver voice. "I'm sure they will. But you will make it absolutely clear, won't you, John, that they've got to be nice to Chris as well."

"Yes, I'll make that perfectly clear at once."

"Because, unless they do promise that, I'm simply not going."

"Nino—I hate to say this when you're feeling so much better —but suppose they won't have you unless you give him up?"

"Then I'll manage somehow by myself," smiling. "There are Homes and places."

"And that's your last word?"

She nodded. The pale green eyes smiled at him in the sweet silent face.

A one-man woman, Nell thought; well, aren't we all? Or most of us. Unfortunately. It seemed to her that the ones who were not had an easier time of it, and it was at that precise moment, while thoughtfully watching the water coming up to the boil, that she wondered if she might not begin trying to turn herself into one of them?

"John!" It was Charles Gaunt's voice, coming from behind the bedroom door, "Is that you? Where in hell have you been these last two nights? I sat up until nearly three waiting for you last night. I've got to talk to you."

"Papa always talks in movie-dialogue, you mustn't mind," Nell heard John observe in a lowered tone to Nerina. "Oh . . . I was out and about, Papa," calling cheerfully. "I'm so sorry you waited up. Can't we talk this evening?"

"No, we can not. I'm due at Ealing in three-quarters of an hour, to take part in a *home-brewed wine-tasting contest*, God help me. I'll see you tomorrow."

The door flew open and he appeared, twitching and gloom- ing, pushing a clean handkerchief into the pocket of his dinner jacket and giving the two, especially Nerina, a sarcastic glower.

"Shall I get you a taxi, Papa?"

"Thank you; a car is coming for me; in three minutes."

John then gracefully introduced him to Nerina, Mrs. Rutton; silent bows were exchanged; Charles-for-god's-sake propped himself dejectedly against the mantelshelf; and then the arrival of the car was announced by John, craning out of the window.

Immediately his father had gone, he told Nerina to put her feet up.

"There," he said, disposing them upon a cushion. "Nell, we'll have the coffee now, thank you. Nerina can drink it while she's listening to me telephoning."

Nell came in with an untroubled face, carrying the tray. Let him show off; Nerina was not even looking at him.

She set down the tray. She was beginning to feel slightly excited, and to feel for Nerina, sitting there with her yellow hair dragged back from her pale, tired face and her feet up. But at the same time she wondered if she *need* feel? Nerina seemed neither apprehensive nor sad; she was looking into her coffee-cup with no expression at all.

John was kneeling on the sofa arranging his overcoat across her feet. When this was done, he got up, and stood looking down at her.

"Well, now if you're comfortable, I'm going to start."

She looked up. Her face was still perfectly calm.

"Oh yes, do," she said. "I rather want to get it over." She made a tiny pause; then looked from one to the other. "You *have* both been kind. The coffee's wonderful, Nell. I . . . shall tell Chris, later on, how kind you both were."

It was the highest reward she could bestow.

But John said quickly, going over to the telephone:

"That's all right, Nino, we don't want to be thanked. I know I said something earlier this evening about your doing something later on perhaps . . . I didn't mean it too seriously, but if you *do* want to please me, be as much in your garden at home as you can. You'll sit in it, won't you? while the baby's swelling or whatever it is they do . . . I like to think of you there. It's your *proper place*."

There was a sound as if the unearthly bell at The Primula were feeling amused.

"Is it? It's lovely, of course, and I used to quite like sun-

bathing there. But gardening itself bores me. And of course it
will soon be winter . . . he will be a spring baby . . . so I shan't
be able to sit out there much. But whenever I do, John, I'll
think of you and remember how kind you were."

"That's all I want, Nino; just to think of you being in your
proper place. And now I'm going to telephone your people."

He turned to Nell.

"Do you know what her real name is? Mary Falconer. Isn't
it a grand, severe, *tall* name, full of *character*? Doesn't suit you
at all, Nino."

"The telephone number is Leatherwell 255, John," she said
tranquilly. "My father is Doctor Falconer and the address is
Mayfields, Leatherwell, Surrey."

"How convenient. I *thought* you looked rather conscious when
I asked if you knew a *reliable* doctor. By the way, have they a
television set? Yes? Right."

But then he turned round once more.

"I don't think I'd better tell them about the baby, had I?
No," as she shook her head, "you can do that in private. Now
don't interrupt, you two."

The preliminaries took a little time. Nell had sat down in a
corner and was watching John. But she was thinking about
Nerina. What was going on inside the round yellow head?
Was she minding at all? Did she feel sorry for having caused
her parents months of the worst kind of anxiety? Wasn't it
rather an awful prospect, to go back to the place you had
grown up in, after living for nearly a year with a young man
and now be going to have a baby?

Nell thought that *she* would never have been able to face it.

I suppose, she mused, I'm not one of the world-well-lost-for-
Love kind, so it will be all the easier to turn myself into the
kind that isn't a one-man woman either; and then it occurred
to her that it might be fun to be the kind that has lots of men;
men Dancing Attendance, as the Edwardians used to say;
admirers; beaux. . . .

"Hullo! Hullo!" said John suddenly. Nerina turned her
head quickly. "Is that Leatherwell 255? Oh . . . Can I speak
to Doctor Falconer, please? It's extremely important. It's a
private matter. Nothing about a patient . . . oh, is that Mrs.
Falconer? How do you do, Mrs. Falconer? This is John Gaunt
speaking; Peggy Fairfax, the T.V. star, is my mother." (Nell
thought it a good thing Peggy Fairfax, the T.V. star, could not

see his expression.)"Yes . . well, I'm a friend of Mary's . . . "

Across the intervening thirty miles of darkening autumnal country, Nell and, presumably Nerina also, could hear the exclamations break out at the other end of the line. But the daughter's face was calm; her head was drooping a little and her long fingers restfully linked. She did not move. She was looking down at her hands.

"No, she isn't ill. She's quite well. As a matter of fact she's here with me in the room—(I'm speaking from my flat in Hampstead) and—Mrs. Falconer? Are you there? the line's rather bad at this end . . . she wants to come home. Yes . . . Yes. . . . But there is one thing . . . Mrs. Falconer, I must make this absolutely clear before we go any further . . . if she comes there must be no question of her giving up Chris Rutton."

He paused, and listened. Nell caught his eye and he suddenly smiled at her. "Yes," he said, nodding; then, "no, he's in the Army. He went in about ten days ago. Yes. . . . Would you like to speak to her? All right; I'll get her. Just a minute . . . hold on. . . . "

He turned, smiling. and holding out the receiver. Nerina got slowly off the sofa and went across the room, and now Nell saw that her face was deep pink.

"It's going to be all right, I think," John said in a whisper, and she looked a little surprised. She took the receiver from him.

"Mummy? Hullo; this is Mary here." The voice was pure silver again. "Oh, I'm all right. Quite well, really. How are you and Daddy and everybody? Oh. I'm sorry. Poor Daddy. Listen, Mummy—you do understand about Chris, don't you? That I'm not giving him up, I mean. You must tell Daddy, and make him absolutely swear that he won't try to make me. Because if he does anything like that I shall simply go away again."

She listened for a little while with bent head. Suddenly she gave an extraordinary little hiccough, gulped, and shut her eyes. Instantly John was beside her, bending over her, mopping her face with his handkerchief. Soon she gently waved him aside, nodding as if to say that she was all right—but he continued to hover assiduously, with an anxious expression. Nell looked with more liking at Nerina now. Her tears commanded respect. In a moment she was saying quietly:

"All right, then, Mummy dear, I'll see you both in about

two hours, then. Oh . . . it's near the top of Hampstead . . . quite easy to find." She gave brief, clear directions. "I shall be quite all right until you come. Yes. John is being very kind and taking good care of me." She smiled at him; her nose was swollen and pink. "And his cousin, Nell, is here too. We're having coffee. All right, then, Mummy. Give my love to Daddy. I'll see you in about two hours. Good-bye."

She replaced the receiver. No one said anything for a moment. Then Nerina yawned, and smiled at John. It was neither a brave nor a piteous smile, but he said instantly:

"You'd better go to sleep until they come. Here." He put his arm round her. "You come and lie down on my bed. Nell," over his shoulder as he led her unresisting away, "get a hot water bottle, will you? (Papa has a perfect regiment of them in the kitchen, in different sizes for different parts of himself where he gets rheumatism . . . he doesn't seem to realize that as life goes on one should *shed* possessions, not *acquire* them . . .) thank you."

When he came back he was plainly very pleased with himself. He took strides round the room, whistled snatches of tunes, put his hands in his pockets and took them out again, and finally fell upon the sofa and thrust his legs over its end—and stared smilingly up at the ceiling.

Nell got up and went to the door; she did not intend to provide the admiring audience for his self-satisfaction. Round came his head at once.

"Where are you going?"

"To get my supper; I've had nothing since two o'clock."

"Stay and eat it here. There is some liver sausage and three stale rolls, I think."

"Thank you." Nell did not pause in her flight.

He was across the room in two strides. An arm like iron went round her waist and he shook her.

"Nello—" looking down imploringly into her face, "please stay with me, darling Nello. I'm so pleased because I've got Nerina back into her proper place and I want someone to enjoy myself with."

You're quite the best person for that purpose, she thought. But it was difficult to say anything while he was close to her; she only nodded, and he gave her one of his quick, rubbing kisses—and released her.

"You lie on the sofa. I'll bring in the feast," he said.

But while she was eating, not the liver sausage and rolls, but some of his step-mother's store of tinned delicacies, his mood changed. The window stood open and uncurtained to the still, damp, autumn air; now and again a heavy leaf detached itself from the branches of the sycamore trees and went spinning slowly down through the soft light of the old street-lamp to lie on the pavement; the road and the house itself were very quiet.

Nell broke a longish silence by holding up her fork with a piece of ham on it.

"Don't you want—?"

He shook his head.

"Merciful heavens, no. We had an enormous dinner at Belsize Park, with wine. . . . I say, do you think I ought to wake her? She seems to have been asleep a long time."

"Not yet." Nell glanced at the clock. "I shouldn't wake her until just before ten."

"I hate *waiting* for people," he said moodily.

He had got up from his place on the floor, against the sofa, and was prowling round the room. " . . . of course, we shan't see Nerina again after tonight, you know. Dear Nino . . . another proper place for her would be with the ballet-people; do you remember that house in Earls Court where a crowd of them were all living high up under the roof, like a cluster of elegant young bats, among the pink shoes and the wreaths of paper roses and the tu-tus and the lettuce and margarine-papers? But she's too old for ballet now, of course. *Now* where are you going, Nello?" pausing in exasperation.

"To get my knitting."

"Well *don't* get it, please; I like to see a girl doing nothing; knitting is only a form of nervous tension," but this time she ignored him.

When she returned he was leaning out of the window. He turned and looked at her dreamily.

"I wonder what they're feeling, driving along those dark roads under the rhododendrons towards London? Mrs. Falconer sounded so pleased . . . she could hardly speak . . . of course, Nello, because I've been so kind to Nerina and arranged to put her back in her proper place, it doesn't necessarily mean that I approve of the way she's been carrying on."

He left the window and came to sit beside her. Nell was knitting swiftly. "Doesn't it?"

"No. . . . It's bad luck on Chris, you know. Now he'll be saddled with *two* of them. And he won't be able to paint properly, because he'll have to earn money to keep the baby. They'll starve, I should think, unless Doctor Falconer and Chris's father allow them something."

"He could go back to being a gardener," Nell said.

"Go back to being a *gardener*? Really, Nello, will *nothing* cure you of being so hopelessly and *painfully* prosaic? Chris is a *painter*. Most of this trouble has arisen from the fact that no-one will *recognize* that he's a painter."

Nell said nothing, and in a moment he went on:

"Of course, if it were me I should simply curse, in spite of Flaubert and his '*Ills sont dans le droit*'. But Nerina's pleased about it already; I knew that, when she forgot about his painting things when we were coming away from that wonderful house. . . . You 'mark my words', Nello; in a few years the baby will come first and Chris will be a rather bad second." He turned restlessly to the window again. "I say, hadn't we better wake her up? It's getting on for ten."

Nell did not want to spend any more time with him in this mood. It was an odd one. She never remembered having seen him in it before. He seemed pleased, yet bitter over something, triumphant, yet disapproving too. She agreed that it was time to wake Nerina up.

There was not time to make more coffee. As soon as Nerina had come back into the room and was sitting on the sofa again—this time John said nothing about putting her feet up—the minutes began to pass quickly, filled with a little gossip about mutual friends, and the coming journey—and quite soon the Falconers were due to arrive. The room began to be charged with the feeling of anxiety.

"You won't mind if I don't ask them up, will you, Nerina?" John said suddenly, and Nell realised that he had not called her 'Nino darling' since she had awoken from her sleep. "It's such a climb up all these stairs . . . and I'm sure they won't want to see strangers or to talk . . . I'll take you down to them in the hall."

Nerina said that she quite understood. But now her calmness did seem to be slightly troubled, and she was beginning to look a little apprehensive. She said that her parents would certainly want to thank him.

"It *was* kind of me, wasn't it?" He was at the window again, watching for the car. "I think I've managed everything very well . . . and it wasn't 'nothing' because I only had three pounds and I've spent nearly two of them on getting you back into the garden in Surrey again. . . . Go on thanking me, Nerina. I love to be thanked."

He drew in his head from the window. Nell was laughing, but Nerina's expression was absent. She was listening.

"I believe that's them," she said, suddenly standing up.

"Not necessarily. This road has plenty of inhabitants with cars. Don't be in such a hurry to leave us," John said, "when once you've gone you'll be lost to The Coffee Dish and Bunjie's for ever, you know. There won't be any coming back. *Eyes, look your last! Arms, take your last embrace!* . . . "

"I'm *sure* it's them, John." She ran to the window and leaned out by his side. "Yes—that's the car. Oh . . . " She drew back. She looked imploringly at him.

"You needn't be so *nervous*," he said, suddenly and angrily, "you're going to be all right. *They love you in the right way.* I'll go down and let them in. Nell, help her on with her coat, will you?"

He caught up the cases and hurried out.

Nell helped Nerina into the shabby schoolgirlish coat. Nerina murmured something about seeing them again soon and Nell said yes, she expected so; she expected nothing of the kind and did not grieve at the prospect of parting for ever with Nino darling; but with some idea of cherishing a prospective mother, she went with her to the top of the stairs.

The upper part of the house was very silent. But up the well came the murmur of voices.

"Don't come down. There's no need to," said Nerina, quickly turning to her.

"All right—if you're sure you can manage," Nell stood with her hands tucked into the sleeves of her jersey; it was chilly out here on the landing.

Nerina hesitated. She was standing on the top stair, looking down into the shadows, keeping her head turned away.

"It's awfully queer, isn't it," she began quickly, "when we were working together all this summer at The Primula, we never thought all this would happen, did we? I mean . . . "

Nell shook her head. She could think of nothing to say but *Don't keep them waiting. Haven't you hurt them enough?*, but she hardly realized that she was keeping the words back. She said briskly:

"Good luck with everything. Good-bye," and at that Nerina looked round and smiled her sweet chilly smile, and said "Good-bye, Nell, and thanks most frightfully for the coffee," and ran lightly down the stairs.

Nell leaned over the well. She could see the brightly lit hall, and someone wearing a camel-hair coat and someone, a man, she thought, in a dark one. John seemed to be waving his arms about a good deal: perhaps he supposed that would help. Then she saw the top of Nerina's yellow head join the group.

She drew back. It was rather sneaky, watching people like this. She went slowly down the stairs and into her bedroom. She thought that she would have a boiling bath and go to bed; it was only half-past ten, but her feet ached and she felt rather concerned about Robert.

It was nice to think that she would not have the little pain any more; at least, it was nice until she realized that she would not have it any more about Nerina. She just shut her mind in time upon the thought that while there was John and while there was Nell there would always be the little pain.

She did not hear the Falconers' car drive away. But when she came out of her bedroom some ten minutes later with her spongebag and towel, she ran straight into John coming up the stairs.

He looked very black. He just turned his head towards her as he passed—then stopped, and came slowly down again.

"Darling Nello," he said, as if to himself, and put his hand gently on her sleeve, and they stood for a moment together while he looked down at her, "how small you are in your little blue dressing gown. Is it flannel?" He moved the stuff lightly between his fingers.

"No, it's seersucker."

"What a fascinating name. It makes one thing of honeysuckle and suckling babies and sheer delight . . . talking of fascination, I am going to see Angie soon, at the house I rescued Nerina from. I'm glad you can't see Angie, Nello. You would be so narrow about her. You would say she's horrible."

"What's the matter, John?" Nell asked.

He looked away. "Oh . . . of course you think I'm in a state because I'm in love with Nerina. Well, I'm not. (My life isn't as simple as that.) It was her parents. If you could have *seen*

them and *heard* them. Awful semi-county types trying to keep
a stiff upper lip and inwardly drooling with joy over the prodi-
gal daughter . . . but rather ashamed too, of course, and
wondering what the neighbours will say . . . I was almost *sick*.
And both so *plain*. At least, I suppose that Mrs. Falconer must
be conceded some remnants of prettiness, but *him*—! No
wonder Nerina ran away. And you could almost *see* Mrs.
Falconer trying not to ask her when she and Chris were going
to be married."

Nell did not say anything. What use to tell him that the
Falconers had only behaved naturally? She put her own
fingers over the ones clasping her sleeve.

"Why need we *have* parents?" he said, still keeping his head
turned away. "Why can't we just *bud off*, like plants . . . or
whatever it is they do. *Bloody* parents, I *hate* them."

Nell kept her fingers closely over his own. She did not clasp
or stroke them, and suddenly he caught her up against him and
pushed his face down into her neck. She could hear mutters—
something about "wanting to get this over" and "liking you
so much", and something as well about "a damned nuisance",
and then she knew what he was asking.

Oh no, was her first and only thought. Never that. If I do
that, I'll never get away again.

She said, as well as she could with her mouth pressed against
the hard young head under the soft stiff brush of hair—"No.
No. I can't. I'm awfully sorry, John, but I can't."

In a moment he let her go.

"Sorry," he said, not looking at her. "I didn't really want
you to. I'm glad you said no. I like you for other things. But it's
such a damned nuisance. All right, let's forget about it. Good
night, Nello dear."

But as he turned away without kissing her and ran down the
stairs, and she heard the front door shut as she went into the
bathroom, she thought that she would never forget about it.

CHAPTER NINETEEN

WRECK OF A HAPPY SHIP

On her way to the café next morning, although not precisely setting in her mind the pleasures of hard and absorbing work against the pains of personal life, she was more than usually looking forward to the day's toil. She put John, and Robert too, out of her thoughts while planning some scheme about new tea-towels.

She had managed somehow to put John's request of the last evening right away. She simply did not let it come upon her at all, now. Each return of the memory during a restless night had brought a turning over of the stomach which she had so strongly disliked that she exerted all her will to banish the recollection; it was like slamming a door quickly; and it went.

As she went down the side lane that led to the back premises of The Primula she was whistling under her breath.

She turned the handle of the garden gate, and pushed. It resisted her; it was locked. That was funny; had Tansy and Mary, both of whom always arrived before herself every morning, been taken ill together? She lifted out the brick in the wall, behind which the key to the gate was always kept; it was not there. Funnier still.

She looked up at the tall, white rear of the house. The fresh chintz curtains appeared demurely drawn back in the morning light. She went round to the front and peered in; the tea-room looked forlorn and neat, as always at this hour. After a prolonged ringing at the bell which met with no result, she was going round to the back again when Tom, a local character who served in the butcher's in the side lane, called to her from the shop door:

"Ah-ha, the birds have flown! Gone up to Tansy's, I saw 'em about a quarter of an hour ago."

Nell made a gesture of thanks, and skimmed off in the direction of Tansy's cottage, pursued by the shout of: "Key's been pinched, I reckon."

Highly unlikely. And why should they have gone up to the cottage? And where was Miss Berringer? *She* couldn't be stewing herself in the tea which any 'state of affairs', however small, demanded that Tansy and Mary should brew, and which was almost certainly now being drunk at the cottage.

The cottage was two hundred years old, just round the corner in the narrowest possible lane at the top of a steep slope overlooking all London. Those on either side of it had a blue door and a yellow door, and cultural objects in their windows, and through these doors, which usually stood open for small children to totter in and out, there floated cultured voices, but Tansy's 'front' was always tightly shut, and on her windowsill between the plastic curtains there was a statuette of a lady in evening dress bending herself backwards.

When Nell tapped at the door, which had no knocker, it opened at once, revealing Tansy in her coat and turban.

"Come in, Nell," she said importantly, "I guessed you'd be round. Mary's here. I'll just shut the door."

She did so. Nell, returning a businesslike "Hullo, Mary," in response to a tragic and portentous gesture from Mary sitting at the table surrounded, of course, by tea, found herself in a tiny dark room furnished mostly in dark green, spotlessly clean, and smelling strongly of mould. The blind white eye of a television set stared inimically at her through the dimness.

"Sit down, Nell. My Julian's at school. Just as well. There's not much he don't miss." She filled a cup and pushed it towards her. "There. You get that down you. You'll need it."

Nell, who disliked tea on the whole and had finished breakfast less than an hour ago, wondered why. She began to sip it, however, knowing that time and argument would be saved by doing so, while looking at Tansy over the cup. Then she said:

"What on earth is all this about?"

Mary made one of her gestures.

"Have ye not seen the paper?" she demanded. "'Tis all there, every word. Would ye not think she would have come to her common-sense at that age?—forty-six?"

"What *is* it?" Nell spoke sharply, and put down her cup with the air of one who is drinking no more.

Tansy whipped out a newspaper from a drawer.

"(Didn't want my Julian to get hold of it.) She's a correspondent. It's all here—look. Muriel Berringer, of Planers Lane, in a divorce with Franklin Farmer, company director, of Reddington Road. It's *Mrs.* Farmer. She must have known about it all along and charged her with it. So no wonder she isn't down at the caff this morning. She must have known this would be all over the neighbourhood (Mary here and me both read about it over our breakfasts, didn't we? We always read the divorces," but Mary made a delicate repudiating gesture), "and gone off somewhere to stay until it's blown over."

"If it does blow over," Mary said.

"To her sister in Cornwall." Tansy was folding the paper together with a sharp rustle, while her lips were pressed into a thin line and her eyes were shining. "So *now* we know why there was all the tantrums and the pickings on everybody."

"Her poor sister," put in Mary lugubriously; "she's not married. It'll be a terrible shock to her, you'll understand."

"But isn't—wasn't the key there?" Nell was beginning to feel rather irritated; wasn't there going to be an ordinary busy, pleasant, profitable day? She needed one: she knew it now; when there seemed the probability that she would not get one. "It might" (she made the unlikely suggestion firmly) "have fallen into the grass."

"It had not," Mary said, "for Tansy and me looked all around, didn't we?" and Tansy nodded.

"She's taken *that* away with her, of course," she said sharply, "you can't be too careful. They're always about. Why, there's some would be round there like lightning the minute they read the news."

"But how are we going to open up?" said Nell.

Tansy shrugged her shoulders.

"She must *want* us to open up and carry on."

Tansy shrugged again, and Mary said soothingly, "Sit down and drink your tea, dear. You mustn't get all worked up. Naturally—a young girl, it's been a shock to ye. . . . "

"Not particularly," Nell said. She turned again to Tansy. "There's sure to be some kind of a message. She can't just have . . . gone off like this. I'm going down to see if there's anything . . . is the post in yet, do you know? . . . but of course we can't get at the letters, even if it is, but she might send a telegram."

She paused. It had occurred to her that Miss Berringer might be in such a state that she had simply forgotten all about the café. But Miss Berringer was hardly that type. "Come along, Tansy," she said.

She was looking more cheerful; if anyone ran the café for a few days while Miss Berringer was away, it was certain to be herself, for neither Tansy nor Mary was capable of it.

"I don't know . . . we'll have the pleece round there before
we can get the coffees started."

"Oh Tansy. Really. The police! What on earth should they
come round for? You come with me and we'll get the place
opened up. I'm sure that's what Miss Berringer would want us
to do. If she's . . . having a spot of bother . . . she'll need the
café running properly, to cheer her up. We'll probably get a
telephone message later this morning. I'll take responsibility
for everything."

"Oh all right. If you'll be responsible." Tansy set down her
large stained cup half-filled with cool copper tea, and stood up.

"Mary, you finish up your tea, and come down afterwards.
Tansy and I will dash ahead," Nell said, opening the front
door.

"The young ones are over-keen on dashing." But Mary
drained her cup and began to heave herself out of her chair,
and by the time Nell and Tansy were hurrying over the steep
cobbled slope, her large form was leisurely following. On the
way down, Tansy explained to Nell that the police was mixed
up in divorces, wasn't they, and might be told to keep a watch
on them what had been in them, and Nell explained to Tansy,
her voice pitched lower than usual as they passed the open
doors and windows of Miss Berringer's neighbours, that it was
not that kind of police. Her eyes were shining, for she was
relishing the prospect of getting the running of The Primula,
if only for a few days, into her own hands.

But when the two came in sight of The Primula, Tansy
stopped short and gripped her by the arm.

The police were there. They had arrived in answer to a
courteous, apologetic letter, and they had broken a door down.
A small crowd—that usual small crowd which appears to consist of human beings and must in truth consist of ghouls—had
collected, and it was watching two men slowly carrying her
out: sensible, bright Muriel Berringer, of the perky blue feather
hat.

Nell had as much responsibility as she had wanted, during
the next five days, and more. There was no-one else to do it,
so she had to talk to the police, and go through the dead
woman's desk to find the address of her sister in Cornwall,
and break the news to her by telephone. She then asked her
to come up to stay at Arkwood Road until she had disposed

of all the necessary business. She told her no more than that her sister was dead—"and we're—they're—afraid that she did it herself."

Miss Chloe Berringer took the news very quietly, answering her in a voice which the presumable shock seemed to have made no fainter than its natural tone. She accepted the offer of hospitality; she would arrive in the late afternoon of that day. When Nell put down the receiver, she felt that the worst was yet to come.

The five days which Miss Chloe Berringer spent at Arkwood Road were a painful and awkward time for everyone: they would have been painful anyway: it was Miss Berringer's terrible shyness and her depth of feeling that produced the awkwardness. Her thinness, her silence, and the colours which she preferred to wear, together with the fact that she owned a flower farm, contrived to produce a personality irresistibly suggesting some dark, fading violet. Although her pet name for her sister, 'Mu', slipped out only once, while she happened to be alone with Anna, during the entire visit, it was plain that their love for each other had been the sole outlet of a nature burdened with passion. There were continual abrupt references to their shared childhood which showed that her thoughts were constantly returning to those days, with a hopeless yearning. Now she had left her her dog, and the flower farm: close human contact, Anna gathered, there was none.

They were all longing for the inquest and the funeral to be over and for Miss Chloe to be gone.

The Primula was closed. She had put it into the hands of house-agents; and was supervising the packing of her sister's possessions, which would go down to Cornwall to rejoin the family nucleus from which they had been separated when the Berringer girls decided to live apart; and the staff of the tea-shop must set about finding itself new jobs.

Nell had been so occupied with the responsibilities laid upon her that she had scarcely realized she was out of work. When she did; when the first pause came in the discussing, the interviews, the arranging, the telephoning; she decided that she would not look for another post until everything was over.

A corner was found for Miss Berringer in Highgate Old Cemetery. She was buried on the Saturday morning, in mild September sunlight, and Nell's strongest memory of the ceremony in after years was the perfect behaviour of Mary.

At the inquest she had worn her best clothes, referring to
Tansy throughout the proceedings as 'Mrs. Tanswood here'
and plainly relishing every minute. But at the funeral the
Roman Catholic faith, effortlessly sweeping Mary Malone up
into its two-thousand-year-old train, kept her in reverence, pity
and love, and against the mechanically grieved air of the few
other mourners, she shone by her faith; forgetful of self and
thinking only of God and the dead. Nell, a Protestant to the
last disc of her backbone, could never have made, or let herself
be made into, the kind of person that Mary became for half
an hour in the middle of that busy Saturday morning, but
from then onwards she never met Mary without hearing her
most innocently spiteful remarks against a background of
timeless, fathomless peace and light.

The ceremony at the graveside being concluded, she decided
against waiting with her parents until 'the sister' should be
ready to accompany them back to Hampstead. She would
walk home alone across the Heath.

She told them so, in a murmur, and was going briskly out
of the lower gates of the cemetery, which lead into Swain's
Lane, with this intention, when she saw John, lurking almost
in a large bush on the opposite side of the road. He waved
to her mysteriously and she waved back.

He wore a black overcoat, too short for him, which he no
doubt believed appropriate to the occasion, and a black Hom-
burg; she thought that both objects must belong to his father.

"Hullo. How are you?" He came out of the bush and crossed
the road.

"I'm all right," she said.

"Where are you rushing away to?" He fell into step with her.
"I say, is that the sister, in the tweed coat?"

"Yes. I'm going to walk back across the Heath."

"How odd; she looks much more the type to kill herself than
poor Lady Bottlewasher, doesn't she? *Don't* go home across
the Heath, Nello; don't go home at all." He slipped his arm
into hers, and she hoped that the parents, now getting into
the hired car with Miss Chloe somewhere in the background,
would not see. "Come and walk about in the old cemetery
with me; it's beautiful there; and then I know a little place,
like a bird's nest under a wall, over in Fortess Road where
we can get egg and chips for our lunch."

"Walk about in a cemetery?"

"Why not? I told you it's beautiful. There's a view from the top, at the back of the church—if it were a view in Italy or South America it would be famous all over the world."

"I rather wanted some air."

But she let him lead her back through the upper gates, made of old, soft iron painted a soft, faded red, and along the deserted paths, wide at first, then becoming narrower as they wound upwards between the neglected graves. The tombstones were almost buried in green plumelike weeds sweeping across them, dark rich moss obliterating once-beloved names glowed in the mild air, sheets of dry faded grass came creeping down to meet the tangle of briar creeping up. The place was deserted; not a step or a voice sounded but their own. Between the toppling stones London could now and again be seen; far below; grey towers rising up from a sunny mist.

John was looking about him with moderate content. "We'll stay here for a little while," he observed, as they came onto the broad, silent, crumbling terrace which crowns the summit of all the little upward-winding paths, and which is directly below the wall of Saint Michael's churchyard, "then we'll go and find some people."

"It *is* rather creepy," Nell said. "I say, ought you to do that?" for he was arranging his father's coat for her to sit on.

"It doesn't matter. He's doing madly well now on I.T.A., he can buy himself another. There. Isn't that a view?"

She looked down on the black cedar tree spreading its flat branches above the turf on a mausoleum of bleached white stone. The still, sunny, misty air fell away beyond it into a gulf, ending in a wall of motionless, heavy, yellowing trees, and then, far below and away—London: towers, spires, colonnades, cubes of chalk that were flats, steeples, the dark blue egg that was the dome of Saint Paul's, pluffets of snowy engine smoke going up, and the low, humble, creeping, droning haze of the city's common people and everyday life spreading far beyond the horizon and filling the gazing eye from end to end. It was all bathed in the sunny haze that Turner loved to paint: a muddle of light that, when it shone, as here, upon actual objects not transformed by a painter's eye, did but make them appear more distinct, and real beyond ordinary reality.

"What are you thinking about?" he asked. "In that little black cap and with your hair, against that background, you

look like a page-boy in an Italian painting. They so often
have queer long noses. What *are* you thinking about?"

"Miss Berringer," reluctantly, at last, in a low tone.

He moved impatiently. "Why do you always feel the ordinary
things, Nell?"

"I am ordinary."

"No, not quite. That's what makes it so—"

"I don't mind being ordinary, John." She turned to him
with an expression that for a moment disconcerted him. "I
like it, you know."

The expression was calm and amused; in fact, Nell felt
neither.

Useless for him to say to her *Let's forget about it*; that particular request is not easy to forget, for some people, and
particularly when it is the first time that it has been made, and
when it has been made by someone about whom there is a
constant, confusing agitation of feeling.

Nell's strength was in the fact that she had no wish, for her
own part, to grant it.

She did not reflect much upon her own feelings, she had never
honestly faced her feelings for John; she only knew that the
reason why she did not want to grant it was because she was
quite sure that, if she did, she would go into slavery. She was
so often cross with him nowadays that she was beginning to
think she might 'stop all this kind of thing' when once he had
gone away into the Army. She was even beginning to hope that
she might. To behave . . . like that . . . if he were to ask her
again, would be sheer lunacy.

She did, now, want to escape. She had a lot to do; to get on
with; she had to find herself a new job, in which she could earn
even more money and try to persuade her mother to have
some outside help with the housework, and to see Elizabeth
before the latter left for Jamaica, to discuss possible mutual
plans for next year . . . there was so much, enjoyably much,
to be done.

But, sitting beside him here alone in the sunlit silence, it was
difficult not to remember what he had asked.

Then she remembered that she had just seen the body of
someone who had given way unrestrainedly to Love being
lowered into the grave. It was impossible to believe, on such a
day as this, that infinite mercy and endless peace were not
for Miss Berringer, but . . . if one yielded utterly, that could

happen. . . . Better, surely, to behave in such a way that one would have safety and honour and peace?

Her thoughts returned, soberly, to Miss Berringer and remained there. But she had fallen into the habit of listening to John when he talked, and he was talking now.

CHAPTER TWENTY

"... AND WITH THE BLOOM GO I!"

" . . . and such a type to kill oneself for; fifty-six—as the papers have kindly told us more than once. And fat. *And* bald. *And* with a distinctly roving eye."

Nell turned to look at him. "How do you know?"

"Oh, I do know practically everything that goes on in our part of Hampstead. (I have my sources of information.) And of course, as for being fat and bald—it's truly dramatic, all those passions seething under the commonplace exteriors. But it takes an artist to see the beautiful *nuances* in an apparently squalid story. Probably he was getting tired of her, you know. (She was pretty old herself.) And then—"

"I don't want to talk about it."

"But I do; don't be selfish. And then, after the divorce, he *turns* on her, and tells her that she has 'Upset his life'! Wonderful expression, isn't it? 'Upset his life!' So the Sleeping Beauty wakes out of her dream—and promptly goes to sleep again—for ever, this time." He laughed.

Nell continued to look at him. Under the coat that he had taken off, he was wearing his usual collection of pale, loose, rather odd clothes. Today they were crumpled and not noticeably clean. His white skin never became tanned, and so she supposed that most of the brown upon it must be dirt. His hair was certainly dirty, and caught in it there were a few minute fronds of fading bracken: he must have been lying on the Heath, and now that she was close to him she caught a faint scent that was not entirely unwashed boy: it *was* bracken; he must have been absolutely rolling in the stuff.

"I do wish you would wash more often," she said, and he laughed again.

"I mean it, John. How *can* you?"

"I '*can*' because I don't notice being dirty— (if I *am*). You should see some of the people I know. And really, Nello, how rude you can be. Talking of dirt, I've heard from Benedict. (Dirt made me think of dear little Gardis.)"

"Have you? Are they still together?"

"Oh yes. They're living with some men who are diving for salvage from a submarine that was sunk in the war, somewhere off the coast of Spanish Morocco. Benedict says the men have built themselves a house out of rubbish, underneath a terrific rock that overhangs the sea shore, and that's where he and Gardis are living. They can hear the sea all day, and the Arabs from a village nearby come down and eat their rice and scraps of meat out of a tin with them. They don't do anything but swim and sunbathe and watch the men diving. Doesn't it sound marvellous?"

"It sounds very uncomfortable," Nell said, "a house made of rubbish," and after reflecting he admitted that he agreed with her. "And of course after a time *I* should get bored with no houses and no conversation. I'm not fond of uncivilized living—at least, I like to know that civilization is there if I want it."

"And have you heard from Nerina?" she asked.

"Not from *Nerina* (I didn't expect to). But I had a letter from her parents." He paused, looking away from her, across the immense valley filled with a city. "It was rather a nice letter. Thanking me, you know, and that sort of bull. They're nice people actually, I think, nice ordinary people (not like television stars or 'characters'), Nerina sent me her love."

"Good." But there was no little pain now. "I expect she'll be all right."

In fact she thought that the worst part of Nerina's experience was yet to come, although it would at least be undergone in the shelter of her home and family. But this led back to those thoughts upon the unwisdom of giving oneself entirely over to Love which she did not wish to pursue, so she remarked that she was getting hungry.

"Are you? I suppose I ought to be. (Nothing since some canapés at someone's party last night, Nello.) I've nearly had enough of it here. But don't let's go just yet."

Nell kept her head turned steadily towards London. The remark about his last meal had brought back her concern for his entire way of living; those glasses of milk bought on borrowed money and gulped with a kind of languid gusto, which had to serve for lunch and supper as well; the chips bolted on the tops of buses or in the cheapest seats at a French film; the ham rolls, the sausages; the apples chewed in the small hours on the sofa in someone's bed-sitter . . . wouldn't it, *wouldn't it* be a relief when he was sitting down to four square meals a day in the Army?

It was the first time that the idea of relief had mingled with the pain of his going away.

In a moment he announced that he had had enough of it now, and stood up, holding out to her, as she sat on the coat, his long powerful hands covered with long red scratches. "Blackberry bushes," was his explanation, "on the Heath."

He pulled her up, and they wandered down the steps and entered the maze of narrow paths winding and twisting among the graves. The hour sounded coolly across the air from the church spire; women in black were now moving between the graves on the slopes below; watering plants, refilling jars, carrying sheaves of flowers.

"It's so nice, your being out of work, Nello," he said as they went handfasted down Swain's Lane, "why must you get another job? I like to have you there whenever I want you."

No comment. What was the use of feeling the sweetness?

"Where do you think of trying for one?"

"The Rosa di Lima, first. They pay well and the tips are simply marvellous. I was talking to La Gouloue about it."

"The red-haired girl? Yes . . . you know, you'll have a good chance of getting taken on there because they choose girls with definite colouring. Haven't you noticed? La Gouloue is red, and Barbara is so blonde, and Katrin is truly black. Your hair is *really* dead-leaf, you know; don't let me ever find you putting horrible little 'rinses' on it to 'brighten' it."

"I think dyed hair is the complete end."

"Oh *no*, Nello. It *can* look *marvellous*, but not on you. The other thing against the Rosa di Lima is that you *are*, and none of those girls are virgins, of course."

Again no comment; it was wiser from every point of view not to say one word.

"And if you get a job such miles away from Hampstead we shall never see each other."

"We shan't see each other at all soon, anyway." She could not resist trying to find out whether he would mind.

"Oh, the bloody Army," vaguely, and after a pause, "yes, I shall miss you horribly." He went on to say in exactly the same tone that he would miss Hampstead and the flat and London horribly too, and she thought it served her right for asking.

He led her through the back streets to Fortess Road; Nell scarcely knew Outer Highgate, and was not attracted by the secretive, melancholy rows of tall brown houses marching up and down steep hills, the quietness, the huge deserted churches built to shelter three hundred people crowning some sooty silent ridge that overlooked the distant Heath, the great grey mansions and old blocks of flats falling in solid ranks down to the roaring main roads. She observed that it was rather dreary, and he smiled.

The café they went to was one of those tiny hollows, scooped in the curve of an arch or clinging, as he had said, like the nest of a bird to a railway hoarding or the precincts of a garage, which abound all over London from Hendon to Bromley. This one just held four customers and the proprietor; in front it was all boarded up with wood 'left over from an air raid', the owner explained, adding without resentment that there wasn't no toilet only the railway bank. Made it kind of awkward, but he was moving out soon. When the shaky door was shut and they could see through the steamy panes the blue of the late summer sky, dimmed yet still royal, and the tea-urn was hissing and the food set steaming before them on the scrubbed table, John looked contentedly about him and observed: "In twenty years there won't be many places like this left."

Nell, naturally interested in her surroundings, made some non-committal mutter. It would not do to offend him by explaining that she was repelled by the extreme, the almost fierce cleanness of everything and the air of poverty just kept at bay and the copiousness of the greasy food.

"These places are some of my favourite ones," he said, and then they ate in silence for a while.

It was nearly four o'clock, but the proprietor seemed content to cook eggs and chips for them, and for two men in dirty white coats who had been doing a removal job and had come in for a late lunch. It was almost peaceful in the tiny, steamy, crowded shed; the men talked in quiet, low, tired voices that nevertheless sounded easily below the cruel grinding roar of traffic going by outside, and John had some French cigarettes which he shared with Nell, who was getting a taste for strong tobacco. They could hardly see, through the smoke, across even that tiny place.

But she thought that the food, which he had eaten at a rate that alarmed her, must have given him indigestion, for his tone was becoming increasingly gloomy.

" . . . that time that I was taking the money at a Horror-Through-the-Ages Exhibition at Southend. They paid me a percentage on the takings because I was a barker, too, you see, roaring out about the horrors through my little ticket window . . . they had a wonderful and horrific Iron Maiden there, Nello, with a man inside her, a real one (that was Monty, he got horribly bored, of course, stuck in a case full of spikes all day and not able to smoke, so they had to pay him more than me). But she was truly wonderful, that Iron Maiden. I used to get into the booth after the show had closed down for the night, and look at her."

Nell said nothing, looking down at her cigarette. The charm of his voice was on her, as it had so often been during the past six months. But now it was September . . . and Benedict, and Nerina and Miss Berringer? The ones who had yielded completely? How was it with all of them? She did not look at him, but only listened; she wanted to look, but something inside herself was stirring faintly and rebelliously, under the spell.

"The light used to come in through a skylight . . . you know, in Southend I don't believe it's ever truly dark; the land all round is so enormous and so is the estuary, there's always a kind of 'darkness made visible'; you can *feel* all that great gulf of air and water, especially if you're somewhere high up, standing in those appalling ornamental gardens, and after a time you can see the water . . . and there *was* a light in the place where the Iron Maiden was, a sort of . . . of absence of darkness, more than light . . . outside you can smell stale fried fish and chips, blowing along the empty streets in the dark. Even the shells down there look grimy. There's a thin coating of grime over everything. They look spoiled, somehow, those shells, not clean and cold like shells by the real sea. It's as if they were *trying* to be clean . . . you know I don't mind dirt much (you said I was dirty, this morning), but I minded those shells. . . . "

He was quiet for a moment. "You *did* say I was dirty, you know."

"I didn't. I said—I wished you would wash more."

"It's the same thing." He half-turned towards the counter, saying in a low tone, "I wonder if the milk here is fresh?"

"John, it *isn't* the same thing." His look and tone had unexpectedly gone to her heart. She actually put out her hand and laid it over his, as it rested on the table. "I didn't mean that, truly."

"You did mean it, I can't rely on you. I can't rely on anyone. There isn't a single person, in all the eight million people living in London, that I can truly be myself with and have them still . . . go on liking me. And you're just like everybody else. No milk? Oh, all right," to the proprietor, "tea will be fine, then. Thanks, Jack."

"John, I do . . . you know it isn't true to say you can't rely on me."

The proprietor, without leaving the counter, handed a cup of tea to the nearest removal man, who made a long arm and passed it over. "Thanks, Jack," John said again.

"Do you know why I liked Nerina so much?" he said, after a silence in which he put a great deal of sugar into the tea, "because she never tried to make me different or asked me to *give* her anything. She never made *demands* on me. I *hate* being *asked* for things; time or attention or liking. I just want to be left *alone*, and to have someone there when I *want* them."

He was looking at her with the eyes of an angry child. "I *was* kind to Nerina, Nello, kinder than you realized (I'm *always* doing things for people I like, only nobody knows about it). Do you know that when I first saw that room of hers, that afternoon, I bloody nearly turned round and ran out of it? I didn't, but I had to lean against the door, it was a frightening door with no lock, to make myself feel better. I kept thinking *I shall die in a room like this, this is the kind of room I'm going to die in*, a tiny room high up in an old house lost in the back streets, with just a bare washstand and a terrible bed and a rag of black carpet on the floor, and the sun pouring in, nowhere near setting for hours yet, through the dirty little window; I shall be like Chatterton, '*the marvellous boy . . . that perished in his pride*', in that painting of him lying dead—it's just getting light, and you can see the roofs of all eighteenth-century London through the attic window—only somehow I feel I'll be older than he is in the picture when I die."

He paused and drank tea. He was not looking at her, and Nell slowly withdrew her hand, from which he had jerked his own away. How short her own, inward withdrawal from him had been. Miss Berringer might be dead, and Nerina carrying an illegitimate child, and Benedict's career threatened by a dreadful girl, but none of this made any difference: N. S. (she was afraid) Loved J. G. She could see the initials scrawled in dim white chalk on a brown London wall. *N. S. Loves J. G.*

"Please don't say things like that, John. You *can* rely on me, truly."

"I'll believe that when you prove it."

They did not talk any more. He drank his tea, staring out through the window at the sooty slope of the railway bank, and Nell thought that she would suggest going home; she had a lot of things to do, and she was beginning to feel she could not bear it here. The removal men finished their meal and went out, one of them winking sympathetically at her as he edged past their table. The grinding of the traffic was swelling towards the rush hour; it came in loudly for a moment, then the door shut it out; it must fit better than seemed likely, that door. How quickly all this had blown up; it had been such a good earlier part of the day.

Which was worse: this feeling, or having him go away?

She still had not made up her mind when he turned his head and looked at her, and smiled.

"I think perhaps we ought to be going. I'll put you on the Tube. It's quite easy from here to Hampstead," he said.

"Aren't you coming?" she said, when they were outside once more. The royal blue sky had faded to white; thin cool clouds had crept up to cover it, but the long brown hoardings hiding the railway were flushed with peach from a hidden sunset; in such a light it was possible to like looking even at Fortess Road.

She had not been able to keep from asking him.

He shook his head.

"I don't think so. I've got to meet someone in the West End who may give me a job to fill up time until the tenth. . . . I'll just put you on to your train. You'll be quite safe, you know, Nello darling."

And that, in one sense, was the last time she ever saw him.

CHAPTER TWENTY-ONE

JOURNEY TO FRANCE

"I THINK it's a bad sign that you *don't* feel tired. You'll probably collapse suddenly and take weeks to recover," said Elizabeth.

"Thanks," Nell said, sitting on the floor in the Knightsbridge flat on an evening or so later; she had been invited to dinner with the double purpose of assisting Elizabeth to pack for her Jamaican visit, and enjoying a gossip.

"Truly, Nell. You really should have at least a fortnight's rest before you start looking again. No-one will give a job to a girl creeping around with a green face."

Nell said that she did not creep, but her tone lacked conviction.

Elizabeth got up lightly from the floor and went over to the bed. "Oh, we *must* get this done; isn't it ghastly? help me, there's a poppet, Nello."

Nell got up with a wooden expression; Elizabeth must have heard him use it, for no-one else did.

"Do you think Jamaica will approve?" Elizabeth held out a yellow playsuit.

"I'm quite sure it will." Nell was neatly stowing away garments in the cases.

"It can thank Uncle James for the sight. If it weren't for him I shouldn't be getting a *smell* of Jamaica. He's always been kind to me; when I was small he used to have an enormous Christmas tree, just for me, in his awful house in Belgrave Square. He lived all alone (except for about eight servants, of course), and the bathrooms had photographs of cricketing teams. Most embarrassing as one got older."

"Why did he go to Jamaica."

"Chest. He can't stand the English winter. Now the eight servants are black, and the house is lovely, and he says he's 'made arrangements for my entertainment', so I suppose there will be some young men. At least, that's my idea of entertainment. It may not be Uncle James's, of course."

Nell folded an evening dress of vivid cotton. She was thinking soberly how nice it would be if she were going to Jamaica, or anywhere else blue and exotic, but she neither expected nor wanted Elizabeth to say *I wish you were coming too.*

Her friend did not really wish for Sely's company in Jamaica, nor indeed, for any female companionship; it might intrude on the entertainment provided by Uncle James.

"You must ask him to buy you an Espresso bar," she said.

Elizabeth sat down suddenly on the bed, which puffed up on either side of her.

"Sely! What an absolutely wonderful idea. You are the most brilliant girl. Of course I will; that's exactly what I'll do. He might, you know, at that." She was staring at Nell with round and sparkling eyes.

"*Would* he, Liz? I was joking."

"Yes, but it was like fools rushing in or Baalam's ass—sorry, I don't seem able to say the right thing—what I mean *is*: you spoke more wisely than you knew. He truly might. You see, he isn't at all one of those blighted bachelor uncles; he's a cheerful, expansive old thing, and he goes all round the family calling me his Heir (it's bad luck on Nicholas, but he has got Grandpapa), and so I might persuade him that if he bought me an Espresso he could do the Inland Revenue out of some death duties. You know the way one does."

She leant forward waving her white hands about. "I shall ask him right out. You can; he's that sort of person. (We're rather alike in some ways. I hate people slithering round the point, too. Of course there's tact, but that's different.) And it will be an interest for him, as well. If I were running an Espresso bar with you I should have masses to write to him about, instead of having to try and think up something besides my latest young man (I've gaffed a beautiful architect, by the way; remind me to tell you)."

"Running it with me?" Nell said.

"Of course," impatiently. "I shall need your help. I don't know one thing about the catering trade. Besides—it's been arranged for ages. You know that."

"But I only have fifty pounds, Liz."

"So have I. But what *you* will put into it as capital will be your experience and knowledge; management of staff, and that sort of thing . . . where shall we have it? In Knightsbridge? Or do you think that's getting overcrowded with them?"

Nell was now sitting on the bed too.

"Oh . . . Knightsbridge or that part of London. . . . I don't think it's too overcrowded yet . . . and competition is healthy, it will keep us on our toes. Oh . . . " she got up and walked quickly round the room, and sat down on the bed again, "unless there really is a chance, *don't* let's talk about it," shaking her head and shutting her eyes.

"There's a very good chance," said Elizabeth.

"Won't he disapprove of an Espresso? Too modern?"

"Oh, he isn't in the least like that. He had a rather dim youth himself; he was too delicate to go to school or to Cambridge; and now he likes to see the young doing what he thinks are dashing things. He adored it when all those girls and boys did *The Frogs*; he took a party to it."

"He sounds nice."

"He is. Oh God, we *must* get this packing done. Now, Sely," beginning to switch clothes into neat piles, "we'll have a plan of campaign. (Strategy. You begin with strategy and tactics is putting it into practice. That's quoting Daddy.) *You* get yourself a good rest and be all full of energy for helping to run the Espresso in the autumn, and *I* will ask Uncle James to buy it for us."

"How soon will you ask him? Or will that *depend*?"

"Almost as soon as I get there. I shan't be able to wait—at least, of course I *could* wait, but I dislike manoeuvring round anything unless it's strictly necessary. (Actually I'm good at manoeuvring, so it makes it rather difficult my disliking it.) And Uncle James doesn't expect me to manoeuvre round him. He would be surprised if I did. He might even be rather hurt. So be prepared for news of one kind or another *soon*, my Sely-bird."

She fitted two rolled pairs of stockings into a space which they exactly filled, and shut the case.

"And I will tell you what I will do," she said, "if it's 'yes', I'll telephone you."

"All the way from Jamaica?"

"All the way from Jamaica. Madly expensive, of course, but Uncle James won't mind; that's the kind of thing he enjoys. (We shan't have to sit on this, it shuts perfectly.)"

So did the other three cases. However, Nell had not anticipated having to sit on any awkwardly bulging suitcase belonging to Elizabeth.

She began the rest cure that night by going to bed as soon

as she arrived home, but was too much absorbed by thought to sleep.

There was excitement, and anticipatory pleasure, but there were also doubts; Nell wondered if she could be as content with an Espresso bar as with a tea-shop. Whenever she had pictured her own place, she had seen white walls, chintz curtains, pieces of old china and tables of stained oak, and always behind the modest vision was the half-realized wish to refresh people. The clients of an Espresso bar would scarcely need refreshment; pepping customers up by giving them a shot of coffee was not the same thing.

It was not that she preferred old trouts as customers. There had been too many old trouts at The Primula. But she thought that she preferred the ordinary mild crowd that frequents tea-shops to the kind of crowd that patronizes the Espresso bars.

Heavens, I can't be *complaining*? She rolled over restlessly.

If he does buy it for us it will be the most marvellous . . .

Then what shall I do about getting a job? Liz and I didn't discuss that. Of course, I could always arrange to leave, if I had to, at a moment's notice. . . .

It was true that she was tired; she had been walking about Knightsbridge and Mayfair all day; looking at places and sizing them up, but doing only that; not going inside to enquire about vacancies. At the moment she felt that she needed, rather than wanted, a job. And she missed The Primula; she missed its staff; and once while she was peering critically into an ultra-smart coffee-bar near Harrods', she had seemed to hear a beautiful voice saying petulantly, *I detest smart places; they're vulgar. Do you want to work in a smart place, Nello?*

She remembered hearing that now, and, as she remembered, her limbs seemed gently to contract, and her heart did the thing called 'missing a beat'. She almost sat up in bed. But she did not; she lay still; and then gave a long, soft whistle.

Today was the tenth; the day that he took his Medical.

How had he got on? And how could she possibly have forgotten? Unbelievable; yet she had forgotten, just as Nerina had forgotten about Chris's painting things when once she knew about the baby. Nell must be more tired than *she* knew.

She did not realize that this was the first time, since their meeting in the freak March fog of six months ago, that she had forgotten anything that had to do with him; she only felt guilty; seeing herself as a false cousin and unreliable friend; and her thoughts were concerned no more with tea-shop or Espresso bar before at last she fell asleep.

In the morning, part of her problems were removed by the arrival in the post of a cheque for two hundred pounds.

It was for Martin, a present from Peggy, who was so very sorry to hear Nell's bad news. He was to do exactly what he liked with the cheque, but *please* would he not be *too* sensible.

It could not have come at a better time, and Nell brought in the tea to hear the parents arranging to take themselves that evening very modestly to the theatre. Wouldn't Nell like to come too? No, thank you; Robert was coming to coffee. Oh yes, said Anna; she had forgotten; and by the way, some-one had been trying to get Nell all day yesterday on the telephone. One of those tiresome people who wouldn't leave a name. A woman.

Nell put down the teapot carefully. All day? It might be someone with a message. . . .

"Do you know how John got on at his Medical?" she asked, sitting down at the table.

Anna shook her head. "His father was asking for him yester-day evening; he seemed in rather a stew. I said *we* hadn't seen him for days." And no more we have, thought Nell, bolting cereal; it's quite three days, nearer four. Faint uneasiness began to steal through her. But there was plenty to discuss; the cheque, and the Uncle James plan, and John was not mentioned again. The day passed quietly; Nell thought she would not go into town; she performed household duties and paid some attention to a wardrobe which the busy summer months had forced her to neglect. Latish in the afternoon Anna went off with Martin to some service. They had secured tickets for that very good play about the Jesuits, with Donald Wolfit, and would go straight on into town from Saint Saviour's, having supper somewhere before the performance.

The house was quiet. It was getting dusk in the road outside. Nell was sitting in her bedroom, mending by the light of her bedside lamp, when the front door bell rang.

She had such a quick, strong feeling that it was John. The uneasiness, which had been growing upon her since she re-membered having seen some of his dangerous friends in their odd, dark, heavy clothes wandering down Oxford Street yesterday in the customary manner, lifted at once. She dropped the mending and ran down into the hall: he must have forgotten his key, as usual.

She saw his tall figure as a dark blur through the clouded glass panels in the front door. But there was something . . . it wasn't quite . . . she opened it quickly, and her heart seemed to stop.

The policeman touched his helmet, looking at her steadily with light, severe eyes. He did not say anything for a moment. Over his shoulder Nell saw the soft dim lights suddenly going up in the blue air of the road.

"Does John Gaunt live here?" he said at last.

"Yes." Her lips felt cold and stiff but her voice sounded ordinary. She did not take her eyes from his.

"Is he in?"

"No. No, he—he isn't."

"When do you expect him in?"

"I don't know, I'm afraid." Now she was all caution. There was one thought: just one: to keep him from them. But what had . . . She shut off the wild questions.

"You are Miss Gaunt? His sister? Or do you just live in the house?"

She explained who she was, and who lived in the house, adding that her parents were out, and John's father and step-mother at present in the country. She knew that it was no use keeping any information back, and also that it would be very silly to make him angry. She spoke in a businesslike way, keeping her eyes always fixed on his, and praying that he would not ask her to tell him about John's habits and the places where he might be, and she did not smile, in case he should think that she was trying to placate him; she did not know that her cool voice was becoming haughtier with each answer and that her face was very pale. The front of her linen blouse was shaking with her heartbeats.

"Well, now I'll tell you what it's about," the policeman said when she had answered all his questions, and in spite of her fear she felt some relaxation in the tension, the severity, of the atmosphere: it did not lessen her apprehension at all.

"He didn't report for his Medical Examination for the Forces yesterday. Is he ill?"

She shook her head. "I don't know."

"It's a serious offence, unless he had an excuse through illness."

Then it came. He looked at her piercingly. "Do you know where he is?"

She shook her head.

"You've not even got an idea where he might be?"

Again she wagged her head, then compelled herself to say, "I have absolutely no idea," thanking God that she hadn't.

"You're sure, Miss Sely? If you have, and you're concealing information, it could be serious for you, you know."

"I haven't seen him—we none of us have—for days."

"Oh? How many days?"

"About—four, I think." Yes, it must be four days; four this evening.

"Four days. Does he often go off for four days like this?" She shook her head once more. "Thank you." He was putting away a notebook. "If he turns up, tell him to report immediately to the place stated on his instructions."

He touched his helmet again and went lightly down the steps; he was a slender man whose narrow foxy face had no trace of the fox mask's furtiveness, not yet old enough to feel pity for a frightened girl. He had rather enjoyed frightening her. He had not liked the cool voice.

Nell shut the door and went and sat down on the stairs. She felt sick, and if John had been there she would have raged at him. Trouble; there was never anything, where he was, but trouble: mystery, intrigue, shadiness, sudden departures, not turning up; he made trouble wherever he went.

But where was he now? Her anger died away as alarm took its place. She remembered the fits of mysterious anguish, the despair which she had not been able completely to dismiss to herself as 'silly', the friends who were rather more than peculiar; suddenly she remembered, having not thought of them again until this moment, her glimpse of the faces when the woman opened the door in that house beside the olive-coloured canal: weazened, blinking, full of absorbing secret life. *Their own affairs*: the words came to her as she sat crouched in the twilit hall: *busy about their own affairs*. Was he with those faces, *at last*?

She straightened herself, and got up and turned on the light. The delicate shadows cast on the wall by the sycamores vanished and the hall looked ordinary again, a place to be passed through on the way to somewhere, to get somewhere, to get something done. . . .

But what?

She felt that the one thing she could not bear was to hang about; waiting; doing nothing.

Only whatever she did—and what could she do?—it must not be anything that would make matters worse for him.

If they could be worse.

It seemed to her that this first foolish step on the wrong side of the law was fatal. It had in itself the threat of a steady downward walk from now onwards. There wouldn't be any turning back.

The telephone bell rang, and in the midst of her half-distracted moving about the hall she started violently.

"Nell? Thank goodness it's you. I've had the police here about John. Do you know where he is?"

"Oh—Aunt Peggy . . . no, I don't. We haven't seen him for days. They've been here too."

After nearly fifteen minutes' talk nothing had been arranged except that if either household had any news of him they would telephone the other at once. Lady Fairfax was so bitter that Nell's own anger faded almost completely: it seemed that her aunt's chief concern was for her career. She had appeared to love John, when talking about him six months ago during Nell's first visit to Odessa Place, but since then she had become even better known: it was hardly possible now to open any kind of paper or pass a hoarding lately without seeing her face or her name, and of course she dreaded the possible ugly publicity. And John's father, she assured Nell, would feel just the same: he was on the up and up now, in the clear again at last; just beginning to get back into the public eye and make a lot of money. He would be absolutely *livid*. And the *fool*-boy; what good did he think *this* would do?

Nell put down the receiver at last. So it looked as though there was no-one now to help John, except herself.

That was a dangerous state of mind to be in. She knew it, afterwards; quite soon after she was on her way to him she knew it, only by then, of course, it was too late. But tonight the reluctant love, denied and ignored throughout the summer, took its revenge: it assumed entire charge of her, so that all she felt was the longing to help him, and to give.

For the moment she could do nothing about that. She ate some bread for her supper, standing by the kitchen dresser staring at the table; she must be very tired; she did not seem able to pull herself together. She kept remembering how she had told him that he could rely on her, when they were in the café. *I'll believe that when you prove it.* She could hear his voice now.

Oh blast. Robert was coming at eight. She roused herself, and crossly got together the cups and the tray and the biscuits . . . why people had to stuff themselves immediately after supper with *biscuits* . . .

Robert gave her a second look when she opened the door to him. He had never yet seen her absent-minded because of some secret distress, but she was so this evening, and if anything could have pushed him into asking her to become engaged (oh, only on trial, just to see how they got on) it was that. He had often imagined himself comforting her, but until now had always seen her in command of herself. He liked her even better like this.

She was undoubtedly worried about something. She was trying to give him her attention, but twice she forgot what she was saying, and she handed him sugar for his coffee, and she was flushed. All the time he was telling her about last Saturday's match at Hitchen, he was wondering if he should ask her if there was anything he could do, or if something was the matter, and he had almost decided that he would, when she started up.

"There's the telephone!" She ran out of the room without another word.

Robert leant forward in his chair and stared at his large clasped hands. That cut he got on Saturday was healing nicely. Not so good; it looked as if she was expecting someone to telephone, and now they had. 'He' had, presumably. But somehow Robert had thought that he would know if ever Nell fell in love. He knew, of course, that she was not in love with him.

"I'm sorry to have been so long," she said briskly, when she came back (and that made him suspicious, too, because she had not been unusually long). "More coffee?" He shook his head.

"I say," he said—knowing it wiser to say nothing, but she looked so utterly stricken—"is anything the matter?"

"Yes." She did not hesitate for an instant. "I've just heard that a friend of mine is very ill." She looked straight at him; and her eyes were hard as the turquoise stone.

"Oh, I'm sorry. Bad luck. Is there anything we can do?"

We! He *wasn't* going to choose this evening to get sentimental? She knew he was being kind; she ought to be pleased; she didn't care *what* he did; all she wanted was to be with John, and help him. She shook her head.

"No."

"I'm afraid you're awfully worried."

"Yes. So if I behave rather peculiarly you must excuse me."

Her voice sounded older; it reminded him of a woman he had once known in Sydney, and he knew then that she loved this friend who was ill. His heart 'sank'; he could almost feel it.

"I expect you'd like me to go," he said. "It must have been a shock."

But she answered quickly. "Oh no—please don't go yet. I like having you here." She smiled stiffly. "The parents won't be back until nearly twelve, and I'd rather you stayed, really."

If she were left alone she might get into a panic and tell someone . . . try to borrow some money . . . do something that would make matters worse. She would try, of course, not to, but she simply was not sure of herself any more. She had never felt like this before. It was love, of course; when once you let love get hold of you, and admitted that it had, everything else went. She had seen it happen to three other people and now it was happening to herself.

So he sat down again and they talked about Uncle James and the Espresso bar; that possibility seemed as unreal as it was unlikely to Nell just now, but Robert thought it would be splendid to have Nell running an Espresso bar even in far-away Knightsbridge; she wouldn't be so keen on settling down then with this friend who was ill. And he might always die. Robert did not exactly *hope* that he would. But he was not going to wish the blighter a speedy recovery. He might have, if the figure's anonymity had not in some way reduced the conception of serious illness; but as it was he only said, "Good-bye; take care of yourself, Doctor Livingstone," as he kissed her gently at the front door. The lightness of his step as he went away did not betray the heaviness of his heart.

Nell did not want to take care of herself. She had always preferred taking care of other people.

She went straight to the telephone and made some enquiries from Victoria Station; wondering as she did so whether the police and the military were tapping the line. Everything sounded easy, so far; she looked out the passport which Elizabeth had insisted upon her securing when there had been that plan for their going in the autumn to Portugal which the Jamaican invitation had altered; she put out warmer clothes ready for the morning; she made sure that she had small change; she even pushed some cheese and bread into her coat pocket. She could get French money, she knew, on the boat.

She arranged a supper for the parents, leaving on the tray a note saying that she was going off at the crack of dawn tomorrow morning to look for work, and had gone to bed early. Then she had her bath, set the alarm and took four aspirins.

She had to sleep. She could not face lying awake for most of the night, hearing over and over again the hoarse faint voice; far-away; despairing—

"Nello, I'm awfully ill. I ran away to get out of my Medical and I must have caught a chill and it's suddenly got worse. Nello darling, you *must* come. The concièrge doesn't speak any English . . ."

Her own suddenly frantic questions, but remembering through the breaking-away of concealment and control to keep her tone low because of Robert in the drawing-room, and the petulant reply in the hoarse but recognizable voice, "In *Paris*. I *told* you. Can't you hear? You *must* come, Nello. Can't you fly over, *tonight*?"

"Yes, of course I'll come. I'll try to come tonight. But . . . John, are you there? Listen, the police have been here . . ."

Then: "Oh *God*," exasperatedly, rather than in alarm, from the other end of the line, and her own hurried begging for the address . . . quick . . . and of course the pencil by the telephone was broken as usual . . . but she had managed to get it down. . . .

"You said I could rely on you, Nello," almost whispering.

"You can, darling. I'll come. Only—John, are you there?—I've just remembered, I've only got about five pounds in cash and isn't it about seven to Paris by air—"

"Nello, you *said* I could rely on you . . ."

"I'll come. I'll come by boat tomorrow. But don't expect me until later. . . ."

"Don't *tell* anyone. You mustn't. Swear."

And her own low trembling voice promising, swearing, not

to breathe a word to anyone; just to get to him somehow, anyhow, tomorrow, as soon as she possibly and humanly could ... and then she had begged him please, *please*, to go back to bed and try not to worry. She would be there. She was coming.

Then she had said, louder, "John?" The line seemed to have gone dead. But it had not; there had been a flood of irritable French in a woman's voice; presumably the concièrge's, and she had refused to listen to Nell's questions, and of course every word of French had gone out of Nell's head, and then there had been the impersonal voices of the operators, English and French, who had made the connections. Then silence.

She had put back the receiver and stood still for a moment. She was compelling herself to make plans, forcing all feeling aside. She mustn't tell anyone. That was the first thing to hang on to. And Elizabeth had flown that morning to Jamaica so there was no hope of borrowing five pounds from her to make up the sum for the journey by air. Air was quite out; she must go by train and sea.

She must not make Robert suspicious by sending him off too early. How late could one make enquiries at the Continental section at Victoria? John was very ill. . . . No. Mustn't feel. Shut it away.

Robert would be suspicious now, perhaps, if she loitered outside much longer. Must go back to the drawing-room.

Thank heaven the telephone was not exactly outside the door.

Then she had composed her expression, or hoped that she had, and gone back to him.

Now, she tried to compose herself for sleep. One of the tablets had melted in her mouth, with its intolerably bitter taste. She was nearly, exhaustedly off, when a whole new plan suddenly reared itself, based on the idea of borrowing her fare for BEA from Aunt Peggy with a series of fantastic lies, and woke her up again. She dismissed it after a struggle, and then heard the parents come in; and one strike; and two. She just did not hear three.

By the time she was half-way across the Channel on the next day, the house still asleep in the morning light and her journey to Victoria by the yet-uncrowded Underground seemed to belong to another world.

It was a cloudy day; the calm sea swung and rolled, and below the sides of the ship it thrust marbley inlays of foam under
the green water, while far on the horizon there sometimes
struck down on the grey expanse a white beam from the sun;
then the clouds closed over once more.

The boat, a French one, was not very crowded, and Nell
could have had a chair, but she was too restless to sit down.
She leant against the rail, with the Selys' smallest suitcase at
her feet (less likely to provoke interest or notice if one carried
some luggage, however exiguous), and stared unseeingly at the
water fleeting past. She never cared much for Nature at any
time, and now the most that the vast, rather melancholy grey
silk sea, the grey voile sky, did for her was to soothe her a little
unconsciously. She admired nothing of what she saw; she
missed entirely the true thrill felt at first standing upon a real
ship; only her visit to the restaurant in search of something to
quench her persistent thirst faintly aroused her interest;
what would it be like to work here? Otherwise, nothing distracted her thoughts from their concentration on the one
object.

The ship was almost half-way across when a voice addressed
her in French. She looked up quickly and dazedly: a slight
fair young man with a fair moustache was leaning on the rail
at her side and smiling at her.

"I'm sorry . . . ?" she said, uncertainly.

"Oh, you're English. I beg your par-don; I thought you were
a *compatriote*. French. *I'm* sorry, mam'zelle."

"It's all right," she said. Then she stopped thinking about it.
He was saying something else; in English this time.

"What? I'm sorry."

"I said that you look French, mam'zelle. It explains the
mistake."

"Do I?" She had not spoken to anyone but officials for so
long that her voice sounded peculiar to herself. She looked at
him with the eyes like turquoise stones.

"Do you mind if I speak with you?" he said instantly. He
had a terrifically sporting check cap, silly, but somehow smart.
If he had a sister she probably wore her hats very well.

"No. It's all right. I'm sorry." Then she pulled herself
together. He would think she was mad, and she must not,
whatever she did, make herself conspicuous.

"I think it's getting a little rougher, don't you?" she said.

"Oh no, I don't think so. I think it will be nice all the way. You are a bad sailor, are you?"

Followed a talk about sea-sickness which he seemed to enjoy, and which Nell did not find irritating. In fact, without knowing it, she was relieved to escape from thoughts and feelings endured now in silence for some eighteen hours. She was not accustomed to fear and anxiety and they had been punishing her cruelly. While chatting with Georges Simon (she managed to avoid giving him her name for a little while, but in the end he got it out of her) she could even forget her half-expectation of being met by the police at Boulogne. She saw them in helmets, though later she realized that they would of course be wearing those peaked caps. . . .

Georges soon began to take care of her. He had less than half-an-hour to do it, but he put her into a chair carefully sheltered from the wind, offered her a Gauloise, and approved her acceptance of it, and then sat down beside her with every appearance of liking to be there.

Nell hardly noticed any of it. But she was still confusedly relieved not to be alone.

Presently Georges said, leaning towards her:

"Mam'zelle, you worry about something. Forgive me I offend you. But I have so many girl-friends (only *pour la camaraderie*, you understand) and they tell me all their *problèmes*. I only know you one hour, but I know you worry."

His small fair face, appearing younger than it probably was because of the silky moustache and the great cap, was full of sentiment and kindness. He looked like a saucy but well-meaning adolescent chicken. Nell, like most Englishwomen, had always heard that Frenchmen were lecherous and cynical, but if Georges were either she would be prepared (the thought surprised her) to eat his cap. She could not of course tell him even *half*, but she found herself answering without hesitation:

"That's very kind of you. I am rather worried. You see, I'm going to Paris to see someone who's—very ill." To her dismay she had to swallow a lump.

"Ah. I drive you there," said Georges in a satisfied tone. "No," holding up a white hand and displaying a pink cuff, "all is arranged. I have to drive myself to Paris and I have my car on board. We go together." Hand and cuff descended in two quick pats on her knee. "You permit? I am your *camarade*: I'll look after you; you'll be quite safe. My family is very well

known in Le Touquet and Calais and Boulogne, all along the
coast. We have chain of hotels—six of them. You can ask the
captain of this ship if you want, or any of the *matelots*, they all
know *la famille* Simon and Monsieur Georges."

As if to prove his words true, here a *matelot* slouching past
saluted him; somewhat, it was true, as if he would have preferred to shout *à la lanterne!* but it was undeniably a greeting.

Georges said cheerfully, "You see? Everybody knows me.
So now I go and see my car. Oh, she is a beauty. You'll adore
her."

Nell had not made up her mind whether to be driven to
Paris or to refuse; only, the more she thought of three hours
in the train, with those feelings and thoughts for company,
the more she feared the journey. But it was the remark
which Georges made over his shoulder as they approached
the deck where the cars were ranged, that made her decide
to accept.

"Of course, we shall be there sooner by car. We can get away
before the train."

There were no police, helmeted or otherwise, waiting for
Nell at the harbour and in less than half an hour the car was
away.

The road was very white; it ran rolling over a country large
and calm and fair, with lanky golden poplars blowing and
bowing and shedding their leaves under an enormous sky
filled with light. The glittering chill grey sea fell behind, and
the dazzling dunes; the red villages with grey churches began,
and blue blouses appeared, bending over the earth of the fields.
It was large and lonely; few cars on the roads; few advertisements anywhere; rank country smells drifting off the farms as
they sped by; few tractors; no villas lining the roads outside
the towns that were grey and old and dirty and dourly self-
contained; there were large red and white villages of houses
with coloured shutters; bicycles, bicycles, and more bicycles.
This was France.

Nell saw it all in a dazed way, for a slight drunkenness was
now added to the strain of twenty hours of unbroken anxiety.

Georges had bought a bottle of wine for their journey, and
produced a glass (he never drank, he assured her, when he was
driving) for herself, and a loaf as long as his arm, and some
sausage slices, and some rather dry oranges. The part of Nell's
mind that retained normal powers of judgement was relieved

to see him greeted in the *épicerie* where he bought these things as a known and respected customer . . . but really, she did not care if he weren't. He would hardly try anything on while he was driving, and she felt quite capable of dealing with him, even in her present state, if he tried while they were lunching; and anyway, she was sure that he was not going to try anything. He couldn't, certainly, have been more kind.

The car, which was undeniably a beauty, sped on steadily towards the heart of France. He drove remarkably well; very fast, with an unshakable, relaxed, indolent sureness of touch that impressed Nell even through her increasing weariness and anxiety.

He did not talk much, but he talked enough to prevent her from falling again into the maze of questions, problems and wonderings, and painful feelings lying like some great illness within herself; she began, in a dazed way, to feel grateful to him, and to Providence that she had met him.

He had just been spending a month in London, he told her, studying the Espresso bars and the Fortes milk bars; his father was considering a scheme for opening some cafés in Boulogne and Calais, and, although they would not of course entirely resemble those Georges had studied in London, he was taking back with him 'many notes' on English equipment and management.

He was naturally very interested when he heard that Nell had been a waitress, though she thought that he gave her an odd dry look. Her disclosure led on to Uncle James, and the Espresso bar, and more interest, comment, and exchange of promises to keep in touch. The hypnotic road unrolled, the engine hummed deeply, the vast white sky drooped to the remote horizon. A château floated by, with fair towers looking out of noble golden woods; the stag, the hounds, and the riding ladies in steeple hats were surely just out of sight; the horn surely sounded even as the vision passed. Georges sounded the car's, at a dilatory horse and cart, and Nell, dozing now, awoke with a start at the mellow sound.

"Soon we are at Longchamps," he said, "and that is not far from Paris."

Nell felt in her pocket for the scrap of paper torn from the front pages of the telephone directory on which she had written the address. '18 rue des Cloches, Paris 8.' Georges knew Paris well; he thought he knew the rue des Cloches. It was a *quartier* devoted to commerce, he believed. But there must be *aparte-ments* there, of course, and *chambres à louer* also. Her friend would doubtless be in one of those.

With delicate tact he asked neither the sex of the friend nor any other details, and Nell, on the few occasions that she could not avoid doing so, referred to 'my cousin'. It was now about half-past two, and the landscape skimming by, the monotonous droning of the engine, and the wine she had drunk were making her drowsy. Her eyelids began to droop. It was delicious to feel unhappiness receding gradually to a distance: remote: unpainful: it was there, she did not feel it: it was just there, nothing more. . . .

Georges gently bumped her so that she slid off him and rested against the side of the car; chivalry was something, but driving to the public danger with a girl asleep on your shoulder was something else again, and so far he had a clean licence. He regretted having to do this: he liked having her there. He sighed, not unhappily. So many girls in the world! and almost all of them nice.

The outskirts of Paris. Wooded hills; then cliffs of white apartments, and railway lines under a gentle haze of domestic, non-industrial smoke. Soon the elegant, grey, peeling houses began, and the tables arranged on the pavements under the cynical city trees. The sun had come out and set their yellow leaves glowing.

"Mam'zelle." Nell stirred, and began to come back to where she was. "Mam'zelle," she opened her eyes to see a quite unfamiliar face with a huge check cap on top of it smiling down at her, "I think you will want to wake up. We are in the next street to the rue des Cloches. I have park the car here and now we must walk to the apartment of your cousin. You will want your mirror. I have it here."

She supposed that she did; it saved time, anyway, not to argue. He had taken it from her bag and now held it while she tidied her hair. She wore no hat, as she followed the fashion; one pale cheek was creased from lying against the side of the car, and her eyes were a little reddened, from sleeplessness and strain.

"You are *élégante*, Nell," Georges observed impersonally, as he put the mirror away. This was the first time he had used her name, which she had observed him repeating, when she told it to him, as if to memorize it.

"*I* am?" but she scarcely heard what he said. She was getting out of the car, and her eyes were already searching the narrow, busy, sunlit street, between the trees, over the tables of the cafés, for the entrance to the rue des Cloches. She was trying to pull herself together, for in a few moments she would see him.

"Certainly. Without a doubt." Georges hopped out of the car after her, and paused to lock it and give it a final loving over-all glance. "When I see you I think, this is a top-flight English mannequin on holiday, in her chic little 'tweed'. When you say you are waitress I do not believe you at once."

She did not hear him. She was standing on the pavement of Paris, looking anxiously about her. "Permit me," Georges took her hand and led her across the road.

The rue des Cloches was much wider than the pretty street in which they had left the car. It was lined with shops containing typewriters and motor-cars and agricultural machinery. And the upper windows of the buildings bore the names of commercial firms which evidently had offices there; shipping lines, solicitors, agents, merchants of all kinds. There were no signs at all of domestic or private life. It was a hard, busy, crowded street, through which the traffic rushed hooting, loudly; a characterless street which might have belonged to any great city in the world. The afternoon light was bright and chill.

"*Numero dix-huit*." Georges had been studying the shop fronts keenly from under the peak of his cap. "Ah, it is lucky. There is the number seventeen and the number eighteen is of course next to it. See," pointing over the road, "it is a shop of wholesale cosmetics. (I have passed through a course in the commercial expressions, therefore that is how I know so many of them.) But . . . "

He checked himself. But Nell was also looking at the windows above number eighteen. They were inscribed in white lettering, *Raoul Frères, Importeurs des Fruits Algériens*, and apparently the firm occupied the building's entire upper storeys. Georges seemed to think some comment necessary, for he said:

"Sometimes there is an *apartement* at the back."

He was leading her across this road now, strolling in what was evidently the accepted Parisian manner in and out of the darting traffic, as coolly as he drove his car. But Nell was hardly seeing the traffic and was noticing neither Georges nor the comforting pressure he was giving to the fingers linked with his. She was thinking of nothing now. In a moment she would be with him.

Should she have brought anything—fruit, aspirin, clean pyjamas? But there hadn't been time to ask him if he wanted anything.

Now they were on the pavement. Georges turned to her.

"You will like to go in alone, won't you? But will you permit me to wait here? I should like to know how the affair goes."

She nodded. But even while she was nodding, she was moving away from him and towards the door of the wholesale cosmetics shop.

Inside, there were green walls, a dirty floor, and set in one of the walls a kind of pigeonhole with a movable slatted trapdoor. There was a table with a tin ashtray advertising some brand of *bière*, a chair, and a strong and rather pleasant scent of verbena.

Nell went across and tapped on the slats of the pigeonhole. Her heart was starting to beat fast. Everything she had ever known suddenly appeared to her as being infinitely far away. But that was not what she was minding.

When she felt she could stand it no longer, the pigeonhole flew up. A dark face with full cheeks, which at first she could not identify as to sex, demanded something brusquely, hardly looking at her; giving an impression of having been interrupted . . .

Nell pulled herself together.

"*Oh, pardonnez-moi . . . est-ce qu'il y a un jeune homme anglais qui demeure ici, s'il vous plaît?*"

"' 'don?'" snapped the man, staring now.

"*Un jeune homme anglais, Monsieur Gaunt. Il m'avait téléphoné, à Londres, hier soir. C'est mon cousin. Il est malade, je pense, et je . . .*"

"*Personne.*" He scarcely looked at her as he shook his head, and added something so rapidly that she could not gather one word of it. The trapdoor slammed down.

She marched out of the door into the street and caught Georges by the arm.

"Please *can* you come and talk to them? I can't understand a word he's saying. . . ."

He hurried after her, looking pleased.

She waited while he talked to the man, her eyes moving stonily from face to face. She knew, by that time, what the end of it was going to be. When Georges turned to her, not smiling, and began apologetically to speak, while the other man now watched with an expression of curiosity, even of sympathy, through his pigeonhole, she interrupted him before he could say it.

"He isn't here." She said it as a statement, not as a question.

"It seems to be that he is not. There are no *appartements* nor *chambres à louer* here at all; the nearest are in the street where we have left the car. All here is for commerce. You do not think ... perhaps, Nell, you have mistaken yourself?"

"Impossible," she said frozenly. "I repeated the number and the name after him, twice. I am sure this is the place ... he said."

Georges shook his head, looking down at the floor.

Nell began to move towards the door before he did. He followed her, having said something to the man at the pigeonhole, and the latter shut it, but more quietly this time.

When they were out in the street again, Nell said composedly:

"I'm so sorry to have given you so much trouble. You have been awfully kind. I hope when you come to London again you'll ring me up."

He took her arm and pulled her into step with him.

"Nell, you try on your *flegme Britannique* with me. You are so calm, so brave. But I do not permit it. No. We are *camarades*. We go back to the car, and I drive you to nice place near the Faubourg Saint Honore for *le thé anglais*. And then we don't talk. But you have your *thé* and you feel better. Then I drive you to the airport and I lend you the money for you to fly home. No?"

He shook her arm lightly, and she nodded.

"You will be at your home by eight o'clock. Now, see how good I get out the car from the street."

She was so angry that she could not think. She watched, carefully and with genuine interest, his skilful manœuvring of the car, and congratulated him with a smile when they were out again on the wide road and driving towards the fashionable quarter of the city. All through the *thé anglais*, the drive to the airport, the securing of her ticket, their almost affectionate good-bye, she was so angry that she could not think.

"*Au revoir*, Georges. Thank you so much again."

"*Au'voir*, Nell. Take care of yourself. *Bon voyage*."

"Oh, I will. And when your uncle comes to London next Wednesday, I'll have the money waiting for him in francs at the Regent Palace. Monsieur Max Simon. I won't forget."

"I shall think often of you, Nell. But we meet again soon, eh?"

"Oh yes. Good-bye, Georges . . . good-bye . . . "

"Good-bye . . . au'voir . . . good-bye."

Lights were beginning to shine down in Paris now, like rivières and pendants lying on blue velvet. They fell behind and away as night rushed up from the dim empty countryside.

She dropped her burning cheek on her hand and shut her eyes at last.

CHAPTER TWENTY-TWO

"YOU'RE FRIGHTENING DANDY"

SHE came slowly up the steps searching in her bag for her key, but before she could touch the door, it opened quickly.

"My dear child, where *have* you been? We've been quite worried." Anna almost pulled her inside.

"I'm sorry, Mother. John telephoned me last night, pretending he was ill in Paris and asking me to go over. So I went this morning." Nell sat down on the stairs and looked up at her mother's incredulous face. "But he wasn't at the address he gave, of course . . . I flew home. A very nice French boy lent me the fare." She smiled faintly. "All quite respectable. Don't worry."

"*John?* But the police are looking for him. We've had an awful day of it, with," she lowered her voice, "Charles and Peggy and Margie here, all squabbling . . . haven't you seen the papers?"

Nell's eyes were fixed on the banner headline of the *Evening News* lying on the hall table. 'Police Seek Lady Fairfax's Son.' She saw it without having any feelings; she could feel no more.

"In Paris?" Anna now said, realizing it. "What an extraordinary . . . " she began to follow Nell down the hall. "What on earth is he . . . but you said that he *wasn't* there?"

"No." Nell opened the drawing-room door, then stopped.

Three very glum faces and one resigned one were turned towards her.

"Well, here's *one* of them turned up," Lady Fairfax said, from a seat by the fire. "You look tired to death, poppet. Where have you been?"

"With John, of course. He makes people look like that." The spite in Margie's voice was embarrassing.

"Have you, Nell? Where is he?" Charles Gaunt demanded.

Nell almost turned and went out of the room again. Had she to admit in public that she had been played up, humiliated, and generally made a fool of? To these people, who none of them cared a damn for anything but their own careers? Well, that was all she cared about now.

"I don't know where he is," she said, looking at Charles. "I haven't been with him."

"Apparently he sent her on some wild-goose chase to Paris." Anna's voice came lightly from the little table where she was testing the coffee-pot for warmth with her clasped fingers. "(Nell, I think there's some left, if you'd like it.) Telephoning that he was at death's door or some such rubbish. She liked the idea of seeing Paris, so she went. But he wasn't there, needless to say, and she borrowed the fare from a charming Frenchman and flew home. It must have been an amusing day."

It was at this point that Nell knew her mother loved her dearly and had learned how to show it. She said "Thank you, Mother," as she took the cup, without looking at her. She *was* grateful, but just now she did not feel it.

"It sounds just like the little beast," Lady Fairfax said vigorously. "Poor Nell. Kind little cousin."

She stretched out a gracious caressing hand which the kind little cousin, wishing that her English relations had some of Georges' French tact, pretended not to see. "So he *isn't* in Paris, then?" Lady Fairfax went on.

"He may be. I didn't stop to look," Nell answered composedly, drinking her coffee.

"What did he say?" Charles asked. "When he spoke to you, I mean."

"Just that he had run away to get out of his Medical and caught a chill that had suddenly got bad, and that he was in Paris, and gave me the address. Mother, is there a biscuit?"

"Probably he was only pretending to be there," Martin, speaking for the first time, exclaimed.

There followed a cross-examination about the telephone call, and the general verdict that it was a clever fake carried out with the help of two or three of his tatty Bohemian friends.

Nell sat calmly smoking one of Georges' packet of Gauloise, which he had given her as a parting present. The smell of it brought back everything she had seen and heard in Paris. One day when she was not burning with anger any more (if that day ever came) she would go back there to enjoy the place. It was difficult, now, to believe that she had been there in actuality; her pictures of houses and cafés and the roads of France all retained the soft, vivid clearness of a dream. Even Georges had the quaintness and logic of a dream figure. The room, now, was dreamlike too. Only her anger burned and burned and was real.

They were still talking about the telephone call. It seemed as if it were going to lead on to a kind of reminiscence-show of his various shady exploits; the people taken in, the acts of effrontery, the half-dishonest tricks and evasions and avoiding of responsibility, and, always, the condemnation of authority.

She sat there, smoking, and listening without thinking. She had been a fool not to see, from the first meeting, what he was.

But she had seen. Hadn't she? Hadn't she always known what he was? and refused to admit it because she loved him?

Well, now she did not love him any more.

Suddenly she felt so exhausted that she could not bear it. They were all exclaiming now; wondering where he was, talking about the police; wondering whether he would turn up tomorrow . . . shaking their heads . . .

Nell got carefully to her feet. Everything around her was as clear as if she were looking at it—as she felt she was— through a sheet of glass. She was about to ask them all to excuse her, because she really was rather tired, when Anna crossed the room, with a little murmur of wonder about who that could possibly be, to answer a soft but clear tap on the drawing-room door.

But even as she went, she made the reassuring comment that of course it must be Miss Lister; because no-one else could get into the house.

It was Miss Lister.

She was standing in the hall as if poised for flight from somewhere in Old Spain, wearing her thick ancient coat and a sort of black mantilla. She was apologetic. Disturbing them.

Very naughty of her. But she wanted to see the girlie. Nell, was she there?

Anna scolded her briskly. It was nearly ten o'clock and pitch dark outside; she might have tripped and fallen coming up the path.

Yes, she knew it was naughty. But she must just see the girlie. It was important.

At that moment Nell came out into the hall.

She scarcely knew Miss Lister. She had seen her two or three times, but most of her knowledge of her existence and her habits had been gained from hearing Anna occasionally talk about her. Now she was in no mood to dally kindly with old ladies. She nodded a brisk, "Hullo, Miss Lister. I'm just off to bed," and turned away towards the stairs.

Miss Lister said clearly, in a firm voice, "I want to speak to you a minute, dear."

Nell thought, blast you, then. She did not get as far as wondering *what about*? Half-turning, with an impatient smile for the poor old thing and her completely unimportant troubles, she said quickly, "Oh—I'm sorry, Miss Lister, but couldn't you possibly tell me tomorrow? I'm rather tired."

A shake of the head.

"It's important, dear."

"I think you'd better, Nell," Anna said, and over Miss Lister's shoulder sent her a glance that said *Better get it over*.

Nell came quickly down the hall. One more effort. Well, one more, then. One more hardly counted, at the end of this day.

"Is it a secret?" she managed to ask, smiling.

Anna had withdrawn back into the drawing-room; and Nell was alone in the dimly-lit hall, looking down from her extra six inches of height on the little figure in the mantilla.

"Yes, it is, dear. But, trouble is, I don't think it *ought* to be. You see, after seeing those splendid chaps of ours on the T.V. this afternoon—your mother kindly invited me in—(I will *not* call it the telly, I *loathe* that expression) I felt I wasn't doing my duty to the dear little Queen. By keeping it a secret, I mean. So I thought I would tell his father. (He's the right person to know, and such a nice face. Trustworthy. I've seen him on that soapflakes programme, I never can remember

its name.) But then I thought, no. A Man. More likely to be
wild with him, poor boy. And I do *not* like his *mother's* face.
Conceited. So as I know you're a *great* friend of his, I decided
to tell you."

She stopped, and peeped up smiling into Nell's face. It
wore simply no expression at all. The dreamlike feeling had
spread until it had covered the scheme of creation, and she
was engulfed in it. She knew at once what Miss Lister was
talking about, but she could neither feel nor speak.

The old voice sank to a whisper. A tiny cold claw came out
and took masterful hold of Nell's wrist.

"So if you'll come with me, dear. Won't take a jiffy . . . only
we must be rather quiet, because I'm supposed to be out
watering my bulbs. Naughty, I'm afraid. Shirking."

Nell pulled back from the pressure of her hand long enough
to open the drawing-room door and call to them in a voice
flat with fatigue, "Come down to Miss Lister's in about five
minutes, will you." Then she shut it, and allowed herself to
be led along the hall.

They went carefully down the iron staircase leading from
the verandah; under the leafless twin sycamores, and along
the dark path covered in dim rustling leaves. Between the
black houses Nell could see necklaces and brooches of light
lying far below on black velvet. But she was not reminded of
an earlier view of Paris at night because by now she was
completely caught up in the dream; she did remember, however, to move more slowly than was natural to her so that her
guide might be less likely to trip over in haste. They went down
between Anna's flower-beds, still in the disarray of early
autumn, towards the light burning faintly in Miss Lister's
cottage.

I don't know why I came, Nell thought, as Miss Lister with
a touch of drama, stealthily but expansively flung wide the
door and waved her into the dimly-lit entry. There was no
reason for turning back now. What was going to happen would
not hurt her. In a dream, nothing could hurt.

She followed Miss Lister down a narrow dark passage, and
they stopped before a closed door whose shape was outlined
with a thread of gold light. The old lady turned to her, mouth-
ing something; Nell could not distinguish what she was saying,
but she thought that it might be an apology; some kind
of an excuse, or something of that sort. People did sometimes

think it necessary to excuse themselves for betraying other people.

"All right; yes;" she said impatiently, nodding, and then Miss Lister began cautiously to open the door.

Nell, standing rigidly in the shadow, saw first a strip of floor, covered in dust, and then the curved leg of an ancient sofa, and then a brown shoe which she recognized. The long graceful body reclining at length on the sofa was breathlessly still; his big hand had stopped caressing the cat lying on his chest as the door began to open. But he must, without looking fully at her, have known at once who was there, for almost immediately his hand resumed the calm, steady stroking of the yellow back.

The cat, alarmed, began to struggle, and John said crossly without looking up:

"Do be careful, Nello. You're frightening Dandy."

She turned, and pushed her way, without speaking, through the four people who were now crowding into the cottage. She went back to the house and upstairs to her room and locked the door.

CHAPTER TWENTY-THREE

FAIR WIND FROM JAMAICA

The El Hacienda Espresso Bar, he thought petulantly as he climbed the High Street in the teeth of the winter wind, laden with the tediously and unnecessarily large mass of gear which the Army insisted upon one's toting around with one almost wherever one went, might have been especially designed to make someone coming home on leave for Christmas, especially someone who had neither written to someone else, nor been written to by them, for three months, feel thoroughly out of things, forgotten, and neglected.

Occupying the best site in the High Street, Uncle James's present was decorated with the usual strings of onions and travel posters and bamboo fences and chianti bottles, and its customers borrowed glamour from its rich pink lighting. As he lingered, looking in, he thought that it was like an

annoying scene from a musical comedy; Elizabeth
Prideaux darting about in twin set and pearls with the cake
trolley and smiling at the customers; and the red-head with
the hard and pretty face (he presumed that this must be Pat,
from Akkro products), waiting swiftly from table to table, and,
sitting raised slightly above the others at the amusing cash-
desk covered in Caribbean straw hats—Nell.

He was a little surprised to find how well he remembered
the long delicate nose, sharing the honours of indicating her
character with the delicate long mouth. During the three
months that the Army had been failing to soften in the least
his supple and obstinate determination to remain himself,
she had neither bloomed nor wilted; grown prettier or plainer;
she had changed in only one way and that had nothing to do
with her looks. Her hair was still his favourite kind and hanging
straightly and smoothly, and, without seeming to, her eyes
still saw most of what was going on.

The way in which she had changed was that she had become
chic; that dress might have been worn by a French-
woman.

But he recalled that she had been on the way to becoming
chic when he had thrown her down. She seemed to have got
up again.

Telling himself that El Hacienda was a smart and vulgar
place, and knowing that the verdict was very largely ren-
dered false by spite, he turned away. He was not going in to
drink their coffee, not he. It was pleasant to see Nell unaltered,
and if he were in the mood he would look in there tomorrow
and make her tell him all about the acquiring, equipping and
opening of their coffee-bar. It would be tedious to listen to,
but they must be established, he and Nell, in their former
friendship. She was among the few things, he knew now, that
he was going to need, a little, for the rest of his life.

He set off slowly, dragging his luggage after him, for Arkwood Road. Between the dark houses he could now see the
city sparkling in her evening lights; if he had known how
greatly Nell was in fact altered, would it have checked a little
the pleasure he now experienced at the sight; as if wings were
unfolding in his breast?

There was a long time yet, he reflected as he went on up the
hill, to be reluctantly cared for by his cousin Nell. Even if the
room with its rag of black carpet and its threat of witnessing

a death like Chatterton's were not more than fifteen years away, that was still a long time when one was not yet nineteen. And Nell, judging by his past knowledge of her at least, was faithful and forgiving.

He strode on up the hill pulling his bundles after him: to charm someone.

THE END